HEATHERBOUND

SCRIPTOR HOUSE
THE EPITOME OF GREATNESS

DORRINE SIMMERING

Scriptor House LLC
2810 N Church St Wilmington, Delaware, 19802
www.scriptorhouse.com
Phone: +1302-205-2043

Paperback ISBN: **979-8-88692-058-1**
eBook ISBN: **979-8-88692-059-8**

To my best friend and editor, both are my husband, Larry. Also to my three children, Gerri, Candace, and Craig, they keep me firmly attached to reality

Chapter One

A Day in Late winter

Dreena was bored with her friends. They didn't want to do anything fun. With a shrug, she left them to find something interesting to do. It was such a bright cold day, perfect for exploring. As she skipped along, she saw a hill covered with glistening snow in the distance. Wouldn't it be fun to run to the very top!

She thought it was heavenly that the air was cold enough to make lace of frost on her lavender coat and her breath to come out in puffs of icy mist. She couldn't help but laugh at the pure pleasure of it. There were prisms of light everywhere, with all the rainbow colors, especially her favorite, aquamarine. Dreena felt so vibrantly alive. Everything was perfect. She loved the crunching sound her feet made when they broke through the crust of ice, the crisp smell of the turpina bushes, and the feel of the muscles in her legs pushing her faster and faster. What a wonderful world this was. She was gloriously happy.

A little out of breath when she reached the top of the hill, she still felt like a princess of all she surveyed. The sun was way off, just a tiny speck. But wait, the sun was getting bigger, and it looked blazing hot. She could see it growing, and she was starting to get too warm. It was getting harder and harder to breathe. Dreena also realized that she was hungry. So very hungry, but she couldn't find anything to eat. Had she forgotten to bring a snack with her?

Dreena opened her eyes and looked around, frightened. Where am I? It's dark, and there's no room to move. She tried to sit up and realized that there was a ceiling to her confinement. Dreena became rigid with fear. Someone put me into a small box. What am I doing here? Was my hill only a dream? Am I still dreaming?

With a muffled cry, she thought, where are my parents? Something is wrong. Why am I confined to this little box? It's so stuffy in here. I can't breathe, and it's too warm. Panicking, she began beating on the ceiling of her box and thrashing around, her mind screaming, Mommy! Daddy! She then tried to push the lid off, grunting, pushing, pounding. It wouldn't budge.

Dreena started to scream and cry in earnest now. The whole world must be hearing her, she thought, but even with all this noise, no one came to help. She was terrified. Suddenly she stopped her frenzy. She remembered. We were put in a cold box to sleep. She wasn't supposed to wake up for a very long time. Was the time up? Would someone be coming for her soon? Where were her Mommy and Daddy?

Her mother had told her to relax and everything would be fine when she woke up. That thought calmed her for a few minutes, but she didn't feel fine, and she couldn't relax. She needed air, and she was so frightened and hungry too. How long was a very long time? Did she need to be in this box longer? Did someone forget to take her out? I want my mommy", she cried to herself. She broadcasted her fear and lack of air, but still, no one came.

Where was everyone? They must have all died, she thought and sobbed quietly with despair. I'm all alone; no one is coming to help me. Am I going to die?

In her struggling, she had bruised fists and knees. She was whimpering now, no longer hysterical. Suddenly she heard a click and a mist of icy crystals began blowing in on her. It smelled like something.... Oh,... she couldn't remember. Was this freezing air good or bad? It felt better, and at least something was happening. Perhaps someone would come. She was getting sleepy now. Her last thought before the cryonic gas took effect was, I wish I had something to eat.

Dreena's Parents, sleeping next to her in their cubicles, were partially awakened by her broadcast of fear. They tried but could not overcome the effects of the cryonic gases that kept them asleep. To them, it seemed a horrible dream.

The maintenance robot had noticed the flashing emergency light above Dreena's cubical. Of course, Dreena didn't know that. He had been trying to adjust her nutritive inputs and raise the level of cryonic gas she needed. The head robot was down for annual maintenance and could not help him. This problem was really beyond his ability, but he kept trying. Finally, something did happen. He wasn't sure what, but the emergency light went out. He went back to his other duties. He noted the correction in his daily log.

Chapter Two

Same Day in the McCreight Manson

On the planet Heatherbound, most of the colonists lived in the Temperate Zone, and the winters were mild. Today was an exception. It was a cold, dismal day with occasional rain-laden gusts of wind that howled around the corners of the mansion like a moaning ghost. The short winter was just about to end. Even so, there were still patches of snow on the ground, but they would soon be gone. The day was the kind that made you want to stay home in a nice cozy room, read a book, and just enjoy the fact that you didn't have to be out in the cold.

There never seemed to be time to do that, thought Sir John McCreight. Never time enough for family, friends, or just dreaming. Now, from where did that thought come? I must really be in a funk. It was almost as if I was running out of time. Maybe what I need is some fresh air.

Suddenly a scream lashed his mind and gave the eerie sensation that death was near. Where were these panicky, anxious thoughts coming from? They were so intense and persistent. He felt he was suffocating.Sir John went to the sliding glass door of his office on the third floor of his mansion. He opened the door and stepped out onto the balcony. A blast of cold air hit him, but it felt good. He leaned on the railing of the balcony and gazed at the park-like grounds that surrounded his home, still thinking these strange thoughts. They were as gloomy as the day, and he derived no pleasure from the winter scene below him.

With a shudder, he turned from the balcony and looked back at his desk. He took several deep breaths, trying to shake off the disturbing, uninvited fears. He began to focus on all the good things in his life; his beautiful young wife, Helen, a family title from his father, and a profitable and growing business. He had the respect and recognition of his worth in the community and his two competitive sons.

Two sons, that alone was reason for happiness. His first wife died in childbirth after having several miscarriages. She had never been able to carry a child to term. Sir John felt a stab of grief that jolted him. Poor Elizabeth, she had wanted children so badly, as did he. She was his first love and died when she was only forty-two.

He met Helen, his second wife after he had been a widow for five years. It was at a social occasion, and he and Helen stood at the side of the room, watching everyone else enjoy themselves. A waiter came by, balancing a tray with one glass on it. They both reached for the same glass of champagne, almost spilling it. Helen burst into laughter and said, "You take it. You look like you need it more than I."

Sir John laughed with her, put out his hand, and said, "Let's neither take it and dance instead."

It was the first dance either had had since the death of their spouses and was the beginning of the end of their loneliness. They made a beautiful couple. John was tall and handsome, with dark hair, strikingly blue eyes, and a quick smile. Helen was a brown-eyed blond, also tall and quite lovely. Helen's first husband and son died in an accident. She had wished she had died with them. Helen was thirty, and he was sixty, but age differences were not as crucial on Heatherbound. Most people lived for more than one hundred and fifty years.

After only a few weeks of courtship, they married. Though Helen wasn't Sir John's first love, they were very happy together and now had two grown sons.

Helen had been desperate to have more children. The loss of her first child almost killed her with grief. When she miscarried their first child, she went into a period of despair. When Sean was born, she wouldn't let him out of her sight for a minute, doting on him, granting his every wish. Two years later, Cameron was born, and Helen relaxed, although she still favored Sean, thought Sir John. She couldn't see or believe that Sean had a mean streak even when given the truth; she said it was just child's play.

These early tragedies did not explain this unreasonable feeling of doom. *Am I worried about my sons? Is this some omen?*

The eldest son, Sean, was ambitious and, Sir John had to admit, a trifle arrogant. According to the law of the land, Sean would inherit all of his father's holdings, wealth, and title. He had difficulty socializing with anyone but his peers, elder sons of wealthy, prominent families. With them, Sean was well-liked and a leader. Despite his guarantee of future wealth, he enjoyed helping manage the manufacturing plant the McCreights owned.

At times Sean was insensitive to the working men who had been with the firm for decades. He thought of them as peasants, expecting them to be subservient and grateful for the opportunity to work for the great McCreight family. Sir John tried to correct this in his eldest son without success.

Their younger son, Cameron, was more interested in the family farms. Sir John knew that Cameron's greatest interest was in roaming the backcountry, researching the abundant plant life of Heatherbound. He is so much like my father, Kendell, thought Sir John.

Sir John would have liked to provide for his second son's financial security but could do very little. Heatherbound's inheritance law prevented him from deeding property or money to any but his eldest. However, he believed, beyond a doubt, that Cameron's resourcefulness and persistence would bring him success.

There had always been trouble between the two, even as early as the first week of Cameron's life. Their nurse had caught Sean hitting his baby brother and yelling at him to go away. When they were a little older, Sean never missed a chance to hit or shove Cameron when he thought no one was looking. Caught many times and scolded, but it never stopped him. He resented his brother for even being born.

Sir John chuckled, remembering things about Cameron. Cameron was quick to learn and quite often turned the trick on Sean. When Cameron was about seven, they took their classes together in the nursery. Sean hated that Cameron was on the same level as him scholastically, even though he was two years younger. When the tutor had his back turned, Sean often reached over and hit Cameron with his ruler. The tutor thought the boys were just playing and scolded them both for inattention.

One day before class started, Cameron moved his chair so that Sean had to lean far over to hit him. When Sean tried his trick, Cameron grabbed the ruler and yanked him out of his chair. Sean landed with a very loud thump on his face and started to cry. He never did that again, but he got even. He threw Cameron's favorite lead soldier in the fire that burned in their nursery.

Another antagonism between them was their celebrated grandfather Kendell. Cameron was interested in everything that Kendell did and said. He read everything his grandfather had ever written. He studied all the discs, data blocks, and books Kendell had brought with him from Earth. Cameron wanted to spend every free waking minute with him. Sean was not interested in his grandfather's work and found his grandfather to be tedious and boring. Still, he felt left out. He resented the closeness between Cameron and his grandfather that he couldn't or wouldn't share.

Cameron was very depressed, Sir John remembered, when his grandfather died at the age of one hundred and eight. He was only twelve at the time, and it was as if the light had gone out of his world. In one way, it was good as he now had more time to spend with his friends, Ian Scott and Kaitlyn McPherson.

What a tomboy she was, Sir John thought. They had like interests and were found exploring the rough, uninhabited, and largely unexplored countryside of Heatherbound. The three were seldom separated, and Cameron usually suggested what to do and where to go.

The wind had picked up, and there were even a few snowflakes falling. Sir John didn't notice them as they dotted his face and clothes; he was so deep in his brown study. He did start walking around the balcony, though, slapping his arms across his body to keep warm while he continued to reminisce.

Kaitlyn must have grown into a beautiful woman while she was away, he thought. At fifteen, when she left for Earth to further her education, she was a thin, gawky child who had eyes only for Cameron. Cameron had missed her terribly. However, she was home now, unexpectedly early. Everyone was looking forward to her and her sister's homecoming ball that was tonight. Sir John hoped she hadn't changed; he cherished the thought that she might be his daughter-in-law someday. Cameron would need someone who adored him; he could be stubborn and single-minded.

In his woolgathering, Sir John recalled the childhood mishap when Sean was ten. It was just one of those tragic accidents. It had been a cold and wet winter day, much like today. Lady Helen wouldn't let the boys outside to play. She was afraid they would catch a chill. Cameron was eight years old at the time and, in a mischievous mood, went into Sir John's study. He had climbed up on a stool to reach his father's sword, which hung above the mantle. He was playing a mock battle with the blade when Sean came up behind him. Cameron pretended to hack his imaginary enemy to pieces when Sean stepped behind him just as Cameron turned to attack the foe behind him. The downward stroke slashed Sean's face. There was blood everywhere.

Overnight it seemed, Sean became a resentful, difficult young man and blamed his brother for all his problems – especially the ugly scar on his face. They rushed him to the emergency hospital, and the doctors put him into a medicube to heal his wounds. The scar remained. Their plastic surgeon said that in time the scar would not be very noticeable. The accident had changed Cameron as well. He was more cautious and thoughtful but rebellious too.

Since that time, the conflicts between Sean and Cameron have been more serious, not just mischievous. Looking at it objectively, Sir John could see that the problems were mainly Sean's fault. No matter what Cameron did, it was not good enough in Sean's eyes. To make matters worse, Sean felt he, being the eldest son, should have the first choice in all things. Cameron should be satisfied with what remained. Usually, Sir John didn't intervene since it was easier to let Sean have his way. And Cameron seldom complained as he could often figure out a way to get what he truly wanted.

Sean's latest complaint was that Cameron did not spend as much time at the factory as he should and that his work was piling up. Though Sir John listened sympathetically, he found this accusation a little hard to believe. Cameron delegated just about everything to his assistant, Esther James, and her team of technologists. They didn't need supervision.

Esther was a gem. – Having been with the firm for fifty years, she knew just about everything there was to know about Steelite and its different uses. Steelite was a plant that produced, with certain chemicals, a metallic solid building material. It also had other uses, such as insulation and fireproofing.

Cameron felt his time was better spent in research and developing alternative uses and products. Sean saw this as only a waste of time. He thought that Steelite was profitable enough as it was. They couldn't grow enough to fill the demands they had now.

Perhaps that was why Sir John was so gloomy and anxious, this constant strife between the two boys. He knew he should have been sterner with Sean, made him share more, but he felt sorry for him. Sean was very competitive and could not bear to lose at anything. He needed to be around people who looked up to him, and his scar made him very defensive, whereas Cameron seemed to need no one. Cameron was able to find ways to fill his own needs and needed little assistance from his father.

Sir John smiled as he thought about one time in particular when Cameron demonstrated his independent spirit. The annual regatta was coming up. There were two events that the young men usually entered. One event required the competitors to build a boat without professional help and then parade it on the river. The boat project was the most prestigious event. The second was a two-person rowing race, and this actually excited the most interest. The rules allowed only one person per family to enter each contest.

Cameron and his friend Ian started to build a boat, Kaitlyn was with them as always. When they were a good way along with the building, Sean caught wind of it. Going to his mother, he said that Cameron had known that he wanted to enter this contest and had tried to preempt him. As usual, Cameron was told to stop planning to participate in that contest this year and allow Sean to enter. Immediately after finding out that Sean was committed to the boat building, Cameron and Ian quietly entered the rowing contest – and won with honors. Sir John suspected this was their goal all along.

After thinking about this anecdote, Sir John felt much better. Cameron will usually find a way. He only hoped Sean would accept his disfigurement and get on with his life. His constant turning away or covering up the side of his face was an annoyance, especially since the scar wasn't that bad. He had noticed that lately that Sean was making an effort to stop these mannerisms. Maybe all would be well after all.

Sir John shook his head, drawing his mind back from his memories. He realized how cold he was getting out here on the balcony. He hurried back into his office and closed the door. The room felt good and warm after the cold of the balcony. The crackling of the fire drew him, and he held his hands to the radiating heat, glad it was there. After a few minutes, he turned and warmed his backside. Sir John did not notice a small puddle on the floor from the snow melting off him.

When he was warm again, he went to his desk and sat down. He opened a drawer and pulled out some papers. Computers were in wide use, but there were always hard copies to be dealt with. He had a lot of work to do but found it hard to concentrate. He still felt he was suffocating. He got up again and opened the sliding glass door a trifle, took a deep breath of fresh, cold air. "There, that's better," he said, turning back to the room.

Looking around the room, Sir John wondered anew at the pleasure it always gave him. It was a beautiful office; two walls were painted forest green and trimmed with precious wood. One of these had a large fireplace with a stone hearth and that friendly crackling fire of Cameron's bamboo burning in it. The fire smelled like applewood, or at least that's what his father used to say. Sir John had never smelt applewood burning. No one would dream of burning natural wood on Heatherbound.

The window wall led off to the balcony, which curved around it. The windows were leaded glass, which reminded Sir John of his father again, and his stories of the family home on Earth. The fourth wall was a wooden bookcase from floor to ceiling. His desk was also wood, similar to oak, and polished to a high sheen. This wood was the first ever to be harvested on Heatherbound. Brass vases filled with flowers were on the occasional tables, and two very comfortable dark brown leather chairs.

Every time he came into this room, he felt a moment of pride. He was not a vain man, but his ostentatious use of wood on a world where very little to be had, made this seem otherwise. It was one of the things that made him seem unpredictable.

Sir John was a hard-working, conscientious man. He was not quite six feet tall, with ruddy hair starting to gray. His eyes were blue-green and reminded one of the Earth's oceans that Sir John had never seen. His nose was crooked from being broken playing football in his youth, but it gave his face an intense look. He had his likes and dislikes but always tried to be honorable and fair in his dealings with others.

Where his eldest son was concerned, he knew he should have curbed Sean's greed and hunger for power. Did he fail to do this because he preferred his younger son? The son who was so much like his own father, Kendell, whom Sir John worshiped? Is this the reason he had been so hard on Cameron, a feeling of guilt?

Maybe this low feeling he had was because he missed his father. He certainly had been thinking a lot about him lately. He had been gone ten years now. It was a shame he died so young.

Enough of this. There was work to do. He needed to clear away some things to have a free mind to enjoy the festivities, a ball tonight to welcome back the McPherson girls, Kaitlyn and Glendora. The last five years seemed to have flown by. It would be grand to have them back, especially Kaitlyn. He had missed her.

After about half an hour of working quietly and getting nowhere, Sir John decided to call his brother-in-law, Edward. He was the lawyer for the firm, and would have to go over these contracts with him. It was the usual problem; Earth wanted exclusive use of Steelite. There was the regular carrot and stick approach, better handled by a lawyer. He would go for a walk and get some air. He suddenly felt a lot better but a little sleepy. A walk would do him good.

Chapter Three
The Same Night

Sir John and Lady Helen were the first guests to arrive at the McPherson's ball. Helen was a slender woman, tall, dark-haired, unselfconsciously poised as if nothing could ruffle her. Her eyes were the deepest blue, and they crinkled at the corners when she smiled. Dressing for the ball, Helen dressed in an empress-style ball gown of dark blue velvet. Her hair with ropes of pearls twined in her hair with a matching pearl necklace, and earrings made her look like an empress. Sir John complemented her wonderfully with his Scottish attire, kilts and all.

Kaitlyn greeted them when they arrived and gave both hugs. "It's wonderful seeing you both. I've missed you so much. It's so good to be home again." After a bit more small talk, Kaitlyn asked, "Where is Cameron? I've been home two days, and I haven't seen him yet."

"I thought Ian would have told you," replied Lady Helen, looking concerned. She took Kaitlyn's hands, "Cameron is off on one of his field trips. We're not expecting him back for a couple more days. He didn't think you would be home for another month. He will be devastated to have missed your homecoming."

"You know how he is, Kaitlyn," said Sir John softly. "He never keeps in touch when he is gone, gets too engrossed in whatever he is doing, and won't be bothered with his radio."

More people arrived, and Kaitlyn said, "I do understand. We'll talk later. If you will excuse me, I must return to my duties and greet the other guests." She turned away quickly, but not quickly enough as Lady Helen saw the brightness of unshed tears in her eyes and the disappointed look on her face.

The delegation from Earth came to the welcoming ball, and so did many of the Elders. That was another reason for the ball. It allowed the Earth delegates to mingle with the Heatherbounders in a more relaxed atmosphere than at the conference table.

The afternoon session had been getting a little heated over the imports and exports on the trade agreement. Earth wanted open immigration and more control over who had priority on the use of Steelite. There had even been suggestions from the Earth delegates that Heatherbound would be better off as a member of the Earth community with the complete protection of Earth's military space fleet instead of being an independent planet.

Before leaving for Heatherbound, the three leading Consortiums on Earth had many conferences, planning their strategy. They wanted to control Heatherbound, just as they did all the other planets in the area. When Heatherbound was colonized, Earth's government didn't believe that it would take very long to seize control because of debts that would accrue. Heatherbound would need manufactured goods and other things for which they had no way to pay. The planet was only an agricultural planet, without any natural resources such as metals, petroleum, or gems. How could they make their payments?

Steelite had made a difference and had also cut into Earth's profits. Then came that damnable wood-like bamboo that cut into their exports to Heatherbound. The demand for Earth's wood decreased since wood was now only a prestige item. The wool from the hybrid sheep was not a genuine concern yet. But more and more people from Earth wanted it. Would they come up with something else? Who knew best to take over the planet one way or another? Heatherbound seemed to be a cornucopia of natural products.

When the Consortiums learned that the McPherson sisters, Glendora and Kaitlyn, were planning to return to Heatherbound, a delegation from Earth would take them home. The McPherson's would feel grateful, and as they were an influential family, the courtesy might help Earth in some way. Also, it was now essential to recruit a spy to gather confidential information for Earth. They needed someone with the credentials to go to the top for information. Finding a disgruntled employee in government who had access to secret documents and could be bribed was their first objective. He would be found. It was just a matter of time.

Chapter Four
Same Day in the Outback

The wind was howling, and gusts kept trying to blow away his tent. Cameron had had a terrible dream of being buried alive with a bear, and the bear kept screaming. The dream woke him up with a start. The tent was cold, and he felt irritable. He ran his hands through his hair and rubbed his face. Might as well get up and make a fire.

There was no way that he could get back to sleep. He wasn't even in the mood to get dressed quickly as he usually did but just pulled his blankets around him before he went outside to the fire ring. He had carefully banked the fire the night before, but there were barely enough embers to get it going again. Cameron was good with fires, and with a bit of effort, he soon had it blazing.

Pansy came out of her blankets, peeked out of the tent, saw the fire, and came out to lie down beside Cameron. She looked up expectantly and meowed softly. Pansy was hungry. The hunting had been very poorly last night, and she hadn't caught anything. She wanted Cameron to feed her. He opened up a can of meat and gave half to Pansy. The other half of the can, he fried, along with two eggs, for himself. His hunger satisfied, he went back to the tent. It was reasonably neat and orderly, as usual, but it looked cold and depressing to him this morning. It had been windy during the night, and a few of his papers were strewn about, but nothing to be upset about. He did not feel any of the joy that he usually felt when on these trips. Even the smell of his breakfast and the warmth of the fire hadn't dispelled the feeling of impending disaster.

What was he doing out here? He hadn't found anything. What a vacation! Ian couldn't get away from work this time, and he missed him. He had only his flute and Kaitlyn's moorcat, Pansy, to keep him company. Even though he had cared for Pansy these last five years, he still thought of her as Kaitlyn's. Cameron had spent playing his flute and watching Pansy's antics, which was usually enough to keep him contented. Now all he wanted was to pack up and go home.

Thinking of the flute made him recall his grandfather, who had made it. Cameron remembered his gnarled hands carving it while telling him the story of the Pied Piper. He loved to sit cross-legged at his feet, big-eyed and expectant. Grandfather whittled and told stories of Earth and their first days on Heatherbound. He also carved a slingshot, which Cameron still carried with him on his camping trips. He felt that he could still smell the scent of the bamboo-reed he smoked and hear the soft voice of his grandfather.

Another thing that his grandfather had made for him was a magic box, or sometimes he called it a puzzle box. He had made it before Cameron was born, and Kendell told him that he had put something very important inside it and that someday when he was older, he would find the key to open it.

The flute and slingshot were made from a reed-like plant that Cameron discovered on one of his and his grandfather's weekend trips into the unexplored areas of Heatherbound. Cameron loved these trips. There was so much beauty and adventure in the wilds. Grandfather Kendell would name the plants and animals that he knew and made sure that Cameron understood what they were and what uses they may have. If they discovered anything new, they would make notes and drawings.

On one of these trips, when Cameron was ten, they had set up camp, and Grandfather had decided to take a nap, allowing Cameron to explore on his own. It was a beautiful day, but hot, not a cloud in the sky. Cameron decided to take a walk down by the river and perhaps take a quick swim. He knew there was one not too far away as he had seen it from the air before they landed.

Knowing they would need water for the campsite, he grabbed a bucket and was on his way. As he approached the top of the hill overlooking the river, he noticed some very tall feathery-looking plants. He had never seen them before and could not remember seeing anything written up in his grandfather's notes about such a plant. All thought of a swim left his mind as he ran down the hill to get a better look.

On closer inspection, the stand of reed-like plants looked a lot like a plant he had seen in his grandfather's books on Earth flora. It was called bamboo. He wondered what uses it may have and tried to break off a piece, but it was too tough. He then decided to climb one and pull off some of the leaves to take back to his grandfather. Climbing made him think of the trees growing so slowly and the discussions on the need for wood. He wondered, could it be used instead of wood. His grandfather would know, he thought, and quickly climbed down and ran back to the camp, leaves in hand.

Cameron could see that Kendell had just gotten up from his nap and was sitting on the cot, just gazing out over the wilds that he cherished. He arrived all out of breath, "Look what I found by the river."

Cameron showed his grandfather the leaves he had torn from the bamboo. "It looks like Earth's bamboo and maybe could be used for wood! What do you think? It's so tough that I couldn't break off a piece to show you. You must come and look!"

Kendell took the leaves from Cameron's hands. "It does look like bamboo. Let's take a hatchet and get some. I wonder why I had never seen this before. Oh well. We can experiment with it to see what properties it may have. I'm intrigued with the thought that it may be a substitute for wood."

They hurried back to the river, taking a hatchet and a saw with them. The reeds were all different sizes, from as small as a finger to so large around that a grown man would not reach around it. The canes were a beautiful ebony, and the leaves a greenish silver that seemed to catch the sun's rays and flicker with life.

They chose a stalk about fifteen inches thick and cut it down. The inside was not hollow like a reed but had a pulpy center that was easily cut away, leaving a tough outer edge about five inches thick that did look like very hard wood. The stalk was about ten feet tall, and they cut it into several pieces and hauled it back to their camp.

They chopped up one of the pieces for firewood to see if it would burn. It did, with a scorching fire and a lovely smell similar to apple-wood, grandfather said. Next, they tried carving it into different shapes and lengths. Everything led them to believe it would act like wood. Even the pulp might be of use to make paper, Kendell said. All they needed to know was if it would last as well as timber and be as strong after it had dried.

The next day they went back to the reed patch and cut a few more to take back home. Kendell also took a few finger-sized ones. "These will make excellent flutes, and I'll teach you how to play. We'll have a duet!"

"Would you make extras for Kaitlyn and Ian?"

"Of course, then we will have a quartet," he said with a laugh.

After stacking them neatly in the hovercraft by their other gear, they were ready to take off. "We should take time to fly over the area. Let's see if there are many of these patches of reeds."

They droned around for the next few hours. Everywhere they looked, there were rivers, and along all the banks were the reeds. "Would you look at that," said Kendell. "The flickering of the leaves makes the reeds look just like more water. No wonder I never noticed them before."

From what they could see, it looked as if there were enough reeds to last hundreds of years if used as needed for wood products, even if they were as slow-growing as everything else that grew on this planet.

When they returned home, all credit for discovering this plant went to Cameron. Here was another proof to Sir Kendell that this grandson, Cameron, had a genuine talent for science and discovery. He tried to talk Cameron's father into sending both boys to Earth to further their education, but the Elders had forbidden it. They were afraid that these boys would be kidnapped and held for ransom for the seeds and formulas of Steelite. Because of this lack of formal education from Earth, Kendell felt he must teach Cameron everything he knew and set up a program to do so. He could only hope he would have enough time.

Cameron had an undeniable love of plants, and he knew that his interest in them came from this wonderful old man. With a sigh, he pushed the thought away. He still felt the loss from his grandfather's death.

He spent his vacations going to far-flung places on the planet, looking for interesting plants. He didn't wish to be bothered by the radio and seldom called in to tell anyone where he was or what he was doing. There were still a few days left of his vacation, but Cameron decided to return home. He couldn't understand it, but he felt depressed.

He dressed in his comfortable old hiking clothes and boots and stepped outside the tent. Pansy had run off while he was thinking. He hoped she hadn't gotten too far. He wasn't in the mood to hunt for her.

Looking up at the dark clouds, he could see that another storm was brewing. The clouds seemed to be pressing down on him, making him feel that he was suffocating. He thought he heard a scream, but it must have been the wind. He pulled up the collar of his jacket and stuffed his hands into his pockets. He kicked a clump of dirt a little peevishly. He had not found anything new, and he had had great hopes, as this was the first time he had gone at the end of winter. What he had primarily found was that winter was cold and wet. Tramping around in the wilderness ended up being muddy and uncomfortable.

One of the clouds he was looking at reminded him of his brother and Sean's scar. The shape of the cloud made him remember again how Sean had gotten that scar. It was a day much like today, cold and windy, but it was also raining that day. He had been bored and wanted to play outside. His mother wouldn't let him. The door to his grandfather's study was closed, which meant that he was either taking a nap or busy. Being in a rebellious mood, he decided to play in his father's study, even though he knew this was forbidden.

Cameron loved the smell of that room, like old books, leather, and, somehow, summer days. He wandered around the room, touching this and that. He sat watching a spider make a web on the ceiling of the window seat and thinking how annoyed that would make Peggy, the maid. He enjoyed hearing the rain drumming on the windowpanes, especially when an occasional gust of wind made them rattle. He pretended it was a ghost trying to get at him, and he bravely dared him to try.

Spying his father's ceremonial sword over the mantle, Cameron thought, why not play soldiers? He looked around the room for something to stand on and decided the stool should work very well. Getting the sword down was hard work. He couldn't quite reach high enough to unhook it. If the truth were told, Cameron could barely reach it. The stool was not tall enough, so he took a chair and put the stool on top. He climbed up, and even though his makeshift ladder was a bit wobbly, he managed to get the sword down and himself off the stool without dropping it.

Feeling very naughty but excited, he unsheathed it and took a few practice swings. He continued slashing this way and that, in a harsh whisper saying, "Take this, you mangy cur, take that," in-between grunts of effort, for the sword was heavy for a small boy.

Sean had heard Cameron in his father's study and, knowing that he was not allowed there, wondered what he was up to. He snuck in quietly and stood behind him, intending to scare Cameron by yelling, pretending to be his father. Just then, Cameron was holding the sword high over his head, and making believe there was an enemy behind him, he swung around and brought the blade down all in one movement.

Cameron didn't realize that Sean was standing behind him. The sword slashed down Sean's face, barely missing his left eye. It put a deep gash from forehead to chin. There was a stunned silence; Cameron dropped the sword, numb with shock. Sean put his hand to his face, felt the warm, wet blood seeping through his fingers, and then the pain hit. Both of the boys started screaming at the same time.

The noise alarmed the servants, Peggy and Dawson. They came rushing in. Peggy was horrified and started also screaming, which only made matters worse. Dawson tore Peg's apron from her waist and pressed it to Sean's face to stanch the bleeding. Then he told Peggy to control herself and stop that caterwauling.

Lady Helen heard the screaming and rushed into the room. She almost fainted when she saw all the blood and the sword on the floor. Lady Helen immediately pulled herself together and, like a general, marshaled her forces. She grabbed Sean and ran from the room, barking orders. She yelled over her shoulder, "Dawson, bring the hovercraft around in front. We must rush him to the hospital. Peggy, get our wraps."

They left Cameron standing alone in the middle of the room; his eyes looked too big for his face. He was trembling and cold from shock. Grandfather Kendell had heard the noise coming from the study. He ran out of his room, which was just down the hall, to see what was going on. Kendell saw Helen running with Sean in her arms, yelling about going to the hospital. He quickly went into the study and saw the blood and the sword. He didn't know what had happened, but he could see the state Cameron was in.

Kendell's face didn't show it, but he was seething with anger. How could Helen have left Cameron alone and in such a condition? Didn't she remember that she had two sons?

He grabbed an afghan that was on the couch and wrapped Cameron in it. Picking him up, he carried him into his room. Still holding Cameron, he pulled the rocking chair closer to the fire and sat in it. He rocked the child gently and listened to his tale of what had happened. The boy was sobbing and stuttering so hard that Kendell could barely understand him. It was quite a long time before Cameron calmed down and, exhausted, fell asleep in his grandfather's arms. Kendell held him close for an even longer time, listened to the fire crackling, and wondered how he could protect this precious child.

Even with the best of medical attention, Sean was left with a scar that made his left eyelid sag at the corner and the left side of his mouth turned down in a perpetual sneer.

It had been an accident. Cameron felt very badly for his brother and wished it had never happened, but he didn't think his brother should hold him to account forever.

That settles it. I will leave this morning. I swore I would never go over that ground again. What a miserable mood Cameron was in. He had been waking up to see the morning sun flaming on the surrounding hills covered with virgin snow, which made his soul soar. But this morning, with the sky overcast and threatening rain or perhaps even snow, he thought he might as well pack up and go home.

It was discouraging, and he decided to spend the rest of his vacation at his farm. Things needed doing there even though he had excellent help from the Stuarts, who worked for him. First, he would stop at the mansion, clean up, and get the latest news about Kaitlyn. Thinking of Kaitlyn made him feel a lot better. She had been a strange gawky little thing, but he liked her.

Cameron whistled and called, "Pansy, Pansy. Come on, Pansy, we're going home."

As he packed up his gear, he was still thinking of Kaitlyn. She should be coming home soon. I wonder if she is still interested in plants and hiking and such. It used to be a good threesome. This trip has made me realize how much I miss her. She was a pain at times but usually carried her load. The best was their ability to know what the other was thinking or feeling without voicing it. I guess Earth has probably changed her. After five years, she was bound to have forgotten him. In any case, it will be wonderful to see her again.

Still wool-gathering, as he was preparing to leave, Cameron wondered if they would spend time together as they did as teenagers. Just Kaitlyn, Ian, and I, together, are making plans for the future. It would be fantastic if they really could go into business together as they had talked of so many times in the past. It was a pipe dream, though where would any of them get the money? Damn it, if they wanted to join him, he would find the money. They would have their partnership and their dreams.

It took Cameron over an hour to pack everything up and ready the campsite before he could leave. The wind gave him trouble while collapsing the tent and putting it in its carrier. Pansy had returned and was leaping around, excited to be on the move and getting into everything. On top of that, he couldn't find his notebooks. After looking everywhere, Cameron decided he must have left them in the tent before he packed it up, so he took the tent apart again, which was a real pain. The damn notebooks were there, and after repacking everything, he was ready to be off and glad of it.

"Oh hell, I have to get the traps I set out," he said out loud. He didn't want some poor animals caught in them and left to starve to death. Removing the traps took a couple more hours, and it was after noon when he finally could take off. " Will I never get off this god-forsaken hill?"

Cameron took his time flying back; it was a beautiful day up above the clouds. His hovercraft was in good condition, and he had few worries. With the sun shining, it was hard to believe a storm was brewing just below. He felt no need to hurry, just enjoyed this last day of freedom. The sunbeams glistening off the clouds had utterly erased the anxious feeling he had had all morning.

He made several side trips and landed once to let Pansy out to hunt and do her thing. She didn't find anything, so he gave her a snack and had one himself. He strolled around a bit just for the exercise until it started to rain. He whistled for Pansy, who came running to his call, and they were off again.

He started thinking about Kaitlyn while flying home, and of the time, he had helped save her life. The lower school, which they all attended during the summer months, was having their annual picnic at Crescent Lake. The swimming teacher had given the children from ages eight to twelve a lesson in scuba diving. After the class was over, Ian and Cameron sat on the dock, talking and goofing around, still wearing their gear. Kaitlyn had taken hers off, and as the boys seemed to be ignoring her, she decided to show off by diving in and swimming underwater.

Cameron was the only one watching her, and when she didn't reappear in a minute, he started to get worried. He turned to Ian, "Kaitlyn dove in and has been under too long, I think. I'm going in and look for her. If you don't see either one of us in a minute, run and get some help. She could be in trouble." So saying, he dove in and swam to where he thought she would be.

Sure enough, she was there and struggling to get free. Her hair had got caught in twigs on a waterlogged branch, and she couldn't get loose. She was wide-eyed and frantic but still holding her breath. Cameron grabbed her and tried to shove the mouthpiece from his scuba gear into her mouth. She fought him at first, still panicking, not knowing what he was trying to do. Cameron grabbed her face and made her look into his eyes, and then he tried again.

She finally understood and gulped the air. Only a moment had passed during the struggle, but it seemed longer. Cameron then tried to break the twigs loose, but they were so soggy they just bent. She was calmer now and insisted he take a little air. He did, and they passed the air tube back and forth while both of them fought to free her hair from the branch.

Cameron wished there was more air in the tank. He knew it must be about empty by now. Ian had better hurry up, not letting Kaitlyn know how close they were to running out of air. He couldn't just leave her with the tank; she was still too terrified.

The rest of the class had gone to the picnic tables for their lunch. The teachers were keeping things in order while the students waited in line at the buffet table. Everyone was talking and laughing. They could smell the barbecued meats and see the tables groaning with food. There was some shoving and pushing in a friendly way, but soon most were sitting down to a well-earned meal. It had been a strenuous morning of swimming, diving, and quite a lot of horseplay.

Ian ran up to the group around the picnic tables. He was wide-eyed and frantic. He yelled, "You gotta help. They're in trouble. You gotta save them." He started to turn to run back when the scuba coach grabbed him.

"Who's in what trouble?"

"Kaitlyn and Cameron are in the lake and haven't come back up. Hurry, they're going to drown."

The scuba coach scooped up his gear and started running toward the lake, still holding on to Ian. He said, "Do you know exactly where they went in?"

Ian wrenched away and ran as fast as he could. He yelled over his shoulder, "I'm not exactly sure where they are, but not too far from the pier, I think."

Several other teachers grabbed gear and ran after them, putting on their equipment as they ran. It was only a matter of minutes before they were in the water and searching for Kaitlyn and Cameron. The water was pretty clear, and with Ian's directions, they soon found them even though the log had drifted down the stream with Kaitlyn attached to it. One of the teachers carried a knife in his gear and cut away the branches that held Kaitlyn. She was free just before their tank was empty, and she and Cameron shot to the surface.

Kaitlyn was crying and trembling from the cold and fear. Cameron held her and swam back to the pier that way, not letting the teachers take her from him.

Chapter Five
Sean's Office, Same Day

Sean was busy at his desk looking through the day's mail when he came across an official-looking letter. I have been waiting for a letter, and this must be it. It's about time, he thought. Picking up his silver letter opener, he ripped it open. No, it's concerning Cameron. They want to give him an honorary degree at the university in recognition of his discovery of that damn bamboo. God Damn it, why does he get everything handed to him on a platter. Well, he is not going to get this. It just got lost in the mail. He wadded it up and threw it in the wastebasket. He felt like throwing the rest of the mail in after but didn't. He angrily ripped open the rest and scanned them. The one he wanted was not there.

He was furious now and depressed, thinking of all the times that Cameron had gotten in his way. He fingered his scar, thinking about how he got it. Cameron again. The scene was as clear to Sean as if it had happened that very morning. The sky was overcast, and the room looked gloomy except for a beam of sunlight coming through a break in the clouds, shining through the bay window. He could even smell the musty books and last night's fire from the fireplace. It amazed him that he could still feel the slight thrill of anticipation of his prank. Then it all went wrong. I was only trying to scare Cameron, who must have known I was behind him and decided to put a scare into me. Well, that backfired on both of us, but I ended up with the scar.

His secretary came bustling into the room. She had papers in her hand. "Here are the morning reports, Sir, and there are some people from that Earth delegation here. They want to have a tour of the facility. Do you want to go with them?"

Shocked back into reality, Sean yelled. "No! Can't you see that I am busy? Just leave the morning report; I'll get to it later."

Her eyes widened with surprise, and she nervously took a step back. "You – You always insist that the reports be ready now." There was a note of hurt confusion in her voice.

"I'm sorry, Alice." He tried to look contrite. "I have some things on my mind. Would you please see to the delegation in your very competent way? Tell them I will see them for lunch when they are through. Oh, have a nice luncheon arranged. Thanks."

Much mollified, Alice left the room, and Sean went back to the mail. Reading a few more carefully, he made a few notes, but he couldn't concentrate. He got up, walked over to the window, and looked out. A shadow fell across his face when a bird flew past the window. The noise of a hovercraft landing and people gathering and talking in the courtyard below should have caught his interest, but he was too far gone in his memories. He didn't see or hear anything. He was still angry and couldn't get Cameron off his mind.

How about that time he tricked me into entering the boat-building contest, he thought. I got even with him on that one too. He pounded a fist into the palm of his other hand and grinned nastily. My friends and I caught him alone and beat the hell out of him. He did get a few good licks in with his feet; I'll give him that. They were holding him by his arms, and he just raised both feet and kicked me. I admit I lost it for a few minutes there. It's a good thing the guys pulled me away. They thought I was going to kill him, and he almost ended up in the hospital anyway. He had a broken jaw and two broken ribs, both of Cameron's eyes were blackened, and I broke his nose.

He never told anyone how it happened because we told him if he did, we would rape Kaitlyn and give Ian a dose of the same beating. We wouldn't have raped Kaitlyn, but Cameron wasn't going to take any chances. As for Ian, I wouldn't have minded giving him a lesson or two. He was too cocky by half.

I have to give him credit, though; as soon as he was well enough, Cameron and Ian went ahead with the boat they had started for the contest. They worked on it all year and did a fine job too. I fixed that, though, with a bucket of gasoline. It made a beautiful bonfire. Cameron knew I had done it, but there was no proof.

Remembering these thoughts of retaliation made Sean feel righteous, and he returned to his correspondence with a smile. That's what he gets for trying to outshine me.

Chapter Six

Ian

Ian stretched his arms up, then put his hands behind his head, looked up, and gazed at the ceiling. It was time for a break. He had been sitting too long in front of his computer again. His eyes felt dry and gritty. I should blink more often, he thought. I'll be glad when we get this new ceramic process completed. My mind thinks that it's sloughing through mud; it's so tedious and boring. If only it were robotics, I'd never be tired or bored. But that was not what his family's firm specialized in. Right now, they needed a stronger ceramic that could withstand heat and friction.

Being the third son had disadvantages on Heatherbound. There was no hope of financial help from his parents, except for the birth trust of two thousand credits. That was one of the central credos of the Heatherbound manifesto. There were two reasons: The family would have continuity by the eldest inheriting, and the younger sons would gain strength by knowing they had to be self-sufficient. The policy thus made a stronger community of independent people. The policy sounded wise and made a lot of sense, but it wasn't easy to get started in your own business without money behind you.

Ian wanted to start a company that manufactured and designed robots, but it would be years before he could save enough money from his salary to fulfill that dream. It was a good thing they were a long-lived race, he thought with a grin, because he would be a very old man before he could put his name on a letterhead.

His family was not wealthy but comfortable. He had three brothers and two sisters, and the birth trusts for so many had made it difficult to expand the business. It seemed every time they needed money to expand, the family expanded instead. He smiled, thinking of that. He had no complaints. The business employed the whole family, and they lived comfortably. They always had plenty to eat, a lovely house, and lots of love and laughter. They even had a few luxuries, such as his hoverbike. He got that for his twelfth birthday.

He got up from his desk, stretched some more, and decided to get a cup of coffee. Right now, all he wanted was to get away from this desk and be out in the backcountry with Cameron. What a lucky dog, four weeks with no one to tell him what to do or where to go. I wonder if he knows that Kaitlyn is back.

His oldest brother, Martin, was getting a cup of coffee at the same time and said, "How are you doing on that report? Think you'll get it done in time to go to the McPherson's ball tonight? You and Kaitlyn used to be pretty close. Have you seen her since she's been back?"

"You've been keeping me so friggen' busy I haven't even had time to call her," Ian said with a grin and poured his coffee, no sugar or cream. "And yes, I will get the report done today. And I'll see her tonight at the ball."

"Bet she's grown up some. Earth does that to you," Martin said and, with a slight questioning frown, continued, "I always wondered what you kids did all the time you spent together. You always came home looking like you had a wonderful time."

"Yeah, we did have some great times together. I remember mostly digging tunnels and making underground secret rooms. Sometimes we would find tall grasses, and we tied them together at the tops for more long tunnels on the surface. We thought no one could ever find us if we ever needed to hide."

"Didn't having a girl tag along cramp your style?"

Ian shrugged and raised his eyebrows. "We never thought of Kaitlyn as a girl, or at least most of the time; we didn't. Cameron was sometimes a little protective of her, worrying that she might get hurt. But most of the time, we didn't give it a thought. She always insisted on doing her share."

Enjoying his memories, Ian continued telling of them. "Oh, another thing I especially liked was the days we took bamboo sleds and slid down the hills of grass. Boy, did we get going sometimes. It seems we slid faster than the wind. We used the same sleds in the winter, too."

"I envy you, your memories. It seemed that all we ever did when we were kids was go to movies, read books, and hang around," said Martin smiling slightly. "Enough with the reminiscing. If we want to go dancing tonight, we'd better get back to work. That report has to be on Dad's desk in the morning."

"O.K., slave driver," Ian said with a smile, and they both went back to their work.

When Ian got back to his desk with his coffee, he stared at the screen of his monitor, not seeing it. Still thinking about his conversation with Martin, he continued reflecting on the wonderful days the three had spent together. He leaned back in his chair with his hands locked behind his head and his feet up on the desk. How about that time that we built a fire to roast wienies, and Cameron's jacket caught on fire? Boy, that was scary. He sure caught it when he got home from that one. His mom grounded him for a week and made him promise not to build any more fires. From then on, building fires was my job. He chuckled quietly to himself, thinking about that.

Sometimes we would just lie on the grass and talk about our futures. We were always going to start a business together, pool our money and talents. I would design robots, Cameron would do research, and Kaitlyn would manage the finances and paperwork. We could spend hours just talking about it and making plans.

Thinking these thoughts, he could almost smell the summer grasses, feel the heat of the sun on his body, and feel grateful again for the vagrant breezes that occasionally cooled them. He remembered the excitement they had in their dreams, the fun they had planning their next day's adventure, and it was always an adventure, it seemed.

"Hey Ian, how is that report coming along?"

Startled, Ian came back to the present with a bang, as his chair fell back and he landed on the floor.

Chapter Seven
That same night

It was after nine when Cameron finally arrived at the family residence. The house looked pretty dark, but there was a light in his window. He was not surprised, his parents were probably visiting friends, and they were not expecting him tonight. All he truly wanted was a long, hot shower, then a hot meal. He was awfully tired of camp food and cold baths. Any information that his parents had about Kaitlyn, Dawson would tell him.

Hurrying to his rooms, with Pansy following him quietly, he found Dawson there. On the bed was his formalwear. It consisted of a heavy black silk jacket with full sleeves with slashes to show the creamy silk shirt he would wear beneath. The jacket had silver buttons with the McCreight crest on them. His pants were of the same material but tightly fitted to show off the shape of his legs. His boots were soft black leather, unadorned. Beside this was his ceremonial sash in Steelite and cobalt blue, the McCreight colors, a cummerbund, and a jeweled sword.

Dawson had been waiting for him. He rushed forward and started tugging at Cameron's coat and said in a querulous voice, "Thank God you've finally come home. I was instructed to wait in your rooms just in case." The look on his face implied that he had been waiting for hours.

"Sir, you must hurry and change. We could not reach you because, as usual, you didn't call in. Why don't you at least answer your beeper? We needed to tell you of the welcoming home ball for the McPherson ladies. They returned from Earth two days ago. We knew you would wish to attend." He pulled Cameron's coat off.

"Quite right, Dawson," Cameron said as he shrugged out of his shirt and began pulling off his boots. "What are they doing home so soon? They were not expected for another month, at the earliest."

Dawson took Cameron's jacket with a look of disgust, folded it carefully to make sure that no debris fell onto the clean carpet.

"A delegation from Earth was coming here and invited the McPherson girls to join them. What difference does it make? You must hurry and get ready," said Dawson in irritation as he yanked at Cameron's pants.

Looking at Cameron's boots, Dawson said, "Tsh, Tsh. It will take me all night to get those boots clean!"

"A delegation from Earth, huh? " Said Cameron, trying to keep from smiling at Dawson's grumbling. "That must have taken some pull. Anyway, thanks. I'm sorry I didn't call, but you know how it is. Time just slipped away. I'll take a quick shower. Could you get me a sandwich or something while I'm getting ready? I haven't eaten much since breakfast. Oh, and a plate of something for Pansy."

Grumbling about the time, Dawson hurried to the kitchen. He returned with a sandwich and plate of leftovers for Pansy just as Cameron was coming out of the bathroom toweling himself. Having shaved before his shower, he was ready to don his clothes, but first the sandwich. He started munching on it, stark naked. Dawson looked at him with disapproval and poured him a glass of wine.

"I see that the chicken is acceptable. I hope you enjoy the wine as well. It was probably wise that you chose to eat undressed, especially since we are in a hurry. I don't have time to do any spotting."

Cameron laughed, stuffed the last of the sandwich into his mouth, drained the glass of wine, and started to get dressed. "Dawson, you're a gem. You are actually getting quite mellow in your old age."

Dawson sniffed and adjusted Cameron's jacket. He then took a brush to the already gleaming boots and handed them to him.

Cameron looked in the full-length mirror in his room to adjust his sword and check his appearance. He saw a tall man, six feet three inches, very tanned from all the time he spent outside. He had piercing blue eyes and a shock of black hair worn in the current fashion of long enough to curl on his neck. His mouth was generous, and his nose slightly crooked, having been broken. He was satisfied with the image. It would do. The formal dress had reverted to feudalism, but damn, it did make an impression. He felt he was ready for anything.

"Thanks again, Dawson," said Cameron as he ran from the room and rushed to his hovercraft. Pansy wanted to go too, but Cameron told her to stay.

A short while later, he arrived at the McPherson mansion. It was a huge house, reminding one of the great houses in England, except this had an efficient central heating system. The house was made of local stone and had two wings, with a portico in the center. One wing was dark. The other had light streaming from all its windows, making the snow on the trees and bushes glisten. The house made Cameron think of a Christmas card he had once seen as a child. The lighted wing held the ballroom, and as he landed, he could hear the music of a waltz.

The receiving line had disbanded, so he went looking for Angus McPherson, Kaitlyn's father, to pay his respects and explain why he was late. He then went to his father and mother, standing with friends near the dance floor, talking.

Sir John and Lady Helen saw Cameron crossing the room and broke away from their friends to greet him. Both reached out their hands to him. He hugged his mother first and then his father. "Thank you, Father, for having Dawson ready with my clothes. I would have hated to miss this. Next time I'll take your suggestion and call in each evening."

"It wouldn't hurt, and your mother would worry less, but I'll believe that when it happens," replied Sir John with a laugh. "You must tell us all about your trip and what you may have discovered, but not tonight. There is dancing to be done."

"Yes," said Lady Helen, "we're so glad that you made it back in time. I didn't think you would. I didn't expect you for a few more days. Kaitlyn has been asking after you as well as a few other young ladies."

While he was talking to his parents, Cameron watched the dancers out of the corner of his eye. He saw Ian dancing with a new face. "Who is that beauty in the blue dress dancing with Ian?"

Sir John looked to see and smiled. "That's Kaitlyn. Grown-up, hasn't she? I doubt that she would climb trees with you anymore,"

Cameron grimaced at the allusion. "If you will excuse me, I think I'll cut in to say hello."

"By all means," said his father, patting Cameron on the back. "You mustn't let Ian get too much of a jump on you."

At that moment, the music stopped. Upon seeing Cameron, Ian, and Kaitlyn came over to their group. Kaitlyn was laughing and looking up at Ian. They made a beautiful couple. Ian was tall, broad-shouldered, with red hair cut much shorter than the current style., and a small mustache. Kaitlyn was petite, only about 5 feet 5 inches, with strawberry blond hair. Her hair was soft and full around her face and worn in a long braid over her shoulder. She had twisted a gold chain of pearls and blue jewels in the braid. Kaitlyn's dress was silk chiffon, tight in the bodice and low cut, which showed her neck and shoulders, also the swelling of her breasts to good advantage. Her skirt was full, which emphasized the smallness of her waist. There was a lightness to her step that he remembered so well, but he had forgotten how graceful she was, or had he never noticed before? His heart pounded at the sight of her, his mouth felt dry, and he felt slightly out of breath.

The next emotion that Cameron felt was a stab of jealousy at seeing them together. He felt an irrational urge to strangle his best friend at that moment.

Kaitlyn extended both hands to Cameron and said, "You finally made it. Your parents said you would be late and may not be able to attend at all. I was devastated, but you're here now. The three of us are together again."

"Kaitlyn, you look wonderful, all grown up. I didn't even recognize you at first." said Cameron, taking her hands and ignoring Ian. "If only I had known you were home, I would have come back immediately. I feel like kicking myself for not calling in and seeing you sooner. We thought you wouldn't be home for another month. What happened?"

"A delegation from Earth was coming to Heatherbound for a conference. Glendora and I were invited to return home with them as they had extra space. We were dying to come home and heartily sick of Earth," said Kaitlyn, a little out of breath with excitement as Cameron still held her hands. Her face was flushed, and her eyes grew large with the sudden passion that surged through her. They had eyes only for each other as if there was no one else in the room.

31

The orchestra started playing again, which broke the spell. Other couples were making their way to the dance floor. "You can let go of the little lady now, Cameron," said Ian, with a smile and turning to Kaitlyn. "I believe we have the next dance."

Both Kaitlyn and Cameron looked at him aghast and then at each other. "Let me see your dance card, Kaitlyn," said Cameron, laughing, as he wrote his name across all the dances. "There must be some mistake, Ian. All the rest of Kaitlyn's dances seem to have been taken by me."

Ian took the card from Cameron, "Sure enough, all have been taken except the next one, which I will relinquish, as the look on your faces goes to my heart." Ian said in a bantering tone.

Chapter Eight
The Following Morning

Cameron had had a restless night thinking of Kaitlyn and the future. It was full of dreams, both good and bad. His sheets were tangled, and so was his mind. When he heard the morning birds chirping, it was a welcome sound. It was the signal that morning had finally arrived, and he could get up.

He knew what he wanted and realized that he had known his feelings for Kaitlyn for a very long time. He hadn't realized it until last night when he saw her looking up at Ian. It cut him like a knife. He'd never felt such primitive rage, barely under control.

She had always been there for him, and now he knew he wanted to marry her. Nothing else in life mattered. He could only hope that she felt the same way. She seemed to last night when he kissed her. She's so grown-up now, though; maybe that reaction was just something she learned on Earth. I wonder if she had a boyfriend on Earth. She must have; after all, she was gone for five years.

Thank God he had an excuse to see Kaitlyn early this morning by bringing the moorcat, Pansy, back to her. He would miss Pansy and was a bit worried that the moorcat wouldn't remember Kaitlyn. Moorcats can be unruly and difficult when not happy. Perhaps he should just keep her. After all, Kaitlyn had been gone all those years.

Kaitlyn had been having similar thoughts all night. She, too, hadn't slept well. She knew he liked her, but could that grow into the love that she bore him? Had he dated much while she was gone? When he kissed her last night, she never wanted it to end. Her body wanted more, much more. She felt that passion again just thinking about him.

After tossing and turning all night, Kaitlyn got up very early and took her morning shower. Going to her full-length mirror, she removed her towel and surveyed her body with a critical eye. Could he see that Kaitlyn had grown up during these last five years? She was no longer that awkward, boyish girl that always tagged along. She was now a grown woman. Her breasts were not overly large but nicely shaped, and her waist was tiny. Turning slightly, she looked at her bottom. It could be a bit bigger, and maybe my legs are a bit too thin. Would he think so?

She went to her closet to pick out what she would wear. Nothing was right. She wanted to be perfect but not too perfect for her early morning date with Cameron. She tried on several outfits, and after much indecision, she finally decided on jeans and a blue sweater, the color of her eyes. Suddenly she had a horrible thought, what if Pansy didn't remember her?

She began watching for them from her window, wishing that time would fly and he would arrive. When she saw Cameron's hovercraft, she ran from her window and out the door to greet them. She met them on the dew lawn covered and knelt beside Pansy, getting her knees wet. She didn't even notice. She reached out for the moorcat to smell her hand.

"Oh, she's so beautiful." She looked up at Cameron with adoring eyes. "You've kept such good care of her. You can't know how much I've missed you both."

Pansy sniffed her hand, then stood on her hind legs and patted Kaitlyn's face with her wet paws. She remembered this was her old gesture of affection. She made a growling-purr sound and settled in Kaitlyn's lap.

Cameron sat down on the grass beside her. "I guess she does remember you after all," with a touch of disappointment. "I was afraid she might not."

Pansy was a native of Heatherbound, and had four claw-like fingers on the paws of her front legs with opposing thumbs. Her hind feet were like a cat's paws. Moorcats could sit up like squirrels to eat and were daytime foragers. They mostly ate nuts, worms, grubs, very small animals, and some vegetation in the wild. Their fur was short and velvety, usually a dark gray with white stripes down the back. The average size was about the same as Earth's bobcat. They were very choosy about mates and didn't mate often.

Cameron, Kaitlyn, and Ian found Pansy on one of their hikes. Kaitlyn had heard a meowing noise that sounded like a cry of pain. "I heard something." She paused to listen. "There is goes again. Do you hear it? Let's check it out."

"Yeah, I heard it too. It sounds like it is over this way," said Ian.

"Sounds like it's hurt to me. Kaitlyn, stay back a little way. It could be dangerous," said Cameron. "Ian and I will see what it is."

"Don't be silly, Cameron. There is nothing out here to hurt us, and anyway, I want to see it too. I heard it first," said Kaitlyn as she ran ahead to investigate.

Kaitlyn got there first and saw a small animal crouching in the grass. "Oh, it's a baby moorcat. She looks half-starved. The poor thing, his hind leg, looks like it's been chewed by something," said Kaitlyn as she knelt beside the small wounded animal.

When the moorcat saw them, she was badly frightened. She tried to get away but was too weak. Kaitlyn talked to her quietly and gently picked her up. The moorcat tried to scratch and bite, but Kaitlyn quickly wrapped her in her scarf. They gave her water, and the moorcat lapped it up frantically. Then Kaitlyn mixed up some bread, meat, and water and fed her several times in the next hour.

Kaitlyn's gentle handling, and soft words of comfort, calmed the moorcat, and she no longer fought to get away. When she seemed strong enough to move, Cameron took off his sweater shirt and made a blanket sling to carry her. He tied the baby moorcat on the back of Kaitlyn's hoverbike.

They named her Pansy, after the skunk in Bambi, because she was black with only one white stripe down her back. Most Moorcats had three. She was also very tiny for a baby moorcat. The three figured because of her difference; she must have been banished from the den.

Kaitlyn fell in love with her, and when they got back from their hike, she took Pansy to her vet. She was stitched up and given antibiotics, then sent home with Kaitlyn. Kaitlyn made a soft bed for her beside her own and looked after her like a mother hen. All three spent the next week in Kaitlyn's room, catering to the little animal. Glendora came in occasionally and was interested in all the details of how they found Pansy. She wanted to design clothes for Pansy, but when Kaitlyn said no, she lost interest.

It wasn't long before Pansy became a fourth member on their hikes. She would run ahead, hunt, and return to them. When Pansy got tired, one of them would carry her. She loved riding on the hoverbikes, too.

Kaitlyn was reminded of this while she cuddled the moorcat. "Cameron, we did have some great hikes, didn't we? It's been so long since I've walked any distance. Do you have time for one now?"

"I still have a couple of days' vacation time, and I had hoped to spend them with you." He took her hand and helped her up. He did not let go of her hand, and she did not try to take it away. They just stood looking at each other for a few minutes.

"Let's take the hoverbikes and go way into the country, as we used to," said Cameron in a slightly husky voice. "Do you still have two, do you think?"

"We must. Dad never gets rid of anything," said Kaitlyn with a laugh.

They walked hand in hand to the garage and, sure enough, found the two bikes. Both covered with old sheets. Kaitlyn's father emptied the gas tanks for storage, but other than that, they seemed ready to go. Nearby they found gas cans and filled the tanks.

"Let's take a picnic lunch. I haven't eaten breakfast, and this way, we can be gone as long as we like," said Kaitlyn. "I'll just go the kitchen and see what we can take."

"Great idea; I haven't eaten either. I'll check out the bikes while you're gone."

Cameron spent a little time making sure that the bikes were working properly, and when Kaitlyn returned with the picnic basket, off, they went. Pansy rode in her old seat behind Kaitlyn. Cameron strapped the picnic basket behind him on his bike.

The ride was thrilling for Kaitlyn. She hadn't been on a hoverbike while on Earth, and she had almost forgotten how much fun it was. They wove in and out with each other, and Cameron flew around Kaitlyn a few times, giving her a little scare. She squealed with delight, like a teenager. The wind pulled a few strands of her hair loose around her face. She never looked lovelier, and she couldn't ever remember being happier.

The sun had come up and burned off the morning dew. It promised to be a warm day. Most of the snow had melted off, and the hills were starting to green. Kaitlyn could hear meadowlarks singing and was dizzy with the smell of the wildflowers. God, she had missed Heatherbound and everything about it.

Soon they arrived at their old stomping grounds. Both were ravenous. Cameron spread out the blanket while Kaitlyn got out their food. Pansy immediately ran off to hunt.

They ate quickly, talking and laughing all the time. Kaitlyn could always make Cameron laugh, and she hadn't lost her touch.

While clearing things away, their hands touched. It was like an electric shock for both of them. Almost fearfully, Cameron pulled her into his arms and kissed her as they lay back down on the blanket. A spasm seemed to run down her body, and she made a slight groaning sound. He put his hand on her breast, wondering if she would stop him. His hand seemed to have a mind of its own and pulled her sweater up. She wasn't wearing a bra, and he gasped at the beauty of her breasts. He wanted to kiss them. He wanted to kiss her whole body. She didn't say no.

For the next few weeks, Cameron was thinking of her constantly. He wanted to be with her every possible minute. Cameron's work was suffering. He couldn't concentrate on it when he tried. He'd go for walks to clear his mind and see things that reminded him of Kaitlyn, such as a scarf in the window of a shop the color of her eyes. He would go in and have them send it to her. He sent her arrays of roses, her favorite flower, and called her five times a day. He never knew that love could be like this. It was painful to be away from her and painful to be with her unless they could be alone.

Kaitlyn was deliriously happy.

Chapter Nine
Troubled Departure

One hundred and seventy years ago, by Earth reckoning, a group of Scots-Irishmen got permission, and some financial assistance, from Great Britain to gather together 3000 people who wished to leave Earth and colonize another planet. Several G-Type suns were near Arcturus, and that was the direction they chose to explore. They intended to use cryonics to keep the expenses down. Cryonics would enable them to transport many people and the animals they would need to start a colony.

The science of Cryogenics was perfected fifty years ago and used in medical circles for short periods of time. The scientists concerned with space took it one step further and experimented with live animals and then human volunteers for much more extended periods. Ninety-nine percent lived through the freezing process and showed no ill effects. The people and their animals could be frozen to the point where their metabolic rate would be so low that no chemical processes would take place. Theoretically, they could live forever in suspended animation.

Cryonics was opening the door to the stars, and this group would be the first to use it. Before, spaceships had to be huge, with large areas for sleeping, recreation, recycling chambers for water and air, and hydroponic gardens. There were crew quarters, a library, a kitchen, and dining rooms. Very few of these spaceships were produced, and they were used only for research and military applications.

Even though the cost to the government was minimal, there was uproar from the general public, fanned by the media, because of the expense and seemingly special consideration for a racial group. There were talk shows on TV and banner headlines in all the newspapers. The spaceport was picketed by special interest groups. Rioting and threats ensued, causing the government to reconsider even its minimal support.

The Leaders of the expedition were called Elders. They wrote letters to the media and tried to get on talk shows to tell their side of the story. They talked to their friends in high places in the government to create more time. It gained them a few extra months as The House of Government debated the issue.

The Mothership had already been manufactured in space and was ready to go. All that was needed was to finish the space pods before the backing was taken away. The project was speeded up. The people in charge knew that if there were any delays, the ship and pods might never go. All of the participants had invested their life savings, and there was little chance of recuperating any of this investment. They had to go.

A strong guard had to be put up to forestall sabotage because of the picketing and rioting. Many safeguards were eliminated from the construction of the space pods themselves. There was still a lot that could go wrong with cryonics, and there were usually two backup systems. Now they only had one. Without both backup systems, there could be a higher death rate or even complete failure of the mission. The future colonists knew this, but most of them were optimistic and were willing to take their chances. The few that decided not to go were easily replaced by more courageous, or perhaps, more desperate people.

These people were scientists, farmers, engineers, and general workers from all walks of life. All of the same faith and desirous of a better place to live and work. Great Britain was only too happy to send off these people in hopes of finding new planets and products, especially if they could do it without any political backlash. Population control was not working. Earth was overcrowded and getting poorer, in need of raw resources and a way to rid itself of dissidents. The colony ship provided this. If they survived, many more could be sent to other planets.

The ship consisted of twenty cryonic pods and fifteen cargo barges attached to the Mothership. The people, animal embryos, and seeds were put into the pods and frozen. The tools, machines, and everything needed to start a colony were put into the cargo barges. The mothership held the Elders and, of course, the crew.

The Mothership had a robotic probe that automatically went out to all planets they passed, which were close enough, to check for viability. It checked not only for a place where humans could live but a planet as near to Earth standards as possible, such as gravity, rotation of the planet, temperature range, water, and arable land.

When the probe found a planet it deemed met the requirements, it returned to the Mothership and revived the Elders for their opinion. The Elders and six crewmembers were also frozen but were to be revived in case of an emergency or when a suitable planet was found. It would be the decision of the Elders which planet would be acceptable.

They were finally ready to go. The cargo barges had already been filled and sent up to the Mothership. So had the entire range of animal embryos and seeds, which were frozen in five of the cryonic pods. All that remained was the people, two hundred in each of the remaining fifteen pods. They had been assigned to their pods and were lined up in an orderly fashion on their allotted day. It was decided that each day three groups would go, expecting that this would forestall last minute problems from the picketers. It was hoped that no one would know exactly when the colonists would be leaving the planet for good. The plan worked, and they were off.

During the long voyage, many planets were checked by the probe and found wanting without consulting the Elders. The probe awakened the Elders three times, and those planets were rejected, also. They had been fortunate during the voyage, and there had been no ship emergencies. The crew had only been revived when helping the Elders explore possible planets.

Finally, after forty-nine years, Heatherbound was found and approved of by the Elders. The pods and the cargo barges were ferried down separately. The Mothership could never land. It was meant to remain in space, orbiting the planet, to be used as a research station.

The Elders, with the help of the crew, revived the colonists. This took time because each person needed personal attention upon awakening. Two hundred and fifty-nine could not be revived. This was a much higher loss than expected, and many people were sick as well. Of the fifteen pods sent out, only five had no loss of life, and one had one hundred percent loss. The would-be colonist had died peacefully, though. They looked as if they had gone to sleep and didn't wake up. It was decided to cremate them and spread their ashes on the planet they so wanted to colonize.

The first six years were touch-and-go for the colony. Some of the supplies that were supposed to have been sent were not. Other supplies did not survive, such as some of the seeds and animal embryos. There was talk of sabotage, but this was discouraged, morale was already low, and the speculation would not help. The things they needed could only be gotten from Earth, which was far away.

Meanwhile, they used what they had to build houses, roads, and everything needed to build a small city. The local stone was quite handsome, and most people opted to use it in building their homes. Others decided to make bricks so that their houses would be more like the home they missed.

A square mile was promised to each colonist, plus a city lot. Any more land needed would have to be bought from the Elders to build up the Colony's treasury.

During the forty-nine years that the colonists were in transit, Earth had changed both politically and economically. Several other colony ships had been sent out. They were faster and better equipped by business Consortiums but not as particular about the type of planet that they discovered. It did not matter to the Consortiums if the planet would barely sustain life for humans; their only concern was the raw resources that could be obtained from the planet. These colonists had found planets and were already sending raw materials back to the mega-businesses that sent them. These transfers were to repay the Consortiums for the initial costs of the expedition and supplies needed by the colonies.

The countries of Earth could no longer afford to send ships or materials to outer space. Only big businesses could afford it, with the expectation of a return, a very profitable return. The companies would only agree to finance the colonists if they vowed to pay back all costs at an interest rate of fifteen percent. Also, the colonists could only buy additional supplies from the Consortium that had originally financed them until the costs were repaid. This led to virtual slavery for most of the colonists on these planets.

Heatherbound colonists were lucky in some ways because they did not have to pay anyone back for equipping the pods, and supplying all the needed material to colonize a planet. The problem was that no one was responsible for keeping them supplied until they were an established colony. Therefore, to get the things they needed to exist on a level above the stone age, Heatherbound's colonists had to come up with trade goods that had enough value or uniqueness to warrant the interest of the Consortiums. That was where Steelite came in. The seeds were as precious as diamonds and guarded as closely.

Kendell McCreight discovered this plant and its properties several years after landing on Heatherbound. He thus saved them all by finding an export that would make this planet worthwhile to Earth for trade. It was said that he died at only one hundred and eight due to the strain from overwork and worries entailed in perfecting this plant.

Steelite was a plant that grew much like cotton, felt like coarse silk, and, when treated with chemicals, had the tensile strength of steel. It was also a perfect insulating material, lightweight, and with better insulating value than anything yet discovered. It could be used in spacecraft for not only insulation in the natural stage but for the entire hull of the ship when treated to be as rigid as steel. It was only one-fourth the weight of steel, and when layered, it was stronger, and strong enough to withstand a nuclear blast. It could also be used in spacesuits or armor when a different chemical formula was used. When woven in its natural state, it could be used like linen or cotton denim, and it was very sturdy. When chemically treated, spun very thin, and woven tightly, it looked like gray, metallic silk.

There were two disadvantages to Steelite. One was its color, a medium-dark gray. Therefore it was usually only used for work clothes or insulation of overcoats, vests, and other items of clothing It was also used in dress clothes when made like silk, but this material was costly and, of course, could only be made in the one color, medium-dark gray. Also, when treated like steel, it had to be molded perfectly before it was set because it could not be cut or melted, or even filed once it had been set. Until the technology for precision-tooled parts made from Steelite was perfected, machined parts from Earth were still in demand.

Chapter Ten
Two Months Later

Cameron was walking on his favorite hill overlooking the fields of Steelite. He was playing hooky from the manufacturing plant again. It seemed such a waste of time to be there when his father and Sean managed very well without him. He hated the noise and seeming confusion of manufacturing. Give him plants, soil samples or test tubes, and he was at home.

God, he wanted to tell Sean where to shove it. He would have to find a way to make a good living before he could do that. The bamboo wood that he had discovered had helped Heatherbound. But because he didn't own the property that it grew on, he received no income from the discovery. The Elders did give him an extra square mile of land next to the plot that was set aside for him when he reached 21. He also received 1000 federal credits.

His farm consisted of these two square miles and was doing reasonably well, but that was considered a small farm, and it made just enough to pay the help and upkeep with a little left over. Not enough to support a family comfortably. His goal was to find another plant like Steelite. He knew he could if only he had the time. His month's vacation and the few stolen moments he had were not enough.

For years he had been trying to find a plant to crossbreed with Steelite. He wanted one that would have some of the same properties and also other colors. He felt, with time, he could find such a plant. He stubbornly kept looking, not only for a possible native plant but also at the McCreight fields and his own fields, for a variation of color.

His constant surveillance had come to fruition. He had been finding rare plants that were a lighter gray. By crossbreeding these lighter gray plants, he could get a wide variety of grays, including an almost pure white. This used a good proportion of his land, which was why he wasn't making much money from it. The discoveries weren't for sale.

Cameron had kept this project a private one because his brother had a way of stealing ideas or putting obstacles in his way. He grew his plants on land that he owned, his farm, which was several kilometers away from the big

43

farms owned by his family. His security system was even more stringent than on his father's farms.

There had been many attempts over the years to steal Steelite seeds. People had tried to bribe workers to disclose the formulas needed to process the plant. It was made public that the formulas were so complex that no one could remember them all, and they were kept in a safe that only opened twice a year on a timer. This was not true, but it was widely believed. Consequently, very elaborate schemes were concocted to gain the secrets of Steelite.

Electrified Steelite fences guarded the McCreight farms, and guard dogs patrolled them. All the seeds not needed for the next harvest were destroyed. Seeds saved for the harvest were coated with a special substance that had to have another chemical added to insure germination at the planting time.

Cameron had great hopes that this year's crops would give him his pure white or at least a very light, silvery gray. With experimentation, he found that the lighter the gray the less effect the chemicals had on the material, it would not harden into steel. Also, the woven material was softer, more silken but not as strong as silk. For some reason the plants in his own fields kept reverting to the dark gray, at least most of them did. This year he had changed the formula for the fertilizer in a few small areas and hoped this would be the difference he needed. If he could devote his full time to this project, he knew he could find what he was looking for.

Cameron had also been searching during this time for the plants his grandfather had found. The records were not clear as to just where they were found, or how he had managed to change them so quickly. Grandfather Kendell was considered to be the greatest biologist and biochemist of his time, and this bit of bioengineering was his crowning achievement. Sir Kendell had found uses for other native plants, but nothing else as important as Steelite.

Cameron felt that if he could find the plants at the source again, he could possibly find a way to get vibrant colors, and make this material more desirable than any precious metal. He wanted it to be a material that people had looked for down through the ages. A material that could not be stained, dirt could not cling to it, almost impossible to tear, yet feel and look like the finest silk. To this date it was still an impossible dream.

While thinking, he had been making his way to a patch of color he had seen in a rocky area near the top of the hill. He thought it might be something he had not found before because the color was a scarlet red. The sound of a hovercraft brought Cameron back to reality. Could he never get away from his brother? He turned back now and watched the hovercraft land. Sure enough, it was Alan Young, foreman of the shipping area of the plant.

"Hey, Cameron, I thought you would be up here," yelled Alan, getting out of the hovercraft, "your brother sent me to fetch you." While walking toward Cameron, Allen was looking around. He shouted, " what a beautiful view, I don't blame you for liking it up here."

Cameron waved and walked reluctantly towards Alan. He made a mental note to come back here soon to look at those plants.

"So Sean is worried that I am not in the office overseeing you, again. Sorry Alan, I'll follow you back."

As they walked towards Cameron's hovercraft, Cameron asked, "Have there been any problems with the shipment of Steelite for the space ship that is being built?"

Alan shrugged his shoulders and said, "No, just the usual. It was big and bulky, but went up as scheduled."

Walking around a mound of soil on the grass-covered hill, Alan said with enthusiasm, "The McPherson's ceramic motors fit our shuttles perfectly and are everything they claimed them to be. It took them long enough to come up with it, but what a fantastic job they did. All it took was that new ceramic that the Scott clan came up with. It was timely, since our metal rockets are about worn out." continued Alan. "With Earth wanting an arm and a leg to replace anything, we sure needed something, or we weren't going to get anything up in space again without selling our souls."

Patting Alan on the back, "I wasn't worried about the shipment, I knew you would have no problems. As for the motors, Federated Consortium is going to be furious. They thought they had us by the short ones, " laughed Cameron. "They sure have tried, haven't they, for the last fifty years. The celebration tonight should be spectacular."

"I probably should have been there for the big send-off of the Earth delegation, using the new ceramic motor, but there were enough people expected. Anyway, I did not want to steal your thunder. You and Esther have worked too long on coordinating this with the McPherson clan. It should put feathers in your caps." Cameron said as he got into his hovercraft. "See you back at the plant."

On arriving at the plant, Cameron went immediately to Sean's office. "You were looking for me?"

"Yes, needless to say, this was a very important occasion and I wanted all of management to be there for the delegation's departure. If you weren't family, I would fire you." Sean said coldly, looking up from some papers he had been working on at his desk. "I guess you felt wandering around the hills was more important than the latest break-through we have had in years in Hi-Tech."

Cameron took a deep breath to hold his temper and still standing said, "Sean, I agree that it was an important occasion. But I don't agree that my presence was needed or required. It was yours and Alan's day. I do the work required of me at the plant, but prefer to work at the farms or on my own projects, as you well know. If you wish to fire me, we will take that up with Dad."

"You waste time on these projects of yours. If you really feel you must experiment, why not work in the company lab with our researchers to find the precision tooling formula?" Looking up from his desk angrily, Sean said, "This is the research that is needed, not color or material."

Cameron wet his dry lips and replied with a tone of voice that implied that this had been discussed many times before. "I have told you Sean, their line of research is a dead end, in my opinion. The answer is in the plant, not the formula."

"Do you think you are as good as Grandfather, or even better? Come down to earth, Cameron. You don't have the education or the genius," said Sean sarcastically. "Even if you did come up with something on your lousy little farm, do you think I would let you take credit for it? You work for McCreight Industries. Anything you might discover with your puny efforts will be mine because you work for me. Remember, you are just part of the

46

team," said Sean with a hateful grin. He was enjoying the look on Cameron's face.

"What I do on my farm, on my time, is mine," said Cameron, white-faced with anger and fear.

"Come up with something, if you can, and we will see what my lawyers have to say about that." Sean laughed. "You couldn't begin to fight me, Cameron."

"If you are quite through, Sean, I will get back to my office," Cameron said coldly as he turned and left the office.

He felt impotent. It hadn't occurred to him that Sean could steal his research, all he had been working for, for the last three years. Well it wasn't going to happen and he wouldn't be frightened into quitting when he was so close. This just pushed him that much closer to leaving McCreight Industries.

Chapter Eleven
Early Years

Heatherbound was an ideal planet in many ways, but it did have a few drawbacks. It was mostly grassy plains with low rolling hills, with plenty of rivers, lakes, and even oceans. There was no natural forest, very little petroleum, and only traces of most metals. There was a wide range of animals, but they were mostly small and herbivorous. The waters were teeming with fish. The flora and fauna were generally digestible and nutritious for humans. This helped save the colonist during the first few years.

Human plants and animals did very well on this planet, but they grew very slowly. The hardwood trees, after all these years, were still young, only a few ready for harvesting. The other plants,, such as hay, vegetables, and even flowers, took much longer to germinate and grow than they did on Earth. Even humans lived longer, about one hundred years longer, and the gestation period was fifteen months. The scientists attributed this to less radiation from the sun due to a thicker ionosphere and to lower gravity. People weighed about a tenth less here and the average height was six feet for men. What this planet lacked in natural resources was more than made up for by the good climate and gentle weather.

There were three main land masses and several smaller island chains. The robots checked all of them and chose the largest land mass. The area that was first settled had long summers and short winters due to the rotation and tilt of the planet. Heatherbound had two small moons that had a mild gravitational pull, enough to stir up the oceans.

When the colonists first arrived, they set up temporary shelters and planted fields of vegetables and groves of fruit trees. Hardwood trees and other lumber trees were planted later, when time allowed. Nothing seemed to happen, and the fields looked dormant. Acres and acres of rich loam plowed in curving lines with not a speck of green after a month.

The Elders had a meeting, and after it was called to order and the roll call taken, the Eldest, looking very solemn, stood up and started the meeting with, "I think that the seeds we brought from Earth must have been sterilized by leaking radiation or something else. We must plow under the fields we've planted and hope the next batch will germinate."

Raising his hand for attention, a less pessimistic Elder spoke. "Before we do something that drastic, we need to bring in the scientists and get their opinions. We planted those seeds on very fertile land, and not even the native grasses have sprouted. That leads me to believe that either the seeds have sterilized the land or it just takes a lot longer for plants to grow on this planet. In either case, it would be useless to replant those fields."

"We should plow new land. We certainly have enough of it, and will see what happens. We are not in danger of starving because we have found that we can eat the native plants and animals."

After much discussion and opinions from the experts in agriculture, it was decided to plant new fields. They tried again in a different area with the same result. Then the scientists tackled the problem with no improvement.

Everyone was frantic, a few of the women had to be watched closely for fear of suicide because, apparently, their fetuses weren't growing. This caused more fear than the seemingly barren fields. What if nothing from Earth could propagate on this planet?

Finally, after three months, they noticed their first fields were sprouting and seemed to look Earth normal, but growing very slowly. The same thing was happening to the embryos, healthy and growing but very slowly. With the greening of the fields and the abundance of available protein, the colonists knew they could live and prosper on this planet. It was true that they would still need help from Earth to be comfortable and keep the standard of living that they were accustomed to, but with God's help and some hard work, they would multiply and prosper.

Chapter Twelve

A Night in Early Summer

Cameron was elated. Tonight was the night he would ask Kaitlyn to marry him. It would be a double celebration, the annual Foundation Day celebration and the joining of the McPherson and McCreight clans.

He took a longer shower than usual and shaved very closely. Too closely, he cut himself twice. He wanted to look his best, and here he was with tissue stuck to his face.

Dawson came into the room just then and took one look at Cameron. "I told you to wait and that I would shave you. Now look what you have done." Tearing off the tissue, Dawson applied some astringent.

"Ow, that hurts."

"Serves you right. You just never listen. Now be quiet and get dressed. I have to help your father and brother, too, you know."

Dawson set out the same dress suit as for the ball, but this time instead of his sword, he wore an ornate leather belt, worked in silver, and his dress jeweled dagger in the sheath. Checking himself in the mirror, he grinned. He felt he was ready for anything.

Turning to Dawson, his eyes glinted with amusement. "Thanks, Dawson. As usual, everything looks perfect. I'm going to miss you when I move to the farm. You know that I hope to marry Kaitlyn soon, and we will live there. Guess I'll have to clean my own boots from then on."

Dawson was busy tidying up the room and looking at the boots that Cameron had just removed. With a shake of his head, he said in a slightly husky voice, "I won't miss your boots, but I'll miss you. At least it will be one less person to clean up after."

During this time, Kaitlyn and her sister, Glendora, were getting dressed as well. They shared a dressing room and now it looked cluttered with slips, dresses, and shoes scattered about. Their maid was fussing with the clothes and them. The room smelled of perfume and powder and the hot iron that the maid had been using.

Kaitlyn chose her dress with great care. Glendora designed the dress, as well as her own. It was the color of her eyes, deep violet, floor length in velvet, full skirt, and low cut bodice with large puffed sleeves. The sleeves were sewn with a lattice pattern of pearls. Tonight she wore her hair pulled through a cap of pearls, like a ponytail, it came to her waist. As the maid placed her plaid, a McPherson plaid, over her shoulder and pinned it at her waist, Kaitlyn thought that soon it would be a McCreight plaid. Tonight she knew, would be the night that Cameron would declare himself. The McCreight plaid should look very nice with her dress, she thought, with a shiver of excitement.

Glendora was thinking similar thoughts as the maid pulled a blue-green dress on her over her crown of golden braids. The braids were entwined with blue topaz and diamonds. She was the more beautiful of the two sisters, but her beauty was marred by the hardness around her eyes and her thin-lipped smile. She was ambitious and had her cap set for Sean. She wanted the power and prestige of being married to the heir apparent of the wealthy McCreight Clan. Combining the two families would make them the true leaders of society.

The fact that Sean was very handsome, with his blond hair and heavy-lidded brown eyes, made the prospect all the better. The scar on his face made him look a little sinister, but that only added spice. The fact that her father's bank had invested heavily in the Scott ceramic business and that the ceramic motor had been proven greatly improved her chances with Sean. The marriage would be perfect for business. Love was for peasants. With that thought, she closed her jewelry box firmly. The diamonds would be perfect.

"Oh, Glendora, this is going to be the most wonderful night," exclaimed Kaitlyn, her eyes shining like stars. "I just know it will be the most important one in my life. I want so much to look irresistible." Twirling, she looked at her sister questioningly.

"Kaitlyn, darling, " Glendora said, laughing as she looked at her sister, "you are always enchanting, especially right now. No man could possibly resist you, and Cameron won't even try." Then in a serious vein, " What do you think of a double marriage, us to the two brothers? I'm thinking quite seriously about Sean."

Kaitlyn was surprised. "You and Sean? Do you love him?"

"Who knows? I could learn to love him."

"But…"

"No buts! We must hurry, or we will keep our parents waiting," Glendora said as she picked up her cape, took Kaitlyn's arm, and left the room.

The McCreight mansion looked dazzling. The windows in every room were lit up and seemed to be welcoming the incoming guests with their warm glow. Hovercraft were coming and going, looking like giant fireflies disgorging people brilliantly dressed in all the colors of the rainbow, then taking off to find a place of rest. Music was already coming from the ballroom and the night air seemed to be perfumed with exotic scents.

The receiving line was in the entrance hall and all the McCreight family were in attendance. It was a magnificent room, with a high ceiling and airy. The floor was tiled with a local gray slate, a winding staircase led to the upper rooms. The walls were paneled in bamboo wood, and there were tables flanking the doors that led off to other parts of the lower floor. These held huge bouquets of flowers. Just off to the right were open double doors that led into the ballroom.

The McPherson family was arriving and Sean frowned when he noticed how attentive Cameron was to Kaitlyn. Somehow, he hadn't thought a romance was growing between them. He had always considered Glendora the better catch; perhaps Cameron knew something that he had missed. He had planned to ask Glendora to marry him if the ceramic motor was a success, but now maybe he should be thinking of Kaitlyn instead.

Cameron always seemed to find ways to get the best of everything. He doubted that Cameron was in love with her. They had been friends forever, it seemed, and therefore it must be to his advantage somehow. He would have a talk with Cameron as soon as possible before this got out of hand.

As soon as the last guest arrived, Sir John turned to his sons and said, "We must go to the workers' party in about ten minutes. I'll be waiting for you at the hovercraft."

Sean pulled Cameron aside, "I want to talk to you. I have been thinking of asking Kaitlyn to marry me. What do you think? It would be good to have the clans wedded, and she is a pretty little thing."

Cameron, alerted by his brother's manner, knew something unpleasant was about to happen. He was surprised by this turn of events and alarmed. Thinking quickly, he replied, "As a matter of fact, Sean, I was thinking along the same lines. I thought that you would prefer Glendora since she is the eldest and would inherit. I'm willing to forgo the pleasure of Kaitlyn for the beauty and wealth of Glendora if that is what you want. Either one would suit me just fine."

Christ, he's done it again. His scar was itching maddeningly and he tried to stop himself from scratching it. Now I don't really know what he wants, thought Sean, or whether he is trying to outmaneuver me with Glendora.

"Only joking, I noticed you giving special attention to Kaitlyn, If you want her, you can have her. And you are quite right. Glendora is the proper wife for the heir of McCreight." So saying, he left Cameron in the hall and went to meet his father at the hovercraft.

When Sean was out of sight, Cameron heaved a sigh of relief. He didn't really think that Sean could do anything about Kaitlyn, but he didn't want any complications. He loved Kaitlyn desperately; just looking at her made him happy. She made him feel larger than life, and with her by his side all things were possible. He hadn't known until now how deeply he felt. The rage within him at the mere thought that anyone, particularly his brother, would try to stand between them shocked him.

Cameron hadn't thought for a minute that Sean would want to take Kaitlyn away from him. He didn't really think he could, but to be on the safe side, he was glad that he had years of experience outwitting Sean. Marriage to Kaitlyn was too important to his future happiness to allow any chance of losing her. This he would fight for. So thinking, he went looking for Ian Scott.

Ian was just coming into the ballroom when Cameron found him. "Ian, I have a favor to ask. In about half an hour could you give Glendora some extra attention, dance with her or talk, whatever, just look interested."

"What's up?" Ian said, with a questioning look on his face.

"Just a little joke on Sean."

Laughing, Ian said, "I'm up for any joke on Sean. That stuffed shirt has no sense of humor, even though he is your brother. Anyway, it would be no hardship giving that beauty some attention. You won't even owe me one."

"Thanks, Ian, I won't forget this," said Cameron, giving Ian a light tap on the shoulder with his fist. He then turned and left the room to meet his father.

After returning from the employees' party, Sean hurried into the ballroom looking for Glendora. His mind was in such a quandary that he didn't even notice how beautiful the room looked. It was a very large room with eight windows and several doors. Between each window was a gilt-framed mirror that caught the swirl of the dancers in a blur of color. At the far end of the room were French doors leading into the garden. There were vases of roses everywhere. This was one flower from earth that had not changed at all, and grew prolifically. The air was filled with the perfumes of the women and the scent of the roses.

He finally saw Glendora dancing with Ian Scott, a man that he had never considered his rival; after all, he was only a third son. The swine had beaten him at the last fencing contest, though, Sean remembered. Glendora was looking up at Ian and laughing in a way that looked like she was really enjoying herself. That settled it. Glendora was the one he would talk to first. He crossed the dance floor and patted Ian on the shoulder, "Mind if I cut in?"

"You may, regretfully," said Ian as he turned to look at Sean. With a slight bow to Glendora, he said, "But only If I may ask for the privilege of another dance with the most beautiful woman in the room."

Glendora's color heightened at this compliment, and she gave Ian a brilliant smile as she turned from his arms into Sean's.

Cameron had followed Sean into the ballroom, seen this quick exchange, and noticing the frown that Sean gave Ian made him feel good. Even so, he watched the couple dancing a while longer before he made his move. He scanned the crowd for Kaitlyn and quickly found her standing by the refreshment table with a group of friends. He joined them and, after a few minutes of polite conversation, asked Kaitlyn to dance.

"Kaitlyn, my darling, you are the loveliest woman in the room, and I am madly in love with you," Cameron said as he whirled her around the room and out the French doors. "We must talk, and in private."

Taking her hand, they quickly walked through the garden and to the maze. Cameron knew this maze so well that they were soon in the center, where there was a stone bench and a tree. Seating Kaitlyn, he sat beside her and took her hands in his. "Kaitlyn, will you marry me? Before you answer, I must tell you that my brother may ask you as well."

Stunned, Kaitlyn turned white with anger. She pulled away from him and stood up. She whirled on him as if she wanted to strike him. "You idiot, there is no man I would marry except you. You should know that! If forced, I would even go against my father to be your wife."

A disgusted look crossed her face. "Your brother!!!.. I can't believe you told me that," she screamed at him. "Especially after what we have meant to each other these last months."

Turning from him and in a quieter voice, she said, "Don't you know that I have adored you since I was eight years old, and you saved me from drowning at Lake Crescent? Remember, you were just ten, but you were the only one that saw me dive in, and when I didn't reappear, you were worried and came in after me." Turning away from him, burying her face in her hands, and sobbing, she continued, "Now you've ruined everything."

Angry and screaming again. "You were my hero, my knight in shining armor, I've loved you ever since. You imbecile!"

"Please Kaitlyn, I love you," Cameron said as he stood up and reached for her, pulled her back down on the bench, and crushed her to him. "Please don't cry. God, I've made a mess of it. I wanted this moment to be perfect."

She resisted him, pushing him away, still angry. "How could you even think I would marry that snake for any reason?"

"I promise you, I would never let you go. You are my life, my reason for breathing. I'd kill Sean before I would let him have you."

He grabbed her back and held her at arms' distance, "Kaitlyn darling, I'm sorry I messed this up. Please forgive me. It's just that Sean has ways of making things very difficult, and let's admit it, I have very little to offer except myself. It is conceivable that someone as beautiful and wonderful as you deserve and wants more."

Furious again, she pushed him away and stood up to leave. "It is not conceivable to me, Cameron Kendell McCreight," she spat at him like an angry cat. "I love you just as you are. I thought you knew that. Now I'm not so sure I want to marry you at all if you think I can be bought by a title and wealth."

He jumped up and grabbed her again. "Please, Kaitlyn! Don't say that! I know I'm an idiot and saying all the wrong things, but I promise you that I will always love you as I do this very minute. Say you'll marry me." He held her and tried to kiss her again. After a slight resistance, she allowed him.

After many long kisses and caresses, Kaitlyn said," Cameron, Love, I will forgive you this time for doubting me for even an instant. I will marry you. Even though this wasn't exactly how I thought this moment would be, it ended up right."

Cameron said in a husky voice, "Hurry, take my plaid. We'll go to your father at once."

They exchanged plaids. He pulled her into his arms again and kissed her, a very long kiss. Reluctantly he let her go and hurriedly, hand in hand, they left the maze in search of her father. Shortly, they found him in the smoking room.

"Sir, I wish to take the hand of Kaitlyn to be my wife."

"Well, it looks to me as if you've already taken her hand," he said laughing, as he looked at them standing there holding hands, "you may as well have the rest of her. You have my blessing." He shook Cameron's hand and then hugged Kaitlyn.

"I am not surprised, seeing the way you two have been looking at each other lately. This is indeed the happiest day of my life. Let's find your mother, and your parents, Cameron. We will make the announcement."

It wasn't long before the two sets of parents and the joyful couple were standing at the head of the room. Sir John had told the orchestra to play a fanfare to gain everyone's attention. "I have an announcement to make. This ball is to celebrate the day of our arrival on Heatherbound, but now I want to reveal that we have a double celebration. My son, Cameron, and Kaitlyn

McPherson have decided to marry. They have our blessings. This is truly a happy occasion. Champagne is being poured and I would like all of you to toast to the future Mr. and Mrs. Cameron McCreight."

Everyone started talking at once, and there were many yells of congratulation to Cameron and best wishes to Kaitlyn. The servants were hurrying around with trays of champagne, and people were maneuvering to get to the happy couple to wish them well.

Ian rushed forward and grabbed Kaitlyn up, and whirled her around. "Whoopee!" Looking at Cameron, he said, "It's about time, old boy!"

Sean was still dancing with Glendora when this happened. He went rigid with anger but quickly recovered. He knew it was too late to do anything about Kaitlyn, but he could take some of the limelight. "Glendora, it seems that my brother has stolen my thunder. I planned to ask you to marry me tonight at a more opportune moment, but now I would like to make it a double announcement. Would you do me the honor of being my wife?"

"It would give me great pleasure to marry you," said Glendora.

With his arm still around her, he led her to the front of the room.

Chapter Thirteen
An Agreement

The next day, Sir John was sitting at his desk in his office. Paperwork, as usual, was piled up, his computer screen was glowing, and several discs lay scattered about. His secretary didn't see how he could find anything, but Sir John always seemed to know exactly where to find whatever he wanted among the clutter.

He felt especially good this morning, and couldn't help breaking into a smile every other minute. He could not be happier. Both sons are engaged to wonderful girls. His wife Helen is in seventh heaven and in a fever to get started with wedding preparations. What more could he ask for, perhaps the thought of grandchildren on his knee?

Suddenly Sean strode into his office unannounced, looking like a thundercloud, his face distorted with anger. He hadn't bothered to knock, nor did he bother to sit down. His fists were bunched, and he leaned on his father's desk with them. He yelled in Sir John's face, "I cannot put up with Cameron any longer. He is never at work, and he is forever getting in my hair." There was cold fury in his voice, and his eyes were blazing with rage.

"Last night I felt like killing him. What right did he have asking Kaitlyn to marry him when he knew that I had planned to ask Glendora at the ball? He only chose that time to upstage me. I had planned it as a perfect time to unite our families. As usual, Cameron was trying to embarrass me. He made my engagement an afterthought."

He pushed himself off the desk and started to pace; whirling back, he said, "That was the last straw. He must go; I can't stand the sight of him. Let him run the farms. It's about all he is good for, anyway. Let me have the factory make the new arrangement for our wedding presents."

Sir John had never seen Sean so angry. He got up and came around his desk, and took Sean by his shoulders. "Calm down, Sean. Cameron meant no harm. He is in love." Sir John said, trying to placate Sean, "I'll talk to him."

Sean pushed his hands away roughly and moved away. Keeping his temper, Sir John shrugged and returned to his seat behind the desk. His happiness had evaporated.

Whirling back to his father, "That's all we ever do. Talk! No, I'm tired of talking." Sean put his fists on his father's desk, leaning toward him again.

Sir John was angry now and stood up again. "Just who do you think you're talking to? I'm still alive, and you haven't inherited yet."

"You're right, but I'm the eldest, and I will inherit, and I can't work with him anymore. If you want me to run the manufacturing plant, I have to have a say in who works there. Anyway," Sean said with a shrug and calmer, "this will probably make him very happy. We can set up some allowance for him, perhaps one-third of the profit of the farms. That should be sufficient. I would even be agreeable to have that set aside for him as his inheritance."

"That does not seem very generous to me." Sir John said, still standing and angry. "I had thought to give him the entire proceeds from the farms. Compared to the manufacturing it is nothing, given that most of our harvest goes to manufacturing without charge. Only a small portion is sold elsewhere, as you well know."

"All right, all right, write it up that five-sixths of the harvest goes to me. He can keep one-sixth to sell as he sees fit in exchange for managing the farms. This I will agree to as his inheritance," said Sean. "The law says that all go to the eldest son, but as I have no interest in managing the farms, I will be generous on this point. But it must be done now."

"You drive a hard bargain, Sean, but it will be as you say. There is one other thing I wish to give him as a wedding present, and that is some property that belonged to your grandfather. It is around Lake Placid. I'll get the lawyers on it this afternoon. Your mother will be upset by this meager amount and will probably have her money go to your brother alone."

"Who cares about Mother's pittance? As for the land around Lake Placid, this is the first time I have ever heard of it, and I am not interested. He can have it for all I care. Just see that it is done today." Sean said angrily, striding from the room.

After Sean left, Sir John was still angry but heaved a sigh of relief. This was pretty much what he had wanted for Cameron all along. He knew that Sean was right that Cameron would be happy with the management of the farms. Sir John only wanted to make sure that Cameron would get some compensation for it, and not be just another hired hand for Sean when he died. Which, he hoped, wouldn't be for some time yet. After all, he was only ninety years old.

One-sixth of the harvest was quite a bit, enough to raise a family comfortably. Also, he was pretty sure Cameron had other irons in the fire. What with Kaitlyn's dowry, they should do all right. Sir John rang for his secretary, "Ask Cameron to come to my office as soon as possible, please."

A few minutes later, Cameron came into the room and sat down, saying, "Hi, Dad. You wanted to see me?" He noticed that his father looked a little grave. He had expected him to be beaming.

"Yes, I have news that I think you will like." Sir John started. "Sean and I have agreed that you will have the management of the farms as your inheritance. This means that for as long as you live, you manage the farms, and this job can never be taken from you. Starting now, you will manage them; five-sixths of the harvest will go to Sean without charge. You will have the rest of the harvest to sell unprocessed."

He cleared his throat, and continued, looking Cameron in the eyes to see how he was taking it. "I know that that cuts the profits, but we don't want the competition to have the formulas, as you know. I think that should be enough for you and Kaitlyn to live on, and I know you would be happier."

"I've always known you hated working at the factory, but I felt that you should know all about the process in case anything happened to Sean or me. Now you no longer have to, and what's more, I don't have to bother with the farms. I have been thinking that it is time I go into politics. It's expected of a man of my age."

"Dad, that's wonderful. You are going to make a great Elder," said Cameron. "As to the farms, I am grateful. I really didn't expect that much. And you were right, I needed to have background knowledge of manufacturing and marketing, but for the last year, I have felt that my time was wasted."

Sir John heaved a sigh of relief, and shaking his head, he smiled at Cameron.

Encouraged, Cameron leaned forward in his enthusiasm, "Joe Ferris, the foreman at the smaller farm, and I have had some interesting talks. He feels, as I do that there is more potential for Steelite, and he has been helping me with some of my research. Now I'll have time to really discover something."

Cameron's face clouded over in remembrance. He ran his hand through his hair and then put his hands on the desk, "There is one problem, though, Dad. Sean has said that he will claim any discovery I make as owned by the McCreight family."

A little heated, he continued. "This is not right. I have been working for three years on my own time and paying for my own lab assistants. I want it in writing that anything I discover will be my own, to do with as I please, not a property of McCreight Industries."

"I didn't think that Sean would be so greedy," said Sir John with a look of disgust on his face. "I will have that stipulation put into the agreement that my lawyers will draw up today. Let Sean try to block that, and I swear I will disown him."

Cameron was shocked at that statement. "Sean can be a bastard, and he may just have been just pulling my chain, but, son." He fiddled with some papers on his desk. "I have confidence that you will come up with your new uses for Steelite. Are you working on something that will allow us to mill it?"

"Yes, that and some other ideas, but they're not ready to discuss yet." Changing the subject, "This is a wonderful wedding present, Dad. I can't wait to tell Kaitlyn."

"That's not your wedding present. When looking through some old papers of your grandfather's the other day, I noticed a deed for some land around Lake Placid." Sir John handed Cameron the papers he had been fingering. "That is your wedding present. Your mother and I hope you and Kaitlyn will like it," said Sir John with a smile.

Cameron reached out and took the deed. "Dad, I'd thought you had given me all grandfather's old papers. I'd love to see anything else you may have."

Cameron looked down at the deed in his hand. "Lake Placid? Never heard of it. Where is it? It doesn't matter,it sounds like a nice place to have a summer cottage. I know we will love it. Thanks again, Dad, Kaitlyn likes getting out in the country, and lake property sounds perfect."

"It's settled then. You'll manage the farms, and Sean will have the manufacturing," said Sir John. "Regarding the details about Lake Placid, bring Kaitlyn to dinner some night soon, and we'll get the map out. At that time, I'll give you any other papers I find."

Chapter Fourteen
The Wedding

The double wedding was the event of the year. No expense was spared. The brides were dressed alike in white satin trimmed with white lace and pearls. The bodice of the dresses was high-necked lace to the throat with a choker collar of pearls. The skirts were very full and studded with seed pearls. Their bouquets were sweetheart roses and orange blossoms. The bridesmaids were dressed in cobalt blue and white, and the maid of honor was in Steelite silk. All the men were splendid in Steelite silk cut in a formal style. Glendora had designed the clothes, and they were very elegant as well as beautiful.

The sisters had decided on an afternoon wedding in the garden at the McPherson home. It was decorated with white and blue bows up the aisle leading to a bower of flowers. All the late spring flowers were in bloom. With the green expanse of lawn and flowering fruit trees, it was truly a beautiful setting for a wedding.

The day was perfect, with just a slight breeze that flirted with the girl's veils and loosened some of the petals from the orange trees, filling the air with their sweet perfume. The reception was held indoors with extra tables set up outside. It was a buffet, and the food counter seemed endless. There were two wedding cakes and champagne flowed like water. Everyone agreed that this was the most beautiful wedding they had ever attended.

The couples had decidedly different ideas about honeymoons. Sean and Glendora went to Paradise, the nearest planet, which was noted for its pleasure domes. They planned to spend a month and try all the attractions. They wished to see as much as possible on this very small planet that had been turned into a playground for the very rich.

Cameron and Kaitlyn decided they would like to see more of their own world and each other. They took a hovercraft and stayed at several good inns that were scattered about the countryside. The entire populace of the planet seemed to know about the double wedding, and all the innkeepers treated the honeymooners royally. The food was wonderful and they always had fresh flowers in their room. Most people were discreet and left the lovers pretty much to themselves. Their days were spent roaming the countryside and talking, and their nights in each other's arms.

They fell in love with one Inn in particular and stayed a week. It was rather isolated in the countryside and catered to the local farmers. It was more a pub than an Inn and had only one room to let. No one paid much attention to them there. During the days, they took picnic baskets and went for long walks. In the evenings, a local girl came in and sang love ballads while she played the guitar. It was perfect, but all too soon, they had to get back to work and their new life.

Chapter Fifteen
Partnership

Their arrival at the farm found a continuation of the goodwill extended to the happy couple. All of Cameron's workers came out to greet them and to meet Kaitlyn. There was another celebration feast. Travis Stuart, Cameron's headman, brought out his fiddle and Cameron his flute, and the dancing lasted into the wee hours.

Kaitlyn was anxious to get started redecorating and looked forward to having her own kitchen with no one to interfere. She loved to cook and had spent many happy hours with her family's cook as a child. She had even copied her recipes. While on Earth, she had had ample opportunity to practice, as she and Glendora had shared an apartment with only a robot for help. Of course, they had an auto-kitchen, but it was also set up for manual in case the occupant wanted to cook as a hobby.

Cameron was surprised and pleased that she would want to cook. He hadn't really thought much about it. With her education and background, he had naturally thought she would not be interested in anything domestic, except of course, children.

Kaitlyn had received as her dowry 200,000 federal credits, a princely sum. As was their custom, it was to be her money to help set up a household. This was a lot of money, and Cameron and Kaitlyn liked to live simply. After the honeymoon, they started to think about how they should invest it.

Soon after getting settled at the farm, which was now their home, the two of them fell into a comfortable routine.. Once the dishes were cleared away, they sat at the big round dining table in the kitchen.. Kaitlyn, on her side of the table, would be organizing the household accounts, and Cameron, on his side, would be looking through some notes on plants that he had seen while they had been hiking on their honeymoon. It was quiet, and the only sound was a rustling of papers, the scratching of a pen, and an occasional beep from Kaitlyn's calculator.

Kaitlyn pushed her calculator aside, rubbed her face, and stretched. She looked at Cameron for a minute and smiled as he pushed a lock of hair from his face. She could see that he was engrossed with his notes; even so, she thought it was time for a break, and Ian had been on her mind.

"Cameron, I have been thinking about the dowry and wondering if you would be agreeable to investing it in Ian. It's quite a lot of money, and I hate the thought of it just sitting idle."

Cameron looked up from his scribbles. "Ian. That's interesting. Just what kind of investing."

"Ian Scott is one of the best robotics engineers on Heatherbound. At least that is what he tells us," said Kaitlyn with a laugh. "I'd like us to talk to him about starting a business. Remember how we three used to talk about a partnership? It was all pie in the sky, until now, with the dowry; we could really start a designing and manufacturing firm. You and I could put up the money, and Ian would supply his talents. You have contacts in manufacturing, and you and Ian could set up the plant. I could do the financial planning and managing." Kaitlyn said as she got up and came around the table.

Cameron pulled her onto his lap. Looking her straight in the face, he said, "Sounds like you have been giving this a lot of thought. Are you sure you want to put that much time and money into a friend?"

"I've always liked Ian. You better, of course," Kaitlyn said playfully, pushing back his hair and kissing him on the forehead. "And it's our money."

"Even with all his playfulness, he has a good head on his shoulders, and he is honest," said Kaitlyn. "We would do very well with him. The way Earth is being so stingy about their robotic advances, we do need to create our own."

"If you're really serious, I'll call him right now and see if the three of us can get together tomorrow," said Cameron. "We can meet for lunch."

"I couldn't be more serious."

Still holding Kaitlyn, Cameron picked up the phone and called Ian. "Are you free for lunch tomorrow? It's on Kaitlyn and me? We have a proposition for you."

"Sure, always up for a free lunch. I missed you guys. How was the honeymoon? And what is the proposition?" said Ian with a laugh in his voice.

"You'll hear everything tomorrow. See you at the Boar's Arms at about one o'clock." Cameron hung up before Ian had a chance to say anything else. Holding Kaitlyn had driven thoughts of commerce from his mind. He picked her up and carried her into the bedroom.

The three of them arrived at the same time in front of the Boar's Arms. Ian grabbed Kaitlyn and gave her a great hug, than shook Cameron's hand. "How's married life? Haven't seen hide nor hair of you since the wedding."

"It's the greatest," laughed Cameron. "You should try it. Let's go in; I'm starved."

The Boar's Arms looked like a pub you would find anywhere in the British Isles, dart board and all. A little on the dark side, with small leaded glass windows,. A large fireplace was blazing on one wall with horse brass hanging by each side. It was a small place with only room for four tables in the main room and a twelve-foot bar with glasses hanging above it. There was a small alcove on the side with only one table. This was fairly private, and they made their way to it.

The bar area was crowded, and there were people at all the tables. The place smelled of beer and good food. The noise of laughter and loud talk was at a low roar. It quieted a little when the three entered. The barman was serving up a beer to a customer. He looked up when he saw them, "Ian, Cameron, and the little lady, what can I do for you today."

"Three steak pies, a few bangers, and pints all around, Bill," yelled Cameron as he looked around. "We'll be sitting in the alcove."

"Coming right up." Moving quickly, Bill checked the oven to see if there were enough steak pies left. "Haven't seen much of you lately, Cameron. The pretty wife must be keeping you mighty busy," He said amid much laughter in the pub.

Cameron laughed but didn't say anything, just waved at Bill. Kaitlyn blushed but was not angry. The trio walked to their table, greeting several friends along the way. There were lots of back slaps and joking. Everyone seemed to be having a good time, especially at Cameron and Kaitlyn's expense. They finally reached their table and got settled when Bill brought them their beer and food. It smelled wonderful, and they set to it with gusto and very little talk.

Putting down his fork and wiping his mouth with a napkin, Ian sat back and looked at Cameron, "That was delicious. We've had our food and some small talk, so now let's get down to business. What was the proposition you two had for me?"

"Ian, remember all the times we've talked about starting a designing firm, with you the engineer and designer, me the idea and moneyman, and Kaitlyn the financial wizard and manager? Well, Kaitlyn and I have decided that we would like to use her dowry to invest in you. Just the way we had planned. You put up your talent, and we put up the working capital. What do you think?"

"What do I think? When do we start? That's fantastic; I can't believe it is really going to happen." Ian said, practically jumping out of his chair, his heart pounding with excitement, then like the canny Scot that he was, "We always talked in terms of equal partnership. Is that still part of the deal?"

"Oh, that sounds good to us. We can discuss all the legalities later." Kaitlyn chimed in. "What we wanted to know was if you were still available and interested. If so, how soon can we get started?"

"Today, tomorrow, as soon as you want. I'm sick of the madhouse where I am working. Now that we have the new ceramics perfected, I'm not really needed. I can give them notice today, and by the time we have worked out the details, I'll be a free agent," said Ian. "As a matter of fact, I know of a terrific piece of land we can buy for the factory and office."

"It's settled then. I have some ideas for what I would like you to design for me, and they would be very commercial as well, I think," said Cameron.

"This is not the greatest place to discuss this in detail. Can you come to our home for dinner tonight?" said Kaitlyn. "Say, make it around seven o'clock?"

"Seven it is. Wow, it's really going to happen!"

Later that night after dinner, the three of them sat around the dining room table in the kitchen, drinking coffee and making plans. It felt good and natural, to be together again, planning the future.

"Ian, there are several different kinds of robots I need for my fields. They'll be expensive, I know, but I feel we need the security. I've still been working on that material made from Steelite I've talked about for so long, and I think I may be coming to a breakthrough soon. There should be a big demand for the material, and I need some robots to ensure that the fences aren't climbed to steal plants. I also think it would be more efficient to use robots for field hands as well. This is all supposition right now, but I feel sure it will happen," said Cameron.

"We will need robots for weeding, planting, and picking. Also, we'll need specialized ones that can think and guard with stun guns, if necessary. I was thinking of something in the mode of small hovercrafts for the guards."

"That's a tall order, guys, but it can be done. All we need is time and money," said Ian.

"Cameron and I have discussed this, and we are going to put up 150,000 credits to be sure we have enough working capital to design these jobs first. We are hoping that we won't need that much to set up the plant and manufacture the robots, but if we have to, we will."

"That's a lot of money. I have been thinking along some of these lines already, especially the security robots. Some of the bigger farmers and ranchers are worried about poaching," said Ian, getting up and walking around the room.

Coming back, he put his hands on the back of his chair, "The ceramics for the motors for your family, Kaitlyn, has kept the Scotts very busy for the last few years. We haven't had too much time for robotics."

"In fact, they have kind of lost interest in robotics," said Ian with a huge grin. "That leaves me free to set up our business without feeling I am stealing from my family. They will be happy that a Scott has partners in another business."

"Wonderful, that part is settled then. Our thoughts on salary and dividends are that Kaitlyn and I won't take a salary or dividends for the first five years or until it looks like we can afford to. We would leave it in the company for working capital at some interest rate we all agree on. We will pay the company for the robots we need or take it out of our profits, whichever makes more sense. You, Ian, would get a decent salary and work full-time. I would come in when needed, no more than two days a week. Kaitlyn would work full-time until the accounting system was set up, and secretaries were trained. She could then come in just two days a week or whatever is needed. What do you think?"

"Kaitlyn, Cameron, this is a chance of a lifetime for me. Whatever you think is fair, I know it will be fair." Ian sat down again. "As for the interest rate, how about ten percent? That's the going rate right now."

"Ian, you're too much, and so is ten percent. Robotic Design and Engineering cannot afford to pay that high a rate. As our accountant, I refuse to pay more than five percent," said Kaitlyn with a laugh.

"Five percent it is, then," said Ian. "Can't argue with the accountant. Robotic Design and Engineering, I like it. No fighting over whose name comes first."

"We'll get this all hammered out with the lawyer tomorrow. I set up an appointment in anticipation of your agreeing to come in with us," said Kaitlyn.

"One thing I will insist on is that we get together once a week for a staff meeting. Each of us will need to know the status of the company and iron out any problems," said Kaitlyn seriously. "Also, we need to agree on how we are going to allot our tax money for the company and our own salaries. You may not want to give one percent to schools since you are not married, Ian."

"I'm not a shirker, Kaitlyn," laughed Ian, "and I hope to marry and have children. Now that I have good prospects to go along with my good looks, perhaps I can catch a wife. I will leave the decision of the company taxes in the reliable hands of our accountant and financial expert. As for mine, it's the usual seven percent plus miscellaneous."

"Now that it's settled and Kaitlyn has named the company, it's time for a toast. I just happen to have a bottle of champagne chilled," Cameron said, getting up to get the wine and chilled glasses. "To friendship and RD&E."

After toasting and reminiscing about childhood escapades, they said their goodbyes. It was an evening well spent.

The tax system on Heatherbound was much different from Earth. Taxpayers expected to know the purpose of the taxes they were paying and to make some input as to what they felt was the proper way to spend them. Every individual and every company or business paid a flat rate of five percent. This paid for the basic government, fire, police, and military. There was a voluntary rate of one percent each for schools, hospitals, and miscellaneous.

Also, there were other minor things that people allotted taxes for on a regular basis, such as political parties, emergencies, etc. There were also taxes that could be voted in for a limited time to pay for specified things such as roads and dams. You were considered a shirker if you paid less than seven percent. The amount paid was posted in the local post office. Not what it was for, that was privileged information, but just the percentage. This seemed to do very well to keep things running smoothly.

Chapter Sixteen

Government

With Kaitlyn at his side, Cameron experienced contentment he had never known before. He had Kaitlyn, the robotics business with Ian, and he could spend more time on his favorite projects while managing the farms.

Finally, he had time to plot out where in the family fields he most often found the variation in colors. He noticed that it was usually in the more inaccessible places. Talking to his foreman about this, he discovered that these places were tough to fertilize. Because the areas were quite small and difficult to reach, such as on tops of a rocky hills, they were pretty much left alone. The fertilizer used was one that his grandfather had formulated.

Cameron took a hovercraft to each of these spots and took soil samples. He then took random samples of the constant areas. He left the farm and took samples of some virgin land. All of this he took to his lab and tested. The unfertilized spots had almost reverted to virgin soil, with just traces of fertilizer. The spots where the most variation was found had reverted.

Cameron came home that night excited, Katlin was in the kitchen preparing their dinner, and he grabbed her up and swung her around, a big grin on his face, " Katlyn darling, I've finally had a real breakthrough. I now understand why there were no changes in our fields. They were too well taken care of.

Laughing, Kailyn said, "That's wonderful dear, Now put me down, dinner is about to burn."

He could hardly wait to get back to his own farm and start a new policy. He wanted to have his farm divided into three areas, one natural, one with a new fertilizer that he had been formulating, and the last with the old fertilizer. He would still need a money crop, at least until his material became known.

There was so much to do, and all of it to his liking. He and Kaitlyn worked at the robotics firm, she five days a week and Cameron one. He worked on the family farm three days a week and in his own lab whenever he could spare a moment. That left only the weekends for his own farm, but his people were good and everything was done as he requested. There was a lot of detailed work to be done, and Kaitlyn and Cameron spent most evenings together doing it. They were busy and extremely happy.

On the days they worked together at the firm, they usually went to lunch with Ian at the Boar's Arms pub nearby. It was frequently a working lunch.

Ian commented at the last lunch, "It's a good thing we have to eat, or we would never have time for our staff meetings, If it is all right with you, I need to hire some people to help me get the projects done faster,".

"You don't have to ask. We expect you to run the company in the best way possible. And, of course, you will need a lot of help."

Ian hired three engineers and two drafting technicians to help him. They were working on the robots that Cameron needed, and after six months of intensive work, they had a working model of the simplest one and were planning to put it into production soon. Most of the others were close to being ready for production. They just needed a few kinks worked out.

Their main problems were in the electrical components and of course, all metal parts. These had to be shipped from Earth, and Ian and his crew were trying to work around them. All of these robots had been perfected years ago on Earth using metals of various kinds, such as copper, silver, and of course, steel. Earth's Consortiums wanted to keep this technology for themselves and refused to sell any of the components.

They would sell the completed robots, but they were prohibitively expensive. Ian was working on his idea for a new technology of ceramics and fused glass with just traces of metal for conducting the electrical impulses to the robotic brain. They were trying to keep nearly all of the plastics out of their models because most of the petroleum products also had to be shipped from Earth.

Ian's designs were working well; even he was rather amazed at what had been accomplished in such a short time. They were now ready to start production of some of the simpler robots. All that was needed was a small shipment of copper and silver from Earth. The expansion of their building to accommodate the manufacturing division had started last month, and this too, was almost completed. If all went well they should be in limited production within the month.

Kaitlyn said as she surveyed the latest robot model, "You are really a marvel, Ian. Earth's robotic companies are not going to be too happy."

Cameron and Ian were just like the majority of people on Heatherbound. They wanted to be independent from Earth as much possible. No one wanted to beg assistance from the mother planet.

Most of the planets that had been colonized by subsidies from the Consortiums were required to send all natural resources back to Earth for processing, the Consortiums would not let them have the equipment or training to do the job for themselves. The people on these planets were getting mighty sick of the stranglehold on them, and there had been talk of rebellion. When they had contracted to settle these planets, they didn't realize that they were practically enslaving themselves and their children forever.

Heatherbound did not want to get involved with this, even though she was sympathetic. This planet was part of the colony of planets and would be expected to side with its neighbors. If this meant war, and it was possible, then Heatherbound would be drawn into it no matter how they felt about it.

Some of the Elders had their heads in the sand and still hoped that an impregnable defense system would be enough to prevent involvement and Heatherbound could remain neutral. After all, it was not Earth, exactly, that was contemplating war, it was the Consortiums, and Heatherbound had nothing to do with them except for trade. They wished to ignore the fact that Earth was now, more than ever, controlled by big business. Heatherbound had little choice but to side with the Consortiums on most issues concerning the space colonies or risk war. It did not have a defense system set up that could protect itself, and it would take a huge amount of money and time to get one.

There also had been a lot of friction between Earth and Heatherbound about immigration. Very strict limits had been set on the number of people allowed to come to Heatherbound, only twenty thousand people a year. Any immigrant would have to have either 10,000 credits or a profession that was needed. Couples were preferred, and people from the British Isles were given priority. This was part of the agreement with Great Britain to help finance the original expedition. They were allowed to bring two children but were expected to invest 1000 credits for each child in that child's name before embarkation. The people of Heatherbound did not want this planet to become overpopulated.

Not only was immigration limited, so was birth. Heatherbound couples were allowed to have only two children unless they bought 100 acres or invested 1000 credits for each additional child before the birth of that child. There was very little grumbling about this because most people felt it was fair. The first three generations of the original colonists were allotted one square mile and a city lot for each of their first two children.

Earth wanted Heatherbound to take many more people a year and felt that it showed discrimination against races other than Caucasian. On the surface, this appeared to be true, but all races had been allowed to immigrate if they met the qualifications. Of the original 3000 colonists, 458 were not Caucasians. There was no race or sex barrier in trade, business or military on Heatherbound. The only qualifications were that you had the training and brains and were physically able to do the job.

Another thing that Earth complained about was the qualifications. They didn't want technical people emigrating to a planet over which Earth had no control. The Consortiums threatened a boycott on trade, but it didn't happen because Earth needed Steelite too much and also liked the wool produced on Heatherbound.

Some people in power were afraid that Earth might decide to use her power to take over Heatherbound someday. These Elders wanted a space navy as well as a defense system. RD&E had already been approached by the military about possible design work to update the robotic satellite weapons and early warning systems. All very tentative, but it was exciting to contemplate. The defense system Heatherbound had now was very primitive and would need a large infusion of talent and money to make it even formidable, let alone impregnable.

Another worry for the Elders was that even with all the precautions taken at the spaceport, a few illegals slipped through every year. Most were stowaways from the nearby planets, uneducated and poor but willing to work and wanting the freedom to save and work for a future for themselves and their children. The authorities discouraged stowaways, but most Heatherbounders tried to help the individuals, and some took advantage of cheap labor.

Occasionally crews from the spaceships caused problems in the port area that was set up for them. It was called Freeport and was mostly bordellos, bars, and sleepovers. It was set up inside an immigration fence. They seldom tried to leave the area, and their ship captains usually took care of any crimes committed.

Drugs and prostitution were legal, but controlled and heavily taxed. Crimes of passion, greed, and lust are found everywhere there are humans, and Heatherbound was no exception. Even so, rape and murder were rare. The main crimes had to do with stolen property.

Chapter Seventeen

Progress

Five years after the double wedding, Sir John felt it was time to semi-retire from the family business and go into politics. Sean was doing more and more in the manufacturing division. He seemed to have a flair for it. Though the men resented him at times, the job did get done. The farms were producing bumper crops, and Cameron was coming up with some innovative ideas. It was time, and he was glad of it. The Council of Elders needed new ideas in the times ahead if Heatherbound was going to avert war. Most people, when they reached ninety, went in for public service, and he was overdue.

Sean and Glendora took the five acres near the mansion he gave them as a wedding present and built a magnificent mansion on it. The boathouse alone was bigger than most cottages. They were still living in the McCreight mansion, and Sir John was looking forward to the day they could move into their new home. Lady Helen was a remarkable mother-in-law, but it was not easy living with two strong women in one household. Sean said that he and Glendora would move in a month whether or not the house was ready.

Sean and Glendora spent several hours a week with the workers building their mansion. They would then spend several more hours poring over the plans and making changes. A real affection grew between them.

Glendora worked at her father's bank three days a week as her father's assistant. The financial enterprise would be hers one day, and she wanted to know exactly what was going on. She had a very good head on her shoulders and had insight into the interaction between different departments. The work was stimulating, and her main talent came through as a generalist, able to see the overall view. She also had a knack for getting the right people together to do the actual project.

Sean was negotiating with a new company that wished to build small space ships. They wanted a guarantee of a certain amount of Steelite each year, and in exchange, they would give stock in the company to McCreight Enterprises. Sean loved the wheeling and dealing of big business, and he was very good at it.

During these five years, Cameron was experimenting in his fields, and he finally got his pure white. The texture was very different, and he wanted to do several experiments with it before he could go into production. He still needed to find plants with color for his material, as even pure white would not take color. It did have all the other advantages that he was looking for, especially the fact that it would not stain.

The light grays in his lab were another break-through. He was convinced that he had the secret of how to make a grade of Steelite that could be tooled. It would not be as strong as Steelite, but it would certainly be comparable to steel. He needed to work with the formulas a bit more to correct the tendency of some of the samples to be brittle. He was confident that within a month or two at the most, he could make his announcements and begin producing tooled Steelite. He would call it Heatherware.

RD&E was doing very well. Kaitlyn negotiated several large contracts, some military and some with the big local farmers. Ian's designs were different from Earth's and he perfected several innovative ways to get around the use of precious metals and plastic. His background in ceramics was crucial in developing these new ideas. Ian's clan, the Scotts, were subcontracted to do the ceramic work. There were still problems with the brain center, and his robots were not as smart as Earth's, but he felt in time they would come up with a solution for that as well.

During this time Cameron and Kaitlyn had a boy, Robert, and a girl, Megan. Sean and Glendora had two children as well, James and Colin. Both couples appeared quite happy with their roles in life. The rivalry had even mellowed between the brothers, as the sisters had a deep affection for each other. They led completely different lives. Cameron could not afford the sumptuous lifestyle that Sean had, nor would he and Kaitlyn enjoy that kind of life. They seldom mixed as couples socially.

Immediately after the marriage, Cameron moved into the house he had built on his own land. It was only a large cottage, but very comfortable. There were four rooms downstairs; living room, dining room, kitchen, and recreation room. Upstairs were four bedrooms. There was also a large attic that Cameron used as his laboratory. It was not pretentious but certainly large enough for their needs. Kaitlyn had only one girl, Glenys, to help her with the house and children, but that was quite sufficient, since Kaitlyn loved cooking and caring of her babies. Glenys was the daughter of Travis Stuart, Cameron's headman at their farm.

Near the house was another one just like it, that was built for the Stuart family. It was rather a cozy arrangement, and Kaitlyn found it very convenient. It was comforting to know someone was always near when needed, especially when she and Cameron were away from the farm.

A stone fence surrounded the houses, with roses growing on it, this softened the look. Both families had gardens with more flowers and vegetables. There was also a fishpond stocked with fish when they wanted them. There was also a barn for their animals and a chicken shed. All in all, it was a good-sized compound.

Cameron and Kaitlyn's favorite room was the very large kitchen. Most evenings, the four of them would be found together there, Rob engrossed in his blocks on the rug, Megan cooing in her cradle, and Kaitlyn and Cameron working at the table.

Pansy was usually not too far away from Rob since his near fatal accident. Kaitlyn was about six months pregnant with Megan and not feeling very well. She was napping upstairs. Glenys was busy cleaning the house, and Rob was supposed to be taking his afternoon nap. He woke up and decided to climb out of his crib, which he had never done before. He had tried to many times but always fell back into the crib. This time he made it by pulling himself up and getting one leg over the side. He gave a real hard push with his other leg, and over he went. The thick rug softened the fall to the floor, it hurt a little, but he didn't cry. Feeling very proud of himself, he got up and walked out of the room.

No one was about, so Rob decided he would go outside and play. He took his teddy bear with him. He knew he could get out by crawling through Pansy's little door in the kitchen door. He had done it before, and that was fun too.

He hadn't realized how cold it was outside, and he had no shoes on. He didn't care how cold it was; he wanted to be outside anyway. He found his ball and threw it up, but couldn't catch it, so he ran after it several times. This was great fun! He threw it again, and it rolled into the fishpond. Oh oh! He knew he wasn't supposed to go in, but he wanted the ball, so in he went. Each time he grabbed for the ball, it went in further toward the center of the pond. The next step he took, the ground fell away, and he went under. He came up sputtering and yelling, "Mommy, Mommy!"

Pansy heard him and came running but couldn't get to him because Moorcats can't swim. She was frantic, running back and forth in front of the pond, meowing loudly. Finally, she ran into the house and found Glenys in the kitchen. She pulled at her apron, making anxious squeaking noises, then ran to the door, looking back at Glenys.

"Go away, Pansy. Can't you see that I am busy?"

Pansy came back and pulled on her apron with all her might, squeaking and growling, trying to drag her to the door.

"All right, all right, I'm coming, but it better be important," said Glenys, grabbing a towel and drying her hands.

Glenys followed Pansy to the door, still grumbling. She had work to finish. She followed her to the fishpond. Pansy kept running back and forth, making sure that Glenys was coming. Glenys got to the fishpond and saw Robby floating face down in it. She screamed and ran right into the fishpond, snatched Rob up, and quickly carried him back to the bank.

He was very pale and limp and didn't seem to be breathing. She laid him on his stomach and started pushing on his back. A great clout of water gushed from his mouth and he started crying weakly.

Glenys picked him up and held him to her breast, rocking back and forth. "Thank God, oh thank God!" and she started to cry. Meanwhile Pansy was running circles around them, still very concerned, and making a yowling racket.

Kaitlyn heard all the commotion and looked out the window of her bedroom. When she saw what was happening, she flew down the stairs, almost tripping, and rushed into the backyard, screaming, "Robby, Robby, oh my God! Is he all right?"

"I don't know, I don't know," cried Glenys as she was rocking Robby back and forth. She was trembling herself and almost in a state of shock. Her clothes were soaking wet, and she had a piece of water lily in her hair.

"He was in his crib sleeping. I don't know how he got out. I should have checked him before cleaning the kitchen. Oh my God, I should have checked." Glenys was weeping so hard that she almost couldn't be understood.

Kaitlyn tried to soothe her. "It's not your fault. How were you to know that he figured out how to get out of his crib? Give him to me, please."

"We must get him into the house quickly where it's warm. We need to get those wet things off him and into some dry clothes. I'll carry him. You run ahead and call the doctor."

Kaitlyn felt like two people at once. One was watching this calm woman taking control, doing, and saying all the right things. The other was wringing her hands and saying, 'What if he dies? I couldn't bear it. I couldn't. I couldn't. Please, God, don't let him die.'

Robby was ice cold, and he kept crying, "I'm sorry, Mommy. I know I wasn't 'posed to go into the fishpond. I won't do it again. I promise. Please don't be mad at me."

"There, there, sweetheart, don't cry. Mommy is not mad at you. But we must give you a nice warm bath and get you back into bed," said Kaitlyn as she undressed him.

Glenys called the doctor, and he said he would come right away. She then drew the bath for Robby and laid out clean pajamas, crying all that time. She still hadn't changed her own wet clothes and wasn't even aware of it. She was so worried about Robby.

The doctor soon came and, after examining Robby, said. "You did the right thing, butting him a hot bath. He'll have to be watched closely for the next few days. There's always the fear of pneumonia, but I think he'll be just fine. Call me if he develops a fever."

Turning to Glenys, he took her face in his hand. "And you, young lady, need to take a hot bath yourself and get into some dry clothes. Quit crying. From the story I've heard, you and that moorcat, Pansy, are heroines."

Chapter Eighteen
A Stone Hut

One day, soon after the harvest, they were in the kitchen as usual. Cameron looked up from the report he was working on and said, "It's as I thought, Kaitlyn. This has been a very good year. We managed to sell the harvest at the best price ever. Bill Overton just got a big contract for uniforms and he took all we had left. It's all well and good to have one-sixth of the fields, but with the limit of not being allowed to process, and the cost of shipping to Earth, our decision to sell only here on Heatherbound has paid off. This year, even after giving the men bonuses, we are in the black. So let's play hooky and take tomorrow off. We'll go on a picnic."

Kaitlyn looked up from her papers and put down her cup of coffee. Coming around the table, she gave Cameron a big hug and sat in his lap. "Wonderful! Where shall we go? I know. We haven't seen the land that your parents gave us for our wedding present. Your father was telling me, just yesterday, how beautiful a place it is. He had fond memories of it when he was a child. Your grandfather especially loved it and went there quite often, stayed at a little hut, even by himself." Kaitlyn frowned. "It's funny. Your father seemed anxious for us to see it soon, too. Let's go there."

"Sweetheart, picnics with grandfather at Lake Placid?" Cameron said with a perplexed look on his face. "Dad never had time to go on picnics with us as kids. And this is the first I've heard that grandfather took him anywhere when Dad was a child. Where is this hut?"

"It's on a bluff overlooking Lake Placid, and that's about all I know about it. Your father said that your grandfather used to go there whenever he needed to think. It was the only place he could be alone. He built a stone hut, and even set up a small lab, but no one other than your father knew that. Dad thinks it is probably still there. It's about a three hour flight from us."

Cameron ran his hand through his hair. "I can't believe this. I have been trying for the last twenty years to find where Grandfather did his experiments. Dad never mentioned this place, and I have asked him a hundred times where he thought Grandfather's notes might be."

"Really, I wonder why he never mentioned it," said Kaitlyn. She got up from his lap and went back to her chair. Still looking at him, she said, "Sounds like our picnic will become a day of exploration as well. I can't wait until tomorrow. I had better finish this report tonight. I want to enjoy tomorrow with a free mind."

"Lake Placid is pretty far off the main stream. I've often wondered why we own half the shoreline. Granddad was a crafty Scot, that's for sure," Cameron said. "Was there anything else you can tell me about your conversation with Dad?" Cameron came around and sat on the edge of the table.

Kaitlyn looked up at him. "Well, he did mention one thing I thought a little strange. Your grandfather told your father he must remember, 'The secret is the secret.' when he visited the stone hut. Your Dad never forgot, but it meant nothing to him. Does it make sense to you, Dear?"

"Not at the moment, but perhaps we will find the answer at the stone hut," said Cameron as he returned to his chair and paperwork. Kaitlyn did too, and the room was quiet again except for Robby, who talked to his soldiers, and the rustle of papers.

The next morning the sun was shining, the air was clear, a perfect day for a picnic. After much scurrying around, everyone was ready. Cameron had the blankets, picnic basket, and baby needs, Kaitlyn held the baby, and Megan and Glenys took Robert's hand. Everyone was in a holiday mood as they climbed into the hovercraft. Cameron, in his careful way, made sure everything and everyone were secure and they were off.

The sky was very blue, with just a few billowy clouds, and Cameron flew high enough so that the land below looked like a patchwork quilt. There were mostly farms closer to the city, plots of vegetables, groves of olives, orchards of peaches, plums, citrus of all kinds, and fields of wheat. Further out were the sheep and cattle ranches.

Most of the Earth's animals ran true to form, but not the sheep. Their wool was longer, and so were their legs and body. Their horns were two-pronged, and these sheep were a much fiercer animal than the earth type. In trying to breed out the fierceness, they found that the quality of the wool lessened. Because the wool was much like cashmere, the ranchers put up with the breed. The shearers had to be macho, indeed, to shear these sheep.

Robert oh'ed and ah'ed about all the pretty farm houses and the small trees, but he really loved the sheep and cows they were seeing. The hours passed very quickly, and they saw the lake, blue and shimmering in the distance. They could see the stone hut near a bluff, as described by Sir John. Cameron landed nearby, and everyone got out. Robert ran around excitedly with Kaitlyn and Glenys, watching him with smiling eyes while they laid out the lunch. Megan was placed on another blanket, where she cooed and kicked her feet and waved her hands about.

Cameron had no thought of the lunch. He made a beeline to the hut, which seemed to be weathered with age, but still in very good shape. There were vines growing all over it, even over the doorway, making it impossible to get in until it cut away. He went back to the hovercraft for tools, puzzling over the message, 'The secret is the secret.' What could it mean?

He got the ax from the hovercraft and went back to the door. He hacked away the vines, and it wasn't long before he could see the entire door. It was made of Steelite and had a cipher lock with a picture of a spacecraft painted beside it. Suddenly the riddle made sense. The secret formula for Steelite must be the combination. Quickly he tried it and was rewarded with a click. With a twist of the handle and the door swung open and with it the smell of fresh air. That surprised him.

Stepping inside, Cameron noticed that everything was covered with dust and cobwebs. He knew that it had been at least thirty years since anyone had been inside this hut. He felt awed and humbled at the same time to think that the great man, his grandfather, had been the last one to enter.

It was not a large hut and had only one room with no windows. Cameron guessed that was for security. He was impressed that the automatic lighting was still working after all these years. The lighting was solar, of course. The solar collectors were set up with a little charge to kill off anything that tried to grow over them. All one side of the room was set up as a lab with test tubes, a microscope, a Bunsen burner, and everything needed for lab experiments. There was also a small safe with another cipher lock. A man in a space suit was painted on the side. Cameron smiled in congratulation to his grandfather, who thought of this for a clue. He tried the formula for space suit material, turned the handle, and again was rewarded with an open door. The inside of the safe was filled with papers. His heart lurched at the sight of them.

Just then, he heard Kaitlyn calling him to lunch. With a shrug, Cameron thought, I have waited for twenty years. Another hour will not hurt me. Leaving everything as he found it, he went to a picnic with his family.

"Darling, Glenys and I kept Rob away so you could get on with it, but we are dying of curiosity. Is it what you hoped to find?" Kaitlyn said as she handed him a plate.

Taking the plate from her hand, he sat down on the grass beside her. "Love, you are a jewel beyond compare to think of this picnic and to suggest this place. And yes, it looks like it may be. I just got into it, and it is unbelievable. Even the lights still work."

"One side of the room is set up with a cot, desk, and chair, the other a complete lab. He must have spent quite a lot of time here. I was surprised that the air seemed fresh since there were no windows. It's awfully dusty, though."

He took a big bite of his sandwich, chewed quickly, and said, "I hope you won't mind, Sweetheart, but after I take you all home, I plan to come back and spend a few days here, maybe longer. Can you handle that?"

"Knowing you, I wouldn't expect anything less," Kaitlyn said with a laugh. "Just wish I could be here with you. It would be like old times. As to coping without you, Glenys and I can manage. And if you're worried we can have one of the security robots assigned to the compound on a twenty-four hour basis while you are away."

"Thanks, Hon, and that's a good idea about the guard. In fact, I think we should have one permanently assigned. We've never had any trouble being so far out, but it doesn't hurt to take precautions. "

"It's really a shame that we have to worry about crime. Dad says that some rich parents send their spoiled darlings to Heatherbound in hopes that they will start anew and become solid citizens. It even happens occasionally. The worst are the riffraff that spend money they brought with them but have no training or education and turn to crime or hope for handouts from the government."

"I read that our Elders are trying to come up with stricter requirements to immigrate here and also to publicize that this is an agricultural planet and everyone has to work. There are no free rides. I am worried that we may have to fight for our land with Earth if we try to close these loopholes," Kaitlyn said pensively.

Kaitlyn realized how serious she was getting and, laughing at herself, said, "I don't want to think about that today, though. It's too perfect here."

Megan started to cry, and Kaitlyn picked her up and proceeded to nurse her. It was a beautiful sight, with Kaitlyn's strawberry blond head bent over the dark-haired baby. Megan's little hands were waving in the air and caught one of Kaitlyn's curls.

When Kaitlyn worked two days a week at RD&E, she took the children with her and Glenys as well. She felt it important for the health and psyche for all three of them to have this nurturing contact.

"Glenys, with Cameron coming back here for a few days and planning to stay in the hut, we had better go in and give it a quick cleaning. We will also need to check on what supplies he may need."

Glenys put her plate down and started to get up. "Sorry, Glenys, not right now. We'll finish our picnic first. I know you are eager to get in there and see it," Kaitlyn laughed, "but we were promised a holiday, and even though it will be shorter than planned, we will have it."

A half-hour later, lunch was finished, and Cameron was itching to get back to the hut. Megan was asleep in her basket, and Glenys had put everything away. Robert had found a stick and was running around pretending that he was riding a horse. "Rob dear, Glenys, your father, and I, are going to be busy cleaning the hut for a little while," said Kaitlyn softly. "Please play quietly by Megan, and let us know when she awakens."

"But Mummy, I want to play with my horsy," Robert said with dismay.

"You may play with your horse, but quietly and close by," Kaitlyn said with a quick pat on his head and a smile.

The three adults walked a very short distance to the hut. Cameron opened the door and showed the ladies in. "My, it is dusty and dirty in here.

Look at all the cobwebs," said Glenys as she wiped her finger along the desktop. "I wonder if there is anything here to clean with."

Kaitlyn was walking around the room, too, and spied a control panel. "Cameron, look at this," making an adjustment, "we have a window after all. It is an air permeate. He had it set at its lowest setting. See, if those vines were cut away, we would probably have a good view of the lake."

"Great, I knew you would find something for me to do while you gals were cleaning," said Cameron with a grin. "Not enough room in here for the three of us anyway. I'll go get the axe."

"Sounds good to me," said Kaitlyn, hitting another button, and a panel slid open to reveal a toilet, sink, and shower stall. The next button revealed a small kitchen. The last button was for the broom closet. "You have all the comforts of home here, Cameron. I won't worry about you a bit."

Glenys was pleased with the broom closet, but the first thing she did was grab the blankets off the cot and said, as she went out the door to shake the blankets, "I'm not at all sure shaking these will be enough. We may have to take them home for a good wash."

Between the three of them, the hut was ready for occupancy within the hour. Kaitlyn had made a list of the supplies that Cameron would need and they were ready to go for a walk and explore the area. Kaitlyn carried Megan in a backpack, and Cameron carried Robert on his shoulders when he got tired. Glenys was on holiday.

After arriving home, Cameron decided to stay until the next afternoon before returning to the stone hut. He wanted to make sure that the guard robot was programmed properly and that all his workers had their instructions for the next week. He promised to keep in touch by radio and could return quickly. Kaitlyn and Glenys packed his supplies and he was off, looking forward to finding out more about his beloved grandfather.

Chapter Nineteen

A Journal

The trip back to the hut was uneventful, although, to Cameron, it seemed endless. While flying, he thought how strange it was that no one had even mentioned the hut, or even much about the picnic. Kaitlyn, Glenys, and even little Rob seemed distracted when he tried to discuss it. Oh well, everyone was very busy getting him ready for the week's stay at the hut.

Everything looked the same when he arrived, and he was soon in the hut. He quickly turned up the window to allow sunshine to come in, and then opened the safe. Now that he had more time, he could see that the safe contained not only papers but also a journal. He was so excited he didn't know where to begin but decided on the journal. With this decision, he went over to the chair, sat down, and started to read.

Dear Grandson,

I say this with the utmost confidence, as only my grandson could get into this safe. There was a mind block put on anyone that showed an interest in the area, and it was to be kept on for a least one hundred years. This was part of my contract with the Dasurainians. When it was time, the mind block on your father would be weakened enough to allow him to tell you about this place, and you could continue my work of helping the Dasurainians to return to their home planet.

To give you a little background, the Colony was getting very low on certain supplies from Earth and had been negotiating with the Mother planet. Earth wanted to be assured that their ships would be filled with some kind of trade goods on the return trip or they couldn't afford to trade with us. They were willing for us to put our planet into hock with them for the supplies, but then Heatherbound would be just another slave planet.

The Elders decided that we would rather go back to the Stone Age than to sell our heritage. Not everyone agreed, and some wanted to be sent back to Earth in the pods. The five best pods had been kept intact for just this purpose, but there was a stipulation, the people who wanted to go back had to try living on Heatherbound for another year.

I had been trying ever since landing to find a native plant that would be unusual enough to be of value for trade. Finding nothing on the main landmasses, I had been flying around to all the islands in hopes of discovering something, anything. I found a lot of possibilities, but it would take years of research and experimentation to make them useful. We did not have years.

I finally tried the island chain that was in the north. This area appeared to have perpetual winter. I flew around all the islands, and except for size, they looked pretty much the same, bleak and desolate. I chose the largest island to land on. It had a very large mountain in the center, the largest I'd ever seen on Heatherbound. This seemed my last chance. It looked hopeless, as the landscape was strewn with rocks and boulders. There were pockets of snow everywhere. The wind was howling like a wolf and cold, cold as a witch's heart. It didn't look like anything could grow there except lichen and a few low-growing bushes.

I unloaded my supplies from the hovercraft and set up a base camp. I planned on a week or two stay. I had a lot of trouble putting up the tent because of the wind and cold. My fingers were numb even through the thick gloves I was wearing. I wished I had taken thermowear with me, but I persevered and finally got the tent up. After a quick meal, I could no longer delay, so I gathered up my gear and started out.

My gear on this godforsaken island was a little more than usual, as I decided that a rope and rock axe could come in handy, along with my knapsack, specimen bags, and trusty walking stick. Off I went, trying to be optimistic. Thank God it was summer here. I couldn't even imagine how it must be in winter.

About a half-hour later, after climbing over many boulders and jumping over some crevasses, I felt this eerie feeling on the back of my neck as if someone or something was watching me. I stopped and looked around. Seeing nothing, I shrugged it off as my imagination due to the weird landscape. A little while later, I felt it again. Stronger, but nothing was there. Why should I be afraid? We had found no large animals on this planet, and this did not look to be a place that could support one. All of a sudden, I heard something, a cry for help. It seemed to be up ahead. Running forward, I came to a crevasse.

On a ledge about twenty feet straight down was what appeared to be a small bear, but I had never seen a bear with lavender fur. It was hurt from the fall, and the call for help was coming from this animal. It was sentient and telepathic because I now realized that what I was hearing was not aloud but in my mind.

Not stopping to think, I quickly tied my rope around a rock and lowered myself down to the ledge, and reached for the small animal. The bear (?), frightened half out of its mind, tried valiantly to defend itself, giving me several deep gashes before it fainted. By this time, I was not in great shape myself. My clothes were badly torn, and I was bleeding in several places. I knew we had to get off that ledge soon before my strength left me. Using my knapsack and an extra length of rope, I managed to tie the limp animal to my back.

Kicking myself mentally for not spending just a few moments to let this animal know that I was only trying to help, I proceeded to try to climb back up. It was slow going as the little bear (I couldn't think of it any other way) was a dead weight, and my right hand was torn and bleeding.

About half way up, I was desperately tired and wasn't too sure that I could make it the rest of the way when I felt the rope being pulled up. I looked up and saw two very large purple bear-like creatures. I was so startled that if I hadn't had the rope wrapped tightly around my waist, I would have fallen. They immediately soothed my mind, and I let them pull us up the rest of the way.

When we were on top and safe, one of them gently removed the small creature from my back. The other picked me up just as gently and, carrying me, followed the first one up the trail. They thanked me and explained that they were trying to find a way to save the child but they were too big to get down the crevasse.

I had lost a lot of blood and was in some pain. The creature told me that he was a Dasurainian and that they were very grateful to me for saving their youngest. Apologizing for my injuries, they promised they would take care of me. Now go to sleep. I did.

I woke up to find myself bandaged and in no pain. I was in a very large cave, lying on a cot, covered with something soft. A Dasurainian was sitting beside me, and assured me that the child I had saved was going to be all right, and I would be too, in a few days. They had sent someone to my camp to get clothing and heating equipment for me because they had none of either, having no need for them.

The Dasurainians had very heavy coats of fur, long and straight, not shaggy but well groomed. The males were a very dark purple, almost black, with a ridge of black fur that started between the eyes and went all the way down the back to a short stubby tail. They weigh about six hundred pounds. The females were all shades of purple to almost lavender, with no ridges. Their hair was longer and silkier. Neither sex wore clothing, just a rather ornate wide belt with many pockets.

The Dasurainians were a lot like a terrestrial brown bears, but with retractable claws and opposable thumbs. Their posture was upright, and they walked with noble grace. Having no vocal cords, they had developed their telepathy to a high degree. This saved them from having to fight many times in their years of exploration. Their race had found numerous other races, and most of these were aggressive and xenophobic.

When my clothes and equipment arrived, the Dasurainian doctor set everything up for me and helped me into a clean shirt. He was very gentle, which surprised me for such a large creature. He then turned my heater on and quickly left me. I could see that even on low heat, he was extremely uncomfortable from the heat. I was soon asleep again, and when I awoke, another Dasurainian was sitting about ten feet from me.

Man, we have been probing your mind to find out just what kind of creature you are, said Drakel when he saw that I was again awake. *For such a young and aggressive race, you have come very far. My kind is no longer warlike and has no wish to contend with yours for this or any other planet. We prefer much colder ones.*

You have a problem, and we can help you, but we must ask a lot of you in return. We need to know as much as possible about your race and we can only accomplish this by a deep study of your mind and body. This is hard on an individual and will reduce your life span by many years. In return, we will give you a plant that can be processed into a steel-like product. We will give you the seeds, also the formulas for different uses, and all data needed to grow this plant. How say you to this contract? said Drakel, who was Captain of the shipwrecked crew.

"I don't know how you have done it, but you have made my mind capable of reading your mind as well as your heart," I said, pushing myself up to a sitting position. The sudden movement made me a little dizzy, but I still felt no pain and noticed that my wounds seemed almost healed. I wondered how long I had slept.

With a slight shudder, for it was cold sitting up even with the heater on, I continued with what I had started to say. "Your mind is as completely open to me as mine is to you. It's daft, but I know that you are telling me the truth when you say you have no desire to compete with my race in any way, war or planet. If there is any way that I can help you, I want to do it. I would be very grateful for any data you can give me on this steel-like plant."

We thank you for this. You must listen to the story of our shipwreck and our problems here in hopes that you will help us further. In the end, I will offer you another plant in exchange for that help.

This is their story.

Captain Drakel and his crew were exploring this area when a meteor holed their ship. They were forced to land on the first available planet that would sustain them, no matter how uncomfortable the planet might be. Twelve of the crew had been killed outright, and ten more were so badly injured that they died within a month, which left forty-seven. Five of the women were pregnant, but only three cubs survived the birth experience.

Food was no problem because their hydroponics garden remained intact. They are vegetarians and eat large amounts of legumes and vegetables. Medicine was in short supply though, as the pharmacy and medical section were in the location where the ship was holed. The small rock that holed them did a lot of damage as it ricocheted around the room. It seemed to have a vicious mind of its own, wrecking machinery and killing at random. This was a freak accident because usually, meteors would just go out the other side leaving two holes. The sudden decompression in that section caused more deaths and injuries. The entire section was ruined, including all but one of their medi-tubes, which was the reason for the loss of most of the injured.

Their medi-tubes were a lot like our medi-cubes. An injured person was put inside and robotic probes diagnosed the problem, needles and arms extended and the necessary repair jobs were seen to, first sedating the patient. The patient was kept in the tube until he was well enough to finish healing on his own. All muscles of the body were regularly massaged during this time to make sure there would be no loss of muscle tone. The patient was usually in better health after leaving the medi-tube than before the need to enter it, as it not only cured the major injuries but anything else the patient may have had wrong with him.

The accident happened about twenty-five years ago. They had discovered, as we had, that this planet had only small amounts of metal ore deposits and that these were very hard to mine. This didn't surprise them too much, and they began experimenting with plants to find the materials they needed to repair their ship and return home.

They would need metal and fuel because most of their fuel had been used in maneuvering for their landing. They needed a large source of fuel to take off and get them home safely. Genetic engineering of plants was their forte, and they knew that eventually, they would be able to tailor plants to fill their needs. The problem was the slow growth on this planet. Also, they were not used to working with heat-loving plants.

They eventually found the plant that became Steelite growing around Lake Placid. After much trial and error, they came up with the formulas needed to turn it into a steel-like product. Steelite exceeded even their highest expectations. It was a discovery that made the time spent on this planet very worthwhile. Their people need never worry about meteors again.

It was difficult for them to plant and harvest in the warm areas of this planet, but not impossible. They were still harvesting the Steelite fields when we colonists arrived. They did not want this planet for themselves since it was too warm, so they did not contest the right of the colonists to settle. But this gave them the problem of keeping their existence a secret. With mind control, on a wide scale basis, they were able to discourage anyone from going to, or even seeing from the air, their Steelite fields. This control also stopped Kendell from finding the plant, which grew only around Lake Placid.

After a few years they had enough Steelite to completely cover their ship, as well as replace most of the interior. They saved the seeds and erased all traces of their planting. This was their usual procedure on populated planets, and they used the land on such planets only on an emergency basis.

They had found the fuel plant on the large island and were still working on it to get enough fuel to go home. The plant was a shrub-like tree with a thick, stubby trunk. They named them Turpina Trees. When the sap was refined, it made a very high grade of oil. Unfortunately, it propagated very slowly, and a lot of fuel was needed. They calculated that they could leave in about a hundred years. The Dasurainians were a long-lived people, but it would be a severe hardship to be awake all that time on a planet too warm for them. Even this island was barely livable for them in the summer, short as it was.

Drakel wanted to trade these oil plants for cryonic equipment and two robots to care for them while frozen. He had read about cryonics in my mind. The Dasurainians had never encountered this method of hibernation before. The robots could be modified to take care of their different physical needs and also to care for the plants while they slept. Most of their own robots had been lost in the accident. Fortunately, their robot engineer was not killed, and they had the means to do all modifications required. There were records of how robot brains were grown, and with the help of the one robot remaining, they planned to build as many more as needed. They also had all the unprocessed Steelite needed to make the bodies.

The shrubs needed very little care, but the sap had to be harvested every three months. Every plant gave about two gallons at each harvest. Of course, this entire island would be covered with this plant in about ninety years, and the plants would produce more as they matured. The plants would have to be replaced about every fifty years. The harvest would be kept in large holding tanks. Meanwhile, the Dasurainians just had to wait and endure the heat and boredom on this small island.

The proposed agreement was that at the end of the one hundred years, the Dasurainians would leave this planet. Instead of erasing all existence of their planting, as was their usual method, they would leave the groves intact. They would also leave all data needed to refine the sap and any robots that had been made to care for them. This would be in exchange for the cryonic equipment, the robots, and help with the revival.

A mind block would be set up to keep people away from the island chain and anything else that might lead anyone to find it. This would include the land around Lake Placid because that is where the Steelite plants were found. It was explained to me that if someone should go to either place, they would immediately forget all about it. If someone other than my programmed descendent should find and read this journal they would not remember a single word.

It was unbelievable, but I believed every word of it.

I agreed to everything they asked for. It was a fair exchange, and my family and friends would benefit greatly. Long life would have been nice, but they assured me that they would tailor my genes to insure that every other generation of my descendants would produce someone like myself, a humanitarian and scientist. Only this person would be able to pass the mind block on this island until the Dasurainians were able to leave this planet. They did not want any of our people to know of their existence.

It took about two weeks for them to retrieve all the information they wanted from my body and mind. I did indeed feel that I had aged thirty years when they were finished but in good health. They even corrected a heart problem that I didn't know I had. When they were finished, I wanted to get back to the colony to fulfill my part of the bargain. I knew that it would not be easy, but what choice, in the long run, did the Elders have?

I guess I looked worse than I felt because when I returned home, everyone claimed that I looked exhausted and wanted to put me in the hospital. I explained to them that I had been pushing very hard but had finally come up with a great discovery. I would need certain equipment to perfect this plant and also the services of our cryonics expert for a month or so. I explained all about Steelite and what we could do with it. The Elders were excited, but some of the people who thought they might want to return to Earth did not want to give up the pods. I told them I needed two pods and six robots.

After much discussion and hand-wringing, I told them that I could probably do with less. I would give half of the profits from the Steelite for the first thirty years of production to the Colony to pay for the equipment. I also said that I would give half the profit for the following ten years for the land around Lake Placid and the four main islands in the chain, which I had named Winter's Grove. This went over very well and we agreed on one pod and four robots.

It was more than I really needed, but I would gladly take it. William Chan, the cryonics expert, said he was willing to come with me, and the Elders would pay him for his time.

The next day I got together my gear, this time including thermo-clothing and gloves for Chan and myself. We were now prepared to return to Winter's Grove. With the help of the robots I managed to get the pod delivered to the Dasurainians.

William followed me with my hovercraft, and when he arrived and saw the Dasurainians, he almost fainted. They quickly assured him that they would not harm him and were grateful that he had come to help them. He saw how difficult the problem would be to convert the sleeping cubicles to fit the Dasurainians, but with a little help from some of the Dasurainian engineers, they soon solved it and the work proceeded.

We stayed with them for a month to make sure that the changes in the cryonic equipment were correct and completely understood by them and the robots. They, in turn, explained the specific requirements that both Steelite and the oil plant needed to grow properly. I took many notes, which you will find in the safe with this journal. The Dasurainians are quite detail oriented and even gave me formulas for the fertilizers, as well as all information needed to process both plants.

Dreena, the little girl cub I had rescued, talked to me from time to time. We became good friends; I was really going to miss her. The saddest part of this whole situation was that I would not be here when they woke up. I would never see Dreena or any of the Dasurainians again. I couldn't even talk about them.

In one of my conversations with Dreena, she explained why she had been so frightened when I came down the rope to rescue her, even though she could read only good thoughts from me. On their home planet, they had an animal that looked a lot like humans. This animal was carnivorous and quite savage. When I smiled at her, revealing my teeth, she was sure I was one of these animals.

I still frightened her a bit when I smiled, so I practiced smiling with my mouth shut. She never talked very long because she was always running and jumping and getting herself in trouble, not like the other two cubs. They were content to move as slowly and surely as the adults did. You may wonder why I called her a cub, considering that she was twenty-five years old. The Dasurainians matured slowly and were not considered adults until they were fifty.

All too soon, everything was ready, even the processing plant for the fuel and extra tanks to put it in. I started to say my good-byes, unhappy with the knowledge that I would never see them again. Also heavy-hearted to think that this was the greatest discovery of my career, and I didn't really discover it. Drakel sensed my feelings and assured me that I would have if given as much time as they had had, and not mind blocked from the source. Believe it or not, I felt better having Drakel say this. I knew he could not lie.

We made sure that all the Dasurainians were fully under the cryogenic gases and that the equipment was working perfectly. I explained to William Chan that he would not remember any of what he had been doing here or the aliens he had met. He was very sad about this but understood, and we left Winter's Grove with heavy hearts.

Since you are reading this the one hundred years must have passed, and you can collect that second half of our legacy from the Dasurainians. I would ask you to figure out some way to give the government of Heatherbound a portion of the profits on the oil plant as I did on Steelite. I think that by the time you read this, Earth may be thinking of taking over this planet one way or another. It would be a sound investment to have a good defense system set up. A defense buildup will take a lot of money, and the government would find it easier to swallow if most of the expenses were already paid.

You will find my last will and testament among the papers in the safe. Everything is the same as in my original one, except you will find that I bought Winter's Grove and bequeath these islands, and all on it, plus any proceeds, to you, the grandson who discovers this will. This bequest was written before I was married or had children and therefore does not come under the inheritance laws. You will find the deed among the papers also, as well as a map of the area.

Good luck, Grandson, and may God protect you.

Chapter Twenty
Discovery

The Dasurainians were a race of explorers. They emerged from a bitterly cold planet. In their beginning they were a lot like our earth bears, omnivores and territorial. Over time they evolved into a telepathic civilized gentle being with opposable thumbs. They no longer needed to fight as they used mind control over their enemies in a compassionate way. With time they became vegetarians, and their scientist's forte was biochemistry.

Captain Drakel circled the closest planet after the meteor strike. *The planet is going to be too warm for us, but we have no choice; we must land. There are some islands in the northern hemisphere that look livable. We will land on the largest island.*

The landing was not a smooth one as it was a mountainous region with very little flat space. The Captain and his crew were very well qualified and managed to land in one piece.

In a strained voice, Drakel said, *Doctor, I have time for your report now.*

The doctor was gray with fatigue. He had one arm in a sling and a bandage on his head. *Sir, there were twelve killed outright. Ten more are severely wounded and may not make it. The five women who are pregnant are in labor. One cub will be premature. We are trying to stop her from delivering to no avail.*

Thank you, doctor, you are dismissed.

Drakel turned to his chief engineer, *Your damage report, Sir.*

Chief Engineer Drafory saluted and stepped forward. His fur was disheveled, and he looked exhausted. *Sir, The medical department is in complete disarray. It will take months to repair even if we have the materials. The meteor ruined all the medicubes except one. Also, our communication room is out of commission.*

We do not have enough fuel to take off and make it back home. The hull is in need of major repair. Fortunately, my men were not injured, and we could start some repairs immediately. None of our flyers were damaged, and I have sent out all four of them with our scientists to look for plants in anticipation of finding some that we can convert to steel and fuel.

Running his hands down his arms, trying to straighten his fur. *I also sent out another group to see if they can make a temporary home for us while the repairs are being made. They have found a cave that can be enlarged and are in the process of doing so.*

Thank you, Chief Drafory. You have been very busy, as have we all. How is your wife doing?

With a broad grin. *Darla is in good spirits. It appears the cub is impatient and will be with us soon. Dr. Dramon is not expecting anymore complications.*

Of the five females that were pregnant, one of them and her cub died. She had been a nurse, and the meteor had torn off her left leg as it ricocheted around the medical center. They tried valiantly to save her and her cub, but both succumbed in less than a week. Another one had been in one of the medicubes that was damaged. In trying to extract her, they discovered to do so would kill her and her cub. Not to do so, she would die anyway. They decided to sedate her and let nature take its course. All were so traumatized they were beyond weeping.

Thank the Holy Mother that the other three mothers are doing so well, even the one that is in labor too early. She sees all and knows we can suffer no more. Dramon said with a bowed head.

Darla named her cub, Dreena. She was smaller than average and very lively. This was very unusual for a Dasurainian cub. Most were very docile and slow-moving, content to be held and cuddled. Not Dreena. When she finished suckling, she wanted to get down and run around. She was into everything and had to be watched constantly.

Everyone loved Dreena, and she loved them back. She would run up to just about any of them and demand to be picked up and taken for a piggyback ride or have a story read to her. Her grin was captivating, and no one could resist her, especially her father. As busy as he was, he found time to talk to her or even take her with him when he inspected the work his men were doing. She especially liked to go with her father on one of the flyers. She enjoyed looking at all the green fields of grass and the splotches of color everywhere from up high. She begged her father to land so she would pick some of these beautiful flowers. He told her it would be too uncomfortable for her because it was so hot on this planet. She insisted, and he did land, telling her, *Just this once.*

Dreena couldn't believe the blast of hot air that hit her when her father opened the door. She stubbornly got out and picked the flowers. She never asked to land again. But she loved the flowers. She was very quiet for a while.

Because of Dreena, the stay on this too-hot planet was not quite so boring, and was bearable. While she was learning to control her telepathy, some of the older individuals in the group felt like strangling her as she was so loud. But her laughter made up for it. It was infectious. They needed her humor and her joy of life.

She spent time with the other cubs, but they soon bored her. All they wanted to do was read books and play with their toys in a quiet way. She tried to get them to come out of the cave and climb on the rocks. Run down to the water's edge and throw rocks to see the splashes. Everything and anything new excited her. She found it difficult to understand why the other cubs weren't interested.

As she grew older, she was willing to sit awhile longer, at least long enough to do her lessons and the few chores she had. Dasurainians were considered cubs until they reached about thirty of our years and her parents sometimes felt that she was never going to grow up to the quiet dignity of their race.

Dreena had more knee scrapes and bruises than the other two cubs put together. Her fur always needed grooming and she hated wearing her tool belt. But if anyone needed a helping hand, she was there. They all loved her.

During the time that Dreena was growing up, the flyers were going out searching for the right plants. They noticed how long it took plants to grow on this planet which made their discoveries that much harder to control. After trial and error, they finally found a plant they called worzell. It grew a lot like our cotton but had more tensile strength and a metallic sheen. After trying many different formulas for fertilizer and processing, they finally came up with steelite. At last, they could start to repair their ship.

They had found the fuel plant quite quickly. It was a small shrub growing on the island they were stranded on. They recognized it properties immediately. Most planets they had discovered had plants similar to this one. The problem with it this shrub was that it was so slow growing. It was going to take, by their calculations, about one hundred years to gather enough fuel to leave.

Chapter Twenty-one
Winter's Grove

After reading his grandfather's journal, Cameron had a lot to think about. He was stunned to realize that he was a clone-like descendent of his grandfather. No wonder he was so interested in plants and science. Did he have any control over his life? Would he have wanted another destiny? He realized that he didn't mind and was even proud. He marveled at the wisdom of his grandfather in predicting the up-coming problems with Earth. It made him all the prouder of his heritage.

The second thing that hit him was that he and Kaitlyn were going to be very rich, much sooner than he had thought. They could set up Hovercraft dealerships and fuel station chains. It was endless. There might even be a use for the residue after extraction of the oil. All the things that are made out plastic could possibly be manufactured on Heatherbound now. It was mind-boggling. It made him excited to think of all the years of research and discovery he had in front of him.

My God, just think, I'll have a grandson to follow in my footsteps just like grandfather did. Only this time, God willing, I'll be able to live long enough to further his education. He couldn't help smiling, thinking of Kaitlyn and their grandchildren.

He then remembered Sean with a feeling of dread. This will drive him mad. He will never accept this as my inheritance. Sean will do everything in his power to take it as his. Cameron envisioned terrible arguments, even court scenes with lawyers on each side enjoying the fight. He would win, though. He had his grandfather's will. It couldn't be broken, he was sure. I wonder how our parents will react to all this.

Suddenly he realized how hungry he was and noticed it was getting late. He got up and stretched. His body felt stiff from sitting too long. Finding the basket of food, Kaitlyn had fixed for him. He pulled out some cold chicken, salad, and fruit. Putting them on the lab table he had been sitting at, he again sat and proceeded to eat while perusing the other papers he had found in the safe.

There was also a thermos of coffee, and he poured himself a cup. He finished off the meal with some berry pie.

When he finished eating, Cameron straightened up the lab table, washed the dishes, and put the leftovers back in the basket. It was still nice out, and he decided to go for a walk. That always cleared his mind and refreshed him. He wished he could discuss this with Kaitlyn or even Ian but knew it would be impossible because of the mind block. He would even have to do what his grandfather did and declare the discovery of the oil plant as his grandfather's. Anything else would have people asking questions he could not answer.

Would Kaitlyn understand, knowing him to be quiet about projects until he was sure of them, or would she be hurt thinking he didn't trust her? She would want all the details of the discovery. And he could not tell her much.

He would have to handle this very carefully. He would also have to keep Sean in the dark until all negotiations with the Elders were completed. Sean would not understand giving away so much money. The chance of a court battle with Sean was almost inevitable. It would not hold up, of course, but it could cause a lot of hard feelings.

This was going to be a big boon to the economy. It will make it easier for just about anyone to own a hovercraft because now the fuel needed would not have to be imported. Of course, the cost was still pretty stiff for the craft itself, as they were mostly made with Steelite. But Ian's family had been doing a lot with ceramics. They even had plans for a ceramic body for the new hovercrafts. Perhaps they could use some of the residues from the oil plant, Turpina, the Dasurainians called it. Good name, even in our language.

Cameron stopped and looked around for the first time. He hadn't realized that he had walked to the edge of the bluff over-looking the lake. The moon, Tristan, was shining on the water, at the horizon was Isolde. One could always tell the moons apart. Tristan had a slight blue cast, Isolde was pinkish and a little smaller. It was so calm and peaceful here. There was a slight breeze that cooled the evening off. Across the lake, he could see a stand of bamboo. This is where he and Kaitlyn would build their mansion. He knew she would love it. Thinking this, he felt optimistic. He knew things would work out. It was only a matter of time.

He walked back to the hut and prepared for bed. He experimented with the control panel and found the small shower cubicle next to the broom closet. The spray was needle-sharp and hot, just the way he liked it. Toweling off, he felt like a new man and slept well the entire night.

He woke up early, as usual, and finished going through the rest of the papers while eating a quick meal of leftovers. He found maps and the coordinates of the Island chain. He had been feeling a slight anxiety all morning and now felt a need to hurry for some reason. He had to get to Winter's Grove as quickly as possible. I wonder if perhaps I'm getting a message that something is happening that needs my urgent attention.

Quickly he packed up the supplies, then went to the broom closet to get the broom. Hanging there were the thermal clothes his grandfather had worn. Neither Kaitlyn nor Glenys had seen them. For some reason, the hair on the back of his neck stood up. It literally brought home to him everything that he had read in the journal. He had believed it intellectually, but now here was proof that it was true.

He took the thermowear out of the closet and looked it over carefully. It was a little dusty but looked to be a perfect fit. He went outside and gave it a good shake. Dust flew everywhere, and a piece of paper fluttered to the ground. It was a note from his grandfather. It read:

My dear Grandson, I had hoped you would find this suit and wear it. You'll need it at Winter's Grove, no matter what season of the year it is. Again, good luck.

He felt a stab of pain on seeing this. His eyes misted as he wished that his grandfather were here with him. God, how he missed that old man. He knew that his grandfather was thinking of him when he wrote this note, knowing that he, Kendell, would not be there to see the end of the story.

His heart ached for this brave man who, even after his death, was trying to keep him from harm's way. I guess he had a lot of time here alone. It must have been hell to never be able to talk about his real discovery, the aliens.

Cameron went back into the hut, straightened it, and put everything back into the safe. Taking the thermal suit, he was ready to go. He wished he could call Kaitlyn to let her know where he was going, but that would take a lot of explaining, and she wouldn't remember it anyway. Taking the supplies, he went to his hovercraft and took off for Winter's Grove.

The island looked a lot different from his grandfather's description. It was covered with shrubs and looked well-tended. Circling the island, he saw two robots harvesting. He wondered how advanced they were and if he could use any of the modifications in his own robots or the new ones coming out at RD&E.

Landing where his grandfather said was the best place to look at the island, he got out and immediately was hit with a powerful smell. It was a combination of citrus and pine. Wonderful, the air was filled with it even though it was also bitterly cold. There was snow everywhere, and the wind was starting to kick up. Though he had donned the thermowear while flying on autopilot, he still felt cold. The feeling of urgency filled him again. No time for exploring. With some haste, he got back into the Hovercraft and flew to the cave.

The cave's entrance was right where the map indicated, and he flew inside. The entrance was quite wide and had a gentle downward grade. He continued down the entrance tunnel until it widened into a huge cave.

He entered the cave through the long tunnel. Lights came on, and he saw the pod his grandfather had written about. Cameron parked his hovercraft and got out to explore. The further he walked in, the more lights came on. He saw some large tanks and several robots around them. In the distance, he saw what looked like a spaceship. This was really a huge cave. He wondered if it were natural or if the Dasurainians had carved most of it out. The mountain must be almost hollow.

He heard a whirring sound behind him and swung around quickly. A robot was coming up to him briskly.

"Mr. McCreight, we were hoping you would come soon. There has been a malfunction in the cryonics equipment. The Dasurainians are still alive, but we have been unable to revive them. There is excess fuel prepared, and we are almost out of tanks for the harvest."

Knowing robots, Cameron knew that this one was agitated or it would never have spoken first. Seeing number one on its breast, Cameron replied, "If you will take me to the Dasurainians, No.1, I will see what I can do. As for the tanks, I will arrange for them to be emptied as soon as possible. You are called No.1, aren't you?"

"No.1 will do for a designation. Please follow me."

No.1 turned around and led him to the pod. Cameron entered and went immediately to look at the aliens. He admitted to himself that the thought of purple bears was rather fantastic, but as everything else had turned out to be correct, this must also be.

He was curious to see these aliens. Going to the nearest of the containers, he wiped the frost that had collected on the view window. Sure enough, there was a very large purple animal inside. He then checked the read-outs, and all the vital signs appeared to be normal. Together they checked all the connections, power supply, and everything Cameron could think of. He asked No. 1 to relate his instructions exactly, and they went through the drill again. No good, they were unable to start the awakening sequence. During this search, Cameron was getting colder and colder. He turned up the heat in his thermowear and that helped at first but he would have to get someplace to warm up, and figure this out.

Cameron then asked for all the paperwork on the cryonics and took it to his hovercraft, turned the heat on full, then spent hours going over them all. He could not find an answer. Everything seemed to be in order. He realized he wasn't going to find the answer himself. If he didn't get a cryonics expert in soon the Dasurainians would never wake up.

He knew of a cryonics company, Cryonics Ltd., which had a small but reputable business. They dealt mostly with people who were very ill and about to die of some obscure illness. These people wanted to be put in cold storage until a cure could be found. There he knew he would find an engineer and a doctor, and by hook or crook, he would bring them back.

While he was going through all the papers, he had No.1 test the fuel for use in the hovercraft. The robot had done so and found that the fuel was better and cleaner than the fuel he was using. It would make the engines last longer, as they would run cooler and yet more efficiently. He then told No.1 to check his fuel and engine and have it ready to fly as soon as possible.

Cameron had now been awake for twenty-five hours. He needed rest. The chill was also continuing to numb him, even though his thermowear. He would have to sleep on the way back. The autopilot controls were usually foolproof, but he had never used them for an eleven-hour flight. He had to take the chance. The threat to the Dasurainians was real, and he had every intention of fulfilling his grandfather's promise to aid them.

"No. 1, I am going to leave you for a short while. I will bring back experts to revive the Dasurainians. Just keep monitoring them as you have been, and I will return as soon as possible."

Chapter Twenty-two

Arrangements

Arriving back in New Edinburgh just before noon, Cameron landed on the roof of his office building. He immediately went to his office where he called Cryonics Ltd., and made a luncheon appointment with the president and his head engineer. They were to meet at the Dunedin restaurant near the spaceport.

Cameron always kept a change of clothes at the office. After showering and shaving, he went to look up Ian. Finding him in the hallway just outside of Ian's office, Cameron started in without any preliminaries. "I can't take the time to explain, but I want you to buy two heavy-duty tanker hovercrafts. Try to get them as cheaply as possible. We don't want to arouse suspicion. I must have them in five hours. Pay cash if you have to. I will also need crews for both." This was a tall order, but he knew Ian could do it, if anyone could.

Ian looked startled, then laughed, "Cameron, that is just like you. No, hello. Nice to see you, Ian. You coast along quietly, and then out of the blue, you come up with something like this. Arouse suspicion. Are you kidding? This will set the tanker business on fire. I can see you are in a hurry, but this takes the cake. I can't believe you are asking the practically impossible so calmly."

"Ian, I know that this will be difficult, but it is important and must be done," said Cameron, resting his hands on Ian's shoulders and looking earnestly into his eyes. "This is not a joke."

"O.K., O.K." Putting his hands up and with a shrug, "I'll do what I can, but I want a complete explanation when you get back."

"Ian, this is not for publication, but if that older brother of yours still has money to invest, he might think about anything to do with supplying fuel for hovercrafts. Also, your family should step up the work they are doing on making ceramic bodies for hovercrafts."

"I have discovered a cheap source of fuel," Cameron said quietly. "I also want you to design a robotic tanker hovercraft, one that has weapons to keep it from being hijacked."

"How much fuel a year are we talking? " Ian asked, sobering immediately. "I've saved quite a bit myself. You'll need fuel tanks and dispensing stations. It's sensational."

"I really don't know exactly, but around six million barrels a year to start with. Kaitlyn doesn't know anything about this yet. Get with her. She's the financial expert. Work out whatever you think is fair. When I get back, I'll explain everything to you and to her."

Cameron started to rush away and then turned back. "That's right. We'll need fuel tanks. Have a couple built while I'm gone. Be sure to have at least one ready for the tankers to empty into when they get back in a couple of days."

"I've got to hurry. Tell Kaitlyn not to worry, that I will be back in about a month. Oh, have a month's supply of food for four people and some cots, blankets, and thermowear, including gloves sent with the fuel tankers," Cameron said as he brushed past Ian on his way to his hovercraft.

"You sound as if you think I'm a magician," said Ian to Cameron's back.

"I always thought you were," laughed Cameron over his shoulder.

Ian stood there for a few seconds looking at Cameron's back, still slightly dumbfounded. Turning, he quickly went back to his office to make some phone calls. The first he made was to Kaitlyn.

Cameron made it to Dunedin with minutes to spare. The waiter said the other two men were already there and waiting for him. He led Cameron to their table, handed him a menu, and left. The other two men stood. One was tall with a bushy black beard. He was dressed conservatively in a gray singlelet; the only bit of color was his belt which was a tartan of the Dugan clan. The other man was Japanese, much shorter and very lean, clean-shaven, with black hair and eyes. He was wearing a singlelet as well, which was the usual business dress. His was brown with a thin red stripe.

Cameron offered his hand to shake. "I am Cameron McCreight. I appreciate your seeing me on such short notice."

"This is Peter Dugan, my chief engineer, and I am Jutaro Komara, President of Cryonics' Ltd., and the chief medical officer," Jutaro said formally, while shaking Cameron's hand.

"Shall we be seated? And let's order. I'm famished," Cameron said with a smile.

They ordered and made small talk while eating, as was the custom, thus getting to know each other. Cameron liked what he saw and was relieved. He could deal with these men. They seemed honest and conservative. He just hoped they would feel the same way and were not too conservative. There might not be enough time to persuade them otherwise.

When making reservations, Cameron had asked for a private table. After the table was cleared and coffee was served, they were left alone. It was time to get down to business.

"You may have guessed that I asked you here today because I have a business proposition for you both. You also may know that I am from the McCreight family that owns the Steelite plants," said Cameron.

"We know of you and your family. You are the second son, but you have a very good business of your own. We did some checking before we come to lunch," replied Jutaro.

"That's good to know and will make what I have to tell you much easier," said Cameron leaning forward in his chair, his hands on the table.

"I made a new discovery with a different plant, but I need some help with cryonics. I'll need an expert on recovery and probably an engineer. I may need a doctor who is an expert in this field as well," Cameron said, holding up his hand to forestall any comment. "Before you commit yourselves, you need to know that the assignment may take as long as a month. Nevertheless, I need an immediate decision as I have an emergency at the site, which could cause loss of lives. I have no time to waste. I plan to leave at five o'clock this evening."

"I know this is a very large demand, but I am willing to pay a very large fee for one month's work. I do not have time to haggle. The plant I discovered provides a fuel suitable for hovercrafts and even spaceships. Some of the equipment that I am using in this project is malfunctioning and it is in your field of expertise."

"I offer you, Dr. Komara, as president of your company and as an expert on recovery, 20,000 Federal credits, for your engineer, Mr. Dugan, 10,000. I hope that I won't need a medical doctor too, but I understand that you are one, Doctor Komara."

There was a stunned silence from the two men sitting across the table from Cameron. "Let me get this straight. You are offering to pay me what I make in one year for one month's service. The offer is also extended to my chief engineer, the amount I pay him for one year," Jutaro said, with a disbelieving look on his face.

"Is it legal?" said Peter Dugan.

"It is perfectly legal. I only offer so much because you must make your decision in the next five minutes. I have a great fear that we may lose some lives and about a million barrels of fuel if I don't get expert help by tomorrow. As you can see, I am being perfectly candid with you both. Needless to say, this must go no further than this room."

"Can you do it?" Cameron asked expectantly.

"It's such short notice. We would have a lot of rearranging to do. With both of us going, it would be difficult but not impossible. I must have a few hours, though. How about you, Peter?" said Jutaro turning to Peter with a question in his eyes.

"Damn, I promised to take the family for a week's fishing trip next week. For that kind of money, they'll just have to understand. Also, with lives at stake, we really have no choice but to go," Peter said, leaning back in his chair and heaving a big sigh.

Peter turned to Jutaro. "Dr. Komara, I'll have to get with some of my men. There are several schedule changes that must be made." He then turned to Cameron, "I will come with you, but I also will need a few hours."

"That's reasonable. As I said, we must leave at five o'clock. It is now two o'clock, we will meet at RD&E at five. That gives you three hours. Do you know where it is?" said Cameron, signaling the waiter for the bill.

Jutaro looked at Peter, who nodded assent, "Yes, we know where it is. We will meet you there at five, with all the necessary equipment. Can you give us a little more information so that we will know how to prepare?"

"I'm afraid not, except to bring thermowear and gloves. Where we are going is freezing cold. Other than that, just bring what you think you will need for a rescue mission. If anything else is needed, we can send back for it. I am sorry to be so secretive, but you will understand when we get there."

The three men stood, shook hands again, and went their separate ways. A lot had to be done in a very short period of time.

Cameron went back to the office. Kaitlyn was there, full of curiosity. Cameron grabbed her and gave her a big hug and kiss while swirling her around.

Kaitlyn laughed and said, "Oh no, you don't. I need some answers." She knew it had to be something to do with what Cameron had found on his trip. Funny, she couldn't remember where he had gone. Her mind kept sliding over that. "Darling, what's going on? Ian's in an uproar, getting together all the supplies he says you are going to need. He's going mad. He also told me that you will be gone for a month. And I am to start setting up business arrangements to take care of millions of barrels of oil. This is fantastic. When did you find time to discover oil?" Kaitlyn said, all in one breath.

"Sweetheart, I don't have time to explain anything now," said Cameron, taking her hands. "Which of the Elders is most interested in arming Heatherbound, and which one has the most influence to push something through council? By the way, you look gorgeous." Cameron said as he took Kaitlyn in his arms and kissed her again.

"You are not going to get around me that easily, but it was nice," Kaitlyn laughed. "Michael Beckett is the military man, but the man with power is Pandit Pahlavi. They are both dedicated men, and honest, but if you want something from them, they will drive a hard bargain. Why do you need to know?"

"You will know all as soon as possible. In fact, I need you to sit in on any discussion I have with them. Do you think you can arrange a meeting with them in the next hour? Your family has a lot of influence with the Elders, and so should mine. It is important."

"You've got to be kidding," said Kaitlyn with a touch of scorn in her voice. "Those men don't jump when asked. They're used to telling people to jump."

Cameron held her at arm's length, looking serious, "It's very important. Would you please try? Tell them I have a military proposition to offer them, which will involve a very large sum of money."

"That just might do it," said Kaitlyn with a shrug. "I'll try."

One hour later, Cameron and Kaitlyn walked into Pandit Pahlavi's office. It was a beautiful office with thick carpets and comfortable leather chairs in front of a huge desk. On the desk was a silver carafe of coffee, porcelain cups and cream and sugar. Michael Beckett sat in one of the chairs, drinking a cup of coffee. He stood up when Cameron and Kaitlyn came in, put his coffee cup on the desk, and extended his hand in greeting. "This is a pleasant surprise, but such haste. I hope it is good news."

"This had better be good. We are not in the habit of dropping everything on a citizen's whim," Pahlavi said after greeting and seating them. "Before we get started, would you care for some coffee?"

"Yes, thank you," said Kaitlyn. "If you would like, I'll pour while Cameron explains why we are here." The rich smell of coffee filled the room.

"I know your time is important, and we appreciate your being able to set aside a few minutes for us," said Cameron. "I'll get right to the point. I have discovered a new plant that my grandfather had worked on. This plant makes high-grade oil, and fuel for hovercrafts and spaceships, depending on how it is processed."

Both Beckett and Pahlavi leaned forward with interest. Cameron continued. "I want to buy all the islands in the Winter's Grove group. I have already inherited the four main islands from my grandfather. In exchange, I will give one-fourth the profit from the plants to the government, for military purposes, for the next ten years. At this time, I think the production will be between three and six million barrels a year. I will have a more exact figure for you as soon as I get organized. This plant is especially slow growing, but I think the yield should double in ten years. This money is only to be used in building an impregnable defense system for Heatherbound."

There was silence for ten long seconds. "When this gets out, we are going to need a defense system all the more," said Beckett, his face turning pale. "A million barrels is about what we import now. We had better continue that, with a gradual lessening for the next few years. God, what a discovery."

Pahlavi got up while Beckett was talking and walked over to his globe of Heatherbound. "That is a rather large piece of real estate you wish to buy for what I calculate to be about fifty million Federal credits. I don't like to appear difficult, but that may not be so easy to put across to the council, especially with the stipulation of only military use. They don't like to be told what do with money from land purchases. It would be easier if you could make that fifty percent."

"That is a very stiff price, but I have an emergency going on at the project, and I don't have time to haggle. I will agree to thirty-three and a third percent if I can also have all the land around Lake Placid for two miles deep. I already own about a fourth of that," said Cameron firmly. "The going price for good land is not that high, and this land is useless to anyone else. I hate to appear rude, but this is my final offer."

"You drive a hard bargain, young man, but I think we can put that through. We have a lot of details to work out before the next council meeting," said Pahlavi. "We four will have to work far into the night on something of this magnitude."

"My wife, Kaitlyn McPherson McCreight, is my financial expert. She will take care of all the arrangements and work with you. I am sure there are a lot of things to set up. She has my Power of Attorney and complete confidence. I'm sorry, I can't stay. I must leave for Winter's Grove at five o'clock this evening. I have an emergency at the site and must get back as soon as possible. I hope this meets with your approval."

"Of course, if that is the way it has to be. We want to talk a little more with you when you return," said Pahlavi. "Winter's Grove, I like that. I'll inform our cartography department tomorrow. When you come up with names for the islands individually, let me know."

'Yes, sir. Now if I could drag my wife away for a few minutes to say good-bye," said Cameron as he helped Kaitlyn to her feet.

"You may use my study; it's just off this office. I'll show you," Pahlavi got up and led them to his study.

When they were alone, Kaitlyn hugged Cameron. "You were magnificent. I was so proud of you. We will have a lot to talk about when you come home."

"I really am sorry that I am leaving you with so much work, but I have to go. I love you, Sweetheart. Give the kids a hug for me and I hope you can explain to them why I will be gone so long."

"I'm not sure I can explain to Rob and Megan when I don't even understand it myself. I'll do my best. I love you." Kaitlyn laid her head against his neck and sighed.

Both were aware that this room was probably bugged, so they said no more. They kissed again, a long lingering kiss, and Cameron held her very close. With a sigh of regret, they returned to the office.

Cameron said his good-byes and was off.

Pahlavi, Beckett, and Kaitlyn were soon immersed in high finance. It was a good thing that Megan could take a bottle because Kaitlyn wasn't going to be home tonight.

Arriving back at RD&E at 4:30, Cameron saw the two tankers with crews. Ian was busy getting them loaded with thermowear and rations. The company hovercraft was already prepared. Seeing Cameron, Ian told his assistant to carry on as he went to greet him.

"As you can see, Cameron, mission accomplished. Unfortunately, they were not cheap, but I had our mechanics check them over, and they are in excellent condition, as advertised. I also arranged for the crew's thermowear and food." Ian said, looking rather proud of himself.

"I wasn't worried a bit. Knew you could do it," Cameron said, with a grin as he punched Ian lightly on the arm. "As soon as my people arrive, we will be taking off. The tankers will follow us."

"I had to fend off an awful lot of questions about the hurry, and I'm a little curious myself," said Ian. "Do you have time to tell me a bit more about what is going on?"

Just then, another hovercraft arrived. It was Jutaro and Peter with an assistant. They all got out and Jutaro came over to talk to Cameron while the assistant and Peter started to unload the craft.

Cameron said, "Sorry, Ian, I don't have time to go into any detail now. You'll just have to trust me. Be sure to get together with Kaitlyn about the distribution of the oil and fuel while I'm gone. It might not be easy because she will be busy with the government. And Ian, make sure she gets some rest. It's going to be a busy month, and I won't be here to help."

Cameron turned to Jutaro and thanked him for being so prompt. Ian's people helped finish unloading Jutaro's hovercraft and the assistant got in and flew away. Cameron introduced everyone. He allowed no time for discussion. The extra gear and equipment were loaded on the company hovercraft, and it was time to go. Ian said good-bye and then instructed the tanker crews to follow Cameron.

The flight was uneventful, and everyone slept part of the way. Peter and Jutaro wanted to get more details, but Cameron put them off, saying it was best for them to see firsthand what the problem was. He suggested that everyone have breakfast in the flight, as they would not have time after landing. He radioed the tanker crew to eat as well.

Chapter Twenty-three

Revival

The flight to Winter's Grove proved to be rather boring for most of the people taking the trip. During the eleven hours, they slept, played cards, told jokes, and read. The time passed.

The first inkling that they had arrived was the sight of several small islands and in the distance, some large ones. Everyone except Cameron, was dismayed at the dismal aspect of the island chain. When they got closer, they could see that the small islands were practically barren, just a shrub here and there. The four large islands were wind-swept mountain crags, virtually covered with shrubs.

The sun had just come up, and the islands had a terrible splendor, but they looked cold and miserable. Winter's Grove was not the least bit appealing to a human being except for its abstract beauty. There was glistening ice and snow everywhere, except where the wind had swept some areas bare. Almost everyone was looking out the windows and couldn't believe that this was their destination.

In the morning light, they observed what looked like several small hovercraft maneuvering around the shrubs, like bees gathering honey. Coming upon the largest island, Cameron flew around to the other side, where a huge cleft could be seen on the side of the mountain. This was the entrance to the cave. Cameron flew in, followed by the two tankers. The opening was quite large, big enough for a medium sized spaceship. The cave itself was enormous; they couldn't even see the far end.

When they got into the cave, the lights came on and the first thing they saw was the pod. Even with the three ships added, it didn't look as if they would be crowded. The men were awestruck by their surroundings; it seemed strange to find so much technology in such a desolate place. They quickly donned their thermowear, glad that it had been supplied. It was cold, cold. They all hurried out of their crafts, curious to see what brought them to such an awesome place.

Cameron heard the whirring sound, turned, and saw No.1 coming up. He told the robot to take the tanker crews and their tankers in hand, and to help them start emptying the storage tanks, then to return to him at the pod. Helping Jutaro and Peter gather their equipment, he took them to the aliens and their work.

Turning to Jutaro and Peter, Cameron motioned them to follow him. "What you are going to see will surprise you, may even shock you. There are about fifty aliens in this pod. The look a little likes bears."

The cryonics men stopped dead in their tracts. "Aliens? What do you take us for? Humans have yet to find any trace of other sentient beings. Are you trying to pull a fast one?" said Jutaro indignantly.

Cameron had braced himself for something like this. "Before you condemn me, come into the pod, look at what is inside the cryonic chambers. If you have questions after examining the chambers and aliens, I'll do my best to answer them."

A look of suspicion and a touch of disgust still on their faces, Jutaro and Peter followed Cameron reluctantly, their curiosity overcoming their suspicions. "This had better be good," said Peter. "I don't like to be made a fool of, even for 10,000 credits."

The three men entered the pod; everything looked the same as when Cameron had left it. The chambers were ticking away, there was a light frost covering them, and the whole complex looked in order. It was extremely cold inside the pod, even colder than the cave itself.

Peter looked quickly around. This place was old and outdated. He wondered how long these people had been frozen. He found the main control panel, laid down his equipment beside it, and immediately got to work checking it out. He still didn't believe in aliens, but there was obviously something alive in these chambers, and he deeply respected life. He broke out into a cold sweat even as cold as it was in the pod. He was trembling with anxiety. For some reason, he felt that he must hurry.

Jutaro also looked round as soon as he entered the pod. This place was ancient, he thought, and the equipment antiquated. What a chance for research. He had never seen anyone that had been in storage for as long as these beings must have been. He turned to Cameron and asked, "How long did you say these beings have been in cryonic suspension?"

After showing the cryonic experts into the pod, Cameron felt relieved. He answered Jutaro with a smile, "Close on to a hundred years, according to my grandfather's journal."

"This is going to be very interesting." Going to the nearest cryonic chamber, Jutaro began feeling a sense of urgency, just as Peter had. He could barely see the outline of something inside, and it was far too large for a human being. He began to think that perhaps Cameron was telling the truth, or perhaps he was just trying an experiment with Earth bears. The life support systems were reporting a far different metabolism than he was accustomed to. The feeling of urgency was growing, he didn't know how, but he knew that he did not have much time to save these people. (Would they be called people?) He quickly started checking the chambers and the lines leading to them.

Both men were working feverishly. Peter took the control panel entirely apart and checked all the main electrical connections. He then took a magnifying glass and started closely inspecting all the microchips. Suddenly he exclaimed, "I've found it. There is a small amount of corrosion on this microchip. It won't allow the defrost command to execute."

Examining it closely, Peter said, "This is an antique, and there is no way it can be repaired. I have some that are similar in my tool kit. I hope I can modify one to fit. It'll take me a few minutes to warm up, though; my fingers are so cold they are clumsy. With this delicate kind of work, I'll have to go back to the hovercraft and defrost or I'll never be able to do it."

A half-hour later, everything was put back together again. Soon the satisfying sound of the gases going through the pipes was heard. The three men heaved sighs of relief.

Pushing hair from his forehead, Cameron sighed, and turning to Jutaro, he asked, "how long will it take for them to wake up?"

"It's hard to tell, with humans, about twenty-four hours, but with these people, I really don't know. Their metabolism is so different. I know one thing, they will be very hungry and will need lots of strong broth for the first day. Cameron, I hate to sound suspicious, but are these really aliens, or are they

Earth bears? I only ask because they are truly going to be hungry and I don't want to be eaten alive."

"Have you ever heard of purple bears on Earth that are telepathic?" Cameron said with a laugh.

"Okay, okay," waving his hand and a slight nod of his head, "I'll reserve judgment until I actually see them. Do you know what they eat?" Jutaro asked with a puzzled expression on his face.

"Yes, as a matter of fact, I do. They are vegetarians. In their space ship they have a hydroponic garden of their own food. The robots must have kept it going for them all these years," replied Cameron. "No.1 and I will check it out."

"Perhaps I had better come also. The broth has to be very strong and full of nutrients. I'll help you make up a pot. They are also going to need lots of fatty solids in a few days. I wonder which of their vegetables are high in fat content." Jutaro said as he followed Cameron out of the pod. "Where is their space ship? I didn't see one when we came in here?"

"It's right over there, about a hundred yards away. You can't see it because they have a mind block on every human but me, for their protection. I'm sure you'll see it in a few minutes. Another thing you will find difficult to believe, and should probably know, is that you won't remember much about this trip. You certainly won't remember a thing about the aliens when you get back."

"This whole trip is difficult to believe and that last is preposterous. How could anyone block my mind to something so fantastic that I can hardly believe it myself?"

Cameron just looked at Jutaro with an elegant shrug and a raised eyebrow that said everything.

"What if I keep a journal?"

Cameron shook his head. "It wouldn't do you any good, you would not remember to read it, and if anyone else read it, they would forget as soon as they put it down. These are powerful people. They only want to be left alone. The Dasurainians have studied our kind and know that they could possibly be in danger if found here. They are not warlike and don't want this planet for their kind. It's too warm. If they did, they would have the right. They were here first."

Back at the pod, Peter made himself as comfortable as possible. He had brought in a pile of blankets and a mattress. He wanted to be on hand in case there was any more trouble. There was not much he could do now except wait. He was getting hungry, though and decided a few minutes away wouldn't hurt. He knew he could grab a Hot-N-Ready pack and bring it back to eat.

He left the pod and went to the hovercraft. Oh, it felt good to be in a warm place again. He took a few minutes to just savor it, and then feeling guilty, he hurriedly took the first thing that came to hand, which was a pot roast dinner. He also grabbed a container of coffee. Looking around for something else, he found a candy bar. With `1these, he hurried back to the pod.

There didn't appear to be any changes. The gases were still circulating, and it would be many hours before even the frost would be off the chambers. Peter pulled the heating strips on both food containers and, three minutes later, settled down to a piping hot meal. It smelled wonderful, and the hot food cheered him up.

Jutaro and Cameron were still looking around the Dasurainians spaceship with No.1. Everything was in order, not a speck of dust anywhere. It looked a lot like the inside of a human ship, except that it was oversized. Both of them wished they could explore more, but that would be for later. Right now, they needed to find the hydroponic gardens. No.1 led them there while carrying Jutaro's small lab.

The gardens were not too different from human gardens either, in the layout, that is. The vegetables were strange to them, and so were the fruit trees. Jutaro picked a little of everything for analysis. He needed to find the food that would make the most nutritious broth. Something kept steering him to the legume looking plants. Being a careful man, he checked everything anyway. He found that the legumes were excellent, almost a perfect food, even for humans. He tasted one. It was delicious, a little exotic, but delicious.

Carrying a sample of the legumes and other vegetables, No.1 then led them to the kitchen. Jutaro proceeded to make a batch of broth. He tasted it and thought it a little flat. Poking around in the cabinets he found something like salt and herbs and added some to the broth. Adjusting this and that, he finally pronounced it delicious. The smell was enticing, something like curried bean soup. And both the men scooped up a bowl and ate their fill.

The preparing of the vegetable soup took only about fifteen minutes. Jutaro wanted it to be at its peak of freshness for the Dasurainians, so they didn't cook the rest of their harvest. There would be plenty of time to get the broth ready and No.1 could do it.

Only six hours had passed since they had arrived, and so much had been accomplished. The sense of urgency had left them all; only sadness remained, like mourning for a lost child. Nobody could understand this, only feel it, and no one wanted to discuss this emotion. It touched Cameron most deeply, he kept feeling his throat close up, and his eyes felt hot, ready for tears. He knew he had to keep occupied, or he would be crying great sobs of grief, and he knew not why but thought that maybe they had lost one of the Dasurainians. God, he hoped it was not Dreena. From reading his grandfather's journal, he felt that he knew her and wanted to get to know her better.

After leaving the spaceship, Jutaro joined Peter in his vigil. While Jutaro had been making preparations for the food, Peter had checked every chamber's connections and made sure that each would defrost on schedule. It would not do to have them all wake at the same time. Each would need a lot of individual attention. There was nothing else to do now except to be there in case of an emergency. Jutaro decided that they would set up cots just outside the pod and take turns sleeping. Once the aliens were awake, they knew they would have no time for anything but the Dasurainians.

Cameron looked in on the tanker crews to see how the work was progressing. Each tanker could hold one hundred thousand barrels of oil. Both were being filled at the same time. The men were sitting around eating and playing cards. They seemed little interested in their surroundings. They really didn't have anything to do until the tankers were filled, and that would take about two more hours. The trip would be eleven hours each way, approximately eight hours to fill-up or empty between trips. It was a boring job, perfect for robots. Cameron planned to have this whole rigmarole automated as soon as possible.

It was still daylight, and Jutaro assured Cameron that he could expect nothing to happen for at least twenty more hours. He decided to check out the shrubs. He had been dying to get to them ever since he had read about them, but this was his first opportunity. Taking No.1 with him, he started out of the cave. He saw, in the distance, several barrel-sized robots flying in. "No.1, what are those robots doing? I didn't notice them before."

"They are bringing the sap in to be refined. Now that there is room in the tanks, we can start production again."

"How long have you been unable to process?"

"It has only been six weeks this time."

Cameron shuddered at the thought of all the wasted fuel over the last few years, "I would like a succinct report on the work you and your fellow robots have been doing here. Also, how many robots there are and what they do."

"The Dasurainians programmed us to maintain the plant, refine the sap, refuel their ship, and use the plant residue to build holding tanks for excess fuel. They programmed No.1 with discretionary decisions concerning production and all robots. No.1 was also programmed to care for the pod's occupants, the spaceship, and the hydroponic gardens."

"Plans were given to us to build the harvesting robots. As the plants multiplied, we spread them over the main island. Old plants were removed and discarded on nearby islands. Some plants reproduce, and most of the other islands are now ready for harvesting."

"We did not have enough robots to do the harvesting, and when the plant is not harvested, the accumulation of metabolic wastes causes senescence. They died in about five years, but their offspring breed true to form." No. 1 continued.

"After the ship was refueled and the one holding tank was filled, we built two more holding tanks. We started building a fourth holding tank. There are five hundred and fourteen harvesting robots, twelve refining robots, and three overseers, including No.1. Was that brief enough for you, sir?" Asked No.1.

"You did very well, No.1, thank you," Cameron said, thinking, thank God that I bought all those other islands. I didn't even know that most of them are already planted. This is bigger than I thought already. Ian will have to drop everything and start making harvesting robots and tankers. I guess K & C Enterprises will be RD&E's biggest customer. K& C Enterprises, I wonder if Kaitlyn will like that name or perhaps come up with a better one.

"No.1, I inferred from what you said before that there was more than one work stoppage. How many times were there stoppages in production, for what reason, and what was the length of time?"

"There were three hundred and twenty-three stoppages. The first was when lighting hit robot No.2. I had to take No.3 off the harvesting line to help me repair No.2. This took four weeks. Twenty-one times the snow was too deep, and we could not get to the plants. These averaged about two weeks and three days. Three hundred and one times, there were short stoppages lasting, on average, fourteen hours. The three hundred and twenty-third stoppage was the latest, of which you have been informed. You asked me to be succinct, so I did not go into detail on each stoppage. If you request, I can give you a written report on each of these events."

"A written report would be valuable for future planning. Please print out one after we get back from inspecting these nearest plants," Cameron replied. They had been walking up the tunnel all during this conversation and had finally reached the entrance. "What do you do with the residue after processing the sap?"

"We made commodities from it. First, the spigots and buckets for each plant, then the holding tanks for the fuel. After the lightning episode, we started making spare parts for the robots, as the resin is non-conductive. We now have 1,500,492 spigot and bucket sets in reserve, spare parts for 564 harvesting robots, 10 refining robots, and 3 overseer robots. We do not have bionic computer chips to finish making the robots needed to harvest all the plants." No.1 answered with an accusing sound to his voice (if that were possible).

"You have been sadly neglected, No.1, but have done a superb job. From now on, you will have the support you need. I want you to report to me whenever you have problems." This was the first time he had encountered a sensitive robot. He wondered how the Dasurainians had altered it.

"The fuel in the spaceship must be pretty old by now. Did you have a way to preserve it?"

"The Dasurainians have a plant on their ship that will preserve anything organic. They programmed me to prepare it and told me how much, per volume, to put in the fuel. Also, how to test the fuel to make sure that it is still viable. Would you like a description of the plant?"

Cameron noticed that No.1 was starting to use the personal pronoun me and I. Perhaps he learns new things by observation. He answered No.1's question. "I would, very much, and later I want to see the plant."

"It is a small bush with purple berries on it. The Dasurainians call it Prussiam. It is an ever-bearing plant. We have a small crop of them growing on the third island. One of the harvesting robots was modified to gather these berries when needed to replenish our supply."

No.1 was a constant amazement to Cameron. He had never encountered a robot like this one. One able to discern problems makes decisions, and follows through. He just hoped he could think of all the right questions. Earth could possibly have some as good, but they were never sold to Heatherbound. He wondered if the Dasurainians would give him the designs. But what did he have to give in exchange? Another wave of sadness hit him just then. He should have been feeling elated. Everything was going better than anticipated. I have to just keep busy, he thought.

They continued walking during this conversation and were now outside. It was bitterly cold. As soon as they left the cave, the force of the wind struck Cameron, and his face was lashed by ice. He was very glad for his thermowear, but he would have to devise something to protect his face if he planned to spend much time out here.

A few minutes later, they came to the first shrubs. As described, the plant was squat and stubby, looking a lot like an oversized bonsai pine tree. Long gray-green needles were on the short branches and the trunks looked like barrels with spigots sticking out of them. On closer examination, Cameron could see that the spigots had almost become part of the plant. Because they were made from the plant's own resin the spigots were accepted and did not appear to harm the plant. As he watched, a drop formed and fell into the bucket. It was iridescent and quite beautiful. For some reason this simple process brought home to Cameron how vast was the knowledge of plants the aliens must have. He wondered how many planets had pine-like trees, such as the Terebinth tree of Earth, from which the best turpentine was made.

He slowly moved from shrub to shrub and was so engrossed with them that he forgot how cold it was and didn't notice that it was getting even colder and darker. He first realized how cold he was when he felt numbness in his fingers. He decided to turn up the heat in his thermowear. A short while later, a gust of wind was so strong that it almost blew him over. He suddenly knew that he could freeze out here, even with the thermowear.

It was starting to snow again, and instead of coming straight down, it was blowing sideways. The wind had come up in sharp bursts, and he couldn't see more than two feet. He also couldn't see No.1. This could be serious, and he hadn't a clue how to get back to the cave or even in which direction to go.

"No.1, where are you? Come to me," yelled Cameron, again and again. After what seemed like hours but had only been about five minutes, he still had no answer. Where was that damned robot? He was getting worried now. Should he try to find his way back or stay and hope that No.1 would know enough to come back? How could he find his way back? He had not paid any attention to where he had wandered or even how long he had been gone. All he knew was that he couldn't stay much longer. He could freeze to death. The thermowear wasn't meant for weather this cold. And with the suit turned all the way up, the battery would not last any length of time.

Was this what the sadness was all about, a premonition of his own death? No, that's too morbid; he wasn't going to die, not without a fight, at least. He made a decision. If the robot didn't come back in five more minutes, he would try to find his own way back. At least moving might keep him warmer.

The five minutes seemed to last forever. He was beginning to think he had made a mistake to wait even that long. His suit seemed to be cooling. Had the batteries died already? He felt something nudge him from behind.

"Sir, I think we should be getting back now," said No.1. He had been standing behind Cameron for a full minute, waiting for Cameron to acknowledge him before he spoke.

Cameron whirled around and said, with a mixture of anger and relief, "Where did you go? I could have frozen out here. Delete the last. You're right; it is time to get back to the cave. Lead the way."

"I went to find No.3, he hadn't checked in on time. His radio is malfunctioning again. We really need more spare parts for the communication systems," replied No.1, in a voice both apologetic and put-upon. "The weather can be quite fierce. Even robots can't work in this. They have standing orders to find shelter when the winds are this brutal. You had better attach yourself to me. Here is a line," said No.1, as he opened a compartment in his torso, withdrew a line, and handed it to Cameron. "We will need to return carefully. Gusts of wind could knock us down."

Cameron took the line and attached it to his belt. He felt like strangling No.1, but knew this was unfair. He was only doing his job. Cameron realized how close to panic he had been. Living in almost perpetual summer, he had never encountered a whiteout, and the feeling of helplessness, of no control, had been almost overwhelming.

"How long does this usually last?" yelled Cameron to be heard as he struggled to keep up. His legs felt numb and clumsy from the cold.

"Usually not more than an hour, but we have had these whiteouts last much longer. It doesn't stop production, though, because we always have on hand enough resin to process," said No.1, as he picked up speed. "We are almost there. Just one minute more."

Suddenly the wind stopped, and Cameron could see more than a foot in front of himself. They were inside the entrance to the cave. Cameron felt like hugging the robot or jumping for joy. He was dizzy with relief and trembling as he leaned against the wall for a moment to catch his breath, but all he said was, "Thank you, No.1, for getting us back safely." The robot would not understand his emotion, or would he? Who knows? At this point, who cares? He was alive and safe.

As they got a little way into the tunnel, Cameron noticed how much quieter it was. He was so concerned with getting back that he had not noticed the roaring of the wind. He now felt almost deafened by the silence. How could anyone stand to live in a place like this? He had read of many places on Earth that were similar, but thank God he didn't have to live in them or here.

He was starting to feel more comfortable but still did not turn down the thermostat on his suit. The batteries needed to be recharged and all he wanted now was a hot bath and a warm fire, but neither was to be had. He knew he had had a very close call and mentally kicked himself for being so stupid.

He began thinking of all the things that needed doing and said, "I want to send the oil tankers back shortly. When it is safe to let them go, please inform me. They will need the exact coordinates and a beacon-homer set up for their return. Please arrange that. Also, check on the status of the pod. You'll find me in my hovercraft or at the pod."

"Yes, Sir. No.2 will stand at the entrance to check the weather. When he says the robots can start gathering again, that will be the time when it will be safe for the tankers to take off. I will so inform you." No.1 whirred away to follow his orders.

After warming up in his hovercraft, Cameron trotted over to the tanker. He still felt cold, and the exercise should help warm him up. What a fantastic cave, he thought, looking at it with fresh eyes. The tankers looked small beside the holding tanks, and the holding tanks were only half way to the ceiling. With the holding tanks, refinery, tankers, pod, hovercraft, and spaceship, there was still enough room left to double the production line.

The tanker crews were in the process of cleaning up after their tankers were filled. They were good crews, and the lines were all neatly stowed away, their area was cleaned of trash, and both crews were ready to depart. He hoped Ian would have the holding tanks on the other end ready for them when these tankers arrived, but he really wasn't worried. Ian would have something ready. He made a mental note to radio Ian to buy two more tankers and to install robot controls in them. This job was so simple that they would not have to be sophisticated.

"There you are, Mr. McCreight; I've been looking for you. We're about finished and will need the coordinates for the return trip," said Joe, the foreman. He was a big black man, built like a wrestler. He had shaved his head but had a full beard. "I've been checking the storage of fuel here, Sir. It looks like we're going to be making over twenty trips. The crew and I were kinda curious why you waited so long to start delivering it."

"It's a long story, Joe, but the gist of it is that I didn't know it was here until a few days ago. My grandfather discovered the plant and set up the process. Somehow the fact that it was here and ready to be harvested slipped between the cracks. I've informed the Elders, and we will soon be selling fuel at a reasonable price for hovercrafts. You might want to tell your crew to buy one now as the prices may go up for a little while."

"We thought it a bit fishy, but if the Elders know, it must be all right," replied Joe. I've put a little money aside, is there any chance of investing in this?"

"I don't see why not, Joe. Talk to my wife, Kaitlyn, when you get back. She is handling all the money matters," said Cameron. "Don't invest in tankers, though; I plan to use robotic tankers for most of the hauling. I will be using these two for quite some time, so you needn't worry about a job for at least a year. If I were in your shoes, I'd try to buy a hovercraft dealership, or a fueling station. Maybe you and your mates could scrape up enough for that. Talk to Kaitlyn; tell her I said you were okay. Maybe she can work out something with an advance on your wages."

"As to the coordinates, No.1 is setting that up and also a homing beacon. You should be able to tune your scanner to that and get back with no problem," said Cameron. "You can understand the need for security and for your own safety. What you don't know, you can't tell, and no one can beat it out of you."

"Sounds like you are expecting trouble, Mr. McCreight."

"Not at first Joe, but what do you think?"

"I think it's going to be an interesting year," replied Joe with a grin. "I like your idea of a dealership. I'll talk to the guys. They may prefer fueling stations. Thanks a lot for your vote of confidence. I will certainly talk to Mrs. McCreight as soon as we get back."

"Sounds like a plan. No.1 will tell you when your tankers can take off. We've got some bad weather out there right now, so it may be a while before you can leave. When you get near RD&E, radio ahead. They'll tell you where you can unload."

No.1 came up and reported. "The weather should be calm enough to take off in about ten minutes. If you take the tankers to the beginning of the entrance tunnel, No.2 will launch you. While you were talking, I installed the beacon system in the lead tanker and instructed the automatic control system on how to lock on. I instructed the second tanker's system to lock on to the first.

"There is no change in the pod." No.1 continued. "All systems are running smoothly. You are asked to report to the pod area in six hours."

"Thank you, No.1. You may go back to your other duties."

Cameron turned back to the tanker boss. "Well, Joe, you'll be off soon. When you get back, tell Ian Scott that everything is bigger than I had anticipated. Tell him we need all the bionics he has for robots, plus many more. Also, tell him that I will send him a letter, next shipment, describing all that is needed here." Cameron shook Joe's hand.

"Frankly, Mr. McCreight, I can't wait to take off," said Joe, looking around. "The atmosphere is kinda depressing in this place, don't you think?

"Yeah, we'll see what we can do about that. Have a good trip."

Chapter Twenty-four

The Dasurainians

"No. 1, I would like to see your inventory of spare parts and extra robots," said Cameron. "Take me to your stockpile or warehouse area. I also need your input on a good location to set up living quarters for six humans. Have you been programmed to know our needs?" Cameron asked as he and No.1 started walking toward the pod.

"The warehouse area is next to the pod," said No.1, slightly shifting direction and leading the way. "I have taken readings of your metabolism since you have been here. It is different from the Dasurainians. You need more light and heat. I would need more information to determine a good location for quarters. How much room does each individual human need to be comfortable, and how high the ceiling? Will the quarters be multipurpose or just for sleeping?"

"Sorry No.1, I will draw you a plan of the quarters needed. I want some place near the stockpile of robots. I plan to have the men put the bionics in to activate them."

"It would not be necessary to have humans here to work on the robots. No.1, No.2, and No.3 are all trained to build replacements. The Dasurainians programmed us to repair or replace ourselves if necessary. They gave us the bionics and specifications to build the other robots, as well."

"You constantly surprise me No.1. I should have realized that was the case. How else could you have made so many robots and maintained this facility all these years alone?" Cameron said, hitting his head with his hand. "We humans have yet to build a robot that was intelligent enough to repair or reproduce itself. Would you be harmed, in any way, if my robotic expert looked at your design and programming?"

"I cannot say if your expert could harm me, but it would be better if I made a duplicate of myself and let your expert work on it. That way, if there were a problem, I would be able to repair it."

"Your logic is faultless, No.1," said Cameron seriously. "I still wish to build quarters for humans, but for only two. The fewer humans that have to come here, the better. But I'll need some place where I can stay when I come to check on your needs and for any expert who may have to come with me."

By this time they had reached the warehouse area. It was huge, spare parts were neatly stacked in many rows, a good-sized machine shop was on one side, and a robot was busily working on a harvesting robot. Cameron was impressed again by the sophistication of the Dasurainian robots. He still found it hard to believe that they had been taking care of this entire project, without human help, for almost a hundred years. There must have been many times when decisions had to be made with no living creature there to help.

"Wow, what an extraordinary machine shop! So much room. This cave is enormous, is it natural, or did the Dasurainians excavate it?" Cameron said with enthusiasm.

"The Dasurainians found a small cave and enlarged it to this extent because they thought they would have to live here, awake, until they repaired their ship and had enough fuel to return to their home planet," replied No. 1.

"I would like to show you an area near the back of this section that has a hot spring. That would be a good place for your sleeping quarters so that you may enjoy the use of the spring."

"Lead me to it No.1. It sounds like the very place."

They walked a short way further and came to another opening. This one looked as if it were a natural opening into a short tunnel. It was dark and started to get warmer a little way in. The Dasurainians had no use for it so they did not set it up with their lighting system. Cameron had a flashlight on his thermowear, and he put it to good use. The tunnel emptied into a sizeable cave. On one side was a small pool. Large bubbles were coming up in its center, with steam rising from them. On the far side, there appeared to be cracks in the rocks where the water could run off. The near shore was a gradual slope ending in large flat rocks and sand. The water lapped the rocks occasionally with a soft sound.

Cameron tested the temperature, and it was warm to the touch near the shore. It seemed an ideal place to bathe. "This will be perfect for the human quarters. I'll make a diagram of our needs for you, No.1. Wish I had a towel. I'd jump right in."

Peter Dugan was checking the chambers again. He had been worried about one for the last fourteen hours. The dials had been fluctuating rapidly, and now he was afraid that the alien in this chamber was dead. There was nothing he could do about it. He couldn't even open the top yet, as it might interfere with the others. The oppressive sense of death was almost overwhelming. He felt so helpless, he wanted to break the chamber open and do anything to revive the child. (Why did he think child?) He knew it was impossible. The lives of forty-nine others were at stake. All he could do was walk back and forth, checking the others and making sure that all connections were working right. He wanted no more deaths.

The numbers registering on the dials were so different from humans that it was maddening for Peter. He was frustrated, but he knew at this point that there was nothing more he could do as long as the system was working on schedule. He wasn't sure if the Dasurainian schedule would be the same as humans, either. All he could hope was that this had been worked out beforehand and that the safeguards were set up correctly.

"Everything looks in order. I only wish we knew more about the physiology of these people," said Jutaro as he walked up to Peter to relieve him. "If they were human, they would be coming around in about eight more hours. But from the appearance of the chambers, it looks to me that they may be ready in less than two. I just don't know, but I think we better have No.1 start preparing food. It must be served lukewarm, and I want it ready and here, when they do start coming out of it."

"Right, I'll find him and get the food started. I need to get away from here for a while anyway," said Peter in a dejected manner.

Jutaro made himself as comfortable as possible in the freezing cold pod and worked on some papers he had brought with him. After about an hour and a half of concentrated work, he got up to check the chambers. It had been so quiet in the pod, just muffled ticking of the controls. He wished that Peter would get back with the food. Suddenly there was a loud click, and one of the chamber lids slowly opened. He started to rush over, then checked himself, fearful of the reaction the alien might have on seeing a human upon awakening. Something told him it was all right to come forward, and he felt reassured.

Jutaro looked into the chamber and saw the alien lying there with its eyes closed. He looked just as Cameron had described but far more intelligent than expected, and the eye sockets were so large. He detached the tubes and gently removed the helmet. There was a light frost on the alien's fur, and looking at the thermostat, he saw that it was set to a very low temperature. Cameron had told him that they came from an extremely cold planet and were cryophilic. That would explain why it took them much less time to recover from the cryonic process.

Jutaro heard a whirring sound and turned to find No.1 with a large container of thick broth. No.1 assured him that it was only lukewarm, even though it was steaming in this cold air.

"Peter is bringing another container full and we have more cooking," said No.1, as he put down the container near the open chamber.

"You just made it in time. The first one is awake and should be ready to eat in about five minutes. I expect the rest to be waking up in fifteen-minute intervals. At least, that is the usual rate. They will be unable to feed themselves the first time, as they will be too weak. Are you programmed to do such tasks? We will need extra help until all are awake and able to feed themselves."

"I have been programmed to do most tasks. Helping to feed the Dasurainians seems a simple one. I brought cups. They should find that the easiest way to consume the broth."

"Good idea, I should have suggested it myself," said Jutaro as he turned back to the alien. He was a bit startled to see that he had his eyes open. Jutaro's first thought was that these aliens were beautiful. The eyes were large and friendly looking, but sad as well. "You are awake. How do you feel?"

Awake I am. It was a long sleep, but I feel healthy and very hungry, as you know. I am called Dramon. He tried to sit up but Jutaro motioned to him to remain as he was. Dramon continued, *The deep sadness you have all been feeling is from the death of Dreena. She has not been doing well for the last seven years. I fear that we did not lower the temperature enough for our kind.

135

We went into deep hibernation instead of the cryogenic state that your kind would have gone into.*

Dreena had always been a very active child and did not have enough fat on her to sustain her body for these extra years. It was a very hard lesson to learn, but she will not have died in vain, as this process will be very helpful for my people in the future.

This reply was broadcast to all in the cave, not just to Jutaro. Cameron heard and hurried to the pod. He felt terrible for them, and even for himself because he felt he had almost known Dreena. He had been looking forward to meeting her and talking about his grandfather.

No.1 came forward and lifted Dramon's head so that he could drink. He drank eagerly, feeling the healing strength of the broth. Jutaro said, "Not too fast. His stomach will not keep it down. They must have a few minutes to wait between each cup. He should not try to get out of his chamber until he has consumed a gallon or more and has had a nap."

Dramon looked at him inquisitively.

"That's right, even though you have been sleeping for almost a hundred years, it isn't the same as normal sleep. Your body needs to build up again. You will find that you will be sleeping a lot in the next three days. It is the normal way, at least for humans. You are so different we will have to monitor you closely to be sure of your progress."

Another chamber clicked open, and Jutaro went quickly to it. No.1 gave Dramon another cup of broth. Peter had just come in with another pot of broth. He was curious about the Dasurainians and went over to see for himself. He noticed a cinnamon smell that made him think of hot apple pie and autumn days. He thought any being that smelled like this must be benevolent. After checking all the tubes and wiring again and seeing that there was nothing more he could do here, he left immediately to prepare more broth.

Cameron entered at this time, out of breath; he had run the entire way. "What can I do to help?"

There were three chambers open now. Jutaro said to him, without turning around, "Grab a cup and start feeding Darla. She will need a cup of broth every five minutes until she needs to sleep. Try to make sure she drinks about a gallon."

"Hello, Darla, I am terribly sorry about your loss. If only we could've heard your call sooner or understood it, we might have saved her. It was so close. I feel responsible. If I hadn't taken that extra day at the compound, perhaps she would have lived," Cameron said, as he lifted Darla's head and fed her the broth.

There is no need to feel guilty. Dreena would have been a vegetable if she had lived. Her brain death is what alerted Drakel enough to start sending a call for help. It wasn't until he could get enough of us awake sufficiently to help him call that it was finally received. It is you we have to thank, not condemn. Drakel feels that the rest of us would have been dead within the next month. Your prompt action saved forty-nine lives. It will not be forgotten. Darla broadcasted this to all as well. She could feel the pain and guilt that all the humans were experiencing and wanted to alleviate it.

All three humans were too busy to fully realize that they were hearing this communication in their minds. For some reason, it seemed natural.

No.1 had called in six more robots to help with the awakening of the Dasurainians. The ten of them were kept busy helping the aliens eat and preparing more broth. All the chambers were now open, and the first few newly awakened Dasurainians were ready to stand for a few minutes. A frantic eight hours ensued, as the aliens needed help not only to eat but also to sit up and get out of their chambers. All took short naps after eating, then wanted to get out and stretch.

The warmth of so many bodies in the confined space was making the Dasurainians very uncomfortable. Many wanted to leave the pod to get some cool air. Jutaro wasn't too sure this was a good idea yet since they were all so weak. He sought the opinion of Dramon, who was the ship's doctor.

Dramon felt that it would be good for them to go outside the pod. Their bedding from the space ship could be arranged for them to rest on near the pod. Also, it was time to start feeding his people a solid diet.

He assured Jutaro that his first thoughts of the Dasurainian needs were correct and complimented him on the mixture of herbs and spices he had used to make the broth taste delicious. Dramon instructed the robots on how to prepare the legumes into a more solid state. He also told the robots to bring over fresh fruit and all the avocado-like fruit there was. He called them Alosas, and they were the fattest food they had and their favorite. Jutaro and Cameron had tested all the different fruits and vegetables, plus nuts and grains. All were edible for humans and, when prepared properly, quite tasty.

Jutaro had been right, it took three days before any of the Dasurainians were strong enough to get around by themselves. They ate large amounts of food, talked about going home and slept. It was a good thing that No.1 had freeze-dried the past harvests. The Dasurainians couldn't seem to get filled. They had all awakened extremely thin for their kind, and it was necessary to build up their reserves. They would also require a good supply of food to take with them on their trip back home.

As soon as the Dasurainians engineers were strong enough, they began to check out their spaceship. They were anxious to get home to their friends and families. It was a slow process, though, as about half of the aliens were very weak, even after two weeks. Their doctor declared all of them free from any lasting harm, but they were suffering from malnutrition. They just needed rest and a nutritious diet of high protein and fatty foods.

The robots had gone back to their usual tasks, as the healthy Dasurainians were now able to help Jutaro and Peter. Their goal was to leave Heatherbound in two more weeks.

While the Dasurainians were recovering, the fuel tankers were coming and going. Between the two, Cameron was constantly on the run. He didn't want the fuel tank crews to know about the Dasurainians and had set them up in the cave off the warehouse. The hot spring was a big attraction and the crew spent a lot of their free time swimming. The fact that this was the warmest part of the cave complex encouraged them to stay there. An added inducement was they didn't need their thermowear.

Cameron imported supplies to build the sleeping quarters in that area, and the crews set that up in their spare time. They brought in their own lounge chairs and turned the cave into a clubhouse. This suited everyone.

The only spare time Cameron had was just before going to bed. He allowed himself time to listen to his classical recordings. His main love was the

Russian composers and Italian Opera from the nineteenth and twentieth centuries.

He was torn between his two desires. He missed Kaitlyn and the children and wished to be home with them, and his other research. But there was so much to learn here, and so exciting. He found the Dasurainians fascinating. It bothered him that he could not share it with Kaitlyn and Ian.

Cameron asked if he could have some seeds of each of the plants in the hydroponic garden. "Humans have colonized some planets that are quite cold and can't grow their own food. Your plants would be a real boon to them. Their major expense is importing food."

Cameron thought if they agreed, this distribution of seeds would have to be done very quietly. If any of the Consortiums discovered my plans, Earth would surely declare war on Heatherbound on some pretext very soon.

You may have the seeds and information needed for raising the plants. With modifications, they can be used for both cold and warm planets. said Captain Drakel. *I was hoping that we could come up with something to trade for the modifications for precision-tooling Steelite that we have lifted from your mind. We could not have used it without a fair trade.*

Jutaro had been thinking about not remembering his experiences at Winter's Grove. "Drakel, Peter and I know how you feel about the rest of humanity knowing of your existence, but we want to remember. Couldn't you just but a block on us so that we would be unable to talk about it?"

We are aware of your desires, and we will honor your request. Remember that you won't be able to discuss us even with each other. I'm sorry.

Chapter Twenty-five

Negotiations

Kaitlyn's time was fully occupied during Cameron's absence. The first few weeks she was running back and forth between the farm, RD&E, and the Central Committee Headquarters. Later she was persuaded to rent a small, furnished apartment, only minutes away from the Federal buildings, and bring the children and Glenys into town to save her time and energy.

Kaitlyn, Michael Beckett, and Pandit Pahlavi had been negotiating the terms of the contract. Timothy, Pandit's secretary, had been to most of the meetings to take notes. The three decided that the sale of the island chain and the discovery of a cheap source of fuel were to be kept secret from the General Assembly because of national security. Pandit had the power to make the sale without the knowledge or consent of the full Assembly, and Michael wished to consult with his security force in-depth before making the discovery of the fuel common knowledge.

The fact that cheap fuel would be available could not be kept secret for long, but the source could. They were in a quandary because though they would have liked to have kept the entire project under wraps, they needed the sale of fuel to raise revenue for their defense system.

The defense system they had now was a joke. It was sparse and consisted of the old spaceship that had brought the colonists to Heatherbound and early warning satellites. These satellites were operative and armed but of limited use because they were so few and widely dispersed. They had to have more satellites to have complete surveillance of the space surrounding the planet. The old spaceship was not really a weapon of defense. It was used to train people to work in vacuum conditions and for research purposes. It wasn't even armed.

With this influx of money, Michael wanted to set up a planet-wide laser system that would knock out anything that might threaten them. This and the completed early warning system should be enough deterrence to discourage Earth from trying a quick takeover. They had the technology and access to the material but lacked the money and men to man the ships. Now they would have the money, but building it would take a few years as well as train people to operate them., and if Earth knew about it she just might not give them that much time.

Michael knew he would have neither the time nor the money to set up much of an offensive system. A couple of warships to patrol the space around the planet were the minimum Heatherbound needed and didn't have. They did have an old transport ship, big, clumsy, and slow, that could be remodeled. And, just recently, a space yacht had been donated and was in the process of being armored. Three spaceships do not a Space Navy make. About all they could do was discourage raiders.

"May I speak to Mr. Sean McCreight? I have some important information that would interest him about his brother, Cameron."

Sean was both irritated and curious. "This is Sean McCreight. This had better be good. I'm a busy man."

"This is too important to discuss over the phone. Could we meet?" said the soft, timid voice.

"I'm not in the habit of meeting people I don't know, but what the hell. Where and when do you want to meet?" Sean couldn't resist information about Cameron. After he hung up the phone, he leaned back in his chair and thought to himself, 'I wonder what Cameron's up to now?"

Michael had been doing a lot of thinking since the last meeting. After everyone was settled for this meeting, and the nit picking details were yet again being discussed, he got up from his chair and came around to Kaitlyn's side. Sitting on the table in front of her, he said, "Kaitlyn, we must get in touch with your husband as soon as possible. As we discussed, we don't want knowledge of his discovery made public. Has he told his tanker crews anything?"

Kaitlyn looked up at Michael, a little startled. "You know as much as I do, Michael. I haven't heard a word from him all this time about the fuel. The letters he sends to me have very little in the way of solid information about anything."

She pushed herself away from the table and stood up, not liking someone to be looking down at her. "But I can tell you this, his men seem confused and vague about what they have been doing except that they asked me to help them set up a dealership for hovercrafts and that Cameron has okayed an advance on their wages to enable them to make this investment. I gather from this that he told them to keep everything to themselves. I must admit that I am surprised at the control he has over them."

While talking, Kaitlyn got up from the table and started pacing the room. It was as if she were a prisoner; the room was small and had no windows. The fact that the door was always locked added to the effect. She thought, I have served my time here, and now we are just rehashing what has gone on before. Nothing more can be done until Cameron returns and briefs them.

"What more do you want from me? I set up the contracts with RD&E for more Smart Satellites, the sale of the islands and Lake Placid has gone through, and the fuel is coming in regularly. More holding tanks are in the process of being built, and an inspector is on each site to verify the amount of fuel brought in to insure that the government would get it's fair share."

Turning to Pandit, she said, "This coming and going of ours, under guard, must be alerting whoever may be interested that something of importance is going on. I really feel that I have to get back to my other duties. If you are worried about security, I will not object to a bodyguard staying with us, but I must get on with my normal routine. Surely you can understand that?"

"My dear Kaitlyn, these are trying times, and you must bear with us just a little longer," said Pandit, getting up from the table and going to her. He put his hands on her shoulders, "Your brother-in-law, Sean, has heard some rumors about all this, and his lawyers have been asking some awkward questions we have not been able to answer."

" As heir to the McCreight fortune, he may have some grounds to stop this transaction and could possibly object to the favorable terms you have given the government. This is why we have been trying to keep you with us until Cameron returns and can explain everything to us. But you are quite right. You must return to your normal life. Could you give us just one week more? Surely Cameron will return by then."

Kaitlyn pushed Pandit's hands from her shoulders indignantly. "Am I being held hostage? I thought this was top secret. How did Sean find out? And anyway, what businesses it of his? What my husband has discovered is his affair. It has nothing to do with his elder brother."

"No, of course, you are not a hostage. As to how Sean found out, we don't know. We are checking into it. And you are quite right. If this is your husband's discovery and not his grandfather's, Sean would have no rights. But if Kendell McCreight was the true discoverer, we may be in hot water, legally. We can only hope that Cameron has excellent proof of ownership," said Michael, leaning forward on the table. "Can you remember anything that Cameron might have said or done in the last few years to indicate that he was working on such a project?"

"I have told you repeatedly that I cannot. Cameron is rather close-mouthed about his research work, and I never pry," said Kaitlyn resignedly. "I really must leave you now and go to my children. I will stay in town one more week, that is all. No more meetings!"

Chapter Twenty-Six

Information Leak

Sean was pacing back and forth in his office like a caged lion. He was restlessly waiting for more information about the new find Cameron had discovered. His source had told him that is was something that his grandfather had worked on, and it involved millions of credits. This would make it his business, and he intended to get to the bottom of it. He was furious that he had had no knowledge of it beforehand, and this giveaway to the government had to stop.

Hearing a knock on his door, Sean quickly went to his desk and sat down. "Come in."

The door opened, and Sean's secret informant came in and stood by Sean's desk, hat in hand. He was a tiny man by any standards, balding and very meek looking, except when you looked into his eyes, which had a hard glitter. "I came as quickly as I could, but I have very little information to give you."

"Please sit down. Would you like a drink?" Sean got up from his desk and went over to the small bar concealed in a cabinet. He looked to the little man for confirmation. Seeing a quick nod, he poured him a large brandy and one for himself. "Just to steady the nerves."

The little man accepted the drink gladly and sat down. Before saying another word, he took a large gulp of the brandy. Then, with a quiver in his voice, "Thank you, Mr. McCreight. This whole business has been more trying than I had anticipated. I thought we agreed to meet in secret. I really don't feel comfortable coming to your office so openly. When you asked me to keep you informed of anything else that may be of interest to you, I had no idea that you would expect me to come to your office."

"Well, I do, and I need to know all the details. It doesn't stand to reason that a private citizen would give five million away to the government unless something illegal was involved. You think that you or you wouldn't be here. The small amount I pay you would not make it worth your while if you didn't feel it was your duty to keep the government straight. Isn't that right," said Sean as he tried to soothe Timothy.

"I gave you a copy of all the documents that have been drawn up between your brother's wife and Mr. Pahlavi. The fact that they didn't want to take it to Central Committee looks suspicious, and I don't take the excuse of national security as valid."

"Until your brother comes back with all the rest of the documents, I have nothing more for you. Of course, their company, RD&E, is getting large government contracts out of this." The brandy had given Timothy courage. He said as he looked Sean in the eye. "In all fairness, there has been some talk that your company may be given a contract for a new warship."

"Yes, yes, we have been negotiating for that contract, but that's all above board, nothing to be devious about. You're not to get interested in that. Are there no rumors? Nothing more you can tell me about the origin of the fuel?"

"No. The lid has been very tightly shut on this. I am afraid that they are suspicious of everyone, even me," Timothy said as he drained his glass and got up to go. "I shouldn't have come here today. I think I may have been followed."

"Sit down. I haven't dismissed you yet," said Seam angrily. "It's been three weeks since you gave me those documents. I find it hard to believe that nothing else has happened. What has Kaitlyn been doing there all this time? What are you holding back? Is it more money you want?"

Timothy did not sit down but continued walking towards the door. "There is no reason to get angry. I know how worried you must be and will take that into consideration for your behavior. I don't know anymore, and I really don't think anyone there does, either. I overheard Kaitlyn say the same thing. Until your brother returns, nothing more can be done. I will contact you at that time, and now I bid you good-bye." Abruptly he was gone, opening and closing the door in equal softness.

Sean was dumbfounded that this little man could stand up to him and had the temerity to leave when he had told him to stay. He thought to himself, perhaps Timothy's reason for helping him was really a misguided sense of duty after all, or did he have some other axe to grind? In any event, he had better revise his manner of handling him.

His lawyers were looking into the matter and advised him that he had very good grounds for taking over the entire business with the fuel. The only possible snag was if his grandfather had made some provision in his will for the proceeds to go to whoever discovered this newest accomplishment in the field of biology. This would only be true if the will had been written before the birth of Sir John. They felt this was highly unlikely.

I just have to be patient, thought Sean. Let Cameron do all the work. I'll step in and reap all the benefits. Just who does he think he is anyway, another Kendell?

When Timothy left, he was kicking himself. He was jeopardizing seven years of spying for Earth for a few extra credits. Sean would probably slow down the Heatherbound's defense building, maybe even stop it. But was that worth losing his job? This was getting too scary. Perhaps it was time to retire. He had a nice nest egg on Earth.

*

Cameron had mixed emotions after reading Kaitlyn's last letter. He wanted to stay with the Dasurainians until they were ready to leave, but he also missed Kaitlyn and the children. Working with these people who knew so much about plants had been exciting and a little humbling. He realized how very little he knew and how much he could learn from them if only he had the time.

He had been gone a month now and really had been too busy to think about his family much. He was cold and exhausted most of the time but had never felt so exhilarated. He felt a little guilty about that, especially since he knew how busy Kaitlyn must have been with all the arrangements with the Central Committee, her work at RD&E, and the children. She had not complained in her letters, but reading between the lines, he could tell that she was about at her limit of patience with the whole situation.

Jutaro and Peter decided to stay until the Dasurainians left. Encountering a group this large, suffering the effects of years of cryonic suspensions, was something they never expected to experience. Even though the Dasurainians were of a different species, there were reams of data to assimilate, so much to learn. This should bring the science of cryonics years into the future. The Dasurainians had been most helpful and explained a lot about their own method of hibernation, which was similar to that of Earth animals.

With the cryonic specialists on hand, Cameron had less reason to stay. He would have to stop at the stone hut on the way back home to get the will, which would delay him a little but was necessary. Kaitlyn's letters said that somehow Sean knew about his involvement with this whole affair. It was a good thing that his grandfather had thought this out thoroughly and wrote what seemed to Cameron an airtight will. Even with the will, he knew that Sean would try to horn in somehow.

It would be another two weeks before the Dasurainians could leave. Cameron had no choice, he had to leave and get proof of ownership back to Pahlavi and Beckett. They were getting more insistent on that proof with each letter he received from them. It was understandable. Large amounts of money were being expended on his word alone. The only thing that made this trip bearable was the thought that he could be back to spend the last week with the Dasurainians.

Sighing, he thought large amounts of money cause equally large problems. He never really wanted to be rich, just wealthy enough to take care of his family comfortably and pursue his research in peace. It was not to be. They were going to be extremely rich. He would give the problem to his brother, but he knew that Sean would not be as far-sighted as his grandfather was. Sean didn't believe in giving so much to the government.

Getting ready to leave his room and donning his thermowear, Cameron thought one thing he would not miss was this infernal cold and his thermowear. He couldn't leave the hot spring area without it, and he was sick of it. As much as he liked the Dasurainians, he would be happy, at that moment, to see them leave. Shaking his head, he laughed softly to himself. This was not true. He really wished that they could be together in a mutually comfortable environment. He knew they were suffering as much as he, only in the opposite direction. He felt an echo of laughter in his head. Drakel was sharing this joke with him, which made him feel better.

This business of having someone able to read his every thought was very difficult at first. Even now, he felt a little wary of it. He could see that there could be no masking of the psyche, no misunderstandings, you always knew where you stood, but he felt a little naked at times. He was not used to everyone knowing his meanest thoughts, his little intolerances. The Dasurainians could see this problem, but in their society, there was no word for privacy. They could not cheat or lie. Any pain they inflicted would be felt by all. Their main source of enjoyment was to obtain recognition, by their peers, for excellent work and achievements in whatever they endeavored to do.

Cameron left the hot spring area and walked toward the spaceship. He saw No.1 and called to him, "I have to leave for a few days. Would you see that my hovercraft is ready? I also want to take your prototype with me. Is he ready?"

"Yes, Cameron," said No.1, as he smoothly came up to him. "He has been assembled, and Drakel gave me the special bionics needed. When you return, will you have time to inspect the other islands? The new robots are working perfectly, and we will be harvesting them in three days."

"Yes. I'll make time. I want to see how those islands are coming along. I hope to be back in three days, but it may be longer. While I am gone, make sure we have enough holding tanks for the additional harvest. We'll have to devise some more efficient way to bring it to the refining area. Perhaps build a small tanker robot that the harvest robots can empty their sap into instead of each making the trip with such a small load." That would be another good idea for Ian to design, and would be useful back home also, to deliver fuel the different fueling stations, thought Cameron.

Knowing this did not require an answer, No.1 went to service the hovercraft. Cameron continued toward the spaceship. Just as he arrived, he saw Dramon leave the ship, "Hello, Doctor, how are your patients coming along?"

All are getting quite fat and ready for the journey home. The children are the slowest to recover, the process was most difficult for them. It will be safe for us to leave in about two weeks, said Dramon with what felt like a relief in Cameron's head. *It has been too long to be away from home.*

"It pleases me to hear that all are well, especially the children. They had us all worried for a time. We will be sad to have you leave, but we understand the need to return home. I, too, must return home for a few days. I do hope to return before you go. Right now, I wish to talk to Drakel. Have you seen him?"

I am in the hydroponics section, Cameron, awaiting your arrival, said Drakel. *I know that you want to go over the information on the various plants. I assigned a robot to learn all that we know about them. This transference of information will take all the time we have left here. He will be programmed to answer only to you. We know about your species' problems of ownership and secrecy. He is your payment for the molded Steelite formulas and the special material. I had Jutaro make a receipt of sale as your people do rely on paper. Also, here is something from your grandfather. It is the key to the magic box he carved for you while he was here.*

There is another gift I wish to give you, the specifications for the bionics of intelligent robots. This is for the music we have heard from you through your mind. We especially loved your classics. We will be working on our telepathic robots to fine-tune them to reproduce those sounds. We find them very soothing. If that is agreeable to you?

"Yes, of course. I can't thank you enough for all this. It will make life a lot better for many humans." Cameron said as he reached out to take the small piece of wood that Drakel gave him. "This is special too. You don't know how many hours I have spent trying to open that box. He did tell me that I would find the key one day. I hadn't realized he meant a real key."

In case you don't get back before we leave, I want to say good-bye now. It has been a pleasure knowing you and your grandfather, said Drakel, shaking Cameron's hand. *We will be meeting you soon, I think. From what we understand, Earth may give you trouble over the technology and plants you have purchased. Because of this, my people feel a need to monitor the situation. To some degree, it is partly our responsibility.*

"Again, I thank you," Cameron said with a nod. "I don't know what you can do, but we are going to need allies."

Chapter Twenty-seven
Homecoming

Cameron climbed into his hovercraft for the journey home. There, seated in the co-pilot's chair, was a duplicate of No.1, "Hello Cameron. I've been waiting for you. My name is No.1+1, if that meets with your approval. If you will instruct me, I can help you fly this instrument to your destination."

"I have been looking forward to meeting you No.1+1. That is a good name, but too long. I will call you +1, and it would be most helpful to have you spell me at the flying task. The first thing we do is get out of this cave. Just be sure to ask any questions if you are not sure of what I am doing." Cameron said as he got behind the yoke and maneuvered the craft to the entrance of the cave. Once they were clear of the island, Cameron turned the hovercraft over to +1 and told him what to do. It didn't take +1 long to learn, and soon Cameron felt he could leave it to him. (He could not think of these intelligent robots as "it.")

Last month Cameron had little time for sleep. He told +1 to wake him when they got to the coordinates of Lake Placid and went to sleep. It seemed no time at all when +1 woke him, and there below was the lake. It was late afternoon; the sun was low on the horizon. Its rays bathed the lake and the surrounding countryside in a fiery hue. There was the stone hut, the window reflecting the sunlight like a welcoming beacon. This seemed like a good omen to Cameron, he took over the controls, and they were soon landed beside the cabin.

Quickly Cameron went to the cabin and got the will his grandfather had left him, and they were off again. Cameron was anxious to get home. It was another three hours. This gave Cameron plenty of time to question +1 and find out if he knew everything that No.1 knew. It was uncanny, but he did. There was so much to find out about what had been going on during the last hundred years on the islands. Before he knew it, his farm was below them. He had radioed to Kaitlyn that he would be home about this time, and there she and the children were, waving to him.

Cameron landed in the courtyard and rushed to his family. He grabbed up Kaitlyn and the baby, Megan, and swung them around, laughing. He then put them down and did the same for Robert. After the excitement of greeting his father, Robert noticed +1, who had left the hovercraft and had been watching the homecoming.

When Cameron could tear his eyes away from drinking in Kaitlyn, he noticed Robert's interest and said, "I'd like to introduce you to +1, my companion on the trip home."

With his arm still around Kaitlyn, he turned to +1, "+1 this is Kaitlyn, my wife, Megan, my daughter, and this young man who is bug-eyed with interest, is my son, Robert."

"Everyone, this is +1. You will find that he is a very unusual robot."

"I am happy to meet you finally. Cameron has talked about you so much that I feel that I already know you," said +1.

Robert blurted, "He talks just like a human. Can he play games?"

"Ask him," said Cameron. " He is a very intelligent robot."

"Do you know any games?" asked Robert, very seriously.

"I do not know what games are, but they sound interesting. I always like to learn new things."

"Super, let's go to my room." Reaching out for +1's hand.

"Whoa there, little man, it is almost your bedtime," said Kaitlyn with a smile.

"Ah, Mom, just one game. I promise to go right to bed when we're finished."

Kaitlyn was standing there with Cameron's arm around her, and the world looked pretty good right now. "All right, just one game, then off to bed. That's, of course, if +1 really would like to learn a new thing."

Megan began fussing just then, and they all went into the house. It was time to put Megan to bed. Cameron followed Kaitlyn into the room and watched her as she dressed his youngest child for bed. He sat quietly and listened to her sing a lullaby. He really had missed this. It was wonderful to be home.

Megan closed her eyes and was sleeping. She looked like a little ballerina lying on her side, one arm over her head and one knee drawn up. Cameron and Kaitlyn smiled down on her, their arms around each other's waists. Kaitlyn leaned over and adjusted Megan's blankets, and then they quietly left the room, leaving the door slightly ajar behind them.

They went to Robert's room. The game was just finished, and with a promise that +1 would play another in the morning, he quit pleading for 'just one more'. Cameron picked him up and took him into the bathroom for his bath. +1 followed, and the three enjoyed talking about the game. Ready for bed, he was tucked in, and it was time for his bedtime story. As much as he loved his father and missed him, Robert was fascinated with his new friend and asked him to read. Cameron said okay if he promised to go right to sleep after one story. He told +1 that he could stay in Robert's room for the night. Enjoying the interaction between the two, Cameron stayed to listen. When the story was finished, Cameron tucked Robert in and went to find Kaitlyn.

Cameron found Kaitlyn in the kitchen. She looked a little agitated but smiled. "Sit down while I fix you something to eat." She went to the counter and started fixing him a snack. "You must be hungry." She knew that he seldom ate much when traveling. "I'll join you with a cup of coffee."

Cameron went to the cupboard for the coffee mugs and put them on the table. He pulled out his chair and sat down to watch Kaitlyn at the kitchen counter. Her back seemed stiff to Cameron, and her movements jerky. The room was quiet. The sound of the clock ticking seemed loud, as did the small noises that Kaitlyn was making preparing the quick meal. Cameron knew that the next half-hour wasn't going to be easy.

Putting a sandwich in front of Cameron, Kaitlyn poured them each a cup of coffee. Sitting down across from him, she said, "Now, we have time to talk. Come on, Cameron, give. What have you been doing this last month, and where did the Teraline come from?"

He hadn't realized how hungry he was until Kaitlyn put the sandwich in front of him. He grabbed it up and took a very large bite while listening to Kaitlyn. He knew she hadn't wound down yet. He took a gulp of coffee, almost burning his mouth, and then another bite. Oh, was it delicious. He had missed her cooking, even sandwiches.

Cameron felt her eyes burning into him as she watched him eat. "Your letters have been pretty scant with information. I have been half frantic trying to keep Michael Beckett and Pandit Pahlavi calm. They are getting very worried about your brother and his claim to ownership of the fuel."

"You realize they have commissioned several spaceships to be built," continued Kaitlyn. "Plus setting up a recruiting and training system for people to man them. Not to mention the radar and missile systems that are in the planning. They've already spent the first three years' profits you guaranteed them."

Cameron noticed that she left her coffee untouched while she continued. "Did you know that Sean threatened to get a court order to stop the disbursement of funds? Your father stopped that for a while, but Sean's lawyers are bringing up prior cases. It is only a matter of time before it goes to court. We must have proof that Teraline is yours."

"It's been a madhouse," Kaitlyn said as she got up and walked back and forth in agitation, her eyes bright with tears of frustration. Cameron had never seen her so upset.

All thought of the other half of his sandwich forgotten in her disturbance, Cameron said, "Kaitlyn, Darling, I do understand what you have been going through."

Getting up from the table, Cameron took her hands in his. He pulled her back to his chair, sat down, and pulled her onto his lap. "It's okay, Honey, I really do have proof that we own the rights to Teraline. Someday I hope to be able to explain everything. But I can't right now. I have a will that my grandfather wrote before he was even married."

Kaitlyn jumped up from his arms and turned on him. She spread her hands as if in supplication. "Why didn't you get that to me immediately? Do you say you knew what I was going through? Did you really?"

He quickly rose from his chair and grabbed her hands. "The will was at the cabin, and I couldn't leave Winter's Grove to get it for you because of…. Well, it's a long story."

She jerked away and glared at him. She sat down in her chair again with a look that said. This had better be good.

"Just listen. My grandfather had reason to believe that a grandson of his would be interested in the same things as he. To this grandson, he gave the rights and responsibilities that were entailed in the owning of Teraline."

" I am that grandson, and I had to fulfill promises he made to a group of people before I earned those rights. These people gave him, and the future grandson, the plants and equipment to manufacture Steelite. They were in a lot of trouble, and it took a month to help them out and fulfill the agreement that had been made by my grandfather. I left them as soon as possible, picked up the will at the stone hut, and came home."

Cameron was happy to see the look of relief on her face. She grinned. "That's wonderful, Darling. We'll take the will to Michael and Pandit tomorrow. The sooner we get that record, the better off we all will be, and so will the defense effort."

With a big sigh, she said, "What a load off my mind. You can't imagine how relieved everyone will be."

Cameron sat down again and started on the second half of his sandwich, thinking, this is going better than I expected.

Kaitlyn started up again with a mixture of hurt and confusion in her voice. "I wish I knew why you are so secretive about all this, but I do trust you. At least I've always trusted you before, and I won't ask anything more right now. It's damn hard though, to understand. Don't you trust me?" Brushing tears from her cheeks, she got up and started her agitated walking again.

"You haven't finished your sandwich. You don't eat enough, Cameron. You're getting skinny." She still had tears in her eyes, and her voice was shaky.

Ignoring her last comment, Cameron said, "Of course I trust you. It's hard to explain, but I'll try. I'm helping a group of people that were stranded here about a hundred years ago. They are very powerful telepaths and have put a mind block on everything to do with their existence. Even if I told you everything, you would not remember it, at least not now."

Cameron got up from the table again and tried to hold her. "Kaitlyn darling, you can't know how difficult this is for me not to tell you everything. You don't know how much I want to share my excitement and joy of this discovery with you, but I have no choice in the matter. You just have to have faith in me," Cameron said, letting go of her and running his hands through his hair. He looked so lost and alone.

Kaitlyn took his hands in hers, feeling very sorry for him. "That sounds really weird, but it does explain why the tank crews seem so evasive. Also, the lack of interest from everyone about where all the Teraline is coming from."

"Promise that as soon as you are able, you will explain every detail to me," said Kaitlyn as she put her arms around his neck and laid her head to his chest, softly saying, "I've missed you so."

Cameron picked her up and carried her into their bedroom. All thought of his unfinished sandwich was gone. "I've missed you too, Sweetheart, and we have better things to catch up on than Teraline."

Chapter Twenty-eight
Betrayal

The next morning Kaitlyn and Cameron left the children with Glenys. They took +1 with them, much to Robert's disappointment, and flew off to RD&E. Cameron spent an hour with Ian to explain as much as he could about what had been happening and what Ian could do with +1. Then they were off again to the War Ministry. They had radioed ahead that they would be there and when they landed, Michael and Pandit were waiting for them on the parking roof. Timothy, Pandit's secretary, was with them.

As soon as the hovercraft stopped, Michael stepped forward, opened the door, and helped Kaitlyn out. Cameron climbed out quickly and shook his hand. Michael said, "It is good to see you again, Cameron. This has been a very long and busy month. I don't want to sound too abrupt, but you do have the proof of ownership with you, I hope?"

"Yes, Mr. Beckett, here it is, and no, it does not sound too abrupt, I can understand your concern," said Cameron as he handed Michael the will.

"It has been a busy month for me too, Sir. I understood that you needed this document, but I really was unable to get away sooner. I had hoped that Sean wouldn't hear about this before I got back. That was wishful thinking I realize now. It really is too big a project to hide for very long."

Michael scanned the will and then handed it to Pandit, saying, "Looks pretty clear to me. There should be no trouble with the inheritance law with this in hand."

Looking a lot more relaxed than he did when they first arrived, Michael said, "What a relief. I was visualizing some pretty nasty scenes this last week, I can assure you. I should have had more faith in you both."

Pandit read the will slowly and with great care. "Yes, everything looks in order." He turned to Timothy, gave him the will, and said, "Take this to Judge Sherman and see that it is recorded before the next court session this morning."

Kaitlyn frowned and said, "That is the only copy we have of the will. I am not too sure we should have it out of our sight."

Pandit gave a condescending smile and said, "Timothy is my most trusted secretary. He will not lose it between here and the courthouse, Kaitlyn. You will have it back as soon as it has been recorded. I promise."

Timothy took the will and immediately left the area. He did not go to the court, though. He went back to his office and took the copies of the files he had been making these last seven years.

He then called the Captain of the spaceship he had hired to be on standby this last month to return him to Earth. "Be ready to leave in three hours."

His work here was finished anyway. It wouldn't be much longer before he was found out. He then hurried to his apartment and finished packing. He had one more telephone call to make before he left for the spaceport.

Timothy made his call and got right through. "Mr. McCreight, I have the document you want. It will cost you 50,000 credits, deposited in my bank account on Earth. You have one week to do this or it will be turned over to your brother."

"Timothy, what are you thinking calling on my private line, and what—"

"Don't interrupt. When the deposit is made, you will receive instructions on where to find the document." Timothy hung up before Sean could reply.

All this didn't take more than two hours, and he was off.

Sean was in a quandary. He didn't have that kind of money. What with the expenses of building his mansion and living as he thought appropriate for his position, he and Glendora spent every credit they made, plus they were in debt up to their ears.

He had to have the proceeds from this new fuel. Even though that old fool of a grandfather gave them to Cameron, he had no right to do so. God Damn it! It should be mine!

Sean rang for his secretary. She came into the room, notebook in hand. She was a little nervous, as Sean had been so grumpy lately. "Good morning Mr. McCreight."

"Would you bring me the account books and the company checkbook?" Sean didn't even look up.

Kaitlyn and Cameron returned to RD&E with easy minds. She was glad to be back to a normal routine. She was so far behind in her work she thought it would take forever to catch up. There were the usual requisitions to fill, bills to be paid, and numerous details that seemed small but must be done. She had been on top of the financial aspects of this whole business, but there were always small details to clear up.

Cameron was anxious to get back to his lab. There were several experiments that he had left with his lab techs, and he hoped that they may have gotten some answers while he had been gone. He wanted to get this done as quickly as possible because he truly wanted to be back with the Dasurainians. He planned to leave for Winter's Grove in the morning.

It was a strain not to be able to talk about the most exhilarating time of his life to Kaitlyn or anyone else, but there it was. She really was one in a million to be as patient and understanding as she has been about the whole circumstance.

Going through piles of disks full of data on his desk, Cameron was completely immersed in his computer when Ian came into his office, very excited. "Cameron, did you know that +1 is so far in advance of anything we, on Heatherbound, know about robotics? His bionics are organic and capable of growing as the need increases. The only limitation is the size of his body cavity."

"According to him, it takes about two years to grow a bionic brain. The brains are very delicate and need a great deal of special handling during the infant stage. With the proper supervision, we should be turning them out by the thousands in two or three years."

Almost musing to himself. "Of course, we are going to need more space, perhaps a special lab built, more lab assistants…." He had been walking back and forth in front of Cameron's desk, too excited to sit down, and stopped in the middle of his sentence.

"This is the most exciting discovery since the Big Bang Theory was disproved," said Ian enthusiastically, as he stopped walking and turned to Cameron and leaned on Cameron's desk with both hands. "He knows so much. It's like talking to a human being."

" How did you find him? Where is he from?" Not waiting for answers, Ian pushed himself away from the desk and started to leave the office. "This is the beginning of a whole new era of robotics."

Ian stopped in mid-stride and turned to Cameron, a look of pure horror on his face. "We do have the rights to this, don't we? It's not something that Sean can try to steal, is it?"

Cameron had been watching Ian all this while with a broad smile on his face. "First, I have papers to prove that he is mine to do with as I please, and second, I give you half the profits from him since you will be doing most of the work."

Ian relaxed with a sigh of relief. "Thank God! The things we can do with this new technology. It's mind-boggling."

Cameron leaned back and locked his hands behind his head. "I know you will find a way to use this in the defensive systems you are working on, and that is priority number one."

He then leaned forward and put his hands on the desk. " I also want those bionics in all my robots, including the oil tankers, but that is pretty far down on the list."

"There will be many new developments with +1's help.. He knows so much and works so smoothly," said Cameron. "I was hoping you could come up with the right questions to ask that would further us along while we are waiting for the brains to grow."

"There are thousands of questions I want to ask him," said Ian. "I just need the time to spend with him. I will have that time, won't I?"

"Yes, of course, +1 is a duplicate of No.1. You may have him for as long as you need him," said Cameron. "You can even dismantle him to see how everything works."

Ian looked a little shocked at this suggestion. "I don't especially want to take him apart until I have had time to really understand his workings. I hope I never have to."

"Right now I have him working on the schematics of his systems. This is going to put us right up on top. Everyone will be vying for our bionics and our robots. I bet Earth isn't this advanced."

Ian noticed the pile of work on Cameron's desk. "Well, I see you're busy, and so am I. I was just so excited I had to talk to you about +1. I'll get back to it now and let you get back to your work." So saying, Ian left the room at a run.

That afternoon Judge Sherman called Pandit and said, "I understand that Cameron McCreight is back. I would like to get this Teraline mess straightened out. Sean McCreight is becoming very insistent that proof of ownership be supplied. I can't hold him off much longer."

Dead silence for a moment and a feeling of dread came over Pandit. "We have the proof. I read the will myself and sent it to your chambers first thing this morning with my secretary, Timothy. Did you not receive it yet?"

Pandit heard the Judge ask his secretary about seeing Timothy or anyone from Pandit's office that morning. He heard the negative reply.

"No, as far as I know, no one in my office has seen either the will or Timothy. Are you sure you gave him instructions to bring it to my attention immediately?"

"Of course I did, judge. I knew how much was riding on that document. I wouldn't have wasted a minute. I'll talk to Timothy. Let me get back to you."

Pandit hung up the phone and sat back in his chair. Oh my God, he thought, I haven't seen Timothy this morning. Could he be the leak in my office? No, there must be some explanation. He rang through to his assistant, "Have Timothy come to my office at once."

"Sorry Sir, he hasn't come in this morning. Didn't call in either or leave any kind of message. I was going to mention this to you, as it is so unusual for him."

"Call his apartment. No, send someone over to his apartment immediately. I must see him. It is on a very serious matter. Also, get me, Mr. Beckett."

A short while later Michael came into the room feeling very relaxed until he saw Pandit's face. Pandit looked ghastly, white, and wild-eyed.

"What's up, you look terrible, are you having a heart attack?" asked Michael.

Pandit shook his head, "I wish it were just a heart attack. I just got a call from Judge Sherman. Timothy never got there with the will. He also did not come back to work this morning."

"But, but—" sputtered Michael.

Pandit put up his hand to stop him, a look of resignation on his face. "I sent someone to his apartment. I can't believe Timothy would betray us. He must have been waylaid or something.

"You read the will too. Do you think they will take our word for it that there really is a valid will in Cameron's favor?" said Pandit, now with a look of desperation on his face." My God, what will happen if they don't? We're ruined." He put his head in his hands.

"Just hold on," said Michael as he took a seat. "We don't know that the will is gone. Give it a little time. Timothy will have an explanation and all will be as before." Trying to reassure Pandit. "Meanwhile, we will call the Judge and ask for a couple more days."

Michael got up and walked around to Pandit and patted him on the back. "Pandit, we have done nothing wrong. We may have acted a little hastily, but it was for the good of Heatherbound, not ourselves. Pull yourself together."

There was a knock at the door, and Pandit's assistant came into the room. "Sir, if I may have a minute of your time?"

"It's all right. You may speak in front of Mr. Beckett."

"The security guard at Timothy's apartment building said that Timothy came home early this morning, and the guard saw Timothy leaving with several suitcases. When the guard asked him how long he would be gone, Timothy told the guard that he was leaving for Earth and he could have what was left in the apartment if he told no one that he was leaving until the next day. It took a bit of persuasion to get this information from him."

There was a stunned silence. Then Pandit said, "Thank you, that will be all for now."

The assistant nodded, turned, and left the room, closing the door softly.

"That clears up one problem. Now we know who was leaking information. I only hope it was just to Sean. You don't think he could have other contacts do you?" Michael said, looking rather sickly himself right then.

"I trusted him. How could he have been so disloyal? What do we do now?" moaned Pandit, hiding his face in his hands.

"I think we must call Judge Sherman, tell him exactly what happened, and that we both read the will stating that Cameron had the right to the Teraline. Let him take it from there. He is on our side. He realizes the threat from Earth to Heatherbound," said Michael.

Judge Sherman was very sympathetic but could do nothing. He called a meeting between Sean and Cameron and their lawyers, with Michael and Pandit included as witnesses for the defense. Sir John McCreight was there as well. It did not go well for Cameron, even though Michael and Pandit swore that they had seen the will and that Timothy had absconded with it.

Sir John McCreight was informed that Sean had very definite rights as the eldest son, even though it was Sir John's inheritance they were talking about. Sean had the right to bring up the question of ownership and to question Sir John's right to give so much away, especially since Sir John seemed to be on the side of Cameron and the Elders.

"I see no reason why Michael Beckett and Pandit Pahlavi would lie or not know a valid will when they saw one. After all Pandit Pahlavi was a lawyer before he became an Elder," said Sir John. "I also feel that Heatherbound needs a defense system and that it was just good business to make sure that one was provided. We certainly can afford it."

"I don't dispute the integrity of Mr. Pahlavi or Mr. Beckett or their ability to read legal documents. But they do have a stake in this. Their careers and reputations are on the line. A forged document is not easy to ascertain on a single reading," said Sean in a reasonable voice.

"I also don't agree that we need a military presence on Heatherbound. Furthermore, I feel that Earth has no real interest in taking over this planet by using force. It would ruin the very thing they want, land and products. I agree that they will do everything in their means, short of force, to acquire us, but only through legal means."

"I intend to bring a suit against Cameron for the Teraline. And I want all contracts that he and Kaitlyn made with the government to be declared null and void. Under the inheritance law, Sir John cannot make decisions of such magnitude without my consent. I have a right to protect my inheritance."

"If you do this," said Sir John, in a voice cold with disgust, "I will have no recourse but to disinherit you."

"Father, I respect and honor you, but if you really believe in our manifesto, you could not disinherit me over an inheritance issue. This would prove to one and all that you are not fit to be an Elder."

Sir John was shocked and sickened by this attack from his eldest son. "I don't believe that the inheritance law meant that the patriarch of the family would not be able to spend his own money in what he considered to be in the best interests of that family."

"This very point will be taken up by my lawyers. I do not wish to hurt you in any way, Father, but I must protect my, and my children's, futures. This giving away so much to the government, for whatever reason, is ludicrous. I reiterate, even though I believe Mr. Pahlavi and Mr. Beckett are honorable men, they could have been duped by a false will, and until a valid copy is shown, there is no proof that one ever existed."

"I request this court to order that all amounts of money accumulated for the sale of Teraline be transferred to the McCreight account. I also demand punitive damages of one million credits from Cameron McCreight. I do not ask for Cameron to be jailed for fraud. I do not wish to dishonor the family name any more than it has been."

"How generous of you, Sean, not asking for your brother to be jailed, just bankrupted," said Sir John sarcastically.

"This will be a glorious prize for the lawyers," said Sir John. "My lawyers will bring evidence that the laws were made to stop large properties from being broken up between the siblings. They were not made to put so much power into the eldest son's hands that the father would be unable to formulate sound business transactions."

"I see no recourse but to put this case to trial," said Judge Sherman. "It is a sad situation, but the law is the law. I am sorry for all of you."

Chapter Twenty-nine
The Trial

If Sean won, this could put the government in a very bad position. In only one month, they had spent several million on the defense systems, and there was no way this could be paid without a massive increase in taxes. They would have to cancel all contracts and take their losses if the judgment went against Cameron.

Heatherbound would be left without an effective defense against any invading force. That was unacceptable. Just having the trial was bad enough for the progress of the defense system because all contracts had to be put on hold until it was settled.

The trial had been going on for six months. During this time, Earth was building up sentiment against Heatherbound among the peoples of Earth. It was claimed that the colonists were not granting immigration to minority races and that they were unjustly upsetting the oil and steel industries by flooding the market with subsidized products. This would put millions out of work, it was alleged. These upstart Heatherbound colonists had to be put in their place before they wrecked Earth's economy.

The propaganda was doing its job. The people of Earth were clamoring for something to be done about Heatherbound. During this time, the Consortiums were using their political muscle to make the countries of the world increase their space forces by adding more ships and training men to man them. This was in expectation that they would have the full backing of the countries of Earth in an invasion of Heatherbound.

Timothy's news about Teraline made the Consortiums lust after Heatherbound. They wanted all rights to this planet for themselves. It was a cornucopia of raw materials, and they wanted it. They were also worried that more new products might be discovered that would further cut into their own profits.

During this time, Cameron was not allowed to leave the capital. Also, all his assets were frozen. RD&E was allowed to continue with the company's contracts, but profits that were in Cameron's and Kaitlyn's names were held in escrow. Sean had never found out about +1 or the organic brain chips for the new robots. If he had, he would have tried to take that too.

The Dasurainians had left, and Cameron did not get a chance to see them again. The Teraline still flowed into the capital, and everything was flourishing along those lines. No one thought it strange that Sean, or anyone else, had not asked to be shown the fields that produced this bonanza.

Cameron was very depressed and worried about his promise to No.1. He knew there would be problems in the fields that needed his input. He decided to send +1 back once a week to carry messages and instructions. That eased his mind a bit while he spent his days in court. The lawyers were having a field day with all their attention to detail.

He and Kaitlyn were using the small apartment that Kaitlyn had rented previously in the capital, and Kaitlyn seldom left him to go back to the farm. If they weren't in court, they were conferring with their lawyers. The children didn't understand why everyone was so unhappy, and the days seemed to drag for them in town, especially for Robert, who kept asking when they could go home.

On weekends they tried to act normal for the children's sake. They attended services in a small church near their apartment on Sundays. On Saturdays and other free days, they might go for a stroll in the park with Robert and Megan. If it was a nice day, they would take a picnic lunch and spread a blanket on the grass under a tree. Robert would run to play on the swings in the playground and hoped he would find some playmates. They had to watch Megan. She would crawl off the blanket and eat grass.

One Friday evening, after a particularly bad day in court, Kaitlyn asked Judge Sherman if she could see him in his quarters. The judge agreed, and when they were secluded, she said, "Judge, you know that Cameron is not a risk to run from these proceedings. This order to not leave the capital is causing problems with my children. Would you please allow us to go to our farm occasionally?"

"You're right; I don't think Cameron is a risk. He has too much to keep him here. It's just a ploy of Sean and his lawyers, and I resent it myself." Judge Sherman got out a form and wrote out the release. "I should have given this to you sooner. I hope you enjoy your weekend."

Kaitlyn rushed home to Cameron, almost giddy with happiness. She exclaimed, "I talked to Judge Sherman today and asked him if you could leave the capital, just for the weekend, to go to our farm. He okayed it, in writing! Let's go right away tonight, even. Nothing much is going to happen."

Cameron was sitting in his chair, both children on his lap, while he was reading to them. He looked up excitedly. "You're kidding. That old goat came through? I can't believe it. You're a miracle worker."

Robert jumped down and ran to greet his mother. Cameron stood up, still holding Megan. "The thought of getting out of this city is almost too good to be true. To think, a weekend at the farm, it's as if the world was lifted off my shoulders. This whole court scene seems like a merry-go-round, and we're not getting anywhere. We'll leave right after dinner. No need to pack or anything."

Robert jumped up and said, "I want to go on a merry-go-round too."

"Sorry, Robert, that was just Daddy's way of saying that this business at court is just going in circles. It doesn't seem to be getting anywhere. We haven't really been on a merry-go-round. But I promise as soon as this is over we'll all go to Pleasure Park and spend the entire day. How does that sound?"

"Super, Mommy. Are we really going to the farm this weekend? Is Daddy coming?"

"Yes, and yes. Now hurry to your room and take what you think you must have for a weekend at home," Kaitlyn said as she lifted Megan from Cameron's arms.

"Glenys, get the kids ready. We're going home for the weekend and leaving as soon as we finish dinner," said Kaitlyn as she and Cameron scurried around securing the apartment.

It was dark when they arrived at the compound, but there were lights on in the house. It looked so welcoming and natural after the confining environment of the capital.

"It's good to be home. From now on we are coming home every weekend if I can persuade Judge Sherman to agree," said Kaitlyn as she got out of the hovercraft. "The lawyers don't really need to confer with us in person all the time. Just have them do their job, and we'll get back to ours."

They went into the house, and the first thing they noticed was the smell of freshly baked bread. In the kitchen on the table was a vase of roses just picked from the garden. Glenys had called her mother and told her that they were coming home for the weekend.

Mrs. Stuart had gone over to the main house and got things ready for them. She always felt that freshly baked bread made everything seem just a little bit better. It was true. With the smells, snacks, roses, and familiar surroundings, suddenly, life didn't seem so desperate.

Both Robert and Megan fell asleep during the trip home. As soon as they got home, they put their children in their beds with a sigh of happiness. Then Kaitlyn and Cameron went for a walk. The air was filled with the heavenly smell of growing plants and newly mown grass. The night air was cool, with a slight breeze. It was a perfect night. They walked hand-in-hand, not needing to talk. They had each other, and they were home.

The following day Cameron was going through the things he had brought home from Winter's Grove and saw the wooden key that Drakel had given him. It looked a lot like the cutouts on the magic box of his grandfather. Could this actually be the key he had mentioned? There was no time like to present to try it. I wonder if it is still on the shelf in my lab, he thought.

Cameron went immediately to his lab and spied the box on the shelf, just as he had remembered. He picked it up and looked at it closely. Sure enough, there was a place that looked like the wooden key would fit. Trying it, he heard a slight click, and then the box came open. Inside was a piece of paper and a letter. It was another will, just like the first one he had found at the lake.

Dear Grandson,

This is the original copy of the will that I made before I married your grandmother. You will see that my two closest friends, Thor Anderdahl and Johana Smidth, signed the will.

The fact that you are reading this letter proves to me that you have met the Dasurainians and Drakel. I hope that all went well for them. My only regret is that I will not live long enough to see these people again. They are an incredible race. It would be to our advantage to become friends with this race, to get to know them. Perhaps we would learn a lot about trust and peace. My friends probably won't remember signing this will, but I have the word of Drakel that anyone seeing this will believe that it is a true and valid document.

Having fulfilled my promise to Drakel for me, you have earned the rights to the Teraline and anything else they may wish to give you.

I hope you have as good a life as I have had,

Your Loving Grandfather,

Kendell McCreight

Cameron sat there stunned. He had been going through living hell for the last six months needlessly. Here was proof all along. Then it hit him. He jumped up and ran to tell Kaitlyn. "Kaitlyn darling, where are you? I have fantastic news."

"What is it, Honey? You sound so excited," said Kaitlyn as she came out of the kitchen, wiping her hands on a towel.

"I've found the original copy of the will. It was in that magic box that Grandfather made for me. I forgot all about the wooden key that Drakel gave to me. I did not recall it while we were gone because of all the problems we had been having, but I remembered it this morning. I tried it, and it fit. Out popped this will."

"Oh God, Kaitlyn, It's over. We can get back to a real-life again." He held her in his arms, buried his face in her hair, and almost wept with relief.

She hugged him to her. "Cameron, that's wonderful. It's been a very rough road, but now it is over or soon will be. Let's not tell anyone yet. Just savor it for the weekend, and this time we have it for ourselves. I'm afraid that this is going to start a whole new set of problems and negotiations. We need these two days."

"My God, you're right. It's going to be another mess. Can you handle it again? I know I'm being a pig, but I must get back to Winter's Grove and see what's been going on."

"Of course, my darling, but not 'til Monday."

Chapter Thirty
The Magic Box

Monday morning, before leaving for the Capital, Cameron faxed the will to several people, Judge Sherman, Pandit Pahlavi, Michael Beckett, both the defense and offense lawyers, Sir John McCreight, and Sean. He also sent a fax to Thor Anderdahl and Johana Smidth, who were now Elders and had signed the will. He hoped that the lawsuit would be thrown out by the time they got to the court.

It was a beautiful morning. There had been rain the night before, and everything looked clean and shiny. Cameron and Kaitlyn felt rested and ready for just about anything. They landed on the roof of the courthouse, which was full of people just waiting for them. When they got out of the hovercraft, all hell broke loose. Arms were waving, and everyone was shouting. They wanted to know where he had found the will, why wasn't it found sooner, and what was going on.

Cameron shouted for attention, "Let's all go inside and calm down. I'll explain everything in detail."

They all trooped into the courtroom and found their seats. Cameron explained about the magic box his grandfather had given him and finding the key at Winter's Grove. Because he had been confined to the capital, he had not had a chance to try the key. He had no idea that it would have anything to do with the case.

He explained that Judge Sherman had given them permission to return to the farm for the weekend. It was the first time in six months that he had been allowed to do so. That was the whole story.

Sean was furious, "Cameron staged the entire episode to make me look foolish and drive a wedge between me and our father. He's grandstanding, too, giving so much away to the government for a defense system when Earth would never be interested in an agricultural planet. Everyone knows they have all the planets they need. Why would they bother with Heatherbound?"

This was going to cost him a lot of money because the loser in a court battle paid all costs. His salary wasn't going to cover it, that was for sure. He still hadn't paid back the money he had taken from the business account and given it to Timothy. Sir John was going to have to bail him out, and this really hurt. He swore he would get even someday.

Michael and Pandit were anxious to get the ball rolling again on the defense system. Too much time had been wasted. From their reports from Earth, it looked as if time was running out for Heatherbound. Earth had sent their ambassador numerous complaints about everything they always complained about, but this time there was saber-rattling as well. This court battle, and Sean's greed and jealousy, may have doomed Heatherbound.

*

Cameron flew to Winter's Grove that very same night. From the air, everything looked the same except that there were some rather large robots on each of the larger Islands. Cameron flew around all the islands in his chain and saw that almost all were filled with the Turpina shrub. He would have to see if there were other remote islands that would grow this plant.

Almost all planets had areas of perpetual snow, and Cameron wanted to export the Turpina plant to all of them. It would be a cheap source of fuel for all of humanity. Boy, would that enrage the Consortiums of Earth. It would certainly reduce their stranglehold on the outer planets. It might even help the people of Earth.

Flying into the tunnel of the main island filled Cameron with excitement. There were so many projects he wanted to do here and so many questions to be answered. He could hardly wait to see No.1 and begin again. He had a moment of rage at Sean for keeping him away from Winter's Grove and the departure of the Dasurainians. He shrugged it off. What's done is done.

After he landed, the first thing he noticed was that the cavern seemed much bigger than he remembered. The Dasurainian's spaceship had left a big hole, not only in the cavern but also in Cameron's heart. The only good part of this was that there was a lot more room to build holding tanks and expand the refinery. No.1 had already started this project. Life had to go on. He only hoped that someday he would see the Dasurainians again.

In the distance, he saw No.1 coming forward with another robot. This other robot looked a lot like No.1 except that he had shorter legs and arms and he was green. Cameron guessed that this was the robot he had been promised. Both robots came to a stop in front of Cameron and waited.

"It is good to see you again No.1. Who is your companion?"

"This is Green. He is your parting gift from the Dasurainians. Green has all the information in his memory bank you required concerning the Turpina shrubs. The Dasurainians experimented with many plants from this planet, and Green has all the data they collected. Green also is able to give you information and seeds of useful plants you may be able to use. He will answer only to you or your equivalent in the following generations."

"Wow, all that in one package," said Cameron reaching out and shaking Green's hand. This gesture confused Green a bit, but No.1 radioed a quick explanation to him. "I have been looking forward to meeting you, Green, and to the many talks we will have. Now, I must spend time with No.1."

"How have things been working out here? I'm sure that +1 has been doing an efficient job relaying my instructions and explaining why I could not come myself."

"All has been going as scheduled. We are keeping up with the fuel barges and have had very few stoppages. I made the robotic barges you suggested. They have been going between the islands and collecting sap from the harvesting robots. This has kept the maintenance of the harvesting robots to a minimum and increased production by twenty percent.

"We have also built another refining factory on the second largest island. That has also increased production, but only by thirty percent. We are in need of supplies to build more robots. We have bionic brains growing and in training. The bionics for harvesting robots takes six months to grow, and we have twenty-five ready to be implanted. The bionics for the—"

"Stop." said Cameron, holding his hands up as if to fend No.1 off. "I should have been more specific. I will hear your full report, but not at this moment. You have been doing an excellent job No.1, and I appreciate it. Is there anything you, yourself, need?"

"I am in need of some minor repairs. This would take approximately two days. No.2 could take over my duties while this is being done. I did not want to shut myself down until you were able to come and inspect this concern, as you may have had questions that No.2 could not answer."

"I would like to inspect everything and have a lot of questions. It is not necessary to wait for your repairs. You are too valuable to me to risk waiting any longer. I am sure you must be way past the time for your maintenance. No.2 could make a list of all questions that he couldn't answer while you are being repaired."

"Thank you, Sir. I will attend to it as soon as I have briefed No.2," said No.1 as he walked away, leaving Cameron with Green.

"Well, we finally meet, Green. I am sure we will have many, many years of conferring on plants and formulas. Right now, I just want to walk around by myself and see what has been happening during my absence. You may go back to whatever you were doing. We will talk later," said Cameron.

Cameron wanted to be alone. He missed the Dasurainians and really wanted to talk to Drakel. A feeling of frustration, and loathing for Sean, came over him. He hated his brother for the lost opportunity and the time wasted. He still couldn't understand his brother's shortsightedness about Earth and his greed. Kaitlyn thinks that Sean is jealous of his way with plants and worried that it would bring more fame and wealth to Cameron, therefore outshining himself. Would Sean be so jealous if he knew that he was practically a clone? This wasn't getting him anywhere. A soak in the hot-springs might help lift his mood.

Chapter Thirty-one

Timing

The Consortiums of Earth had been preparing for an invasion of Heatherbound ever since Timothy had returned with his news of Teraline and the beefing up of the defensive systems of that planet. They knew of the legal battle between the McCreights and how this was affecting the defense buildup for Heatherbound. This lawsuit gave them the extra time they needed to prepare for a full-scale invasion. Timothy had done his job well.

The propaganda scheme had gone over as well as expected. They had the full backing of Earth's governments and military. In another six months, they felt the fleet would be ready. Heatherbound would be just another colony belonging to Earth, ripe for reaping huge profits from penalties and taxes. It's ironic that they would be required to pay all costs for the necessity of a war with Earth.

A meeting was convoked in the boardroom of the Consortiums. This was a very impressive room on the top floor of the tallest skyscraper in New York. Two walls were paneled in dark mahogany; the other two were ceiling-to-floor windows that gave a magnificent view of greater New York City. The only furniture in the room was a massive oval table with ten leather armchairs around it. There was no need for formalities; each man knew where he sat. They filed in quietly and took their seats.

When everyone had arrived and settled, Sergi Rustinkoff, Head of Worldwide Communications, called the meeting to attention. "We've just received the latest information concerning Heatherbound. The trial is over, and Cameron McCreight won. This puts our invasion schedule off. We were assured that the trial would last at least a year. What happened?" He looked around the table at the rest of the men who were heads of their businesses. They, after a stunned silence, all started talking and shouting. Some even suggested that the invasion should be called off.

Sir Kelvin Hardcrow, President of Amalgamated Steel, banged on the table for attention. "Stop this quibbling. This doesn't change anything. It just pushes up the time schedule."

"You should all be happy. You'll be richer that much sooner," shouted Rustinkoff angrily.

"It doesn't matter what happened. We now have to speed up the launch time. Instead of six more months to prepare, we must get launch the invasion as soon as possible. We cannot wait longer than four weeks from now. That will give Heatherbound seven months to prepare while the fleet is en route. This, unfortunately, will mean there will be more loss of life and property. If we can get ships underway this soon, they won't have enough time to fully prepare, and Heatherbound will be ours to divide." As Rustinkoff was saying this, he stood up and leaned forward on the table with both fists.

"You make it sound like child's play," said Admiral Knightson heatedly as he too, got up from the table. "There are ships that are still being constructed that won't be ready for another four months. The stockpiling of supplies has only just begun. We have a hard core of well-trained troops, but the rest still need more training. If we go in one month, as you suggest, it would mean going with fewer ships, men, and supplies. Without the threat of overwhelming odds, we would have to do some serious damage to their major cities, with great loss of civilian lives and property, to subdue them into surrender. I feel—"

"I don't care what you feel. I'm surprised that an admiral would feel squeamish about a little extra loss of life. Isn't that what you are trained to do?" Hardcrow said with a touch of sarcasm in his voice.

The Admiral was furious and started to rebut when Hardcrow interrupted him. "The stakes are too big. We must take advantage of their not being ready. In the long run, you'll see that. We should take a vote now to launch in four weeks," shouted Hardcrow to the rest of the men gathered at the table.

There was much murmuring around the table, but soon the motion was passed. A few of the men looked pale and a little sick, but that didn't stop them. They rationalized that in all battles, the weak must die and the strong shall prevail. They intended to remain strong and in control of all natural resources of this planet and the colonies. They wanted, very intensely, this planet that seemed to have an abundance of valuable plants.

There was a flurry of activity in Admiral Knightson's office these last four weeks. The logistics of speeding up the invasion were almost overwhelming. Through his will alone, he managed to push through the completion of two more ships. He now had twelve ships ready to go, manned and equipped. Granted, a full half of the troops had less than six months of training, but these troops probably wouldn't be needed until after the surrender. They would be used as a peacekeeping force. It hadn't been easy, but the launch would be on schedule tomorrow at 0700.

This entire invasion made the Admiral very uncomfortable. This was not what he had signed up for when joining the Navy. Even if all the propaganda was true, and he had his doubts, Heatherbound was not really a threat to Earth. He had his orders, but by God, he swore to himself there would be as little loss of life as possible in this conflict.

Chapter Thirty-two

Preparations

On Heatherbound, Pandit Pahlavi & Michael Beckett began pouring money into the defense system again. They were informed of the date of the invasion launch through their connections on Earth. It would take six months from that date for the armada to arrive at Heatherbound, and then there would be war.

The military strategists on Heatherbound decided that the first thing Earth's fleet would do is threaten to wipe out New Edinburgh, in the belief that this would cause Heatherbound to surrender. If Heatherbound didn't surrender, at least the bombing would disrupt lines of communication for the defense. They decided that one of their best defenses would be to disperse the populace of New Edinburgh into the countryside.

The people were told of the coming invasion and the possibility of the bombing of their only major city, perhaps even eradication of it. Six months was not much time to move a city of people, but these were very strong and independent people. No one wanted to be controlled by Earth. All had heard what was happening to the other colonies and wanted none of it. Their freedom was valued, and they would fight to the end. The slogan was "No surrender. Ever!"

The next six months were a beehive of activity on Heatherbound. Emergency shelters were being built in ten different locations. All shelters had a complete communications system set up and underground housing as well. All other non-essential work was halted. Everyone that was able pitched in to save their homeland. Money poured in from every household. If they couldn't afford to give money, they volunteered their time, most did both.

Each evening everyone between the ages of eighteen and ninety did military training for two hours. It was mostly guerrilla tactics and hand-to-hand combat. Anyone ninety or older could volunteer to train in communications, supply, or medical support. All were issued weapons and ammunition. It was understood that they would fight to the death.

Pandit Pahlavi & Michael Beckett were heading the military expansion and decided that there was not enough time to build a fleet of space ships. Also, all the Steelite available would be needed to build the shelters. It was used to build the structural supports for the walls and the roofs.

The exodus to the shelters went without incident, especially since about a third of the residents of New Edinburgh refused to leave. They could not, or would not, believe that Earth would be so cruel as to level their beloved home on trumped-up excuses.

*

"It is only two weeks before they arrive," said Sir John. "There are about two million of us again the billions of Earth. We have no chance of course, but it will not be easy for them. And I swear that they will not get the seed or formulas for Steelite. I'll burn the harvest and the seeds first."

Sir John was in his office at home. He was sitting behind his desk, talking to his two sons. He did not look well. His coloring was grayish and he had aged ten years in the last year. Between the war threat and the lawsuit, he had been under tremendous pressure. All his life's work seemed to be going up in flames, and probably the lives of his family.

"You must promise me, Sean, that you will destroy everything."

Sean was in a state of shock. He still couldn't believe that his world was coming to an end. That all he had worked for, the building up of the company, his inheritance, his new home, was for nothing. "I promise, father, to do what is best for the family. I can promise no more."

There was a deathly silence for a moment. Then Sir John said, "You are no longer my son, Sean. I never wish to see you again as long as I live. Now leave my presence and never let me see your face again."

Sean's face turned white except for the scar that seemed to be a banner of red down his face. He whispered, "I'm sorry you feel that way, father. I must do what I think if right for my family." He got up slowly, gave Cameron a murderous glance, and left the room.

After a few minutes, Cameron leaned forward in his chair and said softly, "Dad, perhaps you were a bit hard on Sean. I believe he will do the right thing when the time comes. I think he still doesn't believe the invasion will happen. That's why he fought so long at the trial. He really doesn't believe that Earth could be interested in this plane, at least not interested enough to invade us. So why spend all that money on a defense system was his reasoning."

Sir John turned his head to look at Cameron with a look of disgust, "I'm ashamed of both of my sons. You haven't been around much lately. What have you been doing to help the war effort? You haven't even been on the planet, I hear."

"That's right, Dad, I haven't. I've been to the planet called Snowball." He brushed the hair from his eyes and continued. "You wouldn't believe the conditions those colonists have to live in. It's perpetual winter there, and they can grow nothing except in hydroponic gardens. And it's not enough to feed a quarter of the people."

Sir John had a look on his face that said, I've heard all this before.

Camoner knew that look and continued stubbornly. "I thought the best thing I could do for the war effort was to help take away the stranglehold Earth has on some of the other planets. I gave them some Teraline plants and other plants that are edible. These thrive in the cold and grow even in snow. I also loaned them a robot to teach them what to do with the plants."

Sir John frowned ts, plus so, with a look of interest, and leaned forward in his chair.

Cameron noticed and became even more enthusiastic about his project. "What took the most time was to persuade the Mayor to let me give the plants to them. He was terrified that the Consortiums would retaliate by cutting off supplies or calling in their loans. I made him look at the charter, and nowhere does it say that they can't accept gifts or loans from other planets or people."

"That's all very well and good, son, but how does that help Heatherbound?" said Sir John, still not completely convinced.

"Right now, it doesn't do much, Dad. But in the future, if more of these outlying planets are independent, combined, we could stand against Earth," said Cameron, with feeling.

"I want to go to each of the planets that are being exploited by the Consortiums and give them the same opportunity." Cameron ran his hands through his hair, stood up, and with hands outspread, looked his father in the eye.

"Don't you see? This is the only way we can protect ourselves. We must form a strong alliance of outer planets. This is my contribution to the war effort besides the money I have given to the government. It will do a lot more good, in the long run, than signing up in the army or navy."

Cameron stood up straight and gestured with his hands the frustration he felt. "I don't know how long it will take for the plants to grow before they can start producing enough to be a real help. There will be setbacks, even sabotage, I imagine. But it is a start, and I hope it will let these people see that there is a possibility of being independent."

With a tired look of resignation, Sir John said, "It's a noble act, Son, but too late. In two weeks, we will be just as they are, slaves. What then of your gesture?"

"It will be a beginning. The seed of freedom will be planted," said Cameron, smiling at his pun.

*

Admiral Knightson was standing on the bridge of his Command ship, watching the image of the small planet getting larger as they were approaching it. He hadn't realized that it would look so earthlike. A green and blue sphere wreathed in white clouds. It's so beautiful.

There are only about two million people on that planet, he thought. What right do they have to restrict immigration? So what if it's only been one hundred and fifty years since it was colonized? In that length of time, they could have tripled their population. The people of Earth need the room. It is right that they are attacking a virtually defenseless planet. These people were selfish and needed to be taught a lesson.? Trying to convince yourself that it is all right to commit murder? It's not going to be murder. In two weeks, the fleet would be there. All they needed to do was threaten to drop a few bombs and the government, Knightson ment of Heatherbound would surrender. No one needs to get hurt. They are intelligent people. They know they can't win.

The worst that could happen is that they would have to bomb New Edinburgh, their capital, to show that they really mean business. We might have to send in shock troops to take over the government buildings and communications. It could get messy, but the end is inevitable, and in another week, Heatherbound would belong to the Consortiums, and they would open it up to everyone who wished to come. He might even ask for a large land grant for himself and his family.

The Admiral was having these thoughts while watching everything that was going on around him on the bridge. What were his men feeling if he was having trouble justifying what they were doing?

"Carry on, Captain. I'll be in my quarters if you need me," said the Admiral as he left the command center.

"Aye, aye, Sir," said Captain Adams.

The skeptics on Heatherbound heard the news that the Federation Fleet was only two weeks away. There was panic now, and people who had remained in New Edinburgh were packing up what they could and rushing to leave the capital by any means. The roads were filled with ground vehicles.. The skies with hovercraft. Tempers were short, and there were fights about the right of way and ownership of vehicles.

The ten shelters had given notice that anyone trying to arrive after a week would be turned away. It would have given away the location of the shelters. All would be directed to other temporary camps of tents and hastily thrown-up bamboo shelters.

All the people who had farms in the outlying districts were inundated with refugees begging for housing or any temporary shelter, even the use of their barns. It wasn't complete chaos but close to it. The military had foretold this would happen and had made plans to coordinate with the civilian peacekeepers.

The police and military did what they could to organize the refugees and transport as many as possible to the correct locations. Women and children were given priority and sent to the more secure shelters. Sometimes this meant separating them from their men, but this couldn't be helped.

Chapter Thirfty-three

Encounter

Two weeks later, the Federation Fleet arrived at Heatherbound. All twelve ships were holding orbit above New Edinburgh. Nothing had happened so far to interfere with them. There was a large ship circling the planet. It looked very old and not much of a threat. They knew that it was the Mothership that had brought the original colonists and then had been made into a research vessel. Some armament had been added in the last few years.

There had been no answer from it when the Mothership had been hailed. They also could see two more large spaceships and several smaller ones on the ground that looked to be ready for launching. These were probably the ships that their intelligence had reported to have been built for Heatherbound's defense. There didn't seem to be any surprises except the silence. Why hadn't their hails been answered?

"This is Admiral Knightson of the Federated Union of Earth. We have come to right the insults you have paid to Earth. Surrender your Elders to us, and no one will be hurt."

This time there was an answer. "This is Michael Beckett, Head of the Military and member of the Elder's Council. We will not surrender to you under any condition We have done no wrong to Earth. You are committing an act of aggression against a peaceful planet. What right do you have to invade us?"

The Admiral expected just such a reply. "We do not have to give you excuses to do what is just. You have heard our demands for years. We can no longer stand by and let you continue to disregard them. Heatherbound has flooded the market with Steelite and oil, causing unemployment and unrest on Earth. Also, you have not allowed immigrants of all nationalities to come to your planet in sufficient quantities. We are sure the people of Heatherbound do not wish to continue these policies. We are here to free them from your tyranny."

"We, the people of Heatherbound, have known of your mission of conquest for the last six months. You know, in your heart, that your accusations are a tissue of lies. Steelite is too limited in supply to hurt your steel industry. Also, we haven't shipped an ounce of oil to anyone," Michael said with a touch of scorn. "Your invasion is unjust and motivated by the greed of Earth's Consortiums."

"We have voted to never surrender our planet. You will have to kill every man, woman, and child before you can say you have conquered us. We will burn our fields and our formulas. You will have conquered nothing but ashes."

"We will take your planet. There can be no other outcome. The Federated Union of Earth does not want to harm anyone, but we will if we must. You have twenty-four hours to surrender or we will eradicate New Edinburgh."

With all his rationalization, the Admiral had expected no less. He felt in his heart that he would have said the same thing in defense of his home. It was a shame; he didn't want to bomb New Edinburgh or send in his shock troops to take over the planet. He knew if he didn't that it would be the end of him, not just his career, and then someone else would finish the job. He was not a happy man, but he had orders.

Twenty-three hours were gone and the Admiral was back on the Command Bridge. "Is there still no contact with the planet? They are a bunch of stubborn fools. Try contacting them again."

"Sorry, Sir, there is no answer, and from what we have observed, the city seems to be deserted."

"Try them again every five minutes. Count it down for them. That should get on someone's nerves. Tell them each time that there are so many minutes left before we launch the bombs if they do not surrender."

Everyone was very quiet on the Bridge. The countdown seemed to be doing a job on the crew if nothing else. Each call seemed to wind them up even tighter. The radioman thought, I just want this over with. I don't care what happens, just get it done.

"Federated Command ship calling Heatherbound control, you have five minutes left before we launch our bombs. Please respond."

Suddenly there was the sound of three laud pops. On the viewing screen, they all could see three very large, very alien spaceships come into view. The new arrivals hailed the Earth fleet.

Federated Union of Earth, I am Admiral Cadirex of the Dasurainian Empire. We come in peace and wish you no harm. The people of Heatherbound are our allies. We will protect them. There will be no battle today or any other day. Your weapons will not fire, nor will you be able to launch any missiles or bombs.

All the blood left the Admiral's face; he gripped the arms of his chair so hard that his knuckles were white. *This will be man's first encounter with sentient aliens*, he thought, *and I may have to fight them. This is not how it is supposed to happen.* He was a courageous man and stood his ground. In as firm a voice as he could manage, he said, "Put them on the viewscreen. I wish to talk to them face-to-face."

The screen came on, and everyone gasped. They saw a huge bear-like creature, wearing little else but straps and a belt with many gadgets hanging from it. He was a beautiful shade of purple and had huge black eyes. The most amazing thing about the creature was that he looked so benevolent.

"Where do you come from? How do you know the people of Heatherbound? What do you know of our intentions?" Admiral Knightson said, as calmly as possible, under the circumstances.

The creature didn't move his mouth, but all on board could hear him quite clearly. *We come from a planet that is far from here. We only like extremely cold planets to colonize, so you have no fear of our having conflict over the expansion of our species. We do not make war. We have other peaceful ways to restrain our enemies from harming us.*

We have been monitoring your communications with Heatherbound and cannot allow you to invade them or harm them in any way. A citizen of Heatherbound assisted a shipload of our citizens to return to us, thus saving their lives or at least making their living on Heatherbound endurable.

"I can understand your feeling of gratitude to the person who helped you. But to go to war with another species to fulfill that debt seems to be rather extreme," said the Admiral.

"Also, you may be creating a bad precedent in future dealings with our race by interfering with human problems. This is clearly none of your business."

We do not indulge in armed conflict. We stop it, as we will with this conflict, replied the Dasurainian Admiral. *It is clearly the business of all sentient beings to stop unjust behavior. This, what you are planning to do, is wrong. To kill innocent people for profit is uncivilized. We cannot allow it to happen.*

Admiral Knightson was an intensely unhappy and worried man. He believed the aliens about not fighting, and in his heart, he agreed with everything they said, but he had his orders.

He bristled at the words 'not allow' and said, "We feel that our fight is just. In any event, I don't see how you can stop us. We have our orders and must proceed with the invasion. From what you say, we have no need to fear you. Now, if you will excuse me, I have work to do."

With a sure voice, he gave his orders. "Cut the transmission. Have all ships ready to standby to launch the bombs. Launch."

Nothing happened. It seemed that the weapons officers had forgotten what they were supposed to do. All the weapons officers on the twelve ships just left their stations as if they had been dismissed. The captains called security to take charge of these officers and assigned others to the bombing task. The new officers assigned also looked confused and left their stations without following orders.

Admiral Knightson then told his Captains to do the job. They, too, could not. It appeared that anyone who got near the weapons station became confused or forgetful. They would just walk away.

Admiral Knightson was livid with rage. "See if you can contact the Dasurainian Admiral again."

It was only a matter of seconds, and Admiral Cadirex was back on the screen. *Admiral Knightson, I see that you have discovered that you are unable to employ your weapons. I did warn you that you could not use them. Now that you know your claws are drawn, perhaps we can help you and the government of Heatherbound come to some amicable agreement.*

"Right now, I am not interested in any kind of agreement. I want to know what you did to my crew and my weapons."

I am sorry to hear that you are not interested in settling this armed dispute against a practically defenseless planet, Admiral Cadirex said in a disappointed-sounding voice. *I had hoped for better things from you.*

Cadirex gave Knightson a minute to think about this, then said, *I will give you two of your hours to change your mind. If you do not, I will make your ships turn around and go back to your Homeworld. You will not remember why you returned home without accomplishing your goals. That will be very hard to explain.*

"You are speaking to us telepathically, aren't you? That is how you can control us as well. Is that not true? What's to stop us from turning right around and coming back to finish the job as soon as we are out of your range?"

What you have said is true. We, the Dasurainians, have found that gentle telepathic persuasion is far less harmful and less expensive than weapons of war. As to our range of control, as you call it, you will just have to take our word for it that you will get to your Homeworld and completely forget about us. As a small demonstration, we will make everyone in your fleet forget about us except you.

We no longer need to fight because we can feel the anguish and understand the viewpoint of our potential enemies. We do not wish to fight with anyone. Our only wish is to trade. Admiral Knightson, you have two hours.

"He broke the connection," said Admiral Knightson in disbelief.

"What connection, Sir," the Captain replied, sounding bewildered. "I don't believe that we were talking to anyone on Heatherbound. There has been a no communication from them since you gave them twenty-four hours to surrender."

"I don't mean Heatherbound. I mean the Dasurainians. Those purple aliens we have been talking to," the Admiral said testily.

There was complete silence on the bridge. Everyone turned to the Admiral with shocked looks on their faces, which quickly turned to embarrassment. All turned away in confusion, not wanting to look at each other or the Admiral. The Captain said, "Excuse me, sir, but we haven't been talking to purple aliens or Dasurainians. We have communicated with no one since yesterday."

"My God, they said you wouldn't remember. I am not losing my mind, as you all seem to think. Do you remember our mission, Captain?"

"Yes, of course, Sir," replied the Captain. "We are to take over the planet, Heatherbound. Bomb them into submission if we have to. Secure it with occupation troops, and confiscate all the property of those opposing us."

"That is exactly right, Captain. And do you remember that I gave the government of Heatherbound twenty-four to surrender, or we would bomb their capital, New Edinburgh?"

"Yes, Sir."

"Do you also remember that the twenty-four hours were up several minutes ago? That I gave the order to launch the bombs?"

"Yes, Sir."

"Why haven't my orders been carried out?"

The Captain was very disconcerted by this line of questioning. "I don't know, Sir. The weapons officer seems to have left his post." Red in the face, he turned from the admiral and said, "Ensign Harris, man the Weapons station and commence firing. Lieutenant Wang, inform security to locate Lieutenant Jones. He is to be confined to his quarters until further notice. Commander Winson, contact the other ships and find out why they have not followed orders."

Everyone on the bridge jumped to, including Ensign Harris. When Harris got to the weapons station, he seemed to forget his orders and started to leave the bridge. He didn't even remember to salute the officer in charge or ask permission to withdraw.

"Ensign Harris," yelled the Captain. "Where do you think you are going? I gave you an order."

"I don't know Sir," said the Ensign, turning bright red and looking very confused. "I went to the Weapons station, and somehow I thought I was finished with my shift and should return to my quarters."

"You see, I am not going mad," said Admiral Knightson. "We are being telepathically controlled by Aliens. These Aliens call themselves Dasurainians and have befriended the people of Heatherbound. They will not let us attack the planet."

"Sir, I cannot explain why we have not launched an attack or what is happening to our weapons people, but I assure you I will get to the bottom of it." Captain Adams was very embarrassed but felt he had to continue. "These references to purple aliens, which no one has seen but you, make me think that you have been overstressed."

With the sound of resignation in his voice, Admiral Knightson said, "Captain, I understand how you feel, and if I were in your place, I would feel the need to lock me up in the brig until I came to my senses." He thought a second and then continued. "I want a Senior Staff meeting in the conference room in five minutes." With that, Admiral Knightson got up and left the bridge.

Five minutes later, the Senior Staff convened in the conference room. All stood around talking quietly to each other until the Admiral arrived. Everyone came to attention.

"At ease. Please be seated," said the Admiral as he took his seat. He looked around at his officers, feeling defeated. "I know that all of you have heard that I claim to have seen purple Aliens. I can understand that you all think that I have lost my mind. Humor me; pretend that you believe me." The Admiral held up his hand to forestall any comments.

"Indulge me for a few minutes. Imagine that aliens have control of our ships by telepathically controlling our minds." There was another burst of noise from the staff.

"Wait," said the Admiral, hand up to stop them. "Hear me out. These aliens have given us an ultimatum. We have less than two hours to agree to end our aggression and come to a meeting with them and the government of Heatherbound."

"At this meeting, we are to settle our dispute in a peaceful manner. They will arbitrate. If we do not, the Dasurainians will make us turn around and go back to Earth. Then, they say, they will make us forget why we didn't fulfill our mission."

"With all due respect, Admiral," said Captain Adams, "there are no aliens."

The Admiral ignored the Captain and continued. "Let's use this hypothesis to come up with a solution for just such a contingency. What would we do? If we go back, we would all be court-martialed, if not worse. We would be pilloried and counted as cowards, derelict in our duty to the people of Earth."

"If we agree, and if they allow us to remember them, we would be famous for Earth's first encounter with another species. The people of Earth would be so excited about meeting this benevolent and peaceful species that no matter how much propaganda the Consortiums spread, we would be heroes."

"When you put it that way, we have no choice. We must comply. I, for one, would be glad of it," said Captain Adams. "I wish it were true. There is no honor in killing civilians."

He continued softly but with passion. "I've never liked this mission. It has made me feel more like a murderer than a conqueror. From what we have been told, these people may be shortsighted and greedy, but they have broken no laws, nor have they threatened Earth. What right have we to invade them?"

Commander Winson sat back in his chair and, with a sigh, said, "I don't think the people of Heatherbound are shortsighted or greedy. They left Earth because it was overcrowded and dirty. They wanted a better place to raise their children and their children's children. I, for one, admire them. They left Earth at a time when to do so it was fraught with danger, with no guarantee that they would succeed. They vowed never to let their planet go the way of Earth. Even with their small population, they limit their birth rate. To me, it makes sense. And can you actually believe that this small amount of people can wreck Earth's economy?"

There was more discussion around the table, but all agreed that if the hypothesis were true, they would have to go to the peace table. Many agreed with Commander Winson and were happy that there would be no invasion. The Admiral thanked them and then dismissed them. The Senior Staff returned to their duties, and the Admiral to the bridge.

"Admiral, there is an incoming communication."

"Open up contact on the view-screen."

When the screen came up there were many exclamations of, "Oh my god, he did see them." Some of the crew stood, up some just sat in numbed silence. All felt goosebumps of superstitious fear. Then, almost immediately, they felt foolish. These aliens looked non-threatening and intelligent. Even so, they couldn't help the scalp-crawling fear of the unknown.

The purple creature didn't appear to move his mouth, but all could hear. *Admiral Knightson, have you come to a decision?* said Admiral Cadirex quite calmly. *Your two hours are up.*

"You can read our minds. You know the answer."

We can read minds, as you call it, but we do not unless forced to. We feel it isn't civilized unless permission is granted. It can be a two-sided sword. If you grant us the freedom to read your mind, then we must, in all fairness, allow you to be able to read our minds. There can be no lies or miscommunications. We would know each other's deepest feelings about the subject we are talking about. Is that what you want?

"If I understand you correctly, you would only read my mind on a need-to-know basis. Do not go deeper into personal thoughts or other matters. If this is correct, I am all for it. I will allow you to open up a channel between us on the subject of a peaceful resolution with the government of Heatherbound," said Admiral Knightson after a few seconds of thinking.

Admiral Knightson was so tense that he couldn't sit. He stood and walked towards the view-screen and said, "Do you think that you will be able to get Heatherbound to agree?"

The government of Heatherbound does not know of us. I cannot say what they will do until I contact them. We feel we owe them a debt that they, for the most part, are unaware of, said Admiral Cadirex.

I recommend we both contact their military leader and make arrangements. I will contact them first because they won't believe that we, the Dasurainians, exist. I propose we contact each other again in twenty-four hours.

"That seems the most reasonable thing to do. This will not be easy, but a lot easier than war." Admiral Knightson broke the contact and turned to his men. "I want all Senior Staff to meet again in the conference room in ten minutes."

Ten minutes later, the Senior Staff gathered in the conference room again. There was excited talk about the aliens, and someone even said he wished he could hunt them for that magnificent fur coat. Everyone looked at him aghast. He said he was only joking, but wouldn't his wife love it?

Admiral Knightson entered the room and sat down. He had heard that last remark and had a feeling of disgust for the human race. He knew that many would think the same thing about hunting. It is part of our specie's nature to think that anyone or thing different from the norm is inferior. He didn't say anything but gave them a look that told them exactly what he had been thinking.

"Please sit. We have much to talk about." Looking around the table, he said, "We are the aggressors. We have the might, but we can't use it, not even as a bargaining chip. So what are we going to bring to the peace table that would allow us to go home without disgrace? That is our problem, gentlemen."

There was quiet murmuring among the officers, then silence.

Admiral Knightson sat patiently, waiting for his officers to settle down. "Our orders were to conquer Heatherbound by any means. Send in occupation troops and abolish their government, thus taking this planet under the control of the Federated Union of Earth and in effect, the Consortiums. We cannot do that."

"The people of Earth have been told that this was necessary because of the greed of Heatherbound and their policy of competing with Earth's steel and oil companies to the detriment of the unemployed. They have also been told that Heatherbound is racially biased and doesn't allow minorities to immigrate. You know all this. The media certainly has pounded it into us. I even believed some of it, probably to make it easier to follow orders."

"We know that we cannot complete our mission as ordered. Let's hope we can at least get Heatherbound to agree to end these practices of flooding our markets with steel and oil. They must also agree to allow everyone who wishes to immigrate. I think we also need to have the Dasurainians send an envoy to return with us," said Captain Adams. "No one would ever believe our story otherwise."

There were many other suggestions, and the meeting went back and forth, often heatedly. During all this, the Admiral just listened. He then said, "I have listened to all your comments and advice. I agree with Captain Adams.

We will discuss these terms with the Elders of Heatherbound and the Dasurainians."

Chapter Thirty-four
Negotiations

Meanwhile, Michael Beckett and Pandit Pahlavi, as well as the rest of the Elders, were in the command bunker, preparing for the worst and wondering what was holding up the bombing. This was almost as bad as being bombed. They had not answered the last communications from the Federation fleet. What was there to say? Now all wondered when the Hell would begin.

"There is a communication coming in, but it is not from the Federation fleet."

"Put it on screen," said Pandit. "We will soon find out what is going on."

Suddenly on the screen appeared a very large purple being. Pandit's first thought was that the Federation was pulling some kind of trick, but what could it be?

I am Admiral Cadirex of the Dasurainian Empire. We come in peace and have stopped the Federated fleet from bombing you. They have agreed to a peace conference to stop this war. We wish you to suggest a time and place to accomplish this. We, the Dasurainians, would come to your meeting as a mediator and hope to help resolve your differences.

"Who are you, and why are you helping us?" Pandit said in a state of shock.

It is a long story and best told by Cameron McCreight. Please tell him that all thought blocking has been removed. He will be free to tell you the whole tale if he wishes.

"Thought blocking, what is this? Are you saying that you can block our thoughts?" Pandit was even more agitated, and Michael took over.

"Admiral Cadirex, you must be able to imagine how shocked and confused we are. We had no idea that there were other sentient beings in the universe. We have never come across any. Seeing you and conversing with you is astonishing. What has Cameron McCreight to do with you and this matter?"

He is the grandson of Kendell McCreight, the man to whom we owe friendship. He is also the man who finished the job that Kendell McCreight started over a hundred years ago.

The purple Admiral went on to say, *Admiral Knightson will be contacting you soon. I hope we can arrange a meeting between the three forces in the next twenty-four hours. During that time, you may contact Cameron McCreight for the history between the Dasurainians and the McCreights. To corroborate his story, you may wish to talk to Jutaro Komara and Peter Dugan. We will contact you again tomorrow morning.*

"The alien broke contact. Wait, there is another incoming communication," said the Comm Officer.

The Federation Admiral appeared on the screen looking haggard. "This is Admiral Knightson. By this time, you have seen your ally and now know that we are not going to bomb you or try to invade. We need to confer with each other over our differences so that there will not be another one of these confrontations in the near future. Please discuss this with your Elders and let us know when and where we can meet."

Michael answered for the Elders. "This has come as a complete surprise to us. We knew nothing of the aliens. At least the Elders knew nothing. We will need some time to gather information and to discuss this among ourselves. Our government will contact you in at ten tomorrow morning," said Michael Beckett.

Everyone looked stunned by the events. Michael put his trembling hands to his face to hide his tears of relief. A minute later, he heaved a sigh. He then straightened up and, in a firm voice, said, "Contact Cameron McCreight, Jutaro Komara, and Peter Dugan. Have them meet us here in one hour, if possible. We must hear the entire story before we can do much more. It looks like we have something else for which to thank the McCreights."

The Elder Council reconvened three hours later with the three men. Cameron asked to have Kaitlyn, Ian, and Sir John in attendance as well. This was granted. Cameron brought his grandfather's journal with him and told the story. Jutaro and Peter told of their labors on behalf of the Dasurainians, relieved and elated that they could finally talk about it.

It was agreed that the three forces would meet in two days at the Government Center in New Edinburgh. The meeting would consist of the two Admirals, their aides, and the two Elders, Pandit Pahlavi and Michael Beckett. They would try to hammer out an agreement and then take it to the full Elder's Council.

They met in one of the conference rooms at the Government Center in New Edinburgh. The room was on the third floor and had windows on two sides with a beautiful view of downtown. It was sparsely furnished, just a long table made of Cameron's bamboo cut in long strips and burnished to a high gleam. There were ten comfortable chairs. At each place were legal pads and pens, a carafe of water and a crystal glass.

The humans filed in and found places to sit. It was a rather subdued group, and very little talking was going on. The humans were trying not to think about the problem or how it would be resolved. This was impossible, of course, and that made the humans even more uncomfortable. All were excited and anxious to see and talk to the aliens but wanted to give the appearance that this was something they ran into every day.

Two Dasurainians arrived, Admiral Cadirex and his senior captain, Calan. All the humans rose when they entered and stared. There were a few soft exclamations. "They really do exist! They're so big! They do smell like cinnamon!" This was quickly hushed, and everyone resumed their seats with much rustling and scraping of chairs. The aliens found their chairs also, but the chairs were obviously much too small, and so they had to stand.

Everyone was embarrassed that this small problem hadn't been addressed. Pandit Pahlavi went to the door and asked someone to see about bringing something the aliens could sit on, even if it were just a bench. The Dasurainians said it wasn't important, but within a few minutes, a good-sized bench was brought in and placed at one end of the table. Soon all were seated again.

Still slightly embarrassed, Michael Beckett chaired the meeting and called it to order. "Gentlemen and Gentlebeings, this is a momentous occasion, not only because of actually sitting down with an alien race but because a war was averted through their intervention."

"My only regret is that the Dasurainians are seeing us at are very worst. We are an aggressive race, but I hope that we can prove to them that we can be reasonable." Michael looked at the admiral with concern in his eyes.

We have met several of your race and have been studying you for many years, said Admiral Cadirex. *There are the good and bad in all races. Yours is very young. I will admit to you that we were warlike when young also, and until we developed this form of telepathy, we fought to protect ourselves.*

This planet you call Heatherbound was discovered twenty-five years before it was settled by your colonists. But we do not claim it; it would not suit our needs. It is too warm for us and the heat makes us extremely uncomfortable. There are enough planets to suit our requirements without subjecting our people to discomfort.

Our race is quite sturdy and can withstand discomfort for long periods of time when necessary. We felt that it was necessary for you to see us on your own ground for the first meeting. That is why we are subjecting ourselves to this environment for a short period of time. I would like to adjourn this meeting now, and meet again at the cave at Winter's Grove. If that does not meet with your approval, we can return to our starship and continue via video transmission. He shrugged his shoulders in a veryhuman–like gesture and waved a hand, implying that it made no difference to him.

Our main contribution to this discussion would be to insure that all parties understand each other perfectly. We can do this, if you wish it, by opening up your abilities to hear each other's thoughts on the subject of this conflict, continued Admiral Cadirex.

There was a burst of shouting from most of the humans at this suggestion, and Admiral Cadirex soothed their minds with a quick explanation that only matters of the invasion would be open for all to know.

The Dasurainians waited for a few minutes while the humans calmed down and had quiet discussions among their groups. Then the aliens stood up to leave.

We will leave now and give you a chance to come to a decision. We will expect to hear from you in two hours. with quiet dignity, they turned and left the room. For such large beings, they moved with a graceful, proud motion.

After several minutes of debate with his group, Michael Beckett turned to the Earthmen. He said, "We feel that although it would be interesting to see the cave that the Dasurainians stayed in for one hundred years and the field of Turpina shrubs, it would not really add to our discussion. Winter's Grove is over an eleven-hour flight, and it would be uncomfortable for all, including the Dasurainians. We, of Heatherbound, feel that we can take their second suggestion and continue this conference here with a video link to their spaceship."

Michael looked down and adjusted the legal pad in front of him nervously. "Also, we are not afraid to open our minds to you on this subject of invasion. We have nothing to hide or be ashamed of, and I feel that we can trust the Dasurainians to keep their promise that there will be no eavesdropping on other matters."

Admiral Knightson nodded, looking uncomfortable said, "We of the Federated Union of Earth do not wish to make anyone uncomfortable and agree to continue here with a video link to the Dasurainians. We would also like to have a complete video copy of all transactions between us to take back to our superiors. Whereas I do not like the thought of anyone having access to my mind, I feel, as you do," continued the admiral, "that it would surely expedite our discussions. I need to discuss this a bit further with the Dasurainians on exactly how much of our thoughts will be made available on this subject."

"I do not have the privilege of doing as I wish. My duty is to follow my orders. The private thoughts on this subject from my men, and me, would have no bearing on the case. Therefore I wish to submit to Mr. Beckett the written demands of our world for his perusal." So saying, he handed Michael a portfolio of the demands.

"I move that we adjourn this meeting. We will confer with the Dasurainians before we can commit ourselves on this subject." He and Captain Adams stood and, after looking around the room for permission, prepared to leave.

"Thank you; we will study this," Michael motioned to the portfolio, "before the next meeting. Your concerns are completely understandable. I agree to adjourn this meeting. We shall meet here again after lunch at one o'clock if that meets with your approval," said Michael Beckett. He stood and offered his hand to shake. He respected the Admiral and felt that Knightson was not happy in his present job.

At one o'clock precisely, everyone had arrived and was seated. The video connection had been set up, and all was in readiness, but the meeting was not called to order. The Earthlings had conferred with the Dasurainians, and now the three groups must talk, off the record, before the actual negotiations could begin.

Admiral Cadirex was sitting at his command center on the starship, Calaban. There were other Dasurainians in the background sitting at banks of instruments. Somehow the Admiral looked even bigger than in real life. His dark purple fur looked sleek and well-groomed. He started the informal meeting via the video connection, *Greetings. I see that we are all gathered together again.

As you know, the Earthlings had some questions concerning the telepathy connection. I will endeavor to explain the situation. It is impossible to stop one's inner feelings about a subject from being blocked when an entity has agreed to open up his mind on that subject. The military is expected, in your society, to follow orders without question. This causes a severe conflict of conscience. My only suggestion is that the proceedings be recorded as agreed. The participants are to make no reference to the inner thoughts they will overhear. It is agreed that if I have anything to add to the meeting, Mr. Pandit Pahlavi will render it for the record.*

After a few minutes of whispering between Pandit and Michael, Michael said, "That is agreeable to us. Let the proceedings begin."

Michael shuffled the papers in front of him for a minute and then said, "The demands that you have made to Heatherbound are based on a pack of lies and propaganda. That is a harsh statement, but I have facts and figures to prove beyond any reasonable doubt that this entire fiasco is politically motivated."

There was a shocked exclamation from the Earthmen. Admiral Knightson started to rise to his feet.

Michael ignored them and continued. "First, Earth demands that we stop exporting subsidized oil to Earth. This is easy, since we have not sent one drop of oil, or fuel of any kind, from Heatherbound."

"We are still importing oil from Earth, but that will soon be unnecessary. We only import one million barrels a year now, and for Earth, that is a mere drop in the bucket compared to the oil consumption of your own planet. It is such a small amount that you're not exporting it will not help at all in lowering the price of oil to the common man. If indeed it did help, it would be so little as to be hardly noticeable."

"Second, you say the use of Steelite has disrupted the steel industry of Earth, and Earth demands that they be in control of it. Can anyone honestly believe that the product of one farm, on a planet that has just over two million people, could in anyway effect a worldwide industry as old and established as Earth's with its billions of people?"

"Third, the immigration problem. You say that we are discriminating against minorities, and this practice must be stopped. It is true that only twenty-five percent of the original colonists were of a minority race. These colonists put up their own money to come here, and all of Great Britain and Ireland were invited to participate. The only qualifications were money, skills, an independent spirit, and the courage to participate in the unknown. The first three thousand were accepted. That was all the room available. Our population is still about one-fourth from the minority races."

This was becoming a long speech, and Michael stopped for a drink of water. He then continued, "Great Britain helped the first colonists financially, about ten percent of the cost of the expedition, with the stipulation that we would give people from Great Britain first consideration when accepting immigrants. We still honor that commitment and will continue to do so."

"It has also been stated that we should open up our world to more people than we do at this time, and that it is unfair to allow only the wealthy or skilled to immigrate to Heatherbound. When we emigrated to Heatherbound, our goal was to live on a planet that was unpolluted, with room to expand for our children. We chose an agricultural planet in hopes that it would not tempt anyone to subjugate us."

"Heatherbound was founded by people who had similar interests and were willing and able to work. There are no free rides on Heatherbound, if someone needs temporary help, they must go to the church for it, and the church demands a commitment. We limit our birth rate and will continue to limit our immigration as we see fit. Earth has no right to dictate to us, and certainly not on moral grounds."

Michael quickly looked through the rest of the pages and said, "There are several other demands, but no surprises. Those which I have stated are the main articles, and we have heard them for many years. Heatherbound is a separate and independent world. We do not belong to Earth, nor do we want to. Our desire is to be trading partners on equal terms. Again, I say, this is an agricultural planet. We are no threat to Earth or its people. Our only wish is to be left in peace."

"That was very concise and to the point," said Admiral Knightson after a full minute to be sure that Michael was finished. "Earth does not agree with you on any of the points you have made. We represent your mother planet, and you owe her some consideration. I know what you are saying is what you believe, but I would like to see your facts and figures. Earth would not send a fleet to invade a free society without cause."

"The cause is what we have been accused of, greed," said Pandit Pahlavi in a reasonable voice. He had been sitting quietly, listening to everyone and their thoughts. "Their greed is not only for riches but for power and control. Also, fear. Fear that if this planet can make it on its own, then eventually all the outlying planets will, and together we could be a threat to Earth."

Admiral Knightson looked stony-faced at this accusation. The legal pad in front of him was blank. He hadn't even picked up a pen to doodle. He knew what Pahlavi had said was true, especially the fear for the future. "I do not have the authority to answer any of these allegations. Any agreement we could possibly come to would not be valid. So it is my opinion that this is a waste of time. Earth's leaders, your Elders, and the Dasurainians must hammer this out. I feel my only recourse is to take my fleet and return to Earth and try to explain why I was unable to accomplish my goal."

Dejected but unswerving in his decision, sitting ramrod straight, Knightson co, and what will happen if we try to invade again in the future. I honestly do not think Earth's leaders will go to this expense again, at least not in the near future."

Knightson poured himself some water and drank it. "I can transport any of the Elders that wish to go to Earth for the negotiations. The longer I stay, the more it is costing Earth, so I plan to leave as soon as possible. "The Dasurainians have said they will accompany us. Seeing and talking to them will explain to my superiors what has happened will be as soon as I can refuel and resupply my fleet."

The room was very quiet except for the rustling of papers. Pandit cleared his throat and said, "I will inform the Elders of your decision and make arrangements for your needs for a quick departure. We thank you for the kind offer of transportation, and we will consider it."

"For the record, this threat has caused Heatherbound great expense and disruption of normal life. Reparations will be discussed when we get to Earth." Pandit looked at Michael, a question on his face, asking Michael if there would be a subsequent discussion.

Michael was a little surprised by the speedy conclusion of the meeting but had nothing further to add. He rapped his gavel on the table and said, "Thank you all for joining us. The meeting is adjourned."

There was much scraping of chairs and low murmurings, and then all filed out of the room except Pandit. He sat thinking and making notes on his pad for quite some time.

The Federated fleet and the Dasurainians were on their way to Earth. There had been a batch of radio communications between them and Earth. Even so, much of Earth still did not know of the aliens. The Consortiums, and the governments of Earth, did not want to panic the people; at least, that was their excuse. But rumors had gotten out via the ham operators who had picked up the transmissions, and the news was spreading.

During the last two months, the Consortiums, and the Governments of the world, had been meeting practically around the clock to try to salvage their reputations and businesses. After many recriminations and 'I told you so's', nothing was, nor could be, done. They knew the lies couldn't be covered up, or even made to look respectable. They only thing they could do was say that they were thinking in the long term for the betterment of Earth, and it inhabitants. Some people even believed it.

The Dasurainians fleet could travel much faster than the Federated, so after a month of accompanying the slower spacecraft, the aliens said their farewells and proceeded to Earth. A month later, they arrived in Earth's solar system.

When the Dasurainians popped out of space, they did so over the three most populated areas of Earth, North America, Europe, and Asia. The Earthlings ran out of buildings, excited and wondering. The aliens immediately broadcast a calming effect to all. The people were stunned, but no rioting or panic occurred.

The streets soon became jammed with people looking up at the huge alien ships. It was eerily quiet. People spoke in whispers, but nothing seemed to be happening. They had heard rumors that the Dasurainians were coming, but few really believed it. What could they want? Was this an invasion?

The Dasurainians issued an invitation to the United Federation of Earth Headquarters to all the Heads of State via radio to come aboard Admiral Cadirex's flagship. When all had arrived, and were settled, they were shown the video transcript from Heatherbound. After the showing, not a sound was heard for a few seconds. All knew what they would see. Then President Carver from the United States of America spoke up. "Will this transcript have to be shown to the peoples of Earth?"

We have no interest in how your world is governed, nor will we make that decision. This is something that you will have to negotiate with the representatives from Heatherbound. As you could see from the transcript, we are only interested in stopping a war with our allies. And possibly trade with your planet in the future. Admiral Cadirex said resolutely.

The fleet finally arrived with the Heatherbounders, and the negotiations were swift. The Dasurainians wanted assurances that an invasion wouldn't happen again. The Heatherbounders also wanted this assurance, and that reparations would be made to Heatherbound for the cost of preparing for the illegal invasion.

The Heatherbounders went even further, and asked for punitive damages. These payments to be given to the other four outlying planets that had been unjustly, albeit legally, treated poorly by Consortiums for the last one hundred years. These planets were Snowball, Hades, Leilani and Hemiptera.

All debts would henceforth be forgiven, and they would have the right to trade with whomever they pleased.

The Consortiums countered saying this was too harsh and that Earth would be bankrupted. They, themselves could no longer conduct business, millions would be put out of work. There had to be some compromise.

This argument was countered with the new technology the Dasurainians had, and were willing to trade. One of which was cheap, non-polluting energy. there would be work for all. They also agreed not to broadcast the transcript.

The Governments, and the Consortiums, had no choice but to go along with the aliens. They had been fair and promised prosperity for the future of Earth.

Chapter Thirty-five
Neighboring Planets

Cameron had been gone four months. He had told Kaitlyn that he had to follow his conviction that the only safety for Heatherbound was to be united with the outer planets. She agreed, even though he would be gone for months at a time.

He, and others of like mind, had to help strengthen them. The only way they could was through investments. The charters of these planets were now changed, and they could trade with anyone for their natural resources. Businesses could now locate on these planets. And no one had a monopoly unique products the planets, including Hadean art.

Cameron planned to visit the four nearest planets. He had already been to Snowball. Hades was the next planet on his list. It was aptly named. It was chiefly desert, with high snowcapped mountains that surrounded the oceans. The interior was mostly sand and rocks made harsh by the extremely hot winds that could tear the skin off unprotected flesh. This is where most of the minerals, ores and precious gems were to be found. The Consortiums settled their colonist in this interior hellhole.

Hades had three oceans, small and saline. Nearly all of the water had to be distilled from these oceans. There was very little rainfall except in the Polar Regions, and along the windward side of the mountains. The shores around the oceans were not very wide, and were salt encrusted, with no arable ground. There were underground rivers that ran to the seas, and the colonists could tap into these when they could be found, but the consortiums had withheld the equipment to do so..

The colonists had built vast underground chambers with miles of connecting tunnels in the interior. The chambers and tunnels were created by the mining process, and then converted into living quarters. Most of their food was grown in hydroponic gardens or imported from Earth zt great cost. A little could be grown in the shelter of the mountains, but even this was often wiped out by weather.

It was a hard life, not what they had been promised. Most of the colonists on Hades were miners and geologists. They desperately needed biochemists and farmers. Their only industry besides mining was glass manufacturing. They excelled in this and it was going a long way to helping them get out of their debt to Earth, but the prohibitive cost of shipping was taking most of the profit. Cameron thought there might be a market for this beautiful glass artwork on Heatherbound. He planned to take a shipload back.

The Hadean's had also developed a glass that they could use for the ceilings of the tunnels and chambers that were close to the surface. These were four paned, reflected heat, and made in such a way that when the top pane was too scarred by the wind it was easily replaced. With natural sunlight in many of their tunnels they were happier; they didn't feel so much like cave dwellers.

There wasn't much Cameron could do for them by himself, but he could leave them with seeds from many of the plants he had received from the Dasurainians. He chose plants that were the most highly nutritious, and had high fat and protein content. He also wanted to leave them with a robot that had the knowledge of how to make their hydroponic gardens produce more.

These people were very suspicious of his motives, and couldn't believe he would do this out of the goodness of his heart. What would the Consortiums have to say about it? They had heard about the aliens, and the aborted invasions of Heatherbound. Some didn't believe a word of it, and others didn't see how it would affect them. Cameron got around that by buying their largest underground cavern from the governor, and hired women to work the gardens with the aid of the robot. Business they could understand and the governor could tax.

He set reasonable prices for his produce, and a decent wage for his workers. He knew it wouldn't be long before the women would sell the seeds and knowledge. He hoped that within a few years they would at least have a better, and more stable, supply of food.

Cameron explained about the fuel made from Turpina trees that grew only in freezing climates. He asked permission to buy the tops of the nearest mountains and go into the oil producing business with some of the businessmen there. He would leave the plants and a robot to tend to them. His partners would have to locate a cave for processing and check on the robot monthly.

He wasn't sure how fast the plants would mature on this planet but had hopes that there would be a small harvest within the year. He wished to share fifty percent of the profits with his partners. There was plenty of oil on this planet, but it was very high in sulfur and expensive to refine. He had no trouble finding partners.

'Poor Kaitlyn,' he thought, 'Now she will have to work out contracts and agreements for three more businesses. I wonder if the Dasurainians would be interested in trade in the glass art.

Hemiptera was next on his list. Cameron knew that its main export was a drug called Nirvana made from the carapaces of critters of this planet. With a mild dose of one pill, it relaxed you and allowed one to have a good night's sleep. The second use was for addicts, and this gave a terrific high with two pills. Three pills were used for medical purposes as an anesthesia. The reason it was so much in demand was that it had no side effects. Not even addiction.

Earth wanted it, and the carapaces of the crabs and spiders that lived on this planet were loaded with it. The carapaces had to be ground up with the salts of the seas from this planet. Nothing else seemed to have the same effect.

Cameron circled the planet in search of the spaceport, and waited for permission to land. The security was very strict and the port was small. Hemiptera was mostly a water planet, with many small islands. He had been informed that the seas were shallow and very salty. All water had to be distilled for drinking and even bathing. He wondered how large the population was.

Finally his call was acknowledged and he was given permission to land. Cameron was surprised to see an iridescent barrier surrounding the space station. It was about twenty feet high and very beautiful. He wondered how strong it was.

Armed guards were there to receive him. Their armor looked to be made of the same material as the barrier, stranger and stranger, he thought. He was greeted respectfully, and taken to the commandant of the space station. After looking at Cameron's papers the Commandant Blakeson said rather brusquely, "I see that you are from Heatherbound. What is your reason to come to Hemiptera?"

Cameron understood that this was a no nonsense man. He decided to get down to business immediately and forego the polite small talk. "I am here for trade purposes. We have no need for your drug, Nirvana, but it has its uses, and if you wish to sell it to us, I'm sure there would be a market. Hemiptera has to have a lot of its food imported; we've been lead to believe.

We, that is, Heatherbound wish to become the breadbasket of the outer planets. Because we are so close, the import fees would be much less than Earth's, and fresher."

"You must have heard about the aborted invasion of Heatherbound and the relaxation of the hold that Earth has on these outer planets. Heatherbound feels that by becoming trading partners we could have an alliance which would perhaps deter Earth from trying to take any of us by force again, at least in the near future." Still standing Cameron waited for a reply.

"Please be seated." He waved Cameron to a seat in front of his desk. "We have little association with the outside world. I am afraid my manners are lacking."

"Earth buys all our Nirvana, but I think if we had other markets, Earth might give us a better price. We have little else to bargain with," Commandant Blakeson said, with a gesticulation of frustration.

Cameron said in his most persuasive style, "You have salt, different kinds of salt. Heatherbound has little salt, and needs to import more. I'm sure that Leilani could use some of your special salts to curb the growth of their jungles that constantly encroach on their cultivated lands. I also understand that the crab meat is mostly wasted when you harvest. That also could be processed and exported."

Then with a questioning look of his face, Cameron asked, "If I may be so bold to ask, what is that material you have as a barrier, and why is it necessary? I noticed that your guards wear what looks like the same material as armor."

"That, Sir, is spider silk. When treated with certain chemicals it is as strong as steel and as light as a feather. It is also very flexible. The winds on Hemiptera are very strong at times and loaded with salt. Glass domes did not last long under the onslaughts. We had to come up with an alternative." He said with almost a dismissive air.

"Commander Blakeson you have come up with another trade item. It seems to me that you must have found many uses besides barriers and armor."

"Sir, you have given me a lot to think about. I understand your desire to help Heatherbound, but what's in it for you? People don't just fly around in spaceships for purely humanitarian purposes." said with a note of skepticism in his voice.

"You're right, of course. We had a good scare with the aborted invasion. When I say we, I mean my family and I. We manufacture Steelite, and it has made us very rich. I have a wife and two children and a very good life. I want to keep it that way and I feel an alliance with the closer planets will help insure that."

Commandant Blakeson nodded his head and pursed his lips. "That, I can relate to. Could you stay a few days? I would like to show you about our small world. Perhaps you can come up with even more ideas."

Smiling, Cameron replied, "I'd be happy to. Do you have a hotel here or rooming house?"

"You would be my guest. My wife would never forgive me if I allowed someone as interesting as you to be housed anywhere else."

Cameron arrived with a package for his hostess. It was a modern piece of glass art from Hades. It depicted a man and woman entwined. She was completely enthralled with it. "I've never seen anything so beautiful. It really is too precious. I can't accept it."

"Please accept it. I wanted you to have a piece of this artwork."

Still hesitant, but aching to accept, Mrs. Blakeson said, "How can I thank you? Where is it from?"

"It is from the planet Hades. They hope to export this kind of art work to the other planets. Heatherbound has opened a store just for this artwork. They are hoping to open stores on each of the other planets."

That night the commandant's wife served Cameron a dinner of local foods. They had sea trout, tubers, and a salad from their hydroponics garden. With it was an interesting wine of a deep yellow color. It's taste was difficult to describe, but tasty and seemed quite strong.

Sipping his wine and eating Cameron remarked. "This is absolutely delicious, Mrs. Blakeson." He turned to the Commandant and asked. "Is this a local wine? Its taste is very unusual, but high-quality."

Smiling and with pride, "Yes, it is a local wine. We make it out of a fruit something like a Kumquat. It grows on a bush that is native to this planet." Swirling the wine in his glass and looking at the legs.

"Do you make enough of it to export, do you think?"

"We have five or six breweries on the Islands. I'll check with them and find out."

Cameron spent several more days on Hemiptera and came up with a few more ideas to export. He loaded his spaceship with ten cases of the wine, called Amber, six cases of smoked crab meat, five cases of salt, and two cases of Nirvana. He also took a bolt of the spider silk. For the Nirvana they charged him the same price that they charged Earth, but told him they had high hopes for a better price in the future.

Last, but not least, was Leilani, a humid, hot planet almost covered with rain forest and jungle. There were man-eating plants named Devil-Traps, that could throw their vines at an animal or person and ensnare them. Once captured the plant drew them into its maw and dissolved them with digestive acids. It was not an easy death. Besides these horrible plants, Leilani also had several predatory animals, and large herbivores.

It was about the size of Earth and had one very large land mass and four smaller ones. There were two mountain ranges on the large land mass and that was the safest place for humans to live but the work was in the rain forests and jungles. They were sent to colonize this planet for the medicines found in the plants found there. Earth had completely wiped out all the rain forest on her world, and covered them with cultivated farm lands, but she still needed these medicines.

Even in the mountains, the colonists had to maintain a vigilance against the encroaching vegetation. Earth mandated that only the mountains of this world could be cultivated. The rest of the planet was to be kept free of any form of civilization. To be kept a pristine world for scientific research. Most of the colonists were botanists and biochemists. It was also a hunter's paradise. Earth allowed anyone who could afford it, to come and hunt the animals of Leilani.

Hunting was okay with the colonists. It was a source of income as well as ridding Leilani of some of the fiercest predators. The animal that looked like the saber toothed tiger was the hunters favorite trophy. They also liked the tusks of the elephant like creatures. The colonist did not limit the number of predators they could bag, but limited the herbivores to only one..

Cameron was guided to the spaceport by a beacon. He was met by the governor who knew of the McCreight name. The governor wined and dined Cameron, then took him on a tour of the facilities, including the housing areas, and generally made him feel very important.

In exchange, Cameron gave the governor's wife a piece of the Hades artwork, and the governor a case of Amber wine from Hemiptera. Needless to say they were impressed.

After an especially fine dinner the governor asked Cameron to come into his study. He offered him a brandy and a cigar imported from Earth. After some small talk, they finally got down to business.

The Governor said, "From what I understand you want to start a trading alliance between the outer planets. I like the artwork from Hades and the wine from Hemiptera. What else do they have to offer? And what's more, what do we have to offer in return?"

"Pharmaceuticals is what you have and, of course, the hunters. Leilani is one of the riches of the outer planets. You can afford to buy anything you want. With less shipping costs you can get things cheaper, and the food fresher. I believe the special salt that comes from Hemiptera will stop the encroachment of the jungles that surrounds your compounds. I feel it will also kill the Devil-Traps."

"I've been told that you have tried everything and nothing worked. It wouldn't hurt to try throwing a brick of salt into the maw if captured by the vines. Everyone would have to carry the salt bricks whenever they venture into the jungles."

Cameron leaned forward in his chair. "I can't guarantee it, but I think it's worth a try."

Chapter Thirty-six

Audit

It was two months after the Earth fleet had left. Sir John was in his office talking to his accountant. There had been so much confusion and problems with the trial and the invasion that the biannual auditing of the accounts had been neglected.

The accountant was a tall, thin man who was usually very calm and businesslike. Today he was nervous and looked pained. "Sir John, I, um, I found a discrepancy in the books for a rather large amount of money. Fifty thousand credits, to be exact. My books list this as new equipment, paid to an account on Earth. Your son Sean wrote the check. I can find no invoice for that amount, nor is there any record of equipment received."

"When was the check written?" Sir John asked quietly.

"It was written the day before the trial started." The accountant looked away, not wanting to meet Sir John's eyes. He had his suspicions and hoped that Sir John wouldn't kill the messenger, metaphorically speaking, of course.

Sir John suddenly looked ten years older. "I see. Thank you. I'll look into it. Were there any other discrepancies?"

After the accountant left, Sir John sat there for a few minutes, hoping to God that this was not what he thought. He had his secretary summon Sean to his office. He had followed Cameron's advice and his heart and forgiven Sean. Now he wondered if they had both made a mistake.

Sean had known that the accountant was in to see his father. When he took the money, he was sure that he would win the trial and have more than enough to repay the 'loan'. He knew that he had to put on the act of his life. He went bustling into the office and sat down, a smile on his face. "Hi Dad, what can I do for you?"

Sir John sat at his desk with some papers in front of him. He obviously didn't want to talk about the problem, but it must be faced. "Our accountant just left. He had some very unpleasant news concerning the accounts. Perhaps you can clear it up."

"If I can, I will. What was it? An unpaid bill or an overpaid one." Sean laughed, leaning back in his chair, his hands behind his head, as if he was enjoying this.

"You wrote a check for fifty thousand credits some time back for equipment. We never received the equipment nor can we find an invoice." Sir john was a little annoyed at Sean's flippancy. "Do you think that's funny too?"

Sean sat up straight and looked serious. "Yes, I remember writing a check for that amount. I remember because it was such a large amount. Cameron said he needed new equipment for the farms for security. I thought it was a bit much, but knowing how you felt about security, I went ahead and gave him the check."

"You expect me to believe that you gave a check to Cameron for that large amount without quibbling or coming to me?" said Sir John, a touch of sarcasm in his voice.

"You had been complaining that we don't get along and that I should make some effort to try. This was my big gesture." Sean jumped out of his chair threw and his arms wide. "See what it gets me?"

"You're very good at playing the injured party, Sean. But not this time. I don't believe a word of it, and even if it costs me another fifty thousand credits, I'll get to the bottom of this."

*

Sir John was sitting at his desk in his office, gazing off into space while drumming his fingers on the blotter in front of him. He had found little pleasure in working lately. Was it all for naught? His suspicions of Sean had soured their relationship, and he felt he couldn't trust him. This was breaking Lady Helen's heart. He was waiting for a coded message from Earth that had recently arrived. He dreaded seeing it.

There was a soft knock on the door, and Bigley, his secretary, entered the room. "I believe this is the message you have been looking for, Sir. Would you need anything else?"

"Thank you, Bigley. No, that will be all."

He went to his safe and took out his codebook. After a short while, he found that his worst fears were confirmed. The money had been sent to an account in Timothy's name. It made matters worse to realize that Sean didn't even try to be subtle about his dishonesty.

He buzzed his secretary, "Please tell Sean and his wife to join me in my office at one o'clock today. Also, inform Edward that I will need him around two. Thank you."

Both Sean and Glendora arrived a little early and together. Bigley showed them in, and Sir John dismissed him.

"Please sit down, both of you. I have something rather unpleasant to tell you, and I want you to hear it together." There was a moment of silence, and they both sat down. Sean was very nervous. Glendora was puzzled but not overly worried. She knew nothing about Sean's theft. "Sean, I am going to disinherit you in favor of your eldest son."

"But, but…" sputtered Sean.

Holding up his hand to stop Sean, Sir John continued, "You may keep your position as President of this company, but all checks over five hundred credits will have to be signed by me. I will not embarrass you by making this known. Only our accountant will be aware of it. Your salary will be the same, one hundred thousand credits a year. A sum of ten thousand credits will be deducted until the discrepancy has been paid for. I won't charge you interest."

He waved his hand. "Now you may talk."

Sean had turned very pale, and there was perspiration on his forehead. "Father, let me explain. I really felt that the Teraline should be mine. Grandfather had no right to give my inheritance away as he did. I didn't think this would affect anyone except Cameron."

Sean took a deep breath, " I honestly didn't think that Earth would try to take us over, that the defense effort was unnecessary."

"Even if what you say is true, it doesn't change the fact that you stole from the company." Sir John stood up, leaned over his desk, and pointed at himself. He shouted. "From me!"

Glendora was shocked and angry. She leaned forward in her chair and spoke up then, "Cameron doesn't need the money from Teraline, and we do. Our salaries are just not enough to live in the style expected of heirs apparent. We have major expenses, and we must work for our fathers, not have businesses of our own, as Cameron has."

"You will probably live another eighty years." She was getting rather heated in her argument. Getting up, she walked around her chair. Turning back to Sir John, she said, "How do you expect us to live on what we make during that time?"

Sir John was stunned and sat down again. "I can't believe what I'm hearing. Cameron shouldn't have the money because he doesn't need it as much as you two do. You can't live on two hundred thousand credits a year? You have a position to uphold?"

Sir John was red in the face and practically yelling. "Who says you have to have a mansion twice the size of either of your parents? Why do you have to go off the planet every year to extremely expensive places for your vacations?"

"As to having to work for your parents, that is true, and you are very well paid for it. You could save some of your money and invest it so that you would have other income besides those salaries that you sneer at."

He looked directly at Glendora. "What did you do with the two hundred thousand credits that you received for your dowry, Glendora? Your sister invested hers in a friend."

"That was to set up a household as you very well know!" Glendora said with some heat.

"You know Glendora, you and Sean should thank me. Now that you are no longer heirs apparent of the McCreight family, you don't have to spend so lavishly. Think of all the money you will have now?"

"Your wit is not appreciated, Sir John. We still have my inheritance to live up to!" Glendora was not having it, and was not afraid of her father-in-law.

Sean sat through this dialog, too stunned to say anything.

"Enough! You've heard what I had to say, and your arguments have made me wonder why I was so blind. You're just two greedy, selfish children. Now leave my office. I have an appointment with my lawyer."

He buzzed his secretary. "The McCreight's are leaving. Please tell Edward I'm free now."

"I suppose you had him come immediately after our interview to insure that I didn't kill you tonight before you could change your will?" said Sean savagely.

"One crime often begets another, Sean." Sir John said tiredly. "I'm ashamed to say the thought had occurred to me."

Chapter Thirty-seven

Luncheon

Kaitlyn and Glendora still met for lunch at least once a month. Even with the problems between the brothers, they were close. It was an unspoken agreement that they would not discuss family problems, at least about the brothers. Usually, they talked about mutual friends, parties they had attended, shopping, and bragging about their children. It was a day they both looked forward to, and enjoyed.

Today would be no different, Kaitlyn thought with a smile as she spied Glendora already sitting at their favorite table. Oh, Oh, maybe not. She's already drinking a double martini and smoking what looks like an Ecstasy. That means trouble; she only resorts to drugs when she is really upset.

The waiter met her at the door and said, "This way, Mrs. McCreight, Mrs. McCreight has already arrived."

"Thank you, Andre." She followed him through the crowded room, and they treaded their way to Glendora's table. She saw several people she knew along the way but didn't stop to chat, just waved, as she could see Glendora's agitation.

When she arrived at the table, Glendora did not get up to give Kaitlyn a hug as she usually did. So Kaitlyn leaned down and kissed her on the cheek before she sat down.

Andre gave her a menu and asked, "Would you like something to drink before you order?"

Before Kaitlyn could say anything, Glendora said, "Yes, bring us both a double martini."

"That will be all right, Andre, but first, take us to a private room for our luncheon," said Kaitlyn, thinking fast on her feet. She didn't want another embarrassing scene similar to what had happened the last time that Glendora overindulged.

Andre understood exactly. Taking Glendora's drink and gently helping her to her feet, he led them to a private room with a large window overlooking the park. A low bowl of roses was on the table, and the chairs were upholstered wingback in soft blue velvet. Something about the room made you feel very special.

Glendora had been protesting all the way until she saw the room. "Kaitlyn, why don't we always get this room? Why must you be such a penny-pincher?"

"This will do very nicely," said Glendora sitting down and then turning to Andre. "Now, bring us those drinks."

"Of course, Madam." He said as he put down the drink he had carried for Glendora, handed a menu to Kaitlyn, and then turned to leave.

"Andre, I'll have the Cobb salad," said Kaitlyn. "Have you decided, Glendora?"

"Cobb salad sounds good. I'm not hungry anyway."

As soon as the waiter left, Glendora started in. "As much money as you and Cameron have now. I can't believe you are wearing last year's suit. You can afford to dress better. In fact, you have lots more money than I do. You can just buy lunch today."

Before Kaitlyn could say a word, Glendora continued, "Did you know that your father-in-law just disinherited Sean in favor of our eldest? All because of your Cameron! Some trumped-up embezzlement scheme that was blamed on Sean. Who, I am quite sure, was innocent."

"Now, wait a minute, " said Kaitlyn in a cold voice. "This is the first I'd heard of Sean's disgrace with our father-in-law. And if you are implying that Cameron had anything to do with it, think again. Sean has tried to discredit Cameron from day one. I don't know why Sean is so jealous of him, but he's done everything in his power to make Cameron's life miserable."

"What do you mean jealous? How can the eldest son be jealous of any sibling? He was only fighting for his rights if you're talking about the Teraline."

"I've been talking since they were children, and if you would think back, you would know it too. Some of the things he did weren't just childish pranks."

"Sean was young, foolish. Cameron's no angel!" said Glendora heatedly.

"This isn't getting us anywhere, and we promised not to talk about our husbands." Kaitlyn knew that this could get ugly. She said in a calmer voice. "What's the real problem, Glendora? Why are you so unhappy?"

"What makes you think I am unhappy?"

"You only drink and do drugs together when you are depressed or worried."

Andre arrived just then with the drinks and the salads. He took a bit on himself to bring them together, but he was a very good waiter and knew that these ladies needed privacy. He also put rolls and butter on the table and said, "Will there be anything else?"

"Not right now, thank you, Andre, "said Kaitlyn.

As soon as the waiter left, Glendora's tears started down her cheeks. "I'm worried sick. We are drowning in debt. What with the house, lawyer's fees, court expenses, and day-to-day living? We just can't make it. Sean refuses to cut back on anything, and I haven't bought a new outfit in months." All this came tumbling out. Pushing her salad away, she put her arms on the table and laid her heard on them and wept in earnest.

Kaitlyn patted her arm and waited quietly until Glendora quieted down. When Glendora looked up, took out a tissue, and blew her nose, Kaitlyn said, "I could loan you money, but that wouldn't really help. What you need is another business or two to keep you occupied and bring in more money."

"What business could I possibly go into? I work with my father's business. I don't have time for anything else. My life is just work, work, work, and it's dull, dull, dull."

"I happen to know that you work two, maybe three days a week with Dad. That gives you plenty of time to run another business, with qualified help, of course." She put up her hand to stop Glendora from saying anything.

"It just so happens that I have some contacts with some artisans in Hades. They do really beautiful glass sculptures, vases, what-have-you, and want to open up a market for their wares on Heatherbound. Cameron came back with a shipload of the stuff and wanted me to set up a business. I don't have the expertise in this field, or the contacts you have, to make a go of it."

"Your taste is exquisite and respected by your peers; you could open up a gallery and make a fortune." Kaitlyn could see that she had Glendora's undivided interest, a look of hope started to dawn on her face. "If that doesn't appeal to you, how about a boutique of your own designs? You've been designing clothes since you were five. You made them for our dolls, remember?"

Glendora face lit up with excitement. "My God, you're right! I love both ideas." She stubbed out her Ecstasy. "When can I see the glass? I know a great shop that's up for rent right in the middle of the smartest shopping center in New Edinburgh. It's big enough for both. Maybe I could design some clothes using glass beads or whatever." She grabbed her purse and started to get up. "Let's get out of here."

"No way, I'm hungry, and I am going to eat this wonderful-looking salad first," said Kaitlyn with a chuckle.

They ate and talked for the next half-hour. Kaitlyn took pity on Glendora and skipped the coffee and dessert. Andre presented the bill, and Kaitlyn paid, giving Andre a generous tip.

"First things first," said Glendora. "We'll look at the glass, and then we'll rent that shop. Come with me and see if you like it."

"I'll come with you, with pleasure, but I don't plan on being partners with you if that's what you mean by 'we'll rent the shop.' I really don't have time for any more business ventures.

"Oh, I thought that is what you wanted. That's okay, though. I can swing it on my own. If I needed it, Dad would give me a loan. It will be fun, but I would like your opinion. I don't think I'll tell Sean about this until it's a big success."

The first thing they did was to go to the warehouse where Cameron had stored the glassware. Glendora had workmen open all the crates. She and Kaitlyn spent several hours going through them. Kaitlyn fell in love with a few pieces and kept them. The rest Glendora wanted for her shop.

Glendora was thrilled and couldn't wait to get started. She loved almost every piece. They were exquisite, much better than she expected. She hadn't felt so excited in years. There was so much to do, people to hire, clerks, and seamstresses. Oh, it was going to be the most exquisite shop in the area. She told the workers to pack it all up carefully, and she would give them the address where to send it in a few days.

Next, they went to the store. Glendora walked around, took note of this and that, and rented it. She talked the owner into a ten-year lease and made him promise to do some renovations because of the long lease. She would have plans for him tomorrow, and she wanted to move in the next week.

Glendora took her laptop from her purse, sat down at a desk, and began to draw plans of what she wanted done for her gallery. Kaitlyn said goodbye quietly. She wasn't even sure that Glendora heard her as she slipped out.

When she got home that evening, Cameron ate in the kitchen with the children. Robert was telling his dad all about his adventures at school, and Megan was playing with her food. She was a picky eater and didn't like anything mixed or touched. Mostly she wasn't hungry; she had talked Glenys into giving her a cookie just before dinner.

Glenys knew that today was Kaitlyn's day with her sister and usually came home late. She had made dinner and left for the evening. Kaitlyn fixed herself a plate and joined them. She was dying to tell Cameron all about her day, but that could wait until the children were in bed. Cameron had only been home a few days and cherished his time with them when he was home.

Robert had finished his tale about the school, and Megan wanted to leave the table and have a story read. Robert thought that was a good idea too. Cameron picked them both up and carried them into to living room to read while Kaitlyn straightened up the kitchen.

After the children were in bed, Kaitlyn and Cameron went to sit on the porch. It was a beautiful moonlit night, and the air was filled with the smell of honeysuckle.

Cameron pulled her close and said, "O.K., now that we're alone, you can tell me all the news. I know you've been bursting with it since you got home."

She settled back in his arms and said, "I have? Did you know that your father has disinherited your brother in favor of their eldest?"

Cameron was startled, he pushed himself upright, and away from Kaitlyn, so he could look into her eyes. "What? Why?"

Kaitlyn went on. "Glendora didn't really go into it. Something about embezzling, and she seemed to think it was your fault in some way. She wasn't making a lot of sense because she had had a little too much to drink. She also said they were broke, and she was at her wits end."

"I can't believe it! Dad didn't mention it to me, and I saw him just this afternoon."

He was quiet for a moment. "How can they be broke? Between the two of them they must be making two hundred thousand credits a year. I know they have had a lot of legal expenses, but still, that's a lot of money to spend."

"It doesn't matter how they spend it. They just do. I gave her the glass franchise with Hades. I hope you don't mind. I really don't have the time to do all these businesses you keep coming up with, and she would be perfect for it. Also she's been so bored lately with just my father's business. She really has an artistic bent, and even though she's a whiz at her job with Dad, she needs another outlet."

Cameron pulled away from her and was silent for a few minutes. His bitterness towards his brother clouded his mind. He said sarcastically, "That was very generous of you to help Sean that way."

Kaitlyn understood and pulled Cameron's face towards her. Softly she said, "I didn't do it for Sean. I did it for Glendora, and we certainly don't need the money. And by her account, she does."

"I'm sorry, Honey," Cameron said sullenly. "You're right. It's just that Sean has tried to ruin us for so long, and just about succeeded, that I want nothing to do with him. I wish Glendora weren't your sister at times. And I know that that isn't fair, but I can't help it. If he weren't my brother, I would hate him. I think I do anyway."

"Well, now you can feel sorry for him. He's lost the most precious thing that he felt he had, and that was the McCreight Enterprises."

Chapter Thirty-eight

Stowaways

Ian was expecting a small shipment of silver from Earth. It was about six months overdue because of the troubles. He was engrossed in the data he had been getting from +1 when the telephone interrupted him.

The call was from the spaceport. "This is dispatcher Hamish at the spaceport. Your shipment from Earthworks, Inc. has arrived. Would you like it delivered by courier, as usual?"

Ian had been working his usual ten to twelve-hour days and decided he needed a break. Looking out the window, he noticed for the first time that it was a beautiful day. One too nice to stay cooped up in an office. "No. I'll pick it up myself. See you shortly, and thanks, I appreciate your looking out for me."

"No problem, anything for a good customer," Hamish laughed. "Hey, how about moving my name to the head of the list for a new Pegasus? You are involved with that new ceramic hovercraft, aren't you?"

"You know I am," said Ian, grinning. "What color do you want?"

"Oh wow! Do you mean it?"

"Sure. You've been looking after me for years. It's the least I can do."

"Thanks, Mr. Scott. Make it silver with purple stripes."

"Pretty fancy. Sure, you can afford it."

"Yeah, my wife and I have been saving half our pay each month. Got enough for the down. How soon do you think we'll have it?"

"The first ones came off the line last month. I'd say you'll be notified next month."

"Fantastic! The wife will be good to me tonight! Thanks, Mr. Scott. See you this afternoon." Hamish was so excited he didn't notice that he hung up on Ian.

Ian sat there for a minute with the phone in his hand, grinning. It's nice to make someone so happy. He buzzed his interphone and told his secretary that he would be gone for the rest of the day. I may as well leave right now before I get involved with something else. I'll have lunch at the port. That should be interesting.

Ian enjoyed his walk back to his apartment. It was a particularly beautiful day, crisp and clean after the rain last night. Walking by the small park near his apartment, he could smell the freshly mown grass, and he saw a squirrel run up a tree. This made him realize anew that he was putting in too many hours at work. He needed to get out more. This short walk had been his only exercise for months. Now that the trial was over, perhaps the three of them could get together for a weekend somewhere. He'd love to see Lake Placid.

Arriving back at his apartment, he went to the roof where his hover-craft was parked. He got in and flew it towards the spaceport. There was a pub he used to go to occasionally nearby. He had heard that it had changed hands but that the food was still good. He thought he would try it for old times' sake. He found it immediately, and there was a space right in front to park his hover-craft. Boy, am I lucky today, or what.

After parking, he went inside. The place looked smaller and darker. It reeked of stale beer and rancid food. Not too appetizing, he thought. There were quite a few people, mostly men, all eating and drinking beer. The noise level was pretty high. That was a good sign, at least. He stepped in and waited for a few minutes for his eyes to adjust before he could make his way to the bar.

A thin, ragged-looking waitress was coming towards him. She had raven-black hair with a widows-peak tied back into a ponytail. A few strands had gotten loose and hung straight down. Her heart-shaped face was very pale, and there were smudges of purple under her large dark eyes. Her eyes were so dark he couldn't tell if they were blue or brown. She looked exhausted. She also looked too fragile to be carrying heavy trays, and he wanted to reach out and help her.

She passed him by with a tray of beer in her hand, holding it above her head while holding a dish in the other hand. He watched her place the food on a nearby table and start to swing the beer down. Suddenly a man reached out and grabbed her breast. She screamed and dropped the entire tray of beer on his head. Drenched with beer, the man jumped up, startled and sputtering.

The owner was standing nearby and ran over to see what had happened. Seeing the broken mugs and beer all over the place, he yelled, "Yu dirty slut. Now see what you've done." He hit her, knocking her down, and kicked her for good measure.

"That'll teach yu. Now get up and clean up this mess. That will come out of your wages, yu hear!"

Ian was shocked by the events. Seeing red, he ran over to help the waitress. He grabbed the owner and hit him, knocking him into a table of drunks. The drunks picked the owner up and threw him across the room, flattening the table he landed on. The beer soaked man took a swing at Ian, missing. Ian hit him in the stomach and, when he doubled over, socked him on the chin. He landed on another table, spilling everyone's beer and food. This started a free-for-all, everyone getting into the fight.

The waitress was still on the floor. Ian thought she must be badly hurt. Stooping, he reached down to help her get up. Her face was all puffed up, and it looked like she might soon have a black eye. When she tried to walk, she groaned and swayed, almost fainting. A bottle came flying at them, just missing her head. He picked her up, and with much dodging and darting, ran from the pub. He put her down next to his hovercraft. She started to cry.

"What will I do now," she sobbed, her face in her hands. "I needed that job."

"You can get something better than that. I'll help you," said Ian. "Let me take you home."

"You can't help me. No one can. They'll deport me. Vernon said that if I didn't work here and give him half my wages and tips, he would report me and my family to the immigration authorities." She was crying so hysterically by now that he almost couldn't understand her.

"Stop crying, and get in the hovercraft quickly before the police come. I'll take you to your home. I promise you, I'll think of something," said Ian. He took her arm and helped her into the hovercraft. She struggled a bit and then gave up and sat quietly.

In a very subdued voice, "I live just a few blocks away. I can walk to it if you let me go."

"There is no housing near by." Ian was starting to get a little angry. "What do you take me for? I positively do want to help you. I'm not going to molest you."

She looked up at him. Her one good eye looked defiant. "Honestly, I really do live just a bit away. We live in a packing crate." She hung her head, too embarrassed to look him in the eye after that statement. Making an effort, she stopped crying and seemed calmer. "Just temporary until we can all get some kind of work and get away from the docks," she continued softly.

"O.K., we'll hop over there. Give me directions."

"Go down three blocks and turn left. We are in the alley. Vernon set us up there."

"Who's Vernon," said Ian as he followed her directions.

"He's the man that got us off Snowball. He worked in the hydroponic gardens on his ship and said we could stow away in them. He assured us that we wouldn't be found there, and when we got to Heatherbound, he would find good jobs for us. We gave him all the money we had and believed him."

They had arrived at the alley. Ian parked the hovercraft, came around, and helped her out. She could barely stand, and he half carried her to the crate. He could see three people inside. A man lying down on a blanket, a woman seated next to him on the floor of the crate, and a boy of about six or seven standing, trying to look brave.

"Mom, Dad, don't be frightened. I had an accident, and this kind man helped me." She pulled away from him and went to the little boy. She held the boy in front of her, leaning on him for support.

Ian looked around. There was no food to be seen, and they all looked dirty and very hungry. No blankets except the one the man was on, and it would get colder tonight. Ian couldn't leave them like this. It would be inhumane.

In a no nonsense voice, Ian said, "Pack whatever you have. You're all leaving this place and coming with me. I have a large house that I will take you to tomorrow. Tonight we'll have to make do with my apartment in town."

"When was the last time you ate? No, forget that. First, we'll get something to eat, get you some clothes, and then go to my apartment."

They all looked at him as if he were crazy. Mrs. Wansky sat up a little straighter. "We have no money to pay you, and I won't sell my children. So please just go away. We'll manage, don't worry."

"I'm not going away. I made a promise to your daughter to help you," Ian said with a smile. "And I always keep my promises."

They still didn't believe him and didn't make a move.

"Come on. What do you have to lose? You'll get a meal and a place to stay tonight. If you still don't trust me, you can always leave."

"Momma, he seems nice, and as he says, what do we have to lose," said Laurna. She turned to Ian and reached out her hand, saying, "We haven't been introduced. My name is Laurna Wansky. This is my mother, Kiela, my father, Jakin, and my brother Jonathan. I don't know your name."

"My name is Ian Scott." He made a short bow to Laurna and then to her mother. "It is a pleasure meeting you all, and now I think we must hurry before someone wonders what we are all doing in this alley."

"You're right." So saying, Laurna went to her father to help him get up. The man looked pale and deathly sick. He was missing his left hand, his left shoulder looked misshapen under his shirt, and the left side of his face was badly scarred. His dark hair was long and hid his ear, but Ian thought it was probably missing. This poor man has been in a terrible accident, Ian thought. I wonder why he hasn't been rejuvenated in a medicube.

"Here, let me help you," said Ian. He lifted him up and put his arm around his waist from the right side. "We should get you to a doctor. You don't look well, Sir."

"No! No doctor. They ask too many questions," Kiela said as she helped her husband walk, holding him around the waist on the left side. Jakin was biting his lip to stop himself from groaning from the pain. Ian noticed they both looked a lot like Laurna and so did Jonathan. All had dark hair, deep blue eyes, high cheekbones, a very handsome family.

They hurried to the hovercraft; Ian put the parents and brother in the back, Laurna in front with him. He took off hurriedly and went to the nearest shopping mall. He saw they had nothing to take with them, not even the blanket. Vernon was probably charging them for the use of that, he thought with disgust.

Ian landed the craft and said, "You all stay here. I'll buy some food and some clothes from those vending machines right over there. You can watch me from here. I'll only be a minute."

Ian went to the juice machine first and got real orange juice for them all. He took that back to them. "All they have are ham or fish sandwiches. Oh, and some beef soup. What would you like?"

"Laurna, you go help him. No, on second thought, you're looking worse all the time." Turning to Jonathan, Kiela said, "You help him, son."

Jonathan scooted out. He and Ian got the soup and brought it back. Jonathan asked for some ham sandwiches, too, for later. Ian went back and bought the sandwiches. Next, he went to the machines that had quick clothes changes. He bought pantsuits for everyone, hoping that the sizes he guessed at were close enough.

Ian was hungry too, and ate a sandwich while he flew to his apartment. Landing on the roof, he helped them disembark and led them to his penthouse apartment. It was only two bedrooms but he liked it, and it was close to work. He enjoyed the ten-minute walk twice a day, even when it rained.

The Wansky family was a little intimated by the beauty of the room they could see from the top of the landing. Only the very rich on Snowball had anything like this. A spiral staircase led from the roof down to the living room. The walls were a sand color, and the carpeting was a forest green. In front of a fireplace were two matching couches covered with rich brown leather, a glass table between them. Two walls were floor to ceiling windows, and the view from this tenth-floor apartment was magnificent. They didn't quite know what to do except they knew they were not going to sit on that furniture with their dirty clothes.

"I'm sure the first thing you will want to do is freshen up and get into some clean clothes. There are two bedrooms, and both have bathrooms. The guestroom is clean, but I'll have to change the sheets in my room. Come this way." He led them into the guest room and to the bathroom.

"This shower is new on Heatherbound. I don't know if you have them on Snowball. Anyway, it's a sonic shower. You step in and press this knob, and it cleans you sonically, hair, everything. If you would prefer a wet shower, use this next knob, and you get a warm shower, turn it to the left it get hotter, right, and colder, next you twist this knob if you want to be dried. Or if you prefer, you can use towels. If you want the water shower, you will find soaps and such in this little cubbyhole." He showed them by sliding open the small door in the side of the shower. "The towels are right in that cupboard if you need them. Any questions?"

They looked at him with awe, not saying a word.

"Right. I suggest the women use this bath and bedroom. The men, the other. I will sleep on the couch." Kiela and Laurna protested, but Ian put up his hands and said, "I do quite often anyway, so not to worry."

"After your showers, I suggest you all take naps. You look exhausted. I'll wake you in time for dinner." So saying, he left the ladies to their room and showed Jakin and Jonathan theirs.

"Do you need another run-through about the shower?" Ian took a long look at Jakin. "I didn't think. Mr. Wansky, can you manage a shower by yourself, or would you like me to help you?"

"I thank you for your concern, but Johnathan will help me. I don't quite know what to say about all this and your help." Jakin said with quiet dignity.

"We'll talk later. Now you need to get clean and sleep," said Ian. "I'll bring you each a sandwich and a glass of milk. Try to down them before you go to sleep. Your bodies need the fuel."

Ian went back to the kitchen and got the milk and sandwiches. He then went back and fixed a tray for ladies, adding an icepack for Laurna's face. He knocked on their door, and Laurna answered, "Come in," a little fearfully.

"Thought you should have a snack before going to sleep, and here is an icepack for your face. It should bring down the swelling a little. You'll find some aspirin in the medicine cabinet in the bathroom."

"Thank you, Mr. Scott. I don't know what to say. It's been a long time since anyone has been kind to us." His thoughtfulness had made her eyes swell with tears. Laurna shook her head and straightened her shoulders, denying herself the release of tears.

"Please call me Ian. Things will be different for you now. You can relax and let me take care of everything." So saying, Ian closed the door without a sound.

Laurna leaned against the door, thinking of Ian rushing to her rescue like a red-headed Viking. He is so handsome, she thought, blood rushing to her face. Just then, her mother called, "The bathroom is all yours, honey. Who was at the door?"

"It was Ian. He brought us something to eat and an icepack for my face."

Kiela came out of the bathroom with a towel wrapped around her head. She was wearing a robe that she had found in the guest closet. "That man is too good to be true. I wonder what he wants."

"Oh, Mother, let's take this one step at a time. Just for a little while, let's pretend that this fairytale is true."

"You're right, sweetheart, and so is he. We need food and rest. Let's do as he says. At least until we know what he wants," Kiela said as she picked up a sandwich. "I'll check on your dad while you shower."

Chapter Thirty-nine

Dr. Kevin Fletcher

Ian returned to the kitchen to check on what supplies he would need to feed four extra people. There was plenty in the freezer, but he would need a few fresh things for a salad. He kept remembering the pain in Jakin's suppressed groans and Laurna's swollen face. The hell with it, he thought. I'll call Kevin. He owes me and has that clinic near the spaceport. I bet he helps lots of stowaways.

He went to the phone and called. "Doctor Fletcher's office, may I help you?" said a crisp voice. It was June, Kevin's nurse. A woman of middle age who had been with Kevin since he started his practice. Ian knew her slightly and liked her.

"Hi, June. This is Ian Scott. May I speak to Kevin? It's rather important."

"He's just finishing up a patient. I'll see if he can come to the phone, Mr. Scott." She put him on hold.

A few minutes later, Kevin came on the line and said in a laughing way, "What's up, Ian? June said you sounded serious for a change."

"This is serious. I know of some people who really need to see a doctor but are afraid of questions. I know it's asking a lot, but could you do me a favor and just see them after hours? I'd owe you one."

"I'm always open to helping people, Ian, and I can trust June completely. You won't owe me anything except the bill. You're about the only one I know that can afford me." Kevin said, continuing the banter. "In all seriousness, I want to help if I can. I'll stay until you get here. We should be alone at about six o'clock. Is there anything else you can tell me?"

"I'll rather not. See you at around six."

After he hung up, he stood there looking at the phone, hoping he had made the right decision. How was he going to make them go to a doctor? Guess I'll just have to be extra charming, he thought, with a smile. I'll get them up at five, feed them a quick meal, and off we go. Meanwhile, I have some shopping to do.

He took their dirty clothes to wash them. They came out from the laundry machine mostly rags, but he could see the approximate sizes. These aren't worth keeping, he thought and threw them in the disposal.

There was a small shopping center near his house, and he decided to walk to it. The hovercraft might wake them when he took off. First, he went to the woman's section of the small department store and bought blouses, sweaters, jeans, and underwear. Then he went to the men's and boys' sections and bought clothes for the father and son. Anything that didn't fit could be taken back.

Fully loaded down with packages and bags, he went back to his apartment. All was quiet except for a soft snoring coming from his bedroom. He put the packages in front of their doors and set about fixing a meal.

Ian liked to cook and had extras on hand. He took frozen lasagna from the freezer and popped it into the oven. Next, he spent a little time chopping and mixing a green salad. Last he made some garlic bread. He could have dialed this up on his auto-cook, but it was more fun this way. He didn't have anything for dessert and decided that he would let them choose that from the auto-cook. It would give them a chance to learn how to use it.

All that took time, and it was now close to five o'clock and time to get the show on the road. He woke the ladies first, knocking on the door. "Mrs. Wansky, Laurna, time to wake up. You'll find clothes outside your door. Dinner will be on the table in ten minutes."

He heard a muffled sound through the door, "Okay, we'll be ready."

Next, he did the same at the other bedroom. This time Johnathan answered him. He was already dressed in his new pantsuit and looked as if he had been awake for quite a while.

"My father is still sleeping. I don't think he feels good." Jonathan's eyes were filled with worry. "Can you do something?"

Ian went to look at Jakin. Speaking very softly, he said, "Mr. Wansky, it's Ian. Are you all right?"

No answer. Ian shook him a little. "Wha.., where am I?" He then saw Ian. "Oh yes, Ian. Yes, uh, yes, I'll get up." He tried to sit up but couldn't. "Please, if you will allow me, I'll rest a little longer."

"No hurry, Mr. Wansky. You just go back to sleep."

"Jonathan, I bought some other clothes for you. Please change into them and come into the kitchen when you are ready."

Jonathan still looked frightened, and Ian said, "Don't worry, I will do everything I can to make your father better."

A few minutes later, Jonathan came into the kitchen. He looked like a regular little boy in his new clothes. He had a tentative smile on his face. "Mr. Scott, these are great. May I keep them?"

"Of course, they're yours." Ian's heart bled for the little boy. "Would you like to help?" Jonathan nodded, looking big-eyed and worried again.

"Think you can carry this salad bowl and put it on the table?"

"Wow, I've never seen so many green things at one time. You must be very rich, Mr. Scott."

"Things are different on Heatherbound, Jonathan. We can grow things like that almost year-round. Everyone has all the fruit and vegetables they want here, you'll see."

Laurna came into the room wearing jeans and a soft blue sweater. Her hair was gleaming, she had braided it into a crown on her head, and a few loose strands softened the look. The right side of her face was so swollen that her eye could not open. She stood defiantly straight, daring Ian to say something. "Something smells wonderful," she said. "Thank you for the clothes. How did you know my size?"

"That's our dinner. It's lasagna. Hope you like it. As for the clothes, I checked your old things and guessed."

"You must know a lot about women's sizes." She said with a touch of sarcasm.

"I should. I have two sisters."

"Oh." A blush came to her face. "May I do anything?"

"No, everything is ready just waiting for your mother. Jonathan helped." He led her to the kitchen table.

Laurna sat and picked up her napkin. "She went to see how Dad was doing."

Kiela walked into the room then, looking very good in her new clothing but depressed. "I overheard you saying that dinner was ready. We should sit down then. Your father needs to rest a little longer. He will eat later."

The Wansky family had eaten lasagna before, but never as good as this. And the salad was almost unbelievable to them. When it came time for dessert, the only one who wanted it was Jonathan, but the ladies were interested in how to use the auto-cook. So after clearing the plates and stacking them in the dishwasher, Ian showed them how it worked. Jonathan wanted a banana split. He had never heard of one, but it sounded good.

Ian walked him through dialing in the request, and a few minutes later, the door popped open, and there was the confection. Jonathan was dismayed. Tears came to his eyes. It was so large. No way he could eat that much. "I… I didn't think it would be so much."

"You don't have to eat it all, and it won't go to waste." Ian saw Jonathan's tears. "What we don't want we put in the recycle bin. The machine breaks it down into its components, and when you order something else, it probably contains some of the previous dishes, tasting and looking different. Great, Huh?"

Jonathan wasn't too sure he liked that idea and looked a little dismayed. "You mean ice cream could taste like liver?"

Ian laughed. "No! It would only taste like what you would expect."

"It's okay, Honey. I'd like a couple of bites just to taste it, and I'm sure Mom will help too. With our help, perhaps we can finish it," said Laurna rumpling his hair and smiling. She winced from the sharp pain of smiling.

They went back to the table and sat down while Jonathan tackled the banana split with a little help from his mother and Laurna.

Ian looked nervous and decided the best way was to blurt it out and make them go. "Now that that is settled, I have something to tell you, and you may not be too happy with me. I have a friend who is a doctor and has a small

234

clinic, and he promised to help your father. We will leave here in about ten minutes."

"How dare you! I told you! No doctor. Your precipitous action could endanger us all. He will report us, and we will be deported." Kiela said in a loud, angry voice as she jumped up from the table.

"I'm hoping that my 'precipitous action' will save your husband's life. He is dying, you know," said Ian, losing his temper a bit.

In a softer tone, "You must try to have some trust in me. This doctor has a clinic near the spaceport. I'm sure that he helps people in your situation quite often. In fact, I'm pretty sure that is why he located where he did so that he could help."

"Most of the people of Heatherbound feel for the way your people are treated and would like to aid you in some way, legally. We can't, not until some laws have been changed. Meanwhile, we have unspoken rules of honor, and the officials look the other way as long as the stowaways do not become a burden to the State."

"Now, we don't have time to argue. We are going. If you are too frightened, you may stay here, and Laurna and I will go. I will need someone's help to get him into the hovercraft." Ian got up from the table and started towards Jakin's bedroom.

Kiela started to cry. "You're right. I've been so worried. He made me promise not to go to a doctor for fear of endangering the children."

Laurna took her mother in her arms and said, "Don't cry now, Mother. You've been so strong. Please. You must help me get him dressed and we'll go."

"Don't bother dressing him. You will find a robe in the closet. Just put that around him and we'll be off." Ian said, trying to hurry them.

Jonathan had no appetite for the rest of his banana spit and put it in the recycle bin. I'll never eat another one, he thought. He hadn't known that his father was dying, just awfully sick.

Ian went with the ladies into the bedroom. Jakin had heard the yelling and had tried to get up but was unable to. "What's going on? I thought I heard you yelling, Kiela."

"Don't worry, my darling, I was just excited. We have to leave for a little while and must get you up," said Kiela.

"Here's the robe," said Ian.

They put the robe on him carefully, not even putting his left arm through the sleeve, and carried him up to the hovercraft. It was not easy as Jakin had passed out and was a dead weight. The spiral staircase was beautiful but not built for carrying up an unconscious body.

They finally got him in the hovercraft. Afraid of separation, everyone else wanted to go too. They were soon airborne and, twenty minutes later, landed on the roof of Dr. Fletcher's clinic. Doctor Fletcher and June were waiting for them, and with Ian's help, soon had Jakin inside and on an examining table.

"He looks very bad. We have to get him into a medicube immediately. I only hope it is not too late," said Dr. Fletcher. "I would like to hear the whole story of how this happened." He put up his hands. "I know, no questions, and I promised, but I need to know a little to be able to treat him properly. Also, I want to know how anyone could treat another human being this way."

"He was in a mine blast," Kiela said, looking very worried. "They claimed it was his fault and would not pay his medical bills. We didn't have enough money to put him into a regenerating chamber, and this was all they could do for him."

Dr. Fletcher put him into the medicube. I immediately, the diagnostic arms came out and examined him completely. After about five minutes, a paper scrolled out and gave the prognosis. There were foreign objects in his wounds that were badly infected. His body was fighting, trying to expel them. He was also suffering from malnutrition. The machine didn't know if it could save him, but after three days in the tube, it could give a more accurate evaluation.

Dr. Fletcher didn't hold back any of this information. He felt it best to tell them what he had read. "We really can't promise anything for at least three days. I would say that he will probably need another three after that, if he lives. I'm sorry, I wish I could be more positive."

"Now, I want to put each of you in my other medicube. I don't want any arguments about it, so you all go with Nurse June, and she will get you ready."

When they were gone, Ian said, "Kevin, I appreciate what you are doing. How much does it cost to put someone in one of those machines for a week?"

"Any other hospital, it's four hundred credits a day. I charge two hundred. My clients are mostly poor and can't afford even that, sometimes." He said tiredly.

Ian pulled out his credit card and asked where the credit machine was. He punched in five thousand credits. Kevin raised eyebrows in question.

"I can afford it, and I like to help out too."

"Well, that will certainly pay the bills this month," said Kevin, not trying to dissuade Ian. He looked a little less tired.

June put Jonathan into the medicube first. He checked out fairly well, just malnourished. The machine gave him some large doses of vitamins and minerals and suggested he get plenty of good food and rest for the next month.

Next was Kiela. She was much the same as Jonathan, plus she had high cholesterol due to stress. The medicube gave her the same treatment, plus a statin drug for the cholesterol.

June saved Laurna for last. Her injuries would take longer, perhaps even overnight. She was malnourished, too but had complications with her bruising. There was a fracture in her cheekbone and one in her right thighbone. The machine said this warranted an overnight stay, as surmised.

Kiela and Jonathan looked exhausted and worried. Neither were crying but on the verge. Ian put his arms around both and tried to give them words of encouragement. "I know it looks bad for Jakin, but we got him here, and it's in God's hands now. At least he is no longer suffering, and there is still a chance he may recover. The best thing for you both is to come back to my apartment and get some rest. We'll come back in the morning."

237

Chapter Forty
Laura's Story

Ian called Kevin the next morning, early. "Hi, June. This is Ian. How are my friends doing?"

"Hi yourself, Ian. Laurna looks one hundred percent better, and you can pick her up in about an hour. Dr. Fletcher wants to examine her after he releases her from the medicube. Jakin is still in a bad way. I think he looks a little better, and at least he is not in pain. Thanks for the donation. We just bought that second medicube and weren't quite sure how we were going to make the payments. If you find more friends in need, you know where to go. Do you need to talk to the doctor?"

"No need to talk to Kevin right now. I'll see him in about an hour. And thanks, June, for being there."

Kiela and Jonathan were both still sleeping when Ian was ready to leave. He left them a note telling them to get themselves some breakfast and that he was going to pick up Laurna. The note also told them that Jakin was still holding his own.

When he arrived, June showed him into the examining room, where Kevin and Laurna were talking quietly. Laurna was sitting on the examining table, dressed in the blue sweater and jeans of the day before. She looked so beautiful, he couldn't take his eyes off her, The bruises were gone, and the dark smudges under her eyes were now a mere suggestion.. She smiled when she saw Ian.

Ian stood stock-still. It was as if a thunder stroke had hit him. Here, sitting, was the most beautiful woman he had ever seen. That fragile, ragged girl his heart had told him he had to help had turned into a swan. Her smile was like the sun rising on a dark morning. His heart leaped, and he couldn't breathe.

"Hi, Ian," said Dr. Fletcher as he turned toward Ian when he entered the room, not noticing the flush on Ian's face. "Perfect timing, we were just finished up. Laurna's in good shape now. Just needs some rest and good food. No lasting harm done."

"Thanks, Kevin, I really appreciate it," Ian said huskily. "Those 'cubes do marvelous things, don't they?" said Ian, smiling back at Laurna.

He tore his eyes away from Laurna, looked at Kevin, and said, "How's Jakin doing."

"He's still alive, and that is something I wouldn't have bet upon last night. You got him here not a minute too soon." Kevin had gotten up and was putting away his diagnostic equipment, "Lucky for him that you did. Another hour and he would have been dead. I don't know how he stood the pain. It must have been excruciating."

Laurna looked surprised and then embarrassed. "I really didn't know. He hid it so well, my poor father."

"If you wouldn't mind, Laurna, I would like to hear the entire story of what happened to your father and your family. Would it be too difficult for you to tell me?" Kevin spoke very softly and with obvious interest.

"You both have been so kind. I think I'd like to tell you. It might help me get rid of some of the bitterness to talk about it." She was still sitting on the table,, her long fingers gripping the sides until her knuckles were white. Her eyes were smarting with tears.

Taking a deep breath to calm herself, she began. "Dad worked as the blast commander in Dome Four. It was a well-paid job, and we lived quite comfortably in the dome. That is until the accident. The company was behind quota, and they had started a night shift. The night before the accident, the night crew had gotten everything ready for the morning blasting, even set the dynamite."

"When Dad came on shift that morning, he checked their work. He told them that it wasn't set properly and was too close to the living quarters. He also told them it might do damage to the dome itself. The company boss wouldn't listen, and when Dad told them he wouldn't set it off, they sent someone else to do it. Dad tried to stop the man, but too late."

"The blast killed over a hundred people and injured hundreds more. Dad was lucky to be alive. And so were we. None of us were home that day." Laurna was trembling and hugged herself. The teas won the battle and were streaming down her face.

Ian started toward her, but Kevin held him off with a motion of his hand.

Struggling with her tears, she continued, "Mom and I both worked in the main office with the company computers, and Jonathan was at school. We heard the blast and didn't think too much about it, except it seemed louder than usual. Then we heard the sirens and ran out to find out what had happened. It was very cold in the streets, and we knew that the dome must have ruptured. We ran back to get our cold weather gear, and then went out again to see if there was anything we could do. Mother was frantic for fear it was near Jonathan's school."

Laurna was getting more agitated by the minute. Tears were running down her face. Kevin gave her some tissue and again motioned Ian to keep quiet.

"We grabbed our hoverbikes and followed the ambulances. When we got closer, we could see where the dome had been ruptured and knew that it was the sector where my father worked."

"It was a scene from hell, bodies and parts of bodies everywhere among the rubble. I saw a baby still alive, screaming and waving his arms. He was missing both legs, and the blood was pumping out so fast there was no way to save him."

She put her hands to her face as if to hide her eyes from the terrible scene. "Oh God, it was awful. I can still smell the blood, and foul stench, when I think about it. I'll have nightmares about it the rest of my life."

"Are you sure she needs to go through this now, Kevin," said Ian wanting to crush her in his arms and protect her from any more hurt.

"Be quiet, Ian. She must do this," Kevin whispered.

In a muffled voice, she continued, "We started to help the rescue crews by pulling away slabs of concrete and rubble." She pulled her hands away from the table and put them in her lap, still gripping them tightly, trying to compose herself. "We worked for hours and were exhausted, and yet we could hear the screams of people that were still trapped, fainter now though." She took more tissue and blew her nose. She shuddered and then made herself sit straighter.

Calmer, she continued, "A man came up to my mother late that night and asked if she was Mrs. Wansky. They had found Dad, and he was badly injured but still alive. He led us to him just as they were putting my dad into the ambulance. We wanted to go with him, but there was no room. The ambulance was overcrowded as it was."

"We were too tired to go back to help, and more and more rescuers were arriving. Both of us were worried about Jonathan, so we went home. He was there, anxious and frightened. Mother prepared our supper, but no one could eat. She then went to the hospital, and I stayed with Jonathan."

Laurna was almost composed now, "When Mother got home, she said that she had found Dad and that they had cleaned him up as best as they could, especially the face and neck. There were so many injured they didn't have time to do much more. The medicubes were too few and were used for the most important people." Laurna said this last almost in a whisper.

"They kept Dad in the hospital for a week and then sent him home with a very large medical bill. The company blamed him for the accident and said they would not pay for his medical expenses. Furthermore, they fired both my mother and me as punishment for his carelessness." This was said with bitterness.

"We were evicted from our home, with only the clothes on our backs and what we could carry on our hoverbikes. My parent's savings account was confiscated for the medical bills. Our only recourse was to go to the caves."

"When the company confiscated everything from my parents, they did not touch my savings. So we had some money. And you needed a lot of money in the caves because everything was black market."

"Shortly after we got to the caves, Vernon looked us up. I had met him through work. He sometimes sold extra produce that he had grown in the hydroponic section of the spaceship he worked on. He had heard of our problem and said he could help us by smuggling us aboard the spaceship for a sum of money. We didn't have all of it, and he assured us we could earn money on Heatherbound and pay him the rest when we could. He told us that he knew some people and could get us all good jobs here. We jumped at the chance and went with him." shaking her head at their naivety.

"That night, he stowed us away in the hydroponic section and told us to eat whatever was growing. That sounded wonderful, but unfortunately, nothing was ripe except for some lettuce and a few potatoes.

A look of shock hit her. She put her hands to her mouth and burst into a fit of sobbing. "Oh, my god, how my father must have suffered. We didn't know. He never complained."

Again Kevin stopped Ian from comforting her. "She must continue with her story. It is important for her to try to put this behind her, to carry on with her life."

A few moments later, in a husky voice, she was able to continue. "After a week, Vernon came and said that he knew we didn't have much food, but if my mother and I would agree to come to his cabin occasionally, he and some other members of the crew would gladly share their rations with us. Also, we could start paying him back the money we owed him. We were shocked and embarrassed, telling him we would manage without his help."

"We almost starved, and he never checked on us again during the entire three weeks we were in transit." At this, her mouth twisted with anger and resentment.

"The atmosphere was very hard on all of us, especially Dad. Oh, God!" She beat her hand on her thigh, and looked up to try to stem her tears, and then persevered. "But we lived and finally arrived on Heatherbound."

"Vernon put us in that crate and delivered it to that alley you found us in, Ian." She looked up at Ian and smiled through her tears, her eyes saying that he was a hero.

Laurna hesitated, then continued. "He said he had taken a fancy to me, even though I hadn't been very nice to him on the way here. He would still like to set me up as his space wife in a small apartment with my family, and he would visit me whenever he was in port."

"When I told him no, under any circumstances, he became very angry and abusive. He told me that I would have to work in that dive and give him half of all my earnings. If I continued to resist him, he said he knew where he could sell me and my brother. He would also have my parents deported." She burst into tears again. Ian could stand it no longer and took her in his arms to comfort her.

The room was very quiet except for the soft sound of Laurna's sobbing and Ian's words of comfort. Ian finally said, "I don't know whether to find and kill him or just beat him half to death. He at least got you away from that frozen hell."

"I have one more question to ask. Why was the pub owner so vicious in his attack on you?" said Kevin.

Pink with embarrassment, Laurna hung her head, "He also asked for sexual favors, and when I refused, he was angry. He got even angrier when I slapped a couple of customers for pawing me."

Dr. Kevin Fletcher was very quiet after Laurna's story and then said, "What I find hard to comprehend is how anyone could treat other human beings that way."

"We've heard your story now, Laurna and it's best that you try to get past it. That is easy for me to say, I didn't live through it, but for your mental health's sake, you and your family must try. You are here now, and you have a protector. I know Ian, and he will expect nothing from you except friendship."

"Now, I must check on your father." So saying, Kevin got up and patted Laurna's shoulder, and left the room. Ian helped Laurna down from the table. He kept his arm around her, and she didn't push him away. They followed the doctor out of the room.

Jakin was in a small room, dimly lit. The medicube, and a small cabinet of supplies in the corner, almost filled it. Ian and Laurna looked at Jakin through the glass-enclosed case.

He didn't look too different, except that he seemed relaxed. The readout said that a lot of foreign objects had been removed from his left side and that the poison was being drained from his wounds. The machine said there were many more to be removed, and the subject must remain until the process was completed. He now had a fifty-percent chance of living.

After checking Jakin, Dr. Fletcher turned to Ian with a shrug, hands outspread and palms up. "Ian, if he lives through this, he should go into a regeneration chamber for the ear and hand. I don't have one, and I think it would not be wise to send him to a major hospital. There would be questions."

"You should have one here, Kevin. I'll buy one for you," said Ian.

"That's extremely generous of you, Ian, but I know a little about your finances," said Kevin, as he put his hands on Ian's shoulders, "and it's not possible. The machine costs 150,000 credits. I would have to hire specialists and add a new wing to the building. Also, I would be closely regulated, being that large. I couldn't continue with part of my practice. The part for which you have found a need."

"There must be a way," said Ian, still holding Laurna.

"A group of us are trying to get a rider placed on the immigration laws for hardship cases, such as the Wansky family. What we are trying for is to assure the state that these people can be taken under a sponsor's wing. That sponsor would have to guarantee that he, or she, would take care of these stowaways for the entire first generation."

"But that is the unwritten honor code now," said Ian beseechingly.

"I know, but it's not enough. If someone wants to make things difficult, they can be deported, as it stands now."

Holding up his hand to forestall Ian's protests, Dr. Fletcher said, "Getting back to Jakin. His hand can still be regenerated within two years, perhaps even longer. And there is hope that this new law will pass soon."

"People of Heatherbound have been hearing these horror stories for years, and most have hated having our hands tied. Since Earth tried to invade us, and impose their idea of who should be allowed to come to Heatherbound, there has been even more sympathy for the outlying planets. With the aid of the Dasurainians, we have become less afraid of retaliation. Earth's demand that we refrain from accepting immigrants from satellite planets is backfiring. Heatherbounders are rebelling. They do not like to be told what they can or cannot do, especially by Earth."

Kevin waved his hand and grimaced as if tired of the old story. "Enough of that, as of now, I have to get back to work, and so do you. There is no reason to endanger anyone by stopping to see Jakin every day. In any case, he won't know whether you come or not."

Laurna had been listening to all this and was heartened. When it came to not seeing her father every day, she started to object. "But, but…"

Dr. Kevin stopped her by putting up his hands. "No buts, I will inform you of any changes. Now, I really must go, I have patients waiting." He left them alone.

"Come, Laurna, I'll take you back to the apartment." He pulled her away from her father. "You can explain everything to your mother. Dr. Kevin is right, I to, have to go to work, and you need to rest."

When Kiela heard the hovercraft, she went to the foot of the stairs waiting for them. As soon as they opened the door, she asked anxiously, "is Jakin all right?"

"He has a chance," said Laurna as she rushed down the stairs and took her mother into her arms, busting into tears. "Oh, Mom, I didn't know Dad was suffering so much. I should have done what Vernon asked. He would have gotten him to a hospital or something,"

Kiela pushed her away so she could look into her eyes, still holding her by her shoulders. "Don't be ridiculous. Your father would rather have died." She shook her a little, "You have no reason to feel guilty. The last few months have been almost unbearable, but we're here now, and all's for the best, ."Bravely, holding back her tears, Kiela said, Your father is in God's hands."

Jonathan had come up to them just then. "Boy, do you look better, Laurna? It's great tt Dad's doing better." Turning to his mother. "Can we eat now?" I'm awfully hungry."

Ian had stopped in the middle of the staircase, watching the scene below. When he heard Jonathan, he said, "Didn't you find my note, Mrs. Wansky? You must accept this as your home. Please feel free to use all the facilities without asking for my permission."

Coming down the rest of the stairway, Ian said, "Let's all go into the kitchen and get something to eat. I'm starving too, Jonathan. How about an omelet, I make great ones? "

Chapter Forty-one
Negotiations

During the time, the Federated fleet and the Dasurainians were on their way to Earth. There had been a batch of radio communications between them and Earth. Even so, much of Earth still did not know of the aliens. The Consortiums, and the governments of Earth, did not want to panic the people; at least, that was their excuse. But rumors had gotten out via the ham operators who had picked up the transmissions, and the news was spreading.

During the last two months, the Consortiums, and the Governments of the world, had been meeting practically around the clock to try to salvage their reputations and businesses. After many recriminations and 'I told you so's', nothing was, nor could be, done. They knew the lies couldn't be covered up, or even made to look respectable. The only thing they could do was say that they were thinking in the long term, for the betterment of Earth and it inhabitants. Some people even believed it.

The Dasurainians fleet could travel much faster than the Federated, so after a month of accompanying the slower spacecraft, the aliens said their farewells and proceeded to Earth. A month later, they arrived in Earth's solar system.

When the Dasurainians popped out of space, they did so over the three most populated areas of Earth, North America, Europe, and Asia. The Earthlings ran out of buildings, excited and wondering. The aliens immediately broadcast a calming effect to all. The people were stunned, but no rioting or panic occurred.

The streets soon became jammed with people looking up at the huge alien ships. It was eerily quiet. People spoke in whispers, but nothing seemed to be happening. They had heard rumors that the Dasurainians were coming, but few really believed it. What could they want? Was this an invasion?

The Dasurainians issued an invitation to the United Federation of Earth Headquarters to all the Heads of State via radio to come aboard Admiral Cadirex's flagship. When all had arrived and were settled, they were shown the video transcript from Heatherbound. After the showing, not a sound was heard for a few seconds. All knew what they would see. Then President Carver from the United States of America spoke up. "Will this transcript have to be shown to the peoples of Earth?"

We have no interest in how your world is governed, nor will we make that decision. This is something that you will have to negotiate with the representatives from Heatherbound. As you could see from the transcript, we are only interested in stopping a war with our allies. And possibly trade with your planet in the future. Admiral Cadirex said resolutely.

The fleet finally arrived with the Heatherbounders, and the negotiations were swift. The Dasurainians wanted assurances that an invasion wouldn't happen again. The Heatherbounders also wanted this assurance and that reparations would be made to Heatherbound for the cost of preparing for the illegal invasion.

The Heatherbounders went even further and asked for punitive damages. These payments to be given to the other four outlying planets that had been unjustly, albeit legally, treated poorly by Consortiums for the last one hundred years. These planets were Snowball, Hades, Leilani and Hemiptera. All debts would henceforth be forgiven, and they would have the right to trade with whomever they pleased.

The Consortiums countered, saying this was too harsh and that Earth would be bankrupted. They, themselves, could no longer conduct business. Millions would be put out of work. There had to be some compromise.

This argument was countered with the new technology the Dasurainians had and were willing to trade. One of which was cheap, non-polluting energy. there would be work for all. They also agreed not to broadcast the transcript.

The Governments, and the Consortiums, had no choice but to go along with the aliens. They had been fair and promised prosperity for the future of Earth.

Cameron had been gone four months. He had told Kaitlyn that he had to follow his conviction that the only safety for Heatherbound was to be united with the outer planets. She agreed, even though he would be gone for months at a time.

He, and others of like mind, had to help strengthen them. The only way they could was through investments. The charters of these planets were now changed, and they could trade with anyone for their natural resources. Businesses could now locate on these planets. And no one had a monopoly on unique products on the planets, including Hadean art.

Cameron planned to visit the four nearest planets. He had already been to Snowball. Hades was the next planet on his list. It was aptly named. It was chiefly desert, with high snowcapped mountains that surrounded the oceans. The interior was mostly sand and rocks made harsh by the extremely hot winds that could tear the skin off unprotected flesh. This is where most of the minerals, ores, and precious gems were to be found. The Consortiums settled their colonist in this interior hellhole.

Hades had three oceans, small and saline. Nearly all of the water had to be distilled from these oceans. There was very little rainfall except in the Polar Regions and along the windward side of the mountains. The shores around the oceans were not very wide and were salt-encrusted, with no arable ground. There were underground rivers that ran to the seas, and the colonists could tap into these when they could be found, but the consortiums had withheld the equipment to do so..

The colonists had built vast underground chambers with miles of connecting tunnels in the interior. The chambers and tunnels were created by the mining process and then converted into living quarters. Most of their food was grown in hydroponic gardens or imported from Earth at significant cost. A little could be grown in the shelter of the mountains, but even this was often wiped out by weather.

It was a hard life, not what they had been promised. Most of the colonists on Hades were miners and geologists. They desperately needed biochemists and farmers. Their only industry besides mining was glass manufacturing. They excelled in this, and it was going a long way to helping them get out of their debt to Earth, but the prohibitive cost of shipping was taking most of the profit. Cameron thought there might be a market for this beautiful glass artwork on Heatherbound. He planned to take a shipload back.

The Hadeans had also developed a glass that they could use for the ceilings of the tunnels and chambers that were close to the surface. These were four paned, reflected heat, and made in such a way that when the top pane was too scarred by the wind, it was easily replaced. With natural sunlight in many of their tunnels, they were happier; they didn't feel so much like cave dwellers.

There wasn't much Cameron could do for them by himself, but he could leave them with seeds from many of the plants he had received from the Dasurainians. He chose plants that were the most highly nutritious and had high fat and protein content. He also wanted to leave them with a robot that had the knowledge of how to make their hydroponic gardens produce more.

These people were very suspicious of his motives and couldn't believe he would do this out of the goodness of his heart. What would the Consortiums have to say about it? They had heard about the aliens and the aborted invasions of Heatherbound. Some didn't believe a word of it, and others didn't see how it would affect them. Cameron got around that by buying their largest underground cavern from the governor and hiring women to work the gardens with the aid of the robot. A business they could understand and the governor could tax.

He set reasonable prices for his produce and a decent wage for his workers. He knew it wouldn't be long before the women would sell the seeds and knowledge. He hoped that within a few years, they would at least have a better and more stable supply of food.

Cameron explained about the fuel made from Turpina trees that grew only in freezing climates. He asked permission to buy the tops of the nearest mountains and go into the oil-producing business with some of the businessmen there. He would leave the plants and a robot to tend to them. His partners would have to locate a cave for processing and check on the robot monthly.

He wasn't sure how fast the plants would mature on this planet but had hopes that there would be a small harvest within the year. He wished to share fifty percent of the profits with his partners. There was plenty of oil on this planet, but it was very high in sulfur and expensive to refine. He had no trouble finding partners.

'Poor Kaitlyn,' he thought, 'Now she will have to work out contracts and agreements for three more businesses. I wonder if the Dasurainians would be interested in trade in glass art.

Hemiptera was next on his list. Cameron knew that its main export was a drug called Nirvana, made from the carapaces of critters of this planet. With a mild dose of one pill, it relaxes you and allows you to have a good night's sleep. The second use was for addicts, and this gave a terrific high with two pills. Three pills were used for medical purposes as anesthesia. The reason it was so much in demand was that it had no side effects. Not even addiction.

Earth wanted it, and the carapaces of the crabs and spiders that lived on this planet were loaded with it. The carapaces had to be ground up with the salts of the seas from this planet. Nothing else seemed to have the same effect.

Cameron circled the planet in search of the spaceport and waited for permission to land. The security was very strict and the port was small. Hemiptera was mostly a water planet with many small islands. He had been informed that the seas were shallow and very salty. All water had to be distilled for drinking and even bathing. He wondered how large the population was.

Finally, his call was acknowledged, and he was given permission to land. Cameron was surprised to see an iridescent barrier surrounding the space station. It was about twenty feet high and very beautiful. He wondered how strong it was.

Armed guards were there to receive him. Their armor looked to be made of the same material as the barrier, stranger, and stranger, he thought. He was greeted respectfully and taken to the commandant of the space station. After looking at Cameron's papers, Commandant Blakeson said rather brusquely, "I see that you are from Heatherbound. What is your reason for coming to Hemiptera?"

Cameron understood that this was a no-nonsense man. He decided to get down to business immediately and forego the polite small talk. "I am here for trade purposes. We have no need for your drug, Nirvana, but it has its uses, and if you wish to sell it to us, I'm sure there would be a market. Hemiptera has to have a lot of its food imported. We've been led to believe.

We that is, Heatherbound, wish to become the breadbasket of the outer planets. Because we are so close, the import fees would be much less than Earth's, and fresher."

"You must have heard about the aborted invasion of Heatherbound and the relaxation of the hold that Earth has on these outer planets. Heatherbound feels that by becoming trading partners, we could have an alliance which would perhaps deter Earth from trying to take any of us by force again, at least in the near future." Still standing, Cameron waited for a reply.

"Please be seated." He waved Cameron to a seat in front of his desk. "We have little association with the outside world. I am afraid my manners are lacking."

"Earth buys all our Nirvana, but I think if we had other markets, Earth might give us a better price. We have little else to bargain with," Commandant Blakeson said with a gesticulation of frustration.

Cameron said in his most persuasive style, "You have salt, different kinds of salt. Heatherbound has little salt and needs to import more. I'm sure that Leilani could use some of your special salts to curb the growth of their jungles that constantly encroach on their cultivated lands. I also understand that crab meat is mostly wasted when you harvest. That also could be processed and exported."

Then with a questioning look on his face, Cameron asked, "If I may be so bold to ask, what is that material you have as a barrier, and why is it necessary? I noticed that your guards wear the same material as armor."

"That, Sir, is spider silk. When treated with certain chemicals, it is as strong as steel and as light as a feather. It is also very flexible. The winds on Hemiptera are very strong at times and loaded with salt. Glass domes did not last long under the onslaughts. We had to come up with an alternative." He said with almost a dismissive air.

"Commander Blakeson, you have come up with another trade item. It seems to me that you must have found many uses besides barriers and armor."

"Sir, you have given me a lot to think about. I understand your desire to help Heatherbound, but what's in it for you? People don't just fly around in spaceships for purely humanitarian purposes." he said with a note of skepticism in his voice.

"You're right, of course. We had a good scare with the aborted invasion. When I say we, I mean my family and I. We manufacture Steelite, and it has made us very rich. I have a wife and two children, and a very good life. I want to keep it that way and I feel an alliance with the closer planets will help insure that."

Commandant Blakeson nodded his head and pursed his lips. "That, I can relate to. Could you stay a few days? I would like to show you about our small world. Perhaps you can come up with even more ideas."

Smiling, Cameron replied, "I'd be happy to. Do you have a hotel here or rooming house?"

"You would be my guest. My wife would never forgive me if I allowed someone as interesting as you to be housed anywhere else."

Cameron arrived with a package for his hostess. It was a modern piece of glass art from Hades. It depicted a man and woman entwined. She was completely enthralled with it. "I've never seen anything so beautiful. It really is too precious. I can't accept it."

"Please accept it. I wanted you to have a piece of this artwork."

Still hesitant but aching to accept, Mrs. Blakeson said, "How can I thank you? Where is it from?"

"It is from the planet Hades. They hope to export this kind of artwork to other planets. Heatherbound has opened a store just for this artwork. They are hoping to open stores on each of the other planets."

That night the commandant's wife served Cameron a dinner of local foods. They had sea trout, tubers, and a salad from their hydroponics garden. With it was an interesting wine of deep yellow color. Its taste was difficult to describe, but tasty and seemed quite strong.

Sipping his wine and eating, Cameron remarked. "This is absolutely delicious, Mrs. Blakeson." He turned to the Commandant and asked. "Is this a local wine? Its taste is very unusual but high-quality."

Smiling and with pride, "Yes, it is a local wine. We make it out of a fruit, something like a Kumquat. It grows on a bush that is native to this planet." Swirling the wine in his glass and looking at the legs.

"Do you make enough of it to export, do you think?"

"We have five or six breweries on the Islands. I'll check with them and find out."

Cameron spent several more days on Hemiptera and came up with a few more ideas to export. He loaded his spaceship with ten cases of the wine, called Amber, six cases of smoked crab meat, five cases of salt, and two cases of Nirvana. He also took a bolt of the spider silk. For the Nirvana they charged him the same price that they charged Earth, but told him they had high hopes for a better price in the future.

Last, but not least, was Leilani, a humid, hot planet almost covered with rain forest and jungle. There were man-eating plants named Devil-Traps, that could throw their vines at an animal or person and ensnare them. Once captured the plant drew them into its maw and dissolved them with digestive acids. It was not an easy death. Besides these horrible plants, Leilani also had several predatory animals, and large herbivores.

It was about the size of Earth and had one very large land mass and four smaller ones. There were two mountain ranges on the large land mass and that was the safest place for humans to live but the work was in the rain forests and jungles. They were sent to colonize this planet for the medicines found in the plants found there. Earth had completely wiped out all the rain forest on her world, and covered them with cultivated farm lands, but she still needed these medicines.

Even in the mountains, the colonists had to maintain a vigilance against the encroaching vegetation. Earth mandated that only the mountains of this world could be cultivated. The rest of the planet was to be kept free of any form of civilization. To be kept a pristine world for scientific research. Most of the colonists were botanists and biochemists. It was also a hunter's paradise. Earth allowed anyone who could afford it, to come and hunt the animals of Leilani.

Hunting was okay with the colonists. It was a source of income as well as ridding Leilani of some of the fiercest predators. The animal that looked like the saber toothed tiger was the hunters favorite trophy. They also liked the tusks of the elephant like creatures. The colonist did not limit the number of predators they could bag, but limited the herbivores to only one..

Cameron was guided to the spaceport by a beacon. He was met by the governor who knew of the McCreight name. The governor wined and dined Cameron, then took him on a tour of the facilities, including the housing areas, and generally made him feel very important.

In exchange, Cameron gave the governor's wife a piece of the Hades artwork, and the governor a case of Amber wine from Hemiptera. Needless to say they were impressed.

After an especially fine dinner the governor asked Cameron to come into his study. He offered him a brandy and a cigar imported from Earth. After some small talk, they finally got down to business.

The Governor said, "From what I understand you want to start a trading alliance between the outer planets. I like the artwork from Hades and the wine from Hemiptera. What else do they have to offer? And what's more, what do we have to offer in return?"

"Pharmaceuticals is what you have and, of course, the hunters. Leilani is one of the riches of the outer planets. You can afford to buy anything you want. With less shipping costs you can get things cheaper, and the food fresher. I believe the special salt that comes from Hemiptera will stop the encroachment of the jungles that surrounds your compounds. I feel it will also kill the Devil-Traps."

"I've been told that you have tried everything and nothing worked. It wouldn't hurt to try throwing a brick of salt into the maw if captured by the vines. Everyone would have to carry the salt bricks whenever they venture into the jungles."

Cameron leaned forward in his chair. "I can't guarantee it, but I think it's worth a try."

Chapter Forty-two

Trouble

The alarm woke Ian up to a morning that was overcast and dreary. He sat up, rubbed his eyes and felt the scratchy stubble on his face. He sat there a minute, not really wanting to move. Usually he was anxious to get to work and enjoyed it, but not today. This is ridiculous, I have a lot of work to do and I'd best get going. With this decision, he got up quickly, showered, shaved and dressed. Trying to be quiet so as not to awaken his houseguests, he snuck out of his bedroom. His houseguests had insisted that Jonathan could sleep with them in their room.

Closing the door quietly, he went into the kitchen and there found Laurna, making coffee. He was surprised to see her, and when she turned and smiled at him, the room seemed to glow.

Her bulky robe couldn't hide the slender beauty of her body. His eyes filled with her, his mouth felt dry and he was unable to speak, his loins filled with lust. He had had many girlfriends, but none had ever affected him this way before.

There were still faint smudges of darkness under her eyes from the ordeal she had suffered in the last four months. This did not detract from her smooth forehead, her aquiline nose, or the beautifully curved upper lip, which seemed to emphasize the fullness of her lower lip. He felt he could never tire of just looking at her.

Ian realized he was staring. He felt like an idiot, and turned beet red.

"I heard you stirring and thought you might like some breakfast," she blushed too, seeing Ian's reaction.

Misunderstanding she said, "Am I in the way? You've been so good to us, I feel that I should do something until I can find employment." Laurna thought he looked wonderful standing there so tall and strong, his hair still wet from his shower and his shirt partly unbuttoned. She too felt a rush of passion, and was confused.

"Uh, no, uh, I was just surprised to see you so early in the morning." He quickly buttoned his shirt. "You should be sleeping. The doctor said you needed rest before you could even begin to think of getting a job."

"I'm not tired, really. Would you like some scrambled eggs and toast?"

"Sure, I'll start the toast," said Ian, and both started bustling around the kitchen.

When everything was ready they sat down to eat. They were quiet for a few minutes enjoying the breakfast. Laurna picked up her coffee mug and held it as if to warm her hands and said, "Ian, you know so much about us and we know nothing about you. It's your turn now to tell me all about yourself."

Ian smiled and said, "My life isn't half as interesting as yours. In a nutshell, I'm a partner with my best friends in several businesses. They all seem to be making a lot of money for us. Kaitlyn McCreight is our financial expert, and my best friend's wife. I'd trust her and Cameron with my life, we've been friends since childhood."

He picked up his coffee mug and took a swallow, wishing he could hold her hand. "My main love is robotics, and what I do mostly is research and development in that field."

She had rested her face on her hand, and just enjoyed the sound of his voice. "What about your family? You said you had two sisters. Any brothers, and are your parents still alive?"

"Oh yes," laughing. "We have a big family, and I expect Mom and Dad will be around at least another hundred years. You'll love all of them; I'm sure, especially my sister Michelle. She's about your age, still going to school. She wants to be a doctor."

"Just how old do you think I am?" she said with a slight frown.

"Not old enough to have to take on the responsibilities you have." He put up his hands to forestall her slight protest. "I admire you for it, and I realize you had no choice."

Just then, Kiela and Jonathan came into the room. Kiela said, "Um, that coffee smells good. Any left?"

"Sure", said Laurna and started to get up.

"Sit. I can fix Jonathan and myself some breakfast. Have you called the clinic about Dad yet?"

Ian put down his napkin and stood up. "I was going to call as soon as I had finished breakfast. Would you like to talk to the doctor?"

"Yes, uh, no, oh I don't know. I'm so worried, and I'm afraid I won't ask the right questions." Kiela suddenly looked on the verge of tears. She held onto the back of Laurna's chair to steady herself. Ian was amazed at how much she and Laurna looked alike. She was a little smaller and even more fragile looking than her daughter. She also looked exhausted, as if she hadn't really slept in a week.

"Mrs. Wansky..."

"Please call me Kiela."

"Kiela, I know how worried you are, but everything is being done for your husband that our medical science can do. And that's considerable. You must relax and try to get some sleep and eat. You have to keep your strength up for Jonathan. That sounds trite, I know, but it's still true."

Ian went to Kiela, put his arm around her to steady her, and made her sit in the nearest chair. "Dr. Fletcher said Jakin had improved remarkably when we talked to him yesterday. Remember, he said it was not safe to visit too often, and we would know tomorrow if he is going to pull through."

Laurna had been bustling around fixing something for her mother and Jonathan. "Momma, here's a cup of coffee and some toast. I'll fix some eggs for you and Jonathan. Ian will call Dr. Fletcher, and then you must go back to bed."

Big tears ran down Kaela's face. She couldn't stop them. After four months of horror and worry, the realization that she was safe and her family was in good hands was almost too much for her. She put her head down and sobbed. Laurna started crying too, and knelt down beside her mother to hold her. Jonathan just stood there trying not to cry, very worried and upset.

"There, there, Momma, go ahead and cry. You've been so strong, its time to let someone else take care of things." Laurna rocked her mother in her arms and patted her back.

Ian was at a loss. He felt so helpless. He finally said quietly, "Take your mother back to bed. I'll take care of Jonathan and call the clinic. She needs rest more than anything at the moment."

Ian called the clinic and June said that there had been no change during the night. He then fixed some eggs for Jonathan and a glass of orange juice. A few minutes after Jonathan has finished his breakfast, Laurna came back and said that her mother was sleeping.

Ian said, "That's good. She needs it. I talked to June at the clinic, and she said that there was no change in your father. We just have to wait and see."

Laurna looked forlorn and at a loss for what to say. She wished he would take her in his arms as he had done before to comfort her.

Trying to cheer her up, Ian said, "Jonathan and I had a wonderful idea. Why don't the two of you come with me to work? We'll leave a note for your mother, in case she wakes up, and we will be out of her way all morning."

"It's only a ten minute walk away, and if you get bored or tired, you can make your way home, or I can walk you back. I haven't told Jonathan but there are some real interesting robots that he might like to meet. You could look at the different jobs that are open and see if any appeal to you. Not that I want you to start working soon." The last, Ian said hastily.

"I'll take you to my favorite pub for lunch and then you can both come back here for a nap. How does that sound?" Ian said, looking from one to the other.

Jonathan's eyes got round as saucers. "Real robots! That I can meet and talk to! Wow, that'd be neat."

Laurna perked up immediately. It had been a long time since she had seen a real smile on Jonathan's face and she wanted to be with Ian. She really didn't care where, but seeing where he worked would be a good start to getting to know him better.

"That sounds wonderful," said Laurna. "I wonder what would be the best place to leave a note for Mom. We usually leave them in the message center of our home, but even if you had one, Mom wouldn't know where it was."

"How abut the kitchen table," said Ian.

Jonathan piped up with, "How about the bathroom mirror? Mom would never leave the room without brushing her hair."

"You're right. Bathroom it is." Laurna smiled and ruffled Jonathan's hair.

Kiela woke up slowly, looked around the room. And then, with a start, sat up quickly, wondering where she was. It came back to her. She was sleeping in Ian Scott's guest bedroom. The clock beside the bed read 1:15 p.m. The bed felt wonderful and she wished she could go back to sleep, but she made herself get up. She wanted to check on Jakin and her children.

But first, the bathroom. Picking out the clothes she would wear, she went in and noticed that the room was tidy except for some paper on the floo,r and a smudge on the mirror. Thinking to herself, 'I'll clean that up later, she proceeded to do her morning routine, ending with brushing her hair.

Feeling better and noticing the quiet, she happily thought about how considerate everyone was. She opened the drapes and, noticing sliding glass doors, opened them and stepped out onto a small balcony. The sun was shining, and it was so warm. It's hard to believe this is real and not a simulation under the dome. I love it here. It's so different from Snowball.

Thinking of Snowball put a pall on the day. She had lost her best friend in that accident, as well as her whole way of life. There hadn't even been time to mourn her properly. She suppressed her tears, and after a few minutes, she left the balcony and went back into the bedroom.

Kiela made the bed and left the bedroom. She called out. "Hello, where are you? I'm up now." No answer. Could they be sleeping in Ian's room? She knocked on his door, again no answer. They must have gone out. There must be a message here somewhere. I don't know if Ian has a message center or where it could be. They must have left one in the kitchen. Still not too upset, she went into the kitchen, no message there either.

There's got to be a message. Laurna wouldn't go anywhere without telling me. She looked everywhere she could conceive of, nothing. Maybe Jakin had worsened, and they left in a hurry to see him.

Oh my God, maybe Ian's a white slaver and has taken them to be sold. Vernon said he would if we didn't do as he wished, but I thought he was just trying to scare us. Maybe that really happens on Heatherbound. Oh, I don't know what to think. Ian seemed so sincere and honest. Could he have been just trying to get us healthy for a better price?

She went back into the living room and ran up the spiral staircase to the roof. The hovercraft was still there, so they didn't go far. She went back down the stairs and looked for another way out. She could see a small hallway off the living room and went there. She saw a door with buttons beside it on the wall. Oh, it must be an elevator. She pushed the down button and heard a slight hum, and a few seconds later, the door opened.

Kiela decided to go down. Perhaps someone will be in the lobby who may know where they have gone. When the elevator door opened, she stepped out into a small lobby with a guard sitting at a desk near the door.

The guard looked up with a surprised look on his face. "Did you just come from the penthouse? Mr. Scott didn't mention any guests." He sounded a bit belligerent.

"Yes, my family is staying with Mr. Scott for a few days. Have you seen him? He must have stepped out for a while with my children. Perhaps he left a message?"

"I just came on duty at noon, Mrs....."

"My name is Mrs. Wansky."

"Mrs. Wansky, it's highly unusual for Mr. Scott to have guests and not notify the front desk." The guard started punching things into his computer. "I'll have to call his office. Maybe they forgot to tell us."

"Oh, that's all right. I don't want you to bother him at work. I'll just go back up and wait for him." Kiela was starting to get a bit nervous. She hated officious people, especially guards.

"Can't let you do that, Mrs. Wansky, without authorization. You are not coming up on the computer as anyone living in New Edinburgh. Where do you come from?"

"You saw me getting out of the elevator coming from the penthouse. Why are you so curious about Mr. Scott's houseguests?" She tried to sound imperious, but it came out sounding timid and nervous.

"It's my job, lady. If you don't tell me where you are from and what you are doing here, I'm, going to call the police."

Kiela started to cry, "Don't do that. It would be so embarrassing. Please wait until Mr. Scott returns."

"Too late, lady, I've already called."

Just then, the door swung open, and in walked Ian, Laurna, and Jonathan. Laurna was laughing and looking up at Ian. Kiela saw them and ran to Ian, throwing herself into his arms.

"That man has called the police. He thinks I was illegally in your apartment."

Ian held her at arm's length, turned to Laurna, and pushed Kiela into her arms. "Take your mother back up to the apartment. I'll take care of this."

Laurna got her weeping mother into the elevator, and Ian turned to the guard. "As usual, you did the correct thing, George. A little heavy-handed as always. Is there no kindness in you? Couldn't you see the woman is ill?"

"I'm only doing what I'm paid to do. I don't make the rules."

"Okay! And yes, they are my guests. Now inform the police that there was a mistake, and there are no intruders here."

Ian reached out his hand, "Give me the guest forms. I'll fill them out right now."

Before Ian had finished, the police arrived, and everything had to be explained to them. They were curious about the name Wansky, as it didn't appear on the tax records.

Ever quick on his feet, Ian said, "These friends of mine are from a farming family and didn't make enough money to have to pay taxes. So, of course, they wouldn't be on the tax rolls."

"Oh, all right," the detective said, looking down at his notes. "One other thing, George here said that the woman looked like the description of the waitress who started a brawl in a bar in the port district." He looked up at Ian with a questioning look on his face.

"Do I look like the type that has bar waitresses as guests? " said Ian with a frown.

The detective was still suspicious. "No, but you also don't look like the type to know many poor farmers. What is your connection to these people?"

"Why are you asking all these questions? The women didn't commit a crime, and George is always suspicious of everyone. If you will just check your records, you will see that he calls you in on a regular basis."

"If you have nothing to hide, why do you evade my questions?" The detective said with a cold look in his eyes.

"All right. The woman is the mother of my fiancée. I haven't told my family of my engagement, and I certainly didn't want to blab it to the world until they had been informed."

"That does explain a lot, Mr. Scott. Sorry to have bothered you." The detective folded up his notebook, said goodbye, and he and his partner left.

After a few furious words with George, Ian left and went to his apartment. He didn't know whether to be mad, frightened, or just embarrassed… perhaps all three.

Ian walked into the living room and found the Wansky family huddled together on the leather couch. All were big eyed and frightened. Ian wasn't too happy himself. It was a serious matter to lie to the police, but what choice did he have?

Ian sat down on the couch opposite them, his hands in his lap. He leaned forward as he said, "I'm not going to try to fool you. This could be serious, then again, maybe nothing will happen." He held up his hand to stop Kiela from explaining. "It isn't your fault Kiela, just a lot of little things we should have done. I should have done."

"This isn't a police state, but they do not close their eyes to crime, and being a stowaway, in our law, is a crime. Also, George thought you looked like a person accused of wrecking a bar in the port district."

Kiela started to cry again. Laurna put her arm around her and tried to soothe her by rocking her. Jonathan put his head in Kiela's lap. He was frightened and confused. Kiela kept moaning, "Oh my God, oh my God.

Ian wanted to hold them all, and comfort them, but things had to be said. "George, our guard, is suspicious. It's his nature; he'll push it. He may even monitor my calls. So, no calls to the clinic from here. It could jeopardize Jakin and the clinic. Also, it might not be a good idea to run away today. That would just make George even more suspicious, and he would be sure that you are not legal."

"There's another thing, I had to explain who you are, and I told them you were a poor farming family and that I was engaged to Laurna." Laurna's mouth fell open, and she said, "Engaged?"

Chapter Forty-three
Trouble

George, the Security guard, was angry. He was only doing his job. What right did Ian Scott have to talk to him that way? He sat there for a few minutes fuming and then made a call to McCreight Industries. "Hello, I'd like to speak to Mr. Sean McCreight."

"Who may I say is calling?"

"A concerned citizen, I have some information that may interest him about Ian Scott." This might turn out to my advantage, thought George. There could be money it for me.

"Please hold. I'll see if Mr. McCreight is able to take your call."

The operator came back on the line. "Mr. McCreight is in conference at the moment but will call you back if you would leave a number where you can be reached."

George gave her his number, and within an hour, Sean called. "This is Sean McCreight. You wished to speak to me?"

George was not surprised at the quick response. He kept up on current affairs and knew of the animosity between the brothers. He had also heard that Sean was the type that might make trouble for his brother's friends as well. It was still a small city.

"Yes. I have some information concerning Ian Scott and some possible stowaways. Would you be interested in purchasing such information?"

"I am a concerned citizen too, and yes, I would like to hear more," Sean said with a touch of sarcasm. "I'm a busy man. Give me your information."

"I was hoping for a small donation to a worthy cause," said George.

Sean rubbed his scar in irritation. "Where can I meet you?"

It was decided that they would meet on the corner near McCreight Industries at 6:30 p.m. This was during George's dinner break. George arrived first; he had made a record of Ian's conversation with the police detective and the detective's name. He had also written down his observations and a copy of the story in the newspaper about the bar brawl. George was a very thorough man.

Sean had put on a dark overcoat and wore a hat, in hopes that he wouldn't be recognized. He saw a man in a guard's uniform on the selected corner and asked without preamble. "Where is this information?"

"I have it all right here." George handed Sean a wad of papers. "Where's my donation?" Equally blunt.

Sean gave him twenty credits and started walking away.

"Not very generous," George yelled after him, but he wasn't really unhappy. After all it was a week's wages for him, and more important, he had got his revenge.

Sean didn't even look back but went quickly back to his office. He was alone, having told Alice that she could leave on time for a change. Scanning the material hastily, he was pleased. Laughing out loud, he re-read everything. "Oh boy! This should cause Ian no end of trouble if even half of it were true."

He called a private detective he knew and told him to check up on the Wansky family, probably from Snowball. He wanted to know all about their activities for the last year. Next, he took an envelope off his desk, put the information in it, addressed it to a gossip columnist, stamped it and took it out to the nearest post box. He hadn't felt this good in quite a while.

The next morning when Ian was reading his morning paper, his name jumped out at him. In the gossip column, in all the sordid detail, were the events of yesterday's confrontation with the police in his lobby.

Laurna was sitting across from him and eating her breakfast. She was startled when Ian threw down the paper and said, "Get your mother up. Get her dressed and packed. We have very little time to get you out of here."

"Why? What's happened?"

"I'll explain everything on the way. Hurry! I'll get Jonathan ready."

Ten minutes later, they were in Ian's hovercraft on their way to a house that Ian had recently bought. It was an old house that had been empty for several years. It was in a good neighborhood but neglected because of inheritance problems. The house was three stories with six bedrooms. It lacked some of the modern conveniences and needed painting and redecorating. The front yard was overgrown and wild. There were fruit trees in the back that needed pruning. It also had a greenhouse that was full of dead plants and broken glass.

He felt they would be safe there because he hadn't told anyone yet of his purchase. Fortunately, he had everything turned on, planning to spend his weekends there, working. He had even bought the paint and tools needed to do the work. He hoped they could live in comfort if not beauty, until he could straighten things out.

While in the air, Ian gave Laurna the paper and pointed out the gossip column. She was horrified but decided not to tell her mother anything yet. Kiela had enough to worry about.

"There isn't any food in the house," said Ian. "I know of a store on the way where we can get everything we need. The house is furnished, but you may need fresh linens, so we'll get that too. While you shop, I'll call Dr. Fletcher about your father."

"We can't thank you enough, Ian," said Kiela. "I don't know how or when we will ever repay you."

Ian said in a light tone. "Now, Mother, there'll be no talk of payment. Am I not engaged to your daughter?"

Kiela didn't know whether to laugh or cry at that, and Laurna turned scarlet. She wished it were really true. She didn't know that that was exactly what Ian was thinking.

June had read the paper and was very worried for the doctor and for the Wanskys. "Did you read this? I don't care what the law says," June said, putting the paper down and turning to Kevin. "We can't turn sick people away. We are needed here."

"Yes, I've read it, and it does look like we are going to be in big trouble fairly soon." Kevin put his hands on her shoulders and looked her in the eye. "Let's try to look on the bright side of things. Perhaps this story will hurry the legislation along, and we can legally help these people," said Kevin fatalisti-

266

cally. "It's out now, and there is nothing we can do except tell Laurna's story to the press."

June shrugged off his hands and said, "You can't do that until you get Laurna's permission, and we don't know where to reach her."

"Oh, come on. June. Don't look for trouble. You know they'll call today and soon."

The phone rang just then and it was Ian apologizing for all the trouble he might be causing them. Laurna got on the phone; she too apologized, then asked for her father's prognosis. Kevin told them that there was no change, but that was good, they would know more soon.

"Laurna, I know what you are going through, and the next few weeks could be very unpleasant for all of us. I want to make your family's story known to all of Heatherbound, all the shocking details."

"But, but…" sputtered Laurna.

"Wait, let me finish. I'm sure that Ian has told you about the pending legislation on stowaways. It's a more humane way of handling the problem. We have come up with a law that allows a person to legally take responsibility for a particular stowaway. We've been trying to get this passed for several years. Maybe your story will be just the one to make people see the injustice of sending people back to certain death when we can care for them here without becoming a burden on the taxpayers."

"If we can get this passed soon enough, it could save all of us. I certainly don't want you sent back to Snowball and Ian and I put into jail or fined large amounts. It would put me out of business and hurt a lot of people."

There was silence on the end of the line for a moment, then Laurna said, " Dr. Fletcher, you're right. Of course, we must tell our side of the story. If your people knew just how bad things are on Snowball, perhaps they would help us. You have my permission." She started to cry and gave the phone to Ian.

Taking the phone, Ian was stricken. He couldn't stand to see her cry. "Are you sure this is the only way?"

"How would I know, Ian? It's the only thing I can think of. It has to work."

Ian hung the phone up and turned to Laurna. He took her in his arms to comfort her, whispering into her hair, "I know that we have not known each other very long, but I have fallen in love with you."

Laurna stiffened and started to pull away from him, but he would not let her go.

Ian put his hand under her chin to left up her face. "From the first moment I saw you in that bar, I wanted to take care of you. You looked so fragile and out of place. I saw red when that man grabbed you, and then to top it off, the owner was so vicious. I wanted to tear them both apart. I knew that I had to take you away and protect you. When I told the police that we were engaged, it was wishful thinking and an expression of a real desire to make it come true. Is there any chance that you could learn to love me, Laurna, and become my wife?"

"Oh, Ian, I do love you and will marry you. When you said that you told the police that we were engaged, it was the happiest and saddest moment of my life. I wish it were true, but I thought that you were only trying to help us. I think I have loved you from that first day as well. I felt I could trust you even though we had been badly treated by so many people. I wanted to believe in you."

Ian kissed her then. It started out to be a gentle kiss, but soon it became passionate. He felt her respond to him and knew that her feelings for him were real. It was hard to gently push her from him, but there wasn't time for this. He had to get them to safety.

Dr. Kevin Fletcher had videotaped Laurna while she told her story. He added how she looked when brought in, and the fact that she had just spent fourteen hours in a medicube. He also went into some detail about the injuries of her father and his prognosis. He sent a copy of this to a friend of his, Reese Kanji, who worked as a news anchor at the television station. He also sent a copy of the newspaper gossip column article.

When Reese received the information, he was excited. He had been working on getting the Stowaway Bill passed for some time and thought that this just might do the trick. The people of Heatherbound were already sympathetic to the problems of their neighboring planets, and this could put it into clear perspective. On top of that, it was a real good story and gave an excellent explanation of why Dr. Fletcher had broken the law to help these people.

Within a few hours, Reese had gotten permission to do a documentary on the cruel conditions that Earth had imposed upon these valiant colonists. He dwelled on the exploitation of the colonists, and their hopeless future, forever in debt.

With Laurna's permission, he aired the videotape of the Wansky family and told stories of other atrocities which he had recorded. "How can we stand by and not try to aid these people?" Reese said to his audience with a questioning look.

"The past greed of the Consortiums in their sanctions against the import of essential products, mainly food from the neighboring planets, not only hurt these planets but Heatherbound as well. We should be the bread-basket of the outer planets."

Reese continued, " The fact that all exports of raw material could only be sold to Earth and that all imports would be from Earth, at Earth's rates, was outrageous. These conditions were imposed upon desperate people, anxious to leave a life of poverty and degradation on Earth. They did not understand that Earth would be able to keep them in debt for all time. Even though most of these sanctions have been lifted since the aborted invasion, the outer planets are still in Earth's stranglehold of debt."

"We have a bill that has been pending in the Elders Council for several years which deals with this issue. It is time that they stop being afraid of Earth and help these people."

It was a very well-done documentary, especially considering that Reese had put it all together in just a few hours. The TV station was flooded with calls and was forced to air the program again twice more the same day.

This, coming so soon after the "almost invasion," got the people of Heatherbound riled up. They wanted that bill passed and the immigration laws set up to give priority to people of these planets to immigrate to Heatherbound. The populace was incensed that Earth felt they could dictate who could immigrate to Heatherbound. The Elders were besieged with telephone calls and called a special session. It was only a matter of days before the Bill was passed.

During this time, the police were looking for Ian and the Wansky family. It didn't take them long to find them and the connection to Dr. Fletcher's clinic. They were sympathetic but still took the family, except for Jakin, to a detention center and put Ian and Kevin in jail. They closed down the clinic but let June care for Jakin, as his condition was still too critical to allow him to be moved.

Chapter Forty-four

Retribution

It was a glorious morning at the farm. The sun had burned away last night's low mist, promising a perfect day. Cameron was sitting at the breakfast table reading part of the paper and enjoying his second cup of coffee. He had just finished his breakfast and was looking forward to a day working in the fields. It was close to harvesting time.

Across from him was Kaitlyn, drinking a cup of coffee. She also was quietly reading the morning paper when suddenly Cameron let out a yell. She jumped, spilling some coffee, and looked up quickly at Cameron.

"My God! Did you see this article in the paper about Ian? It says that he broke the law by sheltering some stowaways and lied to the police when they questioned him." Cameron was rigid with anger. He almost threw the paper across the table.

"I can't believe it. Let me see," said Kaitlyn with raised eyebrows and a look of concern as she reached for the paper before it hit the floor. She hadn't seen him this angry in a long time.

"He was in the office yesterday and introduced me to a lovely girl and her brother. He didn't seem the least bit worried. Just the opposite, he looked like he was on top of the world." Kaitlyn said as she scanned the paper, trying to find the article that had upset Cameron.

She found the article in the gossip column and read it quickly. "This looks serious. I wonder how this columnist found out about it so quickly."

"I may be paranoid, but I'll bet Sean has something to do with it." Cameron had calmed down but was still white with anger. He stood up and started towards the phone. "It's just something that little mind of his would find pleasure in doing."

"Oh, Cameron, you don't know that. What are you going to do?" said Kaitlyn, a little wide-eyed.

Cameron turned back to Kaitlyn, cold fury in his eyes. "What am I going to do? If he is behind this, I am going to ruin him. It is bad enough that he has tried to wreck everything I care about, but going after my friends is the last straw."

Kaitlyn stood up and came around the table towards Cameron. "How do you plan to do that?" She put her hand on his arm beseechingly. "Think of your mother. This could break her heart if it's true."

"Don't worry, Honey." Cameron turned from the phone and took her hands in his. "First, I am going to hire a detective I know by the name of Guy Gianardo. He will find out just how the papers got the story. Then, if Sean is behind it, I will expose him for the sneaky low-life he is. Then I will sue him for defamation of character and false testimony in our court case. I didn't press it before because of my parents, but can't you see that unless we do something, Sean will continue harassing us until we are dead."

"We had better both go into the office today. It will be a madhouse," said Kaitlyn.

It didn't take the detective long. That afternoon he called Cameron at work. "I talked to my source at the paper. He told me that the envelope that the information arrived in had a McCreight Industries return address on it. He said, other than that, it was anonymous. No proof that your brother sent it, unless they will let me have it for fingerprints, but who else would have sent it from there?"

"I knew it," said Cameron, with a grimace and shake of his clenched fist. "That bastard!"

The detective continued, "I talked to the police detective that first came upon the case, and he said that the security guard at Ian's apartment building had called about a suspicious person or persons in his lobby. He said that he had reason to believe that she might be a stowaway. He also thought she looked like the woman whose picture was in the paper, who had started a bar brawl in the dock area."

"That son-of-a-bitch should be fired." Cameron ran his hands through his hair in frustration. "He has caused Ian trouble before."

"The guy seems to have a good nose for making trouble," commented the detective.

"When I interviewed the guard, he said he was just doing his job. Seemed to enjoy that part of it, too. After some friendly persuasion and ten credits, he told me that he sold the information to Sean for twenty credits. Says that Sean was a cheap screw."

" He got that right. Thanks, Guy," said Cameron in a quiet voice. "That was fast work."

'That's what you pay me for. Do you want me to try for the fingerprints?"

"Yes, go ahead and get them if you can. I think if he was stupid enough to leave his prints on that envelope, we'd have all the proof we need to ruin him."

After Cameron hung up the phone, he called his secretary. "Have you heard from Ian this morning?"

"Not a word, Sir. I saw that article in the paper this morning. Isn't it awful?"

"It certainly is. If you hear from him or anything, let me know immediately."

"Of course, Mr. McCreight. Will there be anything else?"

"Yes, please get James Morgan, the company lawyer, on the line."

Cameron got up and started pacing the room in agitation. The phone rang, and he rushed to pick it up. "James?"

"This is James. What's up, Cameron?"

"I want to start proceedings against Sean for defamation of character and false testimony." Cameron said and then asked, "Have you read the morning paper? The gossip column about Ian?"

"Yes, I just finished reading the paper and was about to call you about it," answered James.

"I have reason to believe that Sean tipped off the columnist. That scoundrel has gone too far. I've had it with him. It's bad enough attacking me, but now he is going after my friends. It's time to show him that he can't get away with it anymore."

"It doesn't surprise me in the least that Sean had something to do with it," said James in a disgusted voice. "I agree with you wholeheartedly, Cameron. Something should have been done after the hell he put you through last year. I couldn't believe how easy you've been on him. If he hadn't been your brother, I'd have advised you to throw the book at him. It's the only way to stop a person like that. I'll drop everything and get right on it with pleasure."

Two days later, Cameron got a call from Guy Gianardo. "They just arrested Ian and his friend, Dr. Kevin Fletcher. They are at the Central Police Station."

"Thanks, Guy. I'll take care of it."

Cameron called his father and told him of his plans to sue Sean and his reason for it. "Dad, I could use your influence to help get Ian and his friends released. Would you go to the police station with me?"

"Yes, of course, I'll go with you. I also understand your wish to sue Sean. I have been bitterly disappointed with that young man,' said Sir John. "I wonder what I did wrong in raising him. Your poor mother, she is going to be very unhappy. Could you hold off the lawsuit until after the harvest? During that time, I will do everything in my power to help Ian and that family. We've got to get that bill passed to help these people and others like them."

"Of course, Dad," said Cameron with a sigh. "I've already had my lawyer notify Sean, and I doubt that the case will come to trial for at least a month. That will give us plenty of time to finish the harvesting."

Cameron, and Sir John, went to the police station to see about getting Ian and Kevin's release. They were immediately taken to the Captain's office. The police captain was sitting at his desk working on some papers. He got up when he saw who entered, showed them where to sit, and offered coffee. Sir John and Cameron sat down, but declined the coffee. Sir John immediately explained why they were there in his firm and efficient way.

In answer to their request, the police captain shook his head. "I am very sorry, but my hands are tied at this point. They broke the law, and Ian Scott lied to the police. I really do sympathize with them and do realize what lay behind their motives, but the law is the law, and I must stand behind it until it is changed."

"We understand your position. Is there bail we can pay, or can you release them into our custody, with our good name as security?" said Cameron.

The police captain looked very uncomfortable and said, "Their case hasn't gone to court yet. Until then, I can't release them at all. It will be coming up in about an hour, though, and you can be there to speak on the defendant's behalf."

"Could we at least see them?" said Sir John.

"Sorry," the Captain shrugged his shoulders and spread his hands, " but you may wait in my office until their case comes up. I'll make sure you are called in plenty of time. I recommend that you get them a good lawyer."

"Thanks. " said Sir John as he looked around the room. "Could we use your phone?"

"Of course, I only wish I could do more." The Captain closed the door as he left the room.

"The first thing we have to do is call your Uncle Robert. Even though he doesn't deal in criminal law, he will know what to do. Next, I'm going to inform Reese Kenji about what is going on. He could do a follow-up on the story. Between the two, we should have Ian and Dr, Fletcher out in no time," said Sir John, as he reached for the phone,

Laurna was beside herself. Jonathan had been taken from them and put in a separate place for children. Her mother, Kiela, was prostrate with grief and fear. They had been put in a holding cell with ten other women. It was a large, very clean room with twenty beds in it. Small windows were all along one side, near the ceiling, the other three walls were bare except for the locked door in one. Gray walls, gray blankets, and a gray future. She had no way to reach Ian, and no one would tell her what was happening with their case, or with her father.

They had been picked up the night before, and told that they would be deported. Also that Ian was going to jail. Laurna had begged the immigration agents to allow the family to stay together, to no avail. They had been gentle but very firm. Rules must be followed.

The twelve women had been taken from the room twice to the dining room. Neither Laurna nor Kiela could eat a thing. The rest of the women didn't eat much either although the table was groaning with fresh fruits and vegetables, plus meat and rolls. Instead of pleasing the women, it was almost as if they were trying to show the women how much they were going to miss when sent back to their home worlds.

There was very little conversation among the women. Most just lay on their beds, resigned to a bleak future. Nearly all felt that going home would be a death warrant.

Late afternoon of the next day, Laurna was sitting on Kiela's bed holding her, trying to calm her. Kiela couldn't stop crying. She kept saying how sorry she was for causing all the trouble. Both were worried about how Jakin was faring. They didn't even know if he was still alive. And what was happening to Jonathan? He must be frightened to death.

Laurna tried to help her mother deal with the guilt she felt about getting Ian and Dr. Fletcher into so much trouble. Kiela kept saying. "If only I had waited just a little while longer in that apartment, and trusted Ian more."

"Mrs. Wansky?"

Laurna looked up and saw a stout woman dressed in a guard's uniform. Her heart sank to the pit of her stomach. She couldn't stop from trembling. "I'm Laurna Wansky. This is my mother, Kiela Wansky."

The guard could see that Laurna was frightened. "Please don't be afraid. No one is going to hurt you. Would you both please come with me, you have visitors."

Laurna almost burst into tears of relief, but she managed to control herself. She had to be strong for her mother's sake. Helping her up, they followed the guard from the room. They went down a long hall and finally reached another room. No one spoke a word during this seemingly long walk. The guard opened the door at the end of the hall, and Laurna stepped through first. She immediately saw Ian, and burst into tears as she ran to him. He held her, and rocked her in his arms, crooning that everything was going to be all right.

Cameron and Sir John were standing beside Ian. They went to Kiela and sat her down in a comfortable chair. Cameron noticed that Kiela's eyes were red and swollen from crying, and her hair was a mess. Even so, she was still a beautiful woman. With dignity, she pushed back some strands of hair from her face and tried to smile. She accepted the cup of tea that the woman guard offered, but put it down untouched on the small table that was beside her.

Sir John sat dpwn beside her, and said, "Mrs. Wansky we are friends of Ian's, and we are here to help you. We know how much you have suffered these last few months, but it will soon be over. Our Elders have changed the laws about stowaways. The effort of your courageous daughter, and your family's torment, has helped make it come to pass."

Kiela tried not to cry, but tears of relief kept streaming down her face. She was too exhausted, and il, to have the strength to withhold them. She couldn't say anything for a moment, just kept nodding, and wishing that Jakin were there to hold her.

Sir John took Kiela's hand in his. "In just a day or two, at the most, you will be reunited with the rest of your family. Ian agreed to be responsible for you all, and he can certainly afford it."

"Your husband is still in the clinic, Mrs. Wansky," said Cameron, as he handed her his handkerchief. "But Dr. Fletcher says that he expects him to recover."

"Thank God." She took the handkerchief and wiped away her tears. Kiela asked, "And Jonathan?"

"He's in the children's ward and has been told that he will be with you soon. He seems in good spirits. " Sir John took her hand again, and patted it. "Drink your tea. It will make you feel better."

Ian had calmed Laurna, and they came over to where the other three sat. "Laurna I would like to introduce you to my best friend, Cameron, and his father, Sir John McCreight. You met Kaitlyn, Cameron's wife, the other day, when I took you to my office."

He knelt down, and hugged Kiela. "It's going to be all right. Really. I see that Cameron and Sir John have introduced themselves, and are taking care of you."

Kiela buried her face in Ian's shoulder and sobbed. "Oh Ian, I'm so sorry that I started all this trouble for you." She pulled herself away, but held onto his shoulders, looking him in the face. "If only I had trusted you more, none of this might have happened."

"Please Kiela, don't berate yourself up. What has happened to you in the last four months would make anyone suspicious. Perhaps it's even for the best. Your suffering will have helped thousands of others in like circumstances. I hope that doesn't sound pompous or too philosophical. Maybe what I should have said is that now we can be a real family, and not criminals, always wondering when someone will turn us in to the authorities."

Kiela let go of Ian, and he found a seat next to Laurna. She turned to Sir John, her face more relaxed. "You said that we could leave this place in a day or two?"

"Yes. There are some formalities to be taken care of, papers to sign, that sort of thing. It should be completed by tomorrow, and then Ian can take you home," said Sir John.

"Thanks to you, there has been a real outpouring of sympathy for you stowaways among the people of Heatherbound. Thousands of people have volunteered to sponsor the rest of the stowaways that are being held. There will be tests to decide which people would be the best together. Unfortunately most of the men are miners and we have no mining on Heatherbound. They must be retrained. But there is no shortage of jobs here, and with the right combination of detainee and sponsor, we see no real problems."

Laurna leaned forward, very interested. "How long will all that take?"

Sir John turned to her and smiled. He liked what he saw. "It will depend on how quickly we can match people. Some will take longer than others, but I expect that everyone will be placed within a month."

"Is there anything I can do to help?"

"Laurna your bravery in allowing that video to be shown was more than enough. Your family needs you right now. But it was a generous thought."

The next morning Ian came to pick up the Wansky family, and finish the paperwork. His sister Michelle came with him. She wanted to meet the girl that could steal her brother's heart in such a short time. She also wanted to take both women shopping. Ian had told her how little they had when they came to Heatherbound.

Michelle was the athletic type, slim, long limbed, and almost wiry. Her hair was a lovely warm shade of brown, cut very short, almost boyish. She had green eyes and a pixie attitude. She laughed a lot. Being around her lifted people's spirits and they seemed to be more optimistic, for some reason.

The first thing that Michelle did, after the introduction, was give Laurna a big hug. She held her away from herself, and said, "I can see why Ian fell so hard. I was beginning to wonder if he would ever find the right girl."

Michelle turned to Kiela and smiled. "Let's get away from this dismal place, and go eat. Right after lunch we are going shopping. Ian has said no limit, and mother is giving you a welcome party. You must have new dresses for it. We'll go to Glendora's new boutique. A bit pricy, but fabulous designs."

Laurna looked questioningly at Ian.

"Glendora is Cameron's sister-in-law. You'll like her, and her shop," said Ian. "She will see that you are dressed in the latest fashions, and with taste."

Kiela was a little taken back by all this and said, "The first thing I want to do is see Jakin."

I'm sorry," said Michelle. "Of course you would want to see your husband. Did Ian tell you that they expect to have him out of the medicube tomorrow?"

"Oh, that's wonderful," said Kiela, turning to Ian, almost bursting into tears again.

It didn't take long to finish up the release processing, and the five got into Ian's hovercraft and flew to the clinic. Jakin was still in the medicube, but he looked so much better. His color was good, and he looked relaxed and untroubled. Kiela just wanted to stay there, and be near him, but Dr. Fletcher shooed them all out.

"Even though Jakin is under the cube's influence," said Dr. Fletcher as he gently took Kiela's arm, and pulled her away from Jakin, "He could still feel that he was being watched and that could make him uncomfortable."

He pulled her around to a better light. "You are not following my instructions. You need more rest. Are you eating properly?"

After leaving Jakin, Kiela realized that she really was hungry. The five of them went to lunch near Glendora's boutique. Michelle knew of a nice restaurant that served wonderful salads, both the Wansky women wanted that for lunch, Jonathan and Ian wanted hamburgers.. It seemed incredible that so much fresh food was available.

Afterwards the five walked to Glendora's boutique for the shopping. Laura and Kiela kept looking up at the real sky above them, just a bit afraid of all the open space, with no protection from the elements. They had so much to learn, and get used to, on Heatherbound.

Glendora greeted them warmly, and the ladies were thrilled with the clothes. Glendora wisely did not put price tags on her garments, or the Wansky women would have been in a state of shock. They wanted to try on everything. Jonathan was bored, and so was Ian. "Ladies, Jonathan, and I are not needed. I'll take him with me to my office."

Michelle looked up from a dress that she was admiring on Laurna, "First you take him to buy some clothes. He will need a suit for tonight."

"All right. I promise. When you're finished here, take Laurna and Kiela to my apartment. We should be back there around 6:00."

Jonathan wanted to hurry through buying the clothes. He was excited about seeing +1 again, and hated the time it took to shop. Ian understood, and told the store clerk to take Jonathan's measurements and send him the works, suit, underclothes, everything a small boy would need to go to a grownup party. He gave the clerk his address at the office, and said they most be delivered before 5 o'clock. George had been fired, and not replaced yet, so no deliveries at his apartment for a while.

Leaving the store the two got back into the hovercraft and went back to Ian's office. Being away from the office for almost a week had left a lot of work piled up on his desk, and he got right to it. Jonathan asked permission to play with +1.

"Sure," Ian said. "He's down the hall, to the right."

"Super! I want to see if he can play chess." Jonathan rushed out of the office.

Ian smiled as he watched Jonathan leave the room. It amazed him how children could bounce back so easily. It felt good to be back in his routine, especially after the harrowing experience they had all gone through.

When Ian got back to his apartment that night Laurna and Kiela were dressed and waiting. He hadn't thought that Laurna could look any more beautiful, but dressed in Glendora's fashions the impossible had been accomplished. She and her mother looked gorgeous.

With great pride, Ian took the Wanskys to his parent's home to meet his family and friends. His main desire was to get his parents blessing for his upcoming marriage. Everyone liked Laurna immediately, and the only reservation that Ian's parents had was that the whole courtship had been too quick.

Ian's father, Connor, pulled Ian aside. "She's a lovely girl, and your mother and I like her. Her mother and brother seem like fine people, too. But don't you think it's a bit of a rush? You hardly know them. People might talk."

"You may not believe it, Dad, but it was almost love at first sight. When I saw her in that bar I knew I had to take her out of there, and care for her the rest of my life. Rescuing her made me feel suddenly grown up. It's hard to explain, but I suddenly felt that now I had responsibilities."

Connor insisted that they wait at least one month before getting married. Kiela agreed. She said it would take them at least that long to get ready and Jakin to be well enough to attend. Ian and Laurna acquiesced; a longer courtship would make the consummation all the sweeter.

The next day they went to see Jakin. He was out of the medicube, and sharing a room with another man. After everyone greeted and hugged Jakin, they put him into a wheelchair, and took him outside. Jakin didn't remember much of anything, and Ian had to be introduced.

After bringing Jakin up to date, Ian was ready to take the floor. "Mr. Wansky."

Jakin raised his hand to stop him. "Please call me Jakin."

"Jakin, I know this is this rather sudden but Laurna and I have fallen in love. We wish to be married in one month. We would like your permission and blessing."

"Things are going pretty fast here. I just met you, Ian, and you say you wish to marry my daughter." Jakin looked at Laurna. "Is this what you really want?"

"Oh yes, Father." Laurna's face beamed. "I love him."

Turning back to Ian. "In that case, you have my blessing."

All this took time, and Jakin was starting to look tired. They wheeled him back to his room, and got him settled, promising to be back in the morning. Dr. Fletcher wanted to keep an eye on him for a day or two more before they could take him home. He said that Jakin would need help at home for a at least several weeks.

It just so happened that one of the stowaway couples, Greta and Hans Nacht, were from Snowball, and knew the Wanskys slightly. She had been a housekeeper of one of their friends, and he was a handyman. Cameron had read the reports on them and asked to become their sponsors. He then suggested that Ian hire them to care for the Wanskys. The entire matter was expedited quickly, and the Wanskys and the Nachts were ensconced in Ian's house that week.

Ian's apartment felt very lonely with the Wansky family gone. After work he spent most of his time with them at the house. Although he enjoyed Laurna's family, he could hardly wait until the wedding when he and Laurna could be alone. As busy as he was, a month seeded a long time.

The month went by quickly for some, and took forever for others. The wedding was small and simple. Glendora designed Laurna's dress in heavy white satin brocade as a wedding gift. It was a simple empress line with a train attached at the bust line in back. Ian wore the Steelite silk formalwear that he had worn at Cameron's wedding. Cameron was best man and Michelle was maid of honor. Both mothers wiped tears from their faces, and Ian's oldest brother's baby cried. A perfect wedding.

Cameron had built a lakefront house at Lake Placid, and loaned it to them for their honeymoon. Ian taught Laurna how to swim and catch fish. Amid much laughter, they both learned how to cook it.

All too soon they were back to work. Laurna had taken the job as Ian's secretary. She wanted to work at least until they had a baby, which from the looks of things would be in about fifteen months. Ian had thoughts of designing a robotic teddy bear, which he would name Jiminey. This teddy bear would help teach their children in the concepts of right and wrong, and also be a bodyguard to some extent.

Ian saw red every time he thought of Vernon's treatment of the Wanskys, and the bar tender's treatment of Laurna. My God, he was going to do something about it, no one should be allowed to get away with that kind of treatment of another.. He hired Cameron's private detective, Guy Gianardo, to check into it.

Gianardo reported back the next day. It appears that the bar had many complaints lodged against it. Noise, unsanitary, suspicious looking characters, the lot. Because it was in the port area it was given a lot of leeway. Gianardo went to the port authorities and told them Laurna story. This, on top of every-thing else, caused the owner to be fined 10,000 credits. He was also threatened to lose his license if he didn't fire the bartender. and clean up the place.

Finding Vernon took a little longer. He had been fired from his last job and finding him was not easy. He asked around the docks for any knowledge of Vernon. No one would or could tell him anything. No one wanted to be a snitch even though Vernon was not well liked.

After a few days he decided to question a few prostitutes. The third one was one of Vernon's. She was hard looking under all the makeup and scanty outfit. He could see underneath was a scared little girl with no hope in her eyes.

"Do you know a man called Vernon?"

"Yes, but if you want to talk to me, it will cost you" said Rowena.

Guy handed her 10 credits.

Rowena stuffed the money into her brassiere, "He said he would be back in a weeks to collect my wages."

"How long have you been on the job?"

"Just started two weeks ago. I owed Vernon money and he said he would turn me in and I would be sent back to the hell hole I came from if I didn't pay him back quickly."

"Do you know of any other working girls in the area that belong to Vernon?"

"You ask a lot of questions for just 10 credits."

Guy gave her 10 more.

"There are four more girls working for him. We have no choice. It isn't just us, but we have our kids and family here too. So don't think you're so high and mighty."

"I don't think less of you because of what you feel you have to do to protect your family. I want to help all of you."

Guy continued persuasively, "Heatherbound is passing new laws to help stowaways. I promise you if you will all come with me I will see that you are settled with decent jobs and places to stay. You will have to go into a holding area until we can find sponsors for you all. That may take a few weeks, but you would be together, and not on the streets."

"You're pulling my leg. What's in it for you?" Rowena said it with a sneer.

"Two things, I came here to ruin Vernon, and now I have a better cause, and that is to help you girls and your families."

Softly Guy said, "You have to trust someone again. Why not give it a try? At least you would be out from under Vernon."

Rowena burst into tears. She was so tired of trying to be tough.

Guy rounded up the girls, and their families, after calling the emigration authorities and they sent a bus to pick all of them up.. The girls and the families were mistrustful at first, but with gentle persuasion they got into the bus, and were taken to the holding compound. There they were assigned rooms, given clothes, a place to shower, and finally a good meal with lots of fruits and vegetables.

Next they were asked to fill out forms of their qualifications and what kind of job they were looking for. People were still lined up to sponsor these emigrants and there was no shortage of jobs. These poor people felt like shaking themselves out of a fairytale., and come back to the real world. It all seemed too good to be true.

Guy's next job was to go the port authorities and inform them what Vernon had been doing. Having been alerted to this scandal they would be on the lookout for Vernon and any other scoundrels that would do such a thing.

The first thing that the commandant of the port did was have Vernon's itinerary checked. They radioed the Captain of the ship Vernon was on and told him that Vernon would not be allowed to land on Heatherbound again. When the Captain asked them to explain, they did. The Captain left Vernon at the next port they landed on, which happened to be Snowball, and left him there with just his duffle bag.

Ian was more than satisfied with the job that Gay had done. He paid him handsomely.

Chapter Forty-four

Sean's Rebuttal

Sean was in his office when his new secretary, Nieve Locas, (Alice had asked to be transferred to another department) informed him that he had a visitor. He was still feeling good about all the problems he had set in motion for Ian and Cameron. He didn't ask who it was, being preoccupied with his triumph. "Send him in."

The well-dressed young man came into the room and stood in front of Sean's desk. "Are you Mr. Sean McCreight?"

"Yes." Sean looked up smiling. "How may I help you?"

"I have a summons for you to appear in court." The young man handed Sean some papers, and turned to leave the room. Just as he got to the door he turned his head towards Sean, and said, with a grin, "I hope you have a good day."

Sean sat there for a few minutes wide eyed, and open mouthed, with shock. He opened the papers and read them quickly; he then threw them down on his desk, with an oath. "That yellow-livered bastard. He can't beat me any other way, so he takes me to court. It isn't enough that he has almost bankrupted me. Then further humiliates me by allowing my wife to start a business selling one of his damned discoveries, pretending sympathy for Glendora. Now he wants to ruin my reputation.

He was too livid with anger to sit, and his scar itched horribly. He got up abruptly, and started pacing. This habit of his, when agitated, had almost worn a groove in his carpet. He started beating his hip with his fist, as he walked to and fro.

His mind was in a whirl. Cameron's been a thorn in my side since the day he was born. I should have killed him when he was still in his cradle. He slammed his fist into his other palm while thinking these thoughts. The itching on his face was driving him mad, and his rubbing it made the scar stand out very red against the white of his face.

Sean went back to his desk and punched the intercom, "Nieve, please come to my office. I have some papers I want you to fax to my lawyer."

While waiting for his secretary to come into the room, Sean thought. This couldn't be at a worse time for me. I have to deal with the seeds from the harvest, all the orders, everything. I can't believe that he chooses this time to aggravate me.

Nieve came in almost immediately and asked for the papers. She had replaced Alice just recently, and was exceptionally beautiful. Nieve was a petite brunette, with a strong Irish accent. Her face was a perfect oval. Her blue-green eyes were slightly slanted, with long and luxuriant eyelashes, giving her an exotic look. Her family had immigrated to Heatherbound when she was very young, but she still had that lilting accent that Sean loved to hear. She had been his mistress for more than two years.

She looked at the summons and then at Sean with a questioning look on her face. "Will there be anything else, Sir?"

With a shrug, he answered her question. "No! Yes. Hold my calls, except for my lawyer. Thanks Nieve."

The wait for the call seemed interminable. Sean kept checking his watch even though he knew his lawyer hadn't had time to do much about the summons. His mind was in turmoil of emotions. He felt he could do nothing until he had talked to his lawyer.

A half-hour later his lawyer was on the line. "Hello Sean. What did you do to irritate Cameron this time? I hope it didn't have anything to do with Ian's problems with the law. The whole world is up in arms about that!"

"I'll ignore that last remark," said Sean with disgust. "What kind of a case can Cameron make against me after all this time?"

"I think a very good one. After all you did base your whole case against Cameron on hereditary laws when you knew that they didn't apply. You are suspected of bribing a public official for information. Also of obtaining from that official a legal document that proved that Cameron was the lawful owner of Teraline and the entire Winter's Grove, with whatever it held."

"But it's been months since the trial." Sean yelled.

287

"If you choose to bring up the lateness of the suit you could open up a whole can of worms. Such as why Cameron felt the need to sue you at this time,"

"The people of Heatherbound aren't too happy with you because of the way you stopped the defense industry in its tracks. We were just lucky that the aliens saved us. We sure as hell couldn't have. And if you had anything to do with Ian's arrest, the whole country will want to lynch you."

"The truth of the matter Sean, unless you can settle this out of court, you will probably go to jail for perjury, falsifying evidence and defamation of character. The only reason you didn't before was your father's influence."

"You paint a pretty bleak future for me. Sounds like you have me tried and convicted before I even step into the courtroom." Sean was fed up. "Perhaps I need a new lawyer."

"I can't stop you from getting another lawyer, but it won't do you any good. I'll do all I can to keep you out of jail, but you are going to have to make some big concessions to Cameron, and quit this vendetta you have against him."

"I'll see him rot in hell before I apologize for anything I have done." Sean slammed the receiver down.

Sean sat at his desk in a funk. He was not only angry, but a little frightened. This couldn't be happening to him. He was the eldest son of the most prominent family on Heatherbound. I'll find a way to get even with them all, even my father, if it the last thing I do.

He sat there looking at the papers on his desk, not seeing them. Suddenly the word 'seeds' jumped out at him. That's it! I'll steal the Steelite seeds, take them to Earth, and start again. They'll welcome me with open arms. That would teach the people of Heatherbound to look down on me.

It was remarkable how focused Sean became when he was formulating plans. He read the memorandum that said the seeds would be ready for the formulas in three days. They would be divided into two separate areas, as usual. The germinating formula's ingredients would be awaiting his and his brother's arrival to mix them in the first area. The second area would be ready for the disposal formula at the same time. No surprises there.

Good, he thought. That will give me plenty of time to arrange for Cameron's absence from the ritual, and I can use the germinating formula on both areas. I'll put Harrison on the bagging in the disposal area, and arrange for him to drive them to the spaceport. He owes me. I wonder if I can bribe anyone else to help.

It would serve them right if I killed all the seeds I leave them, but that would ruin my son's inheritance. I'll just have to be happy with taking enough seeds to start my own farms on Earth.

He gave a devilish smile then, made more so by his scar. This could turn out to be a good thing for me. It's been so boring here lately. Most of my friends seem to have other things to do. Glendora only has time for her new business, and the boys, not for me. I wonder if she suspects Nieve is my mistress.

It's a good thing I own a space yacht, this caper would be impossible without it. I'd better call the spaceport right now and arrange for it to be serviced and supplied for the long trip. Then I need to think of a way to get rid of Cameron for a day or two. Let's see, if one of his kids would get sick, that would keep him home. Hmm, I think I'll send a box of candy in Grandma's name with just enough poison to make anyone sick but not enough to kill, even if they ate the whole box. That should work, she is away for a few days, so they can't check it out'.

Sean thought about the candy for a few minutes and changed his mind. He really didn't want to harm Robert or Megan in any way. He wasn't completely heartless. I know, I'll arrange for a message from Winter's Grove, saying that Cameron is needed there, urgently. That should do it.

Now, to arrange for Harrison to help me with the seeds and loading the space yacht. I'll ask Nieve to come along. She should get a kick out of going back to the old country. No need to tell her that I am leaving for good. I'd better ask a few of the younger scientists to help me set up my new empire. No one knows that I have been disinherited. They shouldn't be too suspicious. I'll think of some excuse to lure them to come with me. I'll need help that's for sure.

Everything went like clockwork for Sean. He talked quietly to some of his scientists who were not married, and they jumped at the chance to go to

Earth for a short period of time. Nieve was in love with Sean, and even though she was a bit suspicious, was willing to follow him anywhere.

The seeds were ready in their separate areas, and when Cameron came in that morning, he received the urgent message. He left immediately, knowing that Sean could handle the formulas without him. He was glad for the excuse not to be in Sean's presence. In fact, he was not only glad, but also relieved. He did not want to be near Sean at the moment. He wasn't sure how well he could hold his temper. It never occurred to him that this might be a trumped up excuse to get rid of him.

This was exactly what Sean was counting on. He figured it would take about four hours to germinate all the seeds and bag them. The truck that usually took the seed to be disposed of was waiting in its usual place. Harrison had been assigned to drive it that morning, with secret instructions to transport them to the space yacht instead. Sean felt that there was plenty of time to get away before Cameron could radio back that the "urgent" message was a hoax.

All the personnel going with him had been informed to meet at the space yacht that morning, with their luggage. Nieve was to get them aboard and get them settled. The yacht was spacious and very well appointed. Although the staterooms were small, each had its own bathroom, fully equipped with shower and toilet. The social room was also the dining room. The bulkheads of this room were lined with wood from Earth, and the carpet had been woven from Steelite. The tables were also of wood, and beautifully built. They were set with tablecloths, china, and crystal. A long table on the side was covered with a bounteous brunch with plenty of champagne. Everyone was impressed and they were quick to fill their plates and prepare themselves for a pleasurable experience.

The plan went exactly as expected. When Sean came aboard, his people were all settled in their new home for the next six months. He took off immediately for Earth only seven hours after Cameron had left for Winter's Grove. That gave him four hours, at least, to get too large a head start to be brought back.

Sean was very tense and almost reckless with getting the space yacht launched. He continued to drive it at maximum speed for the first five hours when he would be far enough away from the planet to make his first warp jump. After he made the jump, and still saw no pursuit, he was almost giddy with relief, and broke out the champagne.\

While in flight, Sean radioed ahead that he was arriving and wanted to talk to Sir Kelvin Hardcrow head of Amalgamated Steel. He also arranged for his people to be taken to the Ritz Hotel in New York. He was not worried about money for a while, he had wiped out the join checking and savings account that he and Glendora had. He had also taken out a very large loan in their name.

Upon arrival he was met by a limousine-hovercraft which took him straight to Hardcrow's office. The driver said, "Mr. McCreight there is a full bar at your disposal. If you need anything, all you need to do as ask. We should arrive at Sir Hardcrow's office in half an hour, traffic permitting."

"Thanks." Sean fixed himself a drink. "This traffic is a new experience. Even in our capital we aren't concerned with it."

They arrived on time and Sean was taken to a well-furnished office overlooking Central Park. It was a corner office and two walls were windows floor to ceiling. The others were paneled in beautifully carved wood. There were several pedestal tables with Hardcrow's collection of ancient Egyptian artifacts. Hardcrow was sitting behind an enormous desk. He got up to shake hands with Sean as he entered the room.

"It's good to see you Mr. McCreight. I was surprised, and pleased, to hear from you. What brings you to Earth?" He motioned to Sean to seat while he went behind his desk to sit. He offered Sean a cigar, and took one himself. Both lit up before Sean answered.

"It was good of you to have me met at the space port, and to see me on short notice. I've always wanted to come to Earth and now is as good a time as any." Sean leaned back in his chair and puffed his cigar.

"If there is anything I can do for you, just ask."

"There is something. I wish to grow Steelite on Earth and need a large track of land, and a laboratory." said with a poker face.

Hardcrow, with years of experience in negotiations didn't crack a smile. Inwardly he almost choked. "That's rather a big something. If I may ask, why now?"

Sean lied. "I haven't agreed with my father for years about Steelite. I've always felt that we should expand the market. Why not start with Earth first."

"I believe some of the Northern states have plenty of land still and it should grow very well there. I'm sure you must have many contacts that would like to invest in Steelite." Sean said with confidence.

Hardcrow thought there must be something else behind all this. The senior McCreight would never have allowed Steelite to be grown elsewhere other than Heatherbound. "Do you have the seed and formulas?"

"Of course! I also brought a staff of scientists with me who are familiar with Steelite and would be able to make any adjustments needed to grow it on Earth's soil."

"I don't wish to be crass, but where does Amalgamated Steel come in?" Leaning back in his chair, hands on the arms, a firm look on his face.

"I would give you exclusive right to buy all that is grown. At a fair price of course." Sean's cigar had gone out and he reached for the lighter to start it again. "I would keep all the seed and the secret formulas, of course."

"Sounds perfectly fair to me. You have a deal."

Hardcrow sat forward and reached for his phone. Looking at Sean he said. "I'll just call a friend of mine in England. He is a Baron and owns a tract of land in Wyoming that just might be exactly what you are looking for."

While Sean was busy with negotiations, the scientists and Nieve did tourist things in New York. They went to the theatre, great restaurants and shopping. They loved the zoo, spent a full day there. There was the library and museums. So much to do and see. All too soon they were off to Wyoming.

The land was perfect. It even had a large rambling house on it with ten bedrooms, swimming pool, tennis court and a stable of horses. It was completely staffed, cook, butler, stable boy, maids, gardeners, you name it. The Baron had provided. The servants had their quarters in a separate house. There were several guest houses in the compound as well. Sean knew he would be very comfortable here, and so should Nieve.

The scientists set up the lab and got the seeds ready for planting. Sean hired local men to plow the land and plant the seeds. Machines did most of the work and it was soon growing. It surprised Sean how fast the plants were germinating . After the crops were in and the specialized fertilizer had been used, the scientists didn't have much to do. They did test the occasional plant to make sure it was growing as it did on Heatherbound. Sean wanted them stay and monitor the first crop before sending them home. He also needed them to teach the process to lab assistants from Earth.

While waiting for the harvest, they went horseback riding, played tenni,s and went swimming, this was the life. Machines harvested the Steelite and it was no different than that grown on Heatherbound. Everyone hadn't realized that they had been holding their breath s these last few month until this moment.

"Champagne for everyone." Sean shouted the moment he knew for sure.

When the first snows arrived and the scientists learned that there would be about five months of snow and wind, they asked to go home. It had been fun and exciting but they wanted Heatherbound. Sean arranged for them to leave, but not in the luxury they come out in.

Sean had hopes of perhaps two crops the first year. He hadn't counted on the severe winters in Wyoming. He and Nieve were miserable. It was decided that the two of them would see the world of Earth. Both had read about the major tourist attractions and wanted to see them all. They spent the entire five months traveling and at the end, decided they liked their home in Wyoming best.

Chapter Forty-six
Closing the Barn Door

Cameron was not looking forward to seeing Sean at the storage shed for the semi-annual germinating rituals. When he arrived, he found an urgent message waiting for him from No.1. That gave him an excellent excuse to leave before Sean arrived. He fleetingly thought how unusual it was for the robot to do something so contrary to robot protocol as to communicate with him without prior directions. He pushed the thought aside, happy for any excuse to be away from Sean.

After instructing the working crews to have Sean go ahead without him, he left quickly straight to his hovercraft and took off within minutes of receiving the message. He radioed Kaitlyn and left a message informing her that he may be gone for a few days. He asked her to take care of everything while he was gone.

Kaitlyn was surprised at the sudden departure but was used to it. Knowing and loving her husband, she expected the unexpected and accepted it with a smile.

It was with mixed emotions Cameron flew the next eleven hours. He was imagining all the terrible things that could have happened to Winter's Grove. He felt guilty that he had fled from his duties at the farm and ashamed of his feelings about his brother. Creeping in all the time was his happiness at going back to Winter's Grove.

As usual, thinking ahead, Kaitlyn had insisted that Cameron stock his hovercraft with emergency supplies and of course, an extra set of thermowear. He was very glad of it, after a few hours in the air; he realized that he was hungry. Thanking his wife mentally, he set the craft on autopilot and ate. Feeling satisfied, he decided to take a short nap.

The nap turned into a long one. Cameron had been working long hours recently in his lab and hadn't realized how tired he was. He had found that red flower in abundance around his lake property and had been experimenting with different formulas hoping to make purple Steelite.

Cameron woke up when his hovercraft landed at Winter's Grove. He was surprised that he had slept so long but felt great for the rest. Getting out of his ship, with some apprehension, he had been thinking the worst, but everything looked normal as he entered the mountain. No.1 met him when he landed, waited patiently until Cameron had deplaned. "It's good to see you, Sir. We hadn't expected you for another week."

"What?" Cameron said with a frown. "I received a message saying that there was an emergency, and my presence was needed immediately."

"I'm sorry, Sir, that you were caused concern of that nature. No message was sent from this facility. You have expressly given instructions not to bother you unless the place burned down. As that has not happened, I would not have requested you to come."

"Yes, of course, you wouldn't. I guess my brother didn't want to see me either."

"Did you also receive a message from your brother that wasn't really sent? This is very confusing."

"Sorry, No.1, I was just thinking out loud," Cameron said with a smile. 'While I'm thinking about it, let's change that directive. You may call me anytime you feel there is a major problem that needs my attention. Please use your own discretion as to what constitutes an emergency."

"Thank you, Sir, that may be very helpful."

"While I am here, I may as well look around. Please show me what you have been doing recently, and bring me up to date."

No.1 showed Cameron the holding tanks that were recently built. Next, he took him to a new area for growing brains. This took about two hours, and even with his thermowear, Cameron was starting to get cold. He suggested they go to the heated office constructed recently to look at the records.

During all this time, Cameron kept having nagging thoughts about the message and why Sean had sent it if Sean had sent it. I had better radio Kaitlyn and told her that there really wasn't an emergency here. Also, a call to my father to have him check on the geminating process just in case Sean was up to something else, thought Cameron.

After alerting everyone, Cameron put all thoughts of Sean from his mind, and concentrated on Winter's Grove. The entire complex was running very smoothly. No.1 had performed to his usual high standards. With just a tinge of sadness, Cameron realized that he wasn't actually needed there.

He left the office, turned up his thermowear to the warmest, and took a last stroll around. He reasoned that this might be the last time that he would need to return to Winter's Grove. With leaden feet, he returned to his hovercraft for the journey home.

As he climbed into his seat, he noticed a blinking red light on his radio. After strapping in and getting settled, he switched on the radio to hear the message. It was from his father asking him to return immediately. Sean had left Heatherbound and had taken several McCreight employees with him.

Cameron realized instantly what this implied, but he couldn't make himself believe that his brother would betray his own family in such a way. This was not something the McCreight family would want discussed on the airways, so he simply replied that the message was understood and he was on his way home. He should arrive at his father's house around 7 AM.

This was not a pleasant flight home. It seemed to take forever. Cameron did manage to get some sleep, but he was not refreshed when he landed. He kept kicking himself for believing in a message, that in retrospect, could only have been bogus.

His father and Kaitlyn were waiting for his arrival. They both looked drawn as if they too had had a bad night. Cameron hugged them, and all went quietly into the house. The breakfast room had been set up for their meeting. There was a nice fire going, and the morning sun was just starting to shine through the windows. It was a beautiful, sunny room, painted yellow with white wainscoting, but it didn't cheer them up. The room smelled of coffee and bacon, but no one was hungry. Their gloom was too deep.

Sir John spoke first. "Your mother is sleeping. This has been very hard on her."

"I can imagine." Cameron poured himself a cup of coffee and made motions, offering to pour for Sir John and Kaitlyn. Both accepted with a nod. "Did he take all the seeds?"

Sir John accepted the cup and said almost in a whisper. "No just half. From the amount of chemicals used I would have to say that he germinated all the seeds. He must be planning on starting his own company on Earth."

"Your grandfather told me that something like this might happen. He wasn't concerned. The only reason he didn't distribute the seed in the first place to all the settlers was to ensure that food crops would be planted. He was afraid that a cash crop, such as Steelite, would be too hard to resist. The farmers might plant mostly Steelite, and we could be in serious need of food."

Kaitlyn had been quiet up to this point but felt she had to speak her mind. "I know that I have no real say in this matter, but it could be a good thing. Why don't we sell seeds to other farmers now? We could specify that only thirty percent of their arable land could be devoted to Steelite. The McCreight family would still keep the formulas. That way, the other farmers would have to bring their harvest to us to be manufactured. We could still control Steelite, and the farmers would plant other crops we well. We would have to keep the processing a secret to ensure that only so much Steelite would be grown."

"I like it," said Sir John. "That way, the big news will be the sale of Steelite seeds. The people of Heatherbound wouldn't have to know about the disgrace to our family by Sean's thievery and desertion."

"There is one problem," said Cameron. "We might not have enough seeds for everyone who wants them this year. We will need all you have for the main farm, and my farm doesn't have a lot of excess."

"How about an allotment system," said Sir John, "And we will have more seeds than you expect because I have been thinking of putting some of our acreage into that legume of the Dasurainians. It's delicious and would make a good export crop to the outer planets, as well as a gourmet treat for us Heatherbounders. Everyone would jump at the chance to try something from the aliens."

"That sound like a wonderful idea," cried Kaitlyn. "But instead of an allotment system, how about if we advertise the sale as a lottery? Anyone who wanted seeds could put their name in, and we would draw lots. There should be no hard feelings from those who didn't win, and it would generate a lot of goodwill."

"That might be even more exciting, and people would not even think about Sean's defection." Sir John was getting excited and even happy. "This could turn out not as disastrous as I thought. It's really a good idea, Kaitlyn."

The lottery was set up with the money going to Dr. Fletcher's clinic. Everyone knew now that the poor and stowaways mainly used the clinic. With all the publicity about the Wanskys, people felt almost virtuous to buy lottery tickets, but desire for the seed was the main force. Even with the strings that were attached, people were practically breaking down the doors to buy tickets.

Dr. Kevin Fletcher got the money for his new wing and the recuperating chamber with money left over to run it. It was proclaimed that next year there would be even more seeds and another lottery. This calmed down the despair of losing and kept the winners from selling seeds at exorbitant prices. Not that many wanted to sell.

Chapter Forty-seven

Satisfaction

Dr. Fletcher was thrilled with all the support and money that was coming to his clinic. His dreams of having a large clinic to help the poor was coming true.

Within the month, the wing was built and fully equipped with three recuperating chambers, ready for occupants. Jakin was the first in line but wasn't too sure he wanted to go in the recuperating chamber, at this time. He and Hans Nacht were busy renovating the house and cleaning up the orchards. He felt wonderful, and didn't want to miss a minute of the work.

Kiela persuaded him, "Jakin, you must go into the recuperating chamber. You owe it to your family, and to yourself. Think of how much more you could do with two good arms and hands. The house and grounds that Ian has given us will still need a lot to be done when you have recovered."

"It will take a year of my life to go through with it. I am not sure I want to lose so much time without you."

"You're right. It would take at least a year to make you whole again. There would be scars and the hair on the left side of his head would never grow right again, but at least he would be whole.

Kiela went on with her persuasion by reminding him he would be able to hold his grandchild when it was born. Laurna and Ian's baby would be born about the same time. as he would be able to leave his chamber

Laurna was pregnant and due in another twelve months. She wasn't too happy to learn that it took fifteen months to have a baby on Heatherbound. But she was happy to be pregnant. She and Ian wanted a big family. His apartment was not going to be big enough.

Kaitlyn was pregnant too, and the baby was also due in about twelve months. This brought the families even closer if that were possible.

Ian was still working to develop the robot that he had envisioned for his children. He wanted it to be small, like a teddy bear. His main problem was to make the teddy bear soft and cuddly, and then it would be easy to install the commands to be a good bodyguard, nanny, and best friend that always gave good advice.

The Dasurainians were still interested in the humans and wished to continue as allies, for which the people of Heatherbound were grateful. To establish a base closer, they wanted Snowball to colonize their people. They offered to trade the colonists on Snowball, a planet more suitable for humankind.

As a part of the trade, they offered to transport all the inhabitants and their possessions to the new world and help them to get started. The world was smaller than Snowball and further away from Earth. The advantages were that it had mild winters and summers. It also had three moons that were mostly metal and could be mined. (The Dasurainians were not miners.) It was a fair trade and made just about everyone happy. Cameron was elated to have his allies based so close to Heatherbound.

During this year, Cameron was away a lot, trying to help the other planets and being interested in the biosphere of each of them. Sir John finally understood his youngest son's need and the wisdom of aiding the other planets. He was almost ashamed of his short-sightedness.

Sir John worried about his long absences and leaving so many of his responsibilities to Kaitlyn. His worry was needless. She loved the work. That was what she had been trained to do on Earth.

Kaitlyn managed their businesses, and the children, along with her pregnancy, and thought nothing of it. Her workload was lessened by hiring Kiela as her assistant. Laurna also worked for RD&E and planned on working until her baby was born.

Sir John and Lady Helen also were concerned about Sean and hired a detective on Earth to gather information about his affairs. Sean was not forgiven nor forgotten. He was still their son.

The detective came back with a full report.

Sean became a partner with an English land baron who owned thousands of acres in Wyoming, USA. Steelite did well, but only as an insulation material. It needed the extra growing time of Heatherbound to be turned into the steel so much desired. Also, it had only one crop a year, which was thought to be the reason, the winters were too cold. The subject became rich by American standards but was never happy or satisfied. He misses his family and Heatherbound, still blaming his brother for his misfortunes. His secretary and mistress, Nieve, left him at he end of the first winter as did all the engineers that accompanied him, and returned to Heatherbound.

Glendora read the report but never divorced Sean. She was too busy with her chain of boutiques and art stores to bother. The diversity of her stores was well known because of her brother-in-law, Cameron. When he came home with some unusual art or craft, he always brought it to her to sell.

Cameron, Kaitlyn, and Ian were still inseparable, but now they had a fourth with Laurna. Their summers were spent each year at Lake Placid with their growing families.

The lake area was so beautiful and serene, a place to get away and spend quality time with their children. The four loved watching the blue moon Tristan rise in the sky and glisten on the lake, with his mate, the pink Isolde, following soon after. It was so peaceful there, and they needed the break from their hectic schedules during the rest of the year.